Three Faces of Asprin

**BAEN BOOKS
BY ROBERT ASPRIN**

The Time Scout series with Linda Evans
Tales of the Time Scouts (Omnibus)
Tales of the Time Scouts: Vol II (Omnibus)

Myth-Interpretations:
The Worlds of Robert Asprin

Three Faces of Asprin

ROBERT ASPRIN

THREE FACES OF ASPRIN

The Cold Cash War copyright © 1977 by Robert Asprin
The Bug Wars copyright © 1979 by Robert L. Asprin
Tambu copyright © 1979 by Robert Lynn Asprin

"Reminder" copyright © by Robert "Buck" Coulson,
used by permission of the author's estate.

A Baen Books Original

Baen Publishing Enterprises
P.O. Box 1403
Riverdale, NY 10471
www.baen.com

ISBN: 978-1-4767-8164-8

Cover art by Kurt Miller

First Baen printing, June 2016

Distributed by Simon & Schuster
1230 Avenue of the Americas
New York, NY 10020

Library of Congress Cataloging-in-Publication Data

Names: Asprin, Robert, author. | Asprin, Robert. Cold Cash War. | Asprin, Robert. Bug Wars. | Asprin, Robert. Tambu.
Title: Three faces of Asprin / Robert Asprin.
Other titles: Cold Cash War. | Bug Wars.. | Tambu.
Description: Riverdale, NY : Baen Books, [2016]
Identifiers: LCCN 2016010527 | ISBN 9781476781648 (softcover)
Subjects: | BISAC: FICTION / Science Fiction / Short Stories. | FICTION / Science Fiction / Adventure. | FICTION / Science Fiction / General. | GSAFD: Science fiction.
Classification: LCC PS3551.S6 A6 2016 | DDC 813/.54--dc23 LC record available at https://lccn.loc.gov/2016010527

Printed in the United States of America

10 9 8 7 6 5 4 3 2 1

Contents

Three Faces of Asprin

The
Cold Cash
War

This dedication is a formal and public thanks to
GORDON R. DICKSON,
everything in a friend and mentor that
a young writer could ask for, and more!

Chapter One

Tom Mausier was a cautious man. Despite his daydreams of bravery and glorious deeds, he had to agree with his friends that he was one of the most cautious of people. As such, while it surprised everyone that he left his comfortable corporate job to open a business of his own, no one was surprised when it succeeded. Had success not been almost guaranteed in the beginning, he would not have made the move.

Still he had his dreams. He dreamed of being an adventurer. A secret agent. A spy. Lacking the dash and courage to be any of these, he contented himself with the small pride of being his own man and running the business he had built as an espionage and information broker.

His day began at six o'clock in the morning, fully two hours before any of his employees arrived.

This was not difficult for him since his offices were attached to his house. In fact, he could enter his office through a door in his kitchen. However, he never went into the office unless he was properly dressed. It would have been as unthinkable to him as walking outside in his underwear. The offices were another world to him, a world of business and of dreams, while his home was his home.

One could notice a physical change when he stepped through the door joining the two worlds. His home was kept at a comfortable seventy-eight degrees; the office was a more crisp and businesslike sixty-seven degrees. His wife maintained a modest and comfortable early American decor with a few tasteful and functional antiques in their home, but his office—his office was his pride and joy.

Stepping into his office was like stepping onto the deck of a Hollywood spaceship when the budget was both lavish and overspent. While his home was comfortably frugal, he spared no expense on his office. Electronic display screens and their telephone terminal hookups lined the walls as well as machines for recording and storing incoming messages. Gadgetry abounded everywhere, almost all of which he could justify.

His business was his pride, and he started at six o'clock sharp. He didn't require his employees to match his hours, in fact, he discouraged them from coming in early. The first two hours of each day were for him to collect his thoughts, organize the day, and pursue his hobby.

This morning started out the same as any other. Without bothering to turn on the overhead lights, he switched on the first two viewscreens and studied them carefully. The first showed memos to himself of items to be done today. They were either dictated at his desk into the memory file or phoned in by him from one of the phones in his home or a nearby phone booth when a thought struck him. The latter was done with one of the portable field terminals identical to the ones issued to their field agents and it always gave him a secret thrill to use one, even though the data he transmitted to himself was usually of an unexciting nature.

Today's data was as dull as ever. *ISSUE PAYROLL CHECKS . . . RECONCILE PHONE BILL . . . SPEAK TO MS. WITLEY ABOUT HER STEADILY LENGTHENING LUNCH HOURS . . .* He sighed as he scanned the board. Paperback spies never had to reconcile phone bills. Such tasks were magically done by elves or civil servants offstage, leaving the heroes free to gamble in posh casinos with beautiful women on their arms and strange people shooting at them.

One item on the board caught his eye. *CHECK MISSED*

RENDEZVOUS 187-449-3620. He scowled thoughtfully. He'd have to check that carefully. If the agent had missed the rendezvous because of laxness, he would be dropped as a client. Thomas Mausier didn't tolerate laxness. His own reputation was on the line. All of his clients could deal with each other in good faith because Thomas Mausier vouched for them. If a purchasing client didn't pay in full or attempted a doublecross, he would be dropped. If a selling client tried to palm off falsified or dummied information, he would be dropped. When you dealt through Thomas Mausier, you dealt honestly and in good faith. That's part of what you were paying him his ten percent for.

Then again, there might be a good reason why the agent missed the rendezvous. He might be dead. If that were the case, Mausier would have to check to see if the scrambler unit on the agent's field terminal had been somehow neutralized, allowing a rival to intercept the message and set an ambush.

Mausier doubted that this had occurred. He had countless guarantees from the Japanese firm that custom-manufactured the units for him that the scramblers were individually unique and unbuggable, and they had yet to be proven wrong.

Still, it would be worth checking into. His eyes flicked over the agent's client number—187. Brazil. He'd have to pay particular attention to items from that area when he went through the newswire tapes, newspapers, and periodicals this morning.

He was still pondering this as he turned to the second board. This board contained both requests for information and items for sale from the world of corporations which had been phoned in during the night. Again the items were of a routine nature. Now that the Christmas production lines had started, the seasonal rush for information on new designs from rival toy companies was dwindling. The majority of items were from corporate executives checking on each other, frequently within the same organization.

Again an item caught his eye, but this time he smiled. A corporation was asking for information on the design of an electronics gizmo that had appeared in detail in last month's issue of a popular hobbyists' magazine. They were offering a healthy sum. Still smiling, Mausier keyed in the magazine reference and coded it back to the requestor with the footnote, "With our compliments."

There would be red faces when the message was picked up, but what the heck, they didn't have the time for reading that Mausier had. They were chained to a corporation. Better that they got a little embarrassed than if he let one of his agents sell them information that was already public knowledge. He had his reputation to protect.

Again he scanned the board, automatically assigning codes to the items. When his employees arrived, they would spend hours coding the new data into the computers, but he could do it in minutes. After all, he had invented the code.

Each item requested would be encoded with the geographic region for which information was available, the specifics of the information required, the date it was needed, and the offered price. Any agent could then step into a phone booth or pick up a motel phone anywhere in the world, and, using his field terminal, review all requests for information in this area. Similarly, any item offered for sale would be encoded with the general category of interest, the specifics of the information, and the asking price. The buying clients would then use their field terminals to scan for any items that might be of particular interest to them. This system allowed both speculative and consignment espionage to be channeled through his brokerage, with Mausier arranging the details and collecting his ten percent.

With relish he turned on the next board. This board got less use than the corporate one, but was always more exciting. This board was for governments.

There was a new message on the board this morning. It was a request for information. It was a request from the C-Block.

Mausier leaned forward and studied the request. Since the C-Block had gone incommunicado after the end of the Russo-Chinese War, no information had come out, but they were always buying. Even though it was known that their own agents roamed the far corners of the globe, they still dealt with him and probably other information brokers. Whether this was to obtain new lines of information or to check on data sent them by their own agents no one knew, but they were steady customers.

It would be curious to see how his agents would react if they knew how much of their data went to the C-Block. Buying clients were not identified on information requests going out to the agents, for obvious reasons.

The latest information request seemed innocent enough, but then again, most of them did. They wanted lists of any and all new hires or terminations for two specific major corporations in a given region.

It seemed innocent enough. In fact, it duplicated several requests they had made in the past for different corporations. But these were two new lists they were watching, and in a different part of the globe.

Mausier pursed his lips as he studied the request. The C-Block was sharp. They didn't do anything without reason and they didn't waste money or effort on petty items. There was something going on that they were watching, something that he couldn't see.

He studied the board. Two new personnel lists. In a new area. In Brazil. Brazil! The missed rendezvous in Brazil!

Mausier was suddenly excited. Abandoning his boards, he strode hurriedly to his desk and clicked on his doodle screen. He keyed for a clear workspace, then input two items. *Agent missed rendezvous. Personnel hires and terminations.* He leaned back in his chair and stared at the two items glowing brightly on the screen.

Thomas Mausier had a hobby. He never actually handled the information that the clients bartered for, but all the requests and items for sale still crossed his screens even if it was in the vaguest of terms. As a hobby, he put the pieces together.

You didn't have to see the blueprints of a weapon to know a country was hurriedly stockpiling arms. You didn't have to see the actual medical records to know someone was compiling a dossier on someone else. By combining the skeletal information that passed through his offices with the public data he collected from the incredible mass of news tapes, newspapers, and periodicals he subscribed to from all over the world, he could regularly second-guess the next day's headlines. So far he had successfully predicted three border skirmishes, a civil war, two coups, and several assassination attempts. He never did anything with the information, since that would be a breach of confidence with his clients. Still it made an interesting and exciting hobby.

He stared at the two items on the screen. They were probably unrelated. All the same, he would take the time to scan the current events public records for any items concerning either of those two conglomerates or Brazil. The C-Block was watching them for some reason and he was going to puzzle it out.

Chapter Two

Thirty-seven is a lousy age for a corporate executive.

Peter Hornsby grimaced at the busy streets below as he stared out the window of his office. He was taking a break after realizing he hadn't focused on anything all morning. Monday morning blahs, maybe.

Actually, the "window" was a viewscreen with a continuous loop videotape showing on it, the corporate world's answer to the office-status scramble of which executive got a window viewing what. In his depressed, self-analyzing moments such as these, Pete questioned his own choice of views. Most of the other executives looked at a seashore or a morning meadow. He was one of the few who had the "fifty-seventh-story view of city streets" tape, and, to his knowledge, the only one who had the "night electrical storm over the city."

Was this a sign of his waning career? Was this all that was left? Deluding himself with illusions of grandeur?

He shook off the feeling. C'mon Pete, you aren't dead yet. So the promotions aren't coming as fast these last few years. So what? You're getting up there on the ladder, ya know. There aren't as many openings you can move up into. You're just upset because they went outside and hired Ed Bush two years back instead of moving you up.

9

Well, they needed a new person to get the changes in, and even you admit you couldn't do the job Eddie's done. He's a real ball of fire. So what if he's a couple years younger than you.

Pete returned to his desk and picked up a piece of paper, staring at it with unseeing eyes. The trouble with being thirty-seven was you didn't have the option of starting over somewhere else. Nobody hires a thirty-five-to-forty-year-old executive expecting him to go places. That was for the young tigers like—like Eddie. If Pete was going to go any further with his career, it would have to be right here.

His thoughts were interrupted by a tingling on his hand. His ringpager. He grimaced. Dick Tracy was alive and well in the corporate world. He thumbed back the lid.

"Hornsby here."

"Yeah, Pete. Eddie." Eddie Bush's voice was identifiable even with the poor sound reproduction of a three-quarter-inch speaker-mike. "Can you stop up at my office for a minute?"

"On my way, Eddie." He thumbed the ring shut and hit a button on his desk. The wood paneling of the north wall of his office faded, giving him a one-way view of his reception area. For a change, his secretary was at her desk. However, she was covertly leafing through a cosmetics catalogue. He touched the intercom button.

"Ginny!" He was rewarded by seeing her start guiltily before hitting her own intercom button.

"Yes, Pete?"

"I'm heading up to Eddie's office. Hold all calls till I get back."

"How long will you be?"

"Don't know. It's one of his surprise calls."

He clicked off the intercom and started across his office. As he approached the south wall, a portion slid back and he entered the executive corridor, stepping onto the eastbound conveyor. He nodded recognition to another executive striding purposefully along the westbound conveyor, but remained standing, letting the conveyor carry him along at a sedate four miles an hour. Corridor-walking varied by section. Some crews walked, some ran in an effort to show frenzied enthusiasm or pseudoimportance. Eddie set the code for their group. Let the convey do it. We're smoothly run to the point to where we don't have to dash around like a bunch of panicked rodents.

Stepping off onto the platform in front of Eddie's door, he hit the intercom button in the doorframe and got an immediate response.

"That you, Pete?"

"Right."

"C'mon in."

The door slid open and he entered Eddie's office.

Eddie's office was not noticeably larger than Pete's, but much more lavishly furnished. Instead of a panoramic scene, Eddie had a moving opti-print on his viewscreen. The print had always given Pete an uneasy feeling of vertigo, but he didn't say anything.

"Make yourself comfortable, Pete. It's two sugars, no cream, right?"

"Right." In spite of himself, Pete was always pleased when Eddie remembered small details like that.

Eddie punched the appropriate buttons on the Servo-Matic and in a few seconds, the coffee hummed into view.

"That reminds me, Eddie. My Servo-Matic is down. Can you lean on someone to get it fixed?"

"Have you called maintenance?"

"Daily for two weeks. All I get is double-talk and forms to fill out."

"I'll see what I can do. What are you working on right now?"

"Nothing special. Pushing around a few ideas, but nothing that couldn't be delegated or put on hold. Why? What's up?"

"We've had a live one tossed in our laps, and I need that detail brain of yours working on it. I just got back from headquarters— talked with Becker himself.

"Who?"

"Becker, one of the international VPs. Check your conspectus— you'll see his name. Anyway, it seems we've been picked as one of several teams assigned to submit recommendations on this. It's a chance for some nice exposure at the top levels."

"Who else is working on it?"

"Higgins on the East Coast and Marcus in New Orleans."

"Higgins? I thought he got dumped after his last fiasco."

"Just shelved. If you want my guess, someone's using this assignment as an excuse to dump him. I'd be willing to bet that whatever he turns in, it gets rejected. I'm guessing he'll be out by the end of the year."

"It's about time. Who's Marcus?"

"Never met him. He's supposed to be some kind of genius, but the word is he rubs a lot of people the wrong way. If he thinks you're an ass, he'll say so. You can imagine how well that goes over in the brainstorming sessions."

Pete lit a cigarette and exhaled thoughtfully.

"So our competition is a three-time loser and a loud-mouthed whiz kid. If we can't beat that, we should hang it up."

"That's the way I see it. But don't short-sell Marcus. If he's lasted this long, he must have something going for him. There's a chance someone's watching for some real dynamic ideas from him. We'll have to watch close, and if things look like they are leaning his way, decide if we go for the kill or if we want to cover."

"How much time have we got?"

Eddie grimaced.

"Quote, as much time as you need to do a good job, unquote. In other words, whoever submits first is going to be holding up their presentation for the other two teams to tear apart. On the other hand, if we take too long, we're going to look like a bunch of old women who can't make up their minds."

Pete thought it over for a few minutes, then shrugged.

"If that's the rules, that's the rules. We play the cards as they're dealt. Okay, what's the assignment?"

"Are you ready for this? Our everlovin' communications conglomerate has got a war on its hands."

"Come again?"

"You heard me. A war. You know—soldiers, bullets, tanks—a war."

"Okay, I'll bite. What are we supposed to do about it?"

"Nothing much. Just keep a lid on it. We're supposed to come up with a bunch of ideas to keep the public from finding out about it, and at the same time start conditioning the public so that they'll accept it if the word ever leaks out."

"Are you serious? C'mon, Eddie, we're talking about a war! People are bound to notice a war!"

"It's not as wild as it sounds. This thing's been going on for nearly a year—have you heard anything about it?"

"Well . . . no."

"What's more, there are supposedly three other wars going on at the same time—one in Iceland over the fishing rights, one in Africa over the diamond mining, and one in the Great Plains over oil. Corporate wars are nothing new. At least that's what Becker says."

"So who are we fighting?"

"That's where it gets a bit tricky. We're up against one of the biggest oil companies in the world."

"And we're supposed to keep a lid on it?"

"Cheer up. It's being fought in Brazil."

Pete studied his cigarette for a few moments.

"Okay, I'll ask the big one. Who do we get for the task force? Our choice, or assigned?"

"Pretty much carte blanche. Why? Do you have anyone specific in mind?"

"Well, I'll want a personnel listing of anyone in the plant who's been in the service or lost a member of his family in a war; but there is one I'll want if we can get him."

"Who's that?"

"Terry Carr."

"Who?"

"The radical freak back in shipping."

"Him? C'mon, Pete. That kid's got a police record for antimilitary activities. What can he give us besides trouble?"

"Another point of view. I figure if we can sell this war to him, we can sell it to anybody."

Now it was Eddie's turn to look thoughtful.

"Let me think about that one. Say, doing anything for lunch?"

"Not really."

"Let's duck out and grab a bite. There're a few ideas I want to bounce off you."

The two men stood up and started for the door. As he walked, Eddie clapped a hand on Pete's shoulder.

"Cheer up, Pete. Remember, no one's ever gone broke overestimating the gullibility of the general public."

Chapter Three

The sound of automatic weapons fire was clearly audible in the Brazilian night as Major Tidwell crawled silently the length of the shadow, taking pains to keep his elbows close to his body. Tree shadows were only so wide. He probed ahead with his left hand until he found the fist-sized rock with the three sharp corners which he had gauged as his landmark.

Once it was located, he sprang the straps on the jump pad he had been carrying over his shoulder and eased it into position. With the care of a professional, he double-checked its alignment: front edge touching the rock and lying at a forty-five-degree angle to an imaginary line running from the rock to the large tree on his left, flat on the ground, no wrinkles or lumps.

"Check."

This done, he allowed himself the luxury of taking a moment to try to see the scanner fence. Nothing. He shook his head with grudging admiration. If it hadn't been scouted and confirmed in advance, he would never have known there was a "fence" in front of him. The set posts were camouflaged to the point where he couldn't spot them even knowing what he was looking for, and there were no telltale light beams penetrating the dark of the night. Yet he knew that just in front of him was a maze of relay beams which, if interrupted, would trigger over a dozen automount weapons and direct their fire into a ten-meter-square area centering on the point the beams were interrupted. An extremely effective trap as well as a foolproof security system, but it was only five meters high.

He smiled to himself. Those cost accountants will do it to you every time. Why build a fence eight meters high if you can get by with one five meters high? The question was, could they get by with a five-meter fence?

Well, now was as good a time as any to find out. He checked the straps of his small backpack to be sure there was no slack. Satisfied there was no play to throw him off balance, his hand moved to his throat mike.

"Lieutenant Decker!"

"Here, sir!" The voice of his first lieutenant was soft in the earphone. It would be easy to forget that he was actually over five hundred meters away leading the attack on the south side of the compound. Nice thing about fighting for the ITT-iots—your communications were second to none.

"I'm in position now. Start the diversion."

"Yes, sir!"

He rose slowly to a low crouch and backed away from the pad several steps in a duck walk. The tiny luminous dots on the corners of the jump pad marked its location for him exactly.

Suddenly, the distant firing doubled in intensity as the diversionary frontal attack began. He waited several heartbeats for any guard's attention to be drawn to the distant fight, then rose to his full height, took one long stride, and jumped on the pad hard with both feet.

The pad recoiled from the impact of his weight, kicking him silently upward. As he reached the apex of his flight, he tucked and somersaulted like a diver, extending his legs again to drop feet first; but it was still a long way down. His forward momentum was lost by the time he hit the ground, and the impact forced him to his knees as he tried to absorb the shock. He fought for a moment to keep his balance, lost it, and fell heavily on his back.

"Damn!" He quickly rolled over onto all fours and scuttled crabwise forward to crouch in the deep shadow next to the autogun turret. Silently he waited, not moving a muscle, eyes probing the darkness.

He had cleared the "fence." If he hadn't, he would be dead by now. But if there were any guards left, the sound of his fall would have alerted them. There hadn't been much noise, but it didn't take much. These Oil Slickers were good. Then again, there were the explosives in his pack.

Tidwell grimaced as he scanned the shadows. He didn't like explosives no matter how much he worked with them. Even though he knew they were insensitive to impact and could only be detonated by the radio control unit carried by his lieutenant, he didn't relish the possibility of having to duplicate that fall if challenged.

Finally his diligence was rewarded—a small flicker of movement by the third hut. Moving slowly, the major loosened the strap on his pistol. His gamble of carrying the extra bulk of a silenced weapon was about to pay off. Drawing the weapon, he eased it forward and settled the luminous sights in the vicinity of the movement, waiting for a second tip-off to fix the guard's location.

Suddenly, he holstered the weapon and drew his knife instead. If there was one, there would be two, and the sound of his shot, however muffled, would tip the second guard to sound the alarm. He'd just have to do this the hard way.

He had the guard spotted now, moving silently from hut to hut. There was a pattern to his search, and that pattern would kill him. Squat and check shadows beside the hut, move, check window, move, check window, move, hesitate, step into alley between the huts with rifle at ready, hesitate three beats to check shadows in alley, move, squat and check side shadows, move . . .

Apparently the guard thought the intruder, if he existed, would be moving deeper into the compound and was hoping to come to him silently from behind. The only trouble was the intruder was behind him.

Tidwell smiled. Come on, sonny! Just a few more steps. Silently he drew his legs under him and waited. The guard had reached the hut even with the turret he was crouched behind. Squat, move, check window, move, check window, move, hesitate, step into alley . . .

He moved forward in a soft glide. For three heartbeats the guard was stationary, peering into the shadows in the alley between the huts. In those three heartbeats Tidwell closed the distance between them in four long strides, knife held low and poised. His left arm snaked forward and snapped his forearm across the guard's windpipe, ending any possibility of an outcry as the knife darted home under the left shoulder blade.

The guard's reflexes were good. As the knife blade retracted into its handle, the man managed to flinch with surprise before his body went into the forced, suit-induced limpness ordered by his belt computer. Either the man had incredible reflexes or his suit was malfunctioning.

Tidwell eased the "dead" body to the ground, then swiftly removed the ID bracelet. As he rose to go, he glanced at the man's face and hesitated involuntarily. Even in the dark he knew him—Clancy! He should have recognized him from his style. Clancy smiled and winked to acknowledge mutual recognition. You couldn't do much else in a "dead" combat suit.

Tidwell paused long enough to smile and tap his fallen rival on the forehead with the point of his knife. Clancy rolled his eyes in silent acknowledgement. He was going to have a rough time continuing his argument that knives were inefficient after tonight.

Then the major was moving again. Friendship was fine, but he had a job to do and he was running behind schedule. A diversion can only last so long. Quickly he backtracked Clancy's route, resheathing his knife and drawing his pistol as he went. A figure materialized out of the shadows ahead.

"I told you there wouldn't be anything there!" came the whispered comment.

Tidwell shot him in the chest, his weapon making a muffled *pfut*, and the figure crumpled. Almost disdainfully, the major relieved him of his ID bracelet. Obviously this man wouldn't last long. In one night he had made two major mistakes: ignoring a sound in the night, and talking on silent guard. It was men like this who gave mercenaries a bad name.

He paused to orient himself. Up two more huts and over three.

Abandoning much of his earlier stealth, he moved swiftly onward in a low crouch, pausing only at intersections to check for hostile movement. He had a momentary advantage with the two quadrant guards out of action, but it would soon come to an abrupt halt when the roaming guards made their rounds.

Then he was at his target, a hut indistinguishable from any of the other barracks or duty huts in the compound. The difference was that Intelligence confirmed and cross-confirmed that this was it! The command post of the compound! Inside this hut was the nerve center of the defense, all tactical officers as well as the communication equipment necessary to coordinate the troops.

Tidwell unslung his pack and eased it to the ground next to him. Opening the flap, he withdrew four charges, checking the clock on each to insure synchronization. He had seen beautiful missions ruled invalid because time of explosion (TOE) could not be verified, and it wasn't going to happen to him. He double-checked the clocks. He didn't know about the communications or oil companies, but the Timex industry should be making a hefty profit out of this war.

Tucking two charges under his arm and grasping one in each hand, he made a quick circuit of the building, pausing at each corner just long enough to plant a charge on the wall. The fourth charge he set left-handed, the silenced pistol back in his right hand, eyes probing the dark. It was taking too long! The roaming guards would be around any minute now.

Rising to his feet, he darted away, running at high speed now, stealth completely abandoned. Two huts away he slid to a stop, dropping prone and flattening against the wall of the hut. Without pausing to catch his breath, his left hand went to his throat mike.

"Decker! They're set! Blow it!"

Nothing happened.

"Decker! Can you read me? Blow it!" He tapped the mike with his fingernail.

Still nothing.

"Blow it, damn you—"

POW!

Tidwell rolled to his feet and darted around the corner. Even though it sounded loud in the stillness of the night, that was no explosion. Someone was shooting, probably at him.

"Decker! Blow it!"

POW! POW!

No mistaking it now. He was drawing fire. Cursing, he snapped off a round in the general direction of the shots, but it was a lost cause and he knew it. Already he could hear shouts as more men took up the pursuit. If he could only lead them away from the charges. Ducking around a corner, he flattened against the wall and tried to catch his breath. Again he tried the mike.

"Decker!"

The door of the hut across the alley burst open, flooding the scene with light. As if in a nightmare, he snapped off a shot at the figure silhouetted in the door as he scrambled backwards around the corner.

POW!

He was dead. There was no impact of the "bullet," but his suit collapsed, taking him with it as it crumpled to the ground. Even if he could move now, which he couldn't, it would do him no good. The same quartz light beam that scored the fatal hit on his suit deactivated his weapons. He could do nothing but lie there helplessly as his killer approached to relieve him of his ID bracelet. The man bending over him raised his eyebrows in silent surprise when he saw the rank of his victim, but he didn't comment on it. You don't talk to a corpse.

As the man moved on, Tidwell sighed and settled back to wait. No one would reactivate his suit until thirty minutes after the last shot was fired. His only hope would be if Decker would detonate the charges, but he knew that wouldn't happen. It was another foul-up.

Damn radios! Another mission blown to hell!

The major sighed again. Lying there in a dead suit was preferable to actually being dead, but that might be open to debate when he reported in. Someone's head would roll over tonight's failure. As the senior officer, he was the logical choice.

Chapter Four

"Hey, Fred! Wait a minute!"

Fred Willard stopped with one hand on the glass doors and turned to see Ivan Kramitz waving at him from the sidewalk. Forcing a smile, he waved back and waited to see what the son-of-a-bitch wanted.

He hated Ivan with a passion, and knew it was reciprocated. Their dislike for each other was not particularly surprising as the men were physical and cultural opposites competing successfully in identical positions. Ivan was a recent immigrant to America—some said a refugee from the Russo-Chinese War—while Fred was from a long line of fringe-poor Americans. Where Ivan was the image of a Hungarian fencing master in appearance, poise, and arrogance, Fred knew his rounded figure and rolling gait brought to mind a beer-swilling, red-necked cop. Add to this their age difference—Fred in his mid-fifties, Ivan in his early thirties—and the fact that they were employed by rival corporations, and it was inevitable that each saw his rival as the personification of everything he hated and fought against.

However, you couldn't ignore a chance to talk with the second-in-command of Oil's negotiating team outside of the conference room, particularly if you're third in command of the Communications negotiating team. So Fred waited while Ivan closed the distance between them at a leisurely saunter.

"Sorry to keep you waiting, my friend, but I did want to speak with you before you headed in." Ivan smiled through his accent.

Fred returned his smile with an equally insincere toothiness. He had discovered several weeks ago that when he wanted to, Ivan could speak flawless English and only used the accent to irritate Fred.

"No problem, Ivan. What can I do for you?"

"I was merely curious if your team was still interested in that four million barrels of fuel?"

Interested? Damn straight they were interested. They had forty fighter planes grounded until they could get reserves back up.

"I'm not sure, Ivan. I'll have to check with the boys. Why? Are the Oil czars loosening up a bit?"

"Possibly. I've heard a few rumors I might be able to follow up on. Just because they refused your first few offers doesn't mean they aren't interested. Maybe if you offered an exchange instead of a simple purchase. I have relatively reliable information that they might be willing to release the fuel if Communications were willing to share the plans for the throat-mike communicators currently in use."

Bingo! Those bastards wouldn't be so ready to deal if those throat-mike systems weren't giving them real problems. Time to twist the old knife a little.

"I dunno, Ivan. The boys are mighty touchy about those little toys. I don't think they'd be too wild about our trading them off that easily."

Ivan grinned like a barracuda.

"As a matter of fact, Frederick, the rumor I heard stated specifically that your troops were not to be notified of the exchange. You know, a little . . . 'under the table' deal between old friends."

You son-of-a-bitch! You want us to sell our own men down the river! You want us to turn your Oil Slicker wolves loose with those hookups without warning our own troops!

"N-F-W! No fucking way, baby!" He maintained his smile even though it hurt. "No way will we turn those toys loose unannounced for a few crummy gallons of fuel!"

"You disappoint me, my friend. Certainly my superiors are aware that such an exchange would require some additional bonuses for Communications."

"Such as what?"

"Unfortunately those figures are not available at this time. Perhaps we could continue our discussion over lunch?" Without waiting for an answer, he stepped past Fred and disappeared into the depths of the building.

Those figures are not available—damn! That bastard had the pat phrases down cold. In corporate jargon, he had just said, "Eat your heart out, sweetheart. I'm not saying anything more until I'm good and ready!"

Shit! It was times like this you hated being a negotiator. It was clear that the Oilers wanted those hookups and on their terms. And they'd get them. Ivan was far too confident not to be sure his offer would be beyond refusal.

The irritating part was that he had specifically chosen Fred to make his offer to. Not only did he know his offer couldn't be refused, he also knew Fred hated like the plague to give in. If Fred had his way, Oil could offer their entire North American—hell, their whole western hemisphere holdings before he sold their own men down the river.

But he followed orders just like everyone else, and if the Lord High Muckity-Mucks decided it was a good idea, he'd have to knuckle under and accept it. Ivan knew that and was doubtlessly glorying in it.

Not for the first time, Fred contemplated what Ivan's face would look like mashed to a bloody pulp. With a deep sigh he entered the conference room.

It was a spacious room, even with two dozen men in it. Fred smiled at the two groups huddled at their respective ends of the room, murmuring together and casting dark glances at their opposing numbers. He was greeted by the traditional assortment of grunts and vague waves. Really friendly bunch, this. But then again, they weren't being paid to be friendly. Like everyone else in the world of corporations they were paid for results.

The unfortunate part about being a negotiator was that no one was ever satisfied with your results. Everyone could have done better.

Small wonder the rate of casualties due to nervous breakdowns and/or suicide was so high. Of those that survived, most retired young. Fred was the exception, at fifty-three, he was one of the oldest and most respected negotiators in the business.

"Gentlemen, could we get started now?"

It was the Senior Negotiator for Oil, it being Oil's day to chair the meeting. One by one the team members drifted to their seats. There was no hurry as it would take at least fifteen minutes from the time the room was sealed before the electronic detectors could confirm the room was free of listening devices.

Fred dropped heavily into his seat in the move so characteristic of overweight men. As were many of his habitual moves and gestures, this move was theoretically exaggerated to irritate and mislead his opponents. Anyone observing him would dismiss him as a harmless, slightly comical character—that is, anyone who hadn't seen him sidestep an angry longshoreman, then ram the offending party's head through a wall. Fred Willard learned his diplomacy not in a fine old university but on the streets and dockyards of Chicago.

"The meeting will come to order!"

Fred sighed and punched the buttons on his console for his regular morning stimulants. The tray hissed into view bearing his ungodly trio: a glass of orange juice, a cup of black coffee, and a cold can of beer. Fred took private glee in his traditional can of beer among the bloody marys and screwdrivers of his colleagues. He knew it irritated them, and an irritated opponent is a careless opponent.

"The chair recognizes the Third Negotiator for Oil."

Fred groaned inwardly. Those bastards! Why did they always have to start their damn cute maneuvers so early in the morning? The cuter the move, the earlier they started, and this one promised to be a beaut. With a grimace, he punched the record button on his console. Better get this on tape. He'd want to study it later.

The Third Negotiator for Oil was Judy Simmons, an attractive young girl fresh out of college. When she first joined the negotiations, many had ignored her, thinking her to be a "companion" of one of the men. This illusion was short-lived. She had proved herself to be as cold and merciless as any man on the team—maybe a little colder. No one could get a firm line on her background, but it was Fred's theory she had been recruited from one of the campus radical groups—the ones who execute hostages one at a time until their demands are met. Some of the men still speculated privately as to her availability as a bed partner, but Fred had long since reached an opinion: he'd rather sleep with a king cobra than let her near him, even if the opportunity presented itself.

"Gentlemen: as you know we have been engaged for some time in what is essentially a war game—simulated combat. This type of fighting was agreed upon in the early phases of the war as both sides sought to reduce the cost of replacing equipment and troops lost in combat. Through the use of IBM belt computers and Sony 'kill suits,' it became unnecessary to actually kill a man or blow up an installation, but merely prove that you could have done it."

Fred began fidgeting with his beer can as she droned on. He wondered where this history lesson was leading.

"The only condition placed on the use of 'mock weapons' was that if the effectiveness of a weapon was challenged, the side employing the weapon had to be able to produce a functioning model to support its claims." She looked up from her notes to smile toothily at the assemblage.

"Of course, the close adherence of the mercenary forces to the mock combat rules may be at least partially attributable to the knowledge that at the first sign of flagrant violation, the old style of 'live ammo' fighting would be immediately reinstated."

A small titter rippled through the room. Fred wondered how many of them had ever been shot at with live ammo.

"So far this system has proved more than an adequate method for allowing us to settle our differences while keeping costs at a minimum. However, it has been recently brought to our attention that there is a major shortcoming to this system."

Fred was suddenly attentive. Behind the sleepy fat-man exterior he used, a little computer clicked on in his mind. Major policy change . . . initial proposal and justifications . . . record and analyze. Of course he was not alone. An intense silence blanketed the room as Judy continued.

"The problem, gentlemen, is one of logistics. One of the oldest techniques of military intelligence is to watch the enemy's supplies. By watching the amount of supplies drawn and the direction in which they are transported, it's possible to second-guess the next attack and institute countermoves before the attack is actually launched."

One of the closed-circuit screens on Fred's console lit up, indicating an oncoming note from one of his teammates. He ignored it. No sense speculating on what she was about to say next when by waiting for a few more seconds you could hear it. Instead, he centered his attention on her presentation.

"Then, too, there's the guns and butter choice where limited supplies are available. Ammo dumps aren't bottomless. If you've only got a million rounds of ammunition, you can't hit three major targets in one night. You have to choose which one you want the most and how much you're willing to venture on the attack. What we've done with our 'simulated war' is grant the field commanders carte blanche to fight as often as they want, wherever they want. Oil maintains that this is one of the major reasons neither side is able to win this war. We've made it too cheap, too easy to prolong."

There was a low murmur going around the room now, occasionally accented by ill-muffled curses. She ignored it and continued.

"Frankly, gentlemen, we're tired of having the same quote, bomb, unquote dropped on us a hundred times in three different locations four nights a week. To alleviate that problem, we propose the following: to effectively simulate the actual logistics problems found in any war, it ought to be necessary to establish a one-for-one depletion of ammunition and equipment lost in combat. That is, at the end of each conflict, an accurate count must be determined of each side's losses, and an equivalent amount of live ammo or real equipment destroyed. Furthermore, each side has to establish and maintain ammo dumps, and 'replenishment supplies' must be physically transported to the actual site of combat."

"Mr. Chairman!"

It was one of the negotiators for Communications. The Chairman nodded his recognition and the battle was joined.

"We might as well go back to using live ammo. This proposal not only duplicates the cost of a live ammo war, it increases it because of all the necessary records-keeping and controls."

"Not really!" Ivan fielded the challenge for Oil. "In a live ammo war, men are lost, and we all know how expensive they are to recruit and train."

Fred jumped into the fray.

"I don't suppose you have any rough figures handy as to how much this proposal would cost if accepted?"

"That all depends on how straight your men can shoot and how effectively they're deployed. That and how much money Communications is willing to spend to win the war."

"How much ammunition has Oil already stockpiled prior to the proposal of this change in the agreed-upon rules?"

"Those figures are not available at this time."

Fred leaned back and shut his eyes thoughtfully as the battle raged around him. That was that. If Oil had already stockpiled, they'd never back down from this proposal. They couldn't, or all the money spent stockpiling would have to be written off as a loss. Communications would be starting with a handicap, but one thing for sure, they wouldn't let themselves be bought out of the war. It was more than pride, it was survival!

If word ever got out that Communications let themselves be run out of a clash because of high costs, the other corporations would be all over them like wolves on a sick caribou. Everything would suddenly cost triple because the opposition would be trying to back them down on costs. No, they couldn't back out. And the accountants thought that costs-to-date on this war were high now! They hadn't seen anything yet. Fred's only hope was that they could stall accepting the proposal long enough to let Communications catch up a bit on the stockpiling. If they didn't, their forces in the field would be caught short of ammo and overwhelmed.

"Move to adjourn!" he interrupted without opening his eyes.

Chapter Five

The bar was clearly military, high-class military, but military nonetheless. One of the most apparent indications of this was that it offered live waitresses as an option. Of course, having a live waitress meant your drinks cost more, but the military men were one of the last groups of holdouts who were willing to pay extra rather than be served the impersonal hydrolift of a Servo-Matic.

Steve Tidwell, former major, and his friend Clancy were well entrenched at their favorite corner table, a compromise reached early in their friendship as a solution to the problem of how they could both sit with their backs to the wall.

"Let me get this round, Steve," ordered Clancy, dipping into his pocket. "That severance pay of yours may have to last you a long time."

"Hi Clancy, Steve," their waitress smiled, delivering the next round of drinks. "Flo's tied up out back, so I thought I'd better get these to you before you got ugly and started tearing up the place."

"There's a love," purred Clancy, tucking a folded bill into her cleavage. She ignored him.

"Steve, what's this I hear about you getting cashiered?"

Tidwell took a sudden interest in the opposite wall. Clancy caught

29

the waitress's eye and gave a minute shake of his head. She nodded knowingly and departed.

"Seriously, Steve, what *are* you going to do now?"

Tidwell shrugged. "I don't know. Go back to earning my money in the live ammo set, I guess."

"Working for whom? In case you haven't figured it out, you're blacklisted. The only real fighting left is in the Middle East, and the Oil Combine won't touch you."

"Don't be so sure of that. They were trying pretty hard to buy me away from the ITT-iots a couple of months ago."

Clancy snorted contemptuously. "A couple of months. Hell, I don't care if it was a couple days. That was before they gave you your walking papers. I'm telling you they won't give you the time of day now. 'If you're not good enough for Communications, you're not good enough for Oil.' That'll be their attitude. You can bet on it."

Tidwell studied his drink in silence for a while, then took a hefty swallow.

"You're right, Clancy," he said softly. "But do you mind if I kid myself long enough to get good and drunk?"

"Sorry, Steve," apologized his friend. "It's just that for a minute there I thought you really believed what you were saying."

Tidwell lifted his glass in a mock toast.

"Well, here's to inferior superiors and inferior inferiors—the stuff armies are made of!"

He drained the glass and signaled for another.

"Really, Steve. You've got to admit the troops didn't let you down this time."

"True enough. But only because I gave them an assignment worthy of their talents: cannon fodder! 'Rush those machine guns and keep rushing until I say different!' Is it my imagination or is the quality of our troops actually getting worse? And speaking of that, who was that clown on guard with you?"

Clancy sighed.

"Maxwell. Would you believe he's one of our best?"

"That's what I mean! Ever since the corporations started building their own armies, all we get is superstars who can't follow orders and freeze up when they're shot at. Hell, give me some of the old-timers like you and Hassan. If we could build our own force with the corporations' bankroll, if we could get our choice of the crop and pay them eighteen to forty grand a year, we could take over the world in a month."

"Then what would you do with it?"

"Hell, I don't know. I'm a soldier, not a politician. But damn it, I'm proud of my work and if nothing else, it offends my sense of aesthetics to see some of the slipshod methods and tactics that seem to abound in any war. So much could be done with just a few really good men."

"Well, we're supposed to be working with the best available men now. You should see the regular armies that the governments field!"

"Regular armies! Wash your mouth out with Irish. And speaking of that . . ."

The next round of drinks was arriving.

"Say Flo, love. Tell Bonnie I'm sorry if I was so short with her last round. If she comes by again, I'll try to make it up to her."

He made a casual pass at slipping his arm around her waist, but she sidestepped automatically without really noticing it.

"I'll tell her, Steve, but don't hold your breath about her coming back. I think you're safer when you're sulking!"

She turned to go and received a loud whack on her backside from Clancy. She squealed, then grinned, and did an exaggerated burlesque walk away while the two men roared with laughter.

"Well, at least it's good to see you're loosening up a little," commented Clancy as their laughter subsided. "For a while there, you had me worried."

"You know me. Pour enough Irish into me and I'll laugh through a holocaust! But you know, you're right, Clancy—about the men not letting me down, I mean. I think that's what's really irritating me about this whole thing."

He leaned back and rested his head against the wall.

"If the men had fallen down on the job, or if the plan had been faulty in its logic, or if I had tripped the fence beams, or any one of a dozen other possibilities, I could take it quite calmly. Hazards of the trade and all that. But to get canned over something that wasn't my fault really grates."

"They couldn't find any malfunction with the throat-mikes?"

"Just like the other two times. I personally supervised the technicians when they dismantled it, checked every part and connection, and nothing! Even I couldn't find anything wrong and believe me, I was looking hard. Take away the equipment failure excuse, and the only possibility is an unreliable commander, and Stevey boy gets his pink slip."

"Say, could you describe the internal circuitry of those things to me?"

In a flash the atmosphere changed. Tidwell was still leaning against the wall in a drunken pose, but his body was suddenly poised and his eyes were clear and wary.

"C'mon, Clancy. What is this? You know I can't breach confidence with an employer, even an ex-employer. If I did, I'd never work again."

Clancy sipped his drink unruffled by his friend's challenge.

"You know it, and I know it, but my fellow Oil Slickers don't know it. I just thought I'd toss the question out to make my pass legit. You know the routine. 'We're old buddies and he's just been canned. If you'll just give me a pass tonight I might be able to pour a few drinks into him and get him talking.' You know the bit."

"Well, you're at least partially successful." Tidwell hoisted his glass again, sipped, and set it down with a clink. "So much for frivolity! Do you have any winning ideas for my future?"

Clancy tasted his drink cautiously.

"I dunno, Steve. The last really big blow I was in was the Russo-Chinese War."

"Well, how about that one? I know they shut down their borders and went incommunicado after it was over, but that's a big hunk of land and a lot of people. There must be some skirmishes internally."

"I got out under the wire, but if you don't mind working for another ideology, there might be something."

"Ideology, schmideology. Like I said before, I'm a soldier, not a politician. Have you really got a line of communication inside the Block?"

"Well—"

"Excuse us, gentlemen."

The two mercenaries looked up to find a trio of men standing at a short distance from their table. One was Oriental, the other two Caucasian. All were in business suits and carried attaché cases.

"If you would be so good as to join us in a private room, I believe it would be to our mutual advantage."

"The pleasure is ours," replied Tidwell, formally rising to follow. He caught Clancy's eye and raised an eyebrow. Clancy winked back in agreement. This had contract written all over it.

As they passed the bar, Flo flashed them an old aviator's "thumbs-up" sign signifying that she had noticed what was going on and their table would still be waiting for them when they returned. To further their hopes, the room they were led to was one of the most expensive available at the bar—that is, one the management guaranteed for its lack of listening devices or interruptions. There were drinks already waiting on the conference table, and the Oriental gestured for them to be seated.

"Allow me to introduce myself. I am Mr. Yamada."

His failure to introduce his companions identified them as bodyguards. Almost as a reflex, the two mercenaries swept them with a cold, appraising glance, then returned their attention to Yamada.

"Am I correct in assuming I am addressing Stephen Tidwell?" His eyes shifted. "Michael Clancy?"

The two men nodded silently. For the time being, they were content to let him do the talking.

"Am I further correct in my information that you have recently been dismissed by the Communications Combine, Mr. Tidwell?"

Again Steve nodded. Although he tried not to show it, inwardly he was irritated. What had they done? Gone through town posting notices?

Yamada reached into his pocket and withdrew two envelopes. Placing them on the table, he slid one to each of the two men.

"Each of these envelopes contains one thousand dollars, American. With them, I am purchasing your time for the duration of this conversation. Regardless of its outcome, I am relying on your professional integrity to keep the existence of this meeting as well as the content of the discussion itself in strictest confidence."

Again the two men nodded silently. This was the standard opening of a negotiating session, protecting both the mercenary and the person approaching him.

"Very well. Mr. Tidwell, we would like to contract your services for sixty thousand dollars a year plus benefits."

Clancy choked on his drink. Tidwell straightened in his chair.

"Sixty thousand—"

"And Mr. Clancy, we would further like to contract your services for forty-five thousand dollars a year. This would of course not include the eighteen-thousand five-hundred dollars we would have to provide to enable you to terminate your contract with the Oil Coalition."

By this time, both men were gaping at him in undisguised astonishment. Clancy was the first to regain his composure.

"Mister, you don't beat around the bush, do you?"

"Excuse my asking," interrupted Steve, "but isn't that a rather large sum to offer without checking our records?"

"Believe me, Mr. Tidwell, we have checked your records. Both your records." Yamada smiled. "Let me assure you, gentlemen, this is not a casual offer. Rather, it is the climax of several months of exhaustive study and planning."

"Just what are we expected to do for this money?" asked Clancy cagily, sipping his drink without taking his eyes off the Oriental.

"You, Mr. Clancy, are to serve as aide and advisor to Mr. Tidwell. You, Mr. Tidwell, are to take command of the final training phases of, and lead into battle, a select force of men. You are to have final say as to qualifications of the troops as well as the tactics to be employed."

"Whose troops and in what battle are they to be employed?"

"I represent the Zaibatsu, a community of Japanese-based corporations, and the focus of our attention is the Oil vs. Communications war currently in process."

"You want us to lead troops against those idiots? Our pick of men and our tactics?" Clancy smiled. "Mister, you've got yourself a mercenary!"

Tidwell ignored his friend.

"I'd like a chance to view the force before I give you my final decision."

"Certainly, Mr. Tidwell," Yamada nodded. "We agree to this condition willingly because we are sure you will find the men at your disposal more than satisfactory."

"In that case, I think we are in agreement. Shall we start now?"

Tidwell started to rise, closely followed by Clancy, but Yamada waved them back into their seats.

"One last detail, gentlemen. Zaibatsu believes in complete honesty with its employees, and there is something I feel you should be aware of before accepting our offer. The difficulties you have been encountering recently, Mr. Tidwell, with your equipment and, Mr. Clancy, with your assignments, have been engineered by the Zaibatsu to weaken your ties with your current employers and insure your availability for our offer."

Again both men gaped at him.

"But . . . how?" blurted Tidwell finally.

"Mr. Clancy's commanding officer who showed such poor judgment in giving him his team assignments is in our employment and acting on our orders. And as for Mr. Tidwell's equipment failure . . ." He turned a bland stare toward Steve. "Let us merely say that even though Communications holds the patent on the throat-mikes, the actual production was subcontracted to a Zaibatsu member. Something to do with the high cost of domestic labor. We took the liberty of making certain 'modifications' in their designs, all quite undetectable, with the result that we now have the capacity to cut off or override their command communications at will."

By this time the two mercenaries were beyond astonishment. Any anger they might have felt at being manipulated was swept away by the vast military implications of what they had just been told.

"You mean we can shut down their communications any time we want? And you have infiltrators at the command level of the Oiler forces?"

"In both forces, actually. Nor are those our only advantages. As I said earlier, this is not a casual effort. I trust you will be able to find some way to maximize the effect of our entry?"

With a forced calmness, Tidwell finished his drink, then rose and extended his hand across the table.

"Mr. Yamada, it's going to be a pleasure working for you!"

Chapter Six

Mausier paused to wipe the beads of sweat from his forehead, then bent to his task once more. Adjusting the high-intensity lamp to a different angle, he picked up the watchmaker's tool and made a minute change in setting in the field terminal in front of him.

Without removing his eyepiece, he set aside the tool, reached over to the keyboard at the end of his workbench and input the data. Finally he leaned back and heaved a sigh. Done. He flexed his hands to restore circulation as he surveyed his handiwork.

The field terminal was a work of art. It could easily pass for a cigarette case, as it was supposed to. But if you pressed in three corners simultaneously, the inner metal lining folded out to reveal its interior workings, stark but functional. Two wires on mini-retracting reels were concealed in the hinge and could be pulled out to connect the unit to any phone. On the side of the lid was a tiny viewscreen. On the other side of the unit was a small keyboard containing both numbers and letters for data input. There was also the thumb-lock. Once the connection was made, the agent pressed his left thumb onto the metal square which would scan his print for comparison to the one on record in the master file. It would also check his body temperature to see if he was alive and his pulse to see if he was in an agitated state. If any of the three checks didn't match, the unit would self-destruct. Nothing as spectacular as an explosion—merely a small thermal unit to fuse the circuitry.

The Japanese had outdone themselves in producing these units for him. All he had to do was to make final adjustments for the individual's code number before it was issued. This allowed private communication with the individual client in addition to the general announcement postings.

Mausier smiled proudly at the unit. He had come a long way from his coincidental beginning in the business. At a cocktail party, one of his acquaintances had almost jokingly offered to pay him for details on a new machine modification Tom's company was working on. Tom had just as jokingly declined, but expressed an interest in the sincerity of the offer. The result had been an evening-long conversation in which his friend enlightened him as to the intricacies of corporate espionage and the high prices demanded and received due to the risks involved.

A short time after—within the week in fact—another friend of Tom's, this one within his own company, had admitted to him over coffee the dire financial straits he was in and how he was ready to take any reasonable risk to raise more money fast. Tom repeated his other friend's offer and volunteered to serve as a go-between.

In the years to follow, he served in a similar capacity for many similar transactions. Some of the people he dealt with were caught and dismissed for their activities, but he always escaped the repercussions due to the indirect nature of his involvement. Eventually, his clientele grew to the point to where he could quietly resign from the corporate world entirely and concentrate his efforts in this highly profitable venture.

Like most people who went into small businesses, the demands he made on himself were far in excess of any the corporation had ever made, yet he labored willingly and happily, realizing he was working because he wanted to and not because he had to. He was his own man, not the corporation's.

Mausier set aside the field terminal and stretched, rolling his shoulders slightly to ease the cramps from the prolonged tension of his work. It was late and he should go to bed. His wife was waiting patiently, probably reading. If he didn't go up soon, there would be hell to pay. As it was, she had already commented tersely several times in the last week about his lengthening his already long hours.

Finally he made up his mind. To hell with it! A few more minutes couldn't hurt. Having made his decision, he settled in at his desk and turned on his doodle-screen. It never crossed his mind that his wife might grow impatient enough to enter his office and interrupt his work. She might nag or scold or sulk once he entered the house, but she knew better than to interrupt him when he was working.

The workspace he keyed for was by now hauntingly familiar. The Brazil workspace. He still thought of it as that even though by now it had spread to cover other areas. He should call it the Brazil-Iceland-Africa-Great Plains workspace, but the two items from Brazil had gotten him started, and it stayed in his mind as the Brazil workspace.

He concentrated on the screen. From the original two items, it had grown until the items listed covered over half the screen. Still, there were several things about the way the problem was progressing which perplexed him. A pattern was forming, but it wasn't making any sense.

He adjusted the controls on the screen and all the items blinked out except the names of the eight corporations. He leaned back and studied them. It was an unusual assortment of business concerns. There were four oil companies, a fishing concern, two mining corporations, and a communications conglomerate listed. What did they have in common? Some were international while some were local. Some were American in origin while some were based overseas. What was it they had in common?

Mausier frowned and played with the controls again. The eight names sorted themselves into pairs and moved apart, two to each corner of the screen. Now he had the two mining concerns (Africa), two of the oil corporations (the Great Plains), an oil corporation and the fishing concern (Iceland), and an oil corporation and the communications conglomerate (Brazil) grouped together. It still didn't make sense. It couldn't be mergers. The interests of the Iceland pair and the Brazil pair were too dissimilar. What's more, if the articles in the business journals were to be believed, the mining interests in Africa and the two oil concerns in the Great Plains were bitter rivals. It couldn't be mergers. What was the common factor of all eight corporations?

Almost unconsciously his hands twitched across the controls and the notation "C-Block" appeared in the center of the screen and blinked like a nagging headache. Another pass over the controls and solid lines appeared, linking each of the eight corporate names with the C-Block notation.

The C-Block had identical standing offers in for the same information on each of the eight corporations: *Any information on new hires and/or terminations at location.* Mausier's hands moved and new lines grew like a spider web. One of the mining concerns had identical standing orders in for the six corporations at the other three locations, as did the communications conglomerate. Both the oil concern and the fishing interest had identical requests in for the pairs on the Great Plains and in Africa.

Mausier should have been very happy. With duplicate requests for the same information, he could either collect his broker's percent for a double sale or see his fee skyrocketed by a bidding war. He should have been happy, but he wasn't. Whether or not the corporations knew the C-Block was watching them, they knew about each other and were watching each other.

Watching each other for what? What was so vital about the personnel at these locations? It was as if there was a pool of specialized workers that the corporations were passing back and forth, but what could it be? Engineers? They had new engineers beating down their doors with resumes. They could pick and choose at leisure. What was so special about the people at these locations? The geography and climate varied dramatically from location to location, so it wasn't a matter of acquiring a work force accustomed to working under a given set of conditions.

He suddenly realized he was working from negatives. Arriving at a solution by process of elimination was always tedious and often impossible due to the vast number of possibilities. It was always better to work with the facts at hand.

He cleared the screen and keyed for the other information requests coming from the eight corporations in question. He scanned them slowly and was again disappointed. Nothing out of the ordinary here. Just the usual interoffice political bickerings and ladder-climbing. How is a specific executive spending his time away from the office? Does anyone have any inside information on a rival's presentation plans? Any information on plans to shift a meeting site to another hotel? If interoffice communications ever improved, Mausier would lose a sizeable portion of his clientele. Still, there was nothing to add to his speculations.

He cleared the board again, this time using the display of a newspaper article. This was one of the few hard fact items in this file. He leaned forward to study it for the twentieth time.

His agent had not been lax or killed when he missed the rendezvous. He had been involved in a traffic accident and was still in the hospital. This article from a Brazilian newspaper gave the details of the incident. It all seemed very aboveboard. His agent had been stopped at a red light when another car hit him from behind, pushing him out into several lanes of busy cross-traffic. Nothing suspicious, except . . . except the driver of the car that hit him from behind was an employee of one of the corporations everyone was watching.

Mausier studied the article again, then shook his head. It had to be coincidence. He remembered what the rendezvous had been about, the sale of plans for some piece of electronics gear being used by the communications conglomerate. The driver, a Michael Clancy, was an employee of the Oil Combine. If he had been aware of the transaction, he would have either allowed it to happen or made some attempt to steal the information himself, which he hadn't done. It must be just what the article said it was—an accident while the employee was out joy riding with some waitress he had picked up in a bar.

Mausier suddenly realized he had been at the doodle-screen for nearly two hours. There would be hell to pay when he went home. Still, there was one more thing he wanted to check.

He cleared the article and keyed for one more item—today's entry to the file. There had been a new request on the board today from the

C-Block, another request for personnel new hires and terminations. The group under study was a group of Japanese business concerns.

Mausier scowled at the request. It bothered him on several levels. First, it was a new factor in his already complicated puzzle, a new front, a new location. But there was something else that concerned him. One of the Japanese businesses listed was the company that manufactured his field terminals. For the first time, Mausier began to feel deep concern for the security of his scramblers.

Chapter Seven

"It's Pete, Eddie. Can I talk with you for a few?"

"C'mon in, Pete. I've been expecting you."

The door slid open, and Pete stepped into Bush's office. The optiprint on the wall was blue today, matching Eddie's suit. Pete ignored it and sank into one of the numerous chairs dotting the office.

"Okay, boss, what went wrong?"

"With the meeting?"

"Yes, with the meeting. What happened?"

"You sound mad."

Pete blew a deep breath out, relaxing a little.

"A bit. More puzzled. I'm trying to be level-headed about all this, but I get the feeling I'm not playing with all the cards."

"The meeting didn't go that badly . . ."

"It didn't go that well either. And it isn't just the meeting, it's the last couple weeks. All of a sudden you're dragging your feet on this thing. I just want to get the air clear between us and find out why."

Bush didn't answer immediately. Instead, he rose from his desk and keyed a cup of coffee from the Servo-Matic machine in the corner. Pete refrained from pointing out that there was already a steaming cup on the desk. He knew better than to crowd Eddie while he was collecting his thoughts.

"I guess you could say that I'm having second thoughts about our approach to this thing."

"The implementation or the basic idea?"

"Both. More the basic idea, though."

Pete closed his eyes and took a deep breath. The team had been busting their butts on this thing, but it wouldn't go if Number One didn't believe in it.

"Okay, let's take it from the top. We all agree that if this thing blows up in our faces, we've got to have public support behind us. Right?"

"Right. And mass media is the fastest way to get it." Eddie's voice sounded mechanical.

"Now then, to do the job up front, to set the stage and create the atmosphere, we're proposing a saturation campaign of movies and specials, all on a military theme, stressing the right of the individual to protect his personal property and emphasizing the evils of government intervention."

"Whoa! Right there. Our whole strategy is based on the assumption that something will go wrong, that word will get out. At best, it comes off as negative thinking. At worst, it sounds like an open accusation of poor security or lack of employee loyalty. We aren't going to be able to sell this program if we come on hostile."

Pete tried to hide his impatience.

"That's why we slant the entire presentation on a 'better safe than sorry' format. C'mon, Eddie. We've been through all this before."

"And that government intervention thing. Why drag the government into it?"

"Okay, from the top. If this thing hits the news, our problem isn't going to be with the Oil Combine. There we've already got the white hats on. We're clear on everything we've done because all we've done is protect our own property. First, we sent the mercenaries in to protect our copper mines when the revolution threatened them; then we merely continued to defend the mines when Oil got the idea of using their mercenaries to take over the mines themselves. Everything we've done can be publicized as being for the good of the customer, us keeping costs down to keep prices down. Hell, even using our own mercenaries fits the pattern. We're paying for this out of our own pockets instead of using vital taxpayer dollars by lobbying for government troops. It was even our idea to rent land from Brazil to fight the war on instead of endangering the mines with on-site combat. As far as us against the Oil Combine, we've got nothing to worry about."

"I thought it was their idea to use Brazil for the fighting."

"It was, but we got it in writing first. That puts it in our pocket as far as history or the press is concerned. We've got 'em cold."

"That's well and good, but what's that got to do with government intervention?"

"If word of this thing gets out, the real battle is going to be with the government. You know Uncle Sammy—anything he can't tax he doesn't like, and anything he doesn't like he meddles with. It's within possibilities that he'll try to make us compromise with the Combine and divvy up the mines. If that happens, there will be a brawl, both in the courts and in Congress. If we're going to win that fight, we've got to have public support solidly behind us. That's where the saturation campaign comes in. If we can get the spark started before the specific case becomes public knowledge, it will be easy to fan it and point it in a direction. Hell, Eddie, you were the one who pointed it out in the first place."

"Well, I was just . . ."

"You were just asking questions that we answered in the first week we had this assignment. Now I thought we had a pretty good working relationship going, Eddie. I could always count on you for a straight answer no matter how unpleasant it was. I'm asking you plain—what's going wrong? If you can't tell me, say so and I'll back off, but don't give me a smoke screen and pretend it's an answer!"

Bush was silent for a few moments, his eyes not meeting Pete's glare. Finally he sighed.

"You're right, Pete. I should have leveled with you sooner."

He opened a drawer on his desk and withdrew a sheaf of papers, tossing them on the desk in front of Pete.

"Here, look at these."

Pete picked up the sheets and started leafing through them. They were photocopies of the rough drafts of some documents. Crossed-out paragraphs and note-filled margins abounded. Whatever they were, they were a long way from presentation state.

"What are they?"

"That's some of the rough drafts of Marcus's presentation."

Pete raised his eyebrows in inquiry.

"Don't ask how I got them. Let's just say they got detoured past a copier on their way to the shredder."

"Do you have stuff from Higgins too?"

Eddie made a disparaging gesture.

"Some, but not as much. He's pushing for a joint effort with the Oil people to save cost. Frankly, I don't think it has a snowball's chance in hell of being accepted. Marcus is the man I'm watching."

"Okay, what's he got here?"

"It all boils down to one assertion. He says we should win the war."

"Win the . . . really? Just like that?"

"Oh, there's lots of back-up. He works off the same supposition that we do—that if the war lasts long enough, the word will leak out. But instead of trying to cover up afterward, he wants to finish it before it leaks."

"Does the boy wonder bother to mention how we're supposed to do this?"

"Rather explicitly. We're supposed to outgun them."

"Hire more mercenaries? We've already . . ."

"No, outgun them. Better equipment. So far everybody's been fighting with government surplus weapons modified for simulated combat. Anything really new the governments are keeping under top security wraps. He's saying we should go directly to the designers and manufacturers and outbid the governments for the new stuff. That would give us enough of an edge to finish the fight once and for all."

"That'd cost us an arm and a leg!"

"Not as much as you'd think. He points out how much the corporations pad any bill going to the government and suggests by exerting a little economic pressure, we could drive the price down considerably. Then again—pull page four out of that stack for a minute."

"Got it."

"What you have there is a document he intercepted. Apparently the bastard has inside information from the negotiating sessions."

Pete was scanning the page.

"What's a 'One-for-One Proposal'?"

"It's some new rule the Oil types are trying to push through. Basically it means the mercenaries would have to destroy equipment and ammunition as if it had actually been used."

"That's insane!"

"Our negotiating team is giving it an eighty percent probability of passing. If it does, cost estimates for continuing the war go as high as fifty thousand dollars a day."

Pete whistled appreciatively.

"With that tidbit under his arm, Marcus's proposal doesn't sound nearly as expensive."

"So where does that leave us?"

Eddie pursed his lips.

"That's what's been bothering me. This proposed program has a lot of sparkle and romance to it. It's going to get a lot of support. If we decide to fight it, it's going to be an uphill battle."

A warning bell went off in the back of Pete's mind.

"Did you say 'if we decide . . . '?"

Eddie sighed.

"There's one more bit of information that I haven't told you. It seems that Becker, Mr. Big himself, has been talking with Marcus at least once a week, sometimes daily. If he's taking a personal interest in seeing Marcus get ahead, we might want to think long and hard about our own careers before we set out to try to make the golden boy look bad."

Chapter Eight

The cliff towered grim and foreboding, fully the height of a three-story building. Except for a few scrawny weeds dotting its face, indicating outcroppings or crevasses, it was a sheer drop onto the rockslide. It was enough of an obstacle that even the strongest of heart would take time to look for another route.

The man at the top of the cliff didn't look for another route or even break stride as he sprinted up to the edge of the precipice. He simply stepped off the cliff into nothingness, as did the three men following closely at his heels. For two long heartbeats they fell. By the second beat their swords were drawn—the world-famous Katanas, samurai swords unrivaled for centuries for their beauty, their craftsmanship, and their razor edges. On the third heartbeat they smashed into the rockslide, the impact driving one man to his knees, forcing him to recover with a catlike forward roll. By the time he had regained his feet, the others were gone, darting and weaving through the straw dummies, swords flashing in the sun. He raced to join them, a flick of his sword decapitating the dummy nearest him.

The straw figures, twenty of them, were identical, save for a one-inch square of brightly colored cloth pinned to them, marking five red, five yellow, five white, and five green. As they moved, each man struck only at the dummies marked with his color, forcing them to learn target identification at a dead run. Some were marked in the center of the forehead, some in the small of the back. It was considered a cardinal sin to strike a target that was not yours. A man who did not identify his target before he struck could as easily kill friend as foe in a firefight.

The leader of the band dispatched his last target and returned his sword to its scabbard in a blur of motion as he turned. He sprinted back toward the cliff through the dummies, apparently oblivious to the deadly blades still flashing around him. The others followed him, sheathing their swords as they ran. The man who had fallen was lagging noticeably behind.

Scrambling up the rockslide, they threw themselves at the sheer cliff face and began climbing at a smooth effortless pace, finding handholds and toeholds where none could be seen. It was a long climb, and the distance between the men began to increase. Suddenly the second man in the formation dislodged a fist-sized rock that clattered down the cliffside. The third man rippled his body to one side and it missed him narrowly. The fourth man was not so lucky. The rock smashed into his right forearm and careened away. He lost his grip and dropped the fifteen feet back onto the rockslide.

He landed lightly in a three-point stance, straightened, and gazed ruefully at his arm. A jagged piece of bone protruded from the skin. Shaking his head slightly, he tucked the injured arm into the front of his uniform and began to climb again.

As he climbed, a small group of men appeared below him. They hurriedly cut down the remains of the straw dummies and began lashing new ones to the supporting poles. None of them looked up at the man struggling up the cliffside.

They had finished their job and disappeared by the time the lone man reached the top of the cliff. He did not pause or look back, but simply rolled to his feet and sprinted off again. As he did, five more men brushed past him, ignoring him completely, and flung themselves off the cliff.

Tidwell hit the hold button on the videotape machine and the figures froze in midair. He stared at the screen for several moments, then rose from his chair and paced slowly across the thick carpet of his apartment. Clancy was snoring softly on the sofa, half-buried in a sea of personnel folders. Tidwell ignored him and walked to the picture window where he stood and stared at the darkened training fields.

The door behind him opened and a young Japanese girl glided into the room. She was clad in traditional Japanese robes and was bearing a small tray of lacquered bamboo. She approached him softly and stood waiting until he noticed her presence.

"Thanks, Yamiko," he said, taking his fresh drink from her tray.

She gave a short bow and remained in place, looking at him. He tasted his drink, then realized she was still there.

"I'll be along shortly, love. There's just a few things I've got to think out."

He blew a kiss at her, and she giggled and retired from the room. As soon as she was gone, the smile dropped from his face like a mask. He slowly returned to his chair, leaned over, and hit the rewind button. When the desired point had been reached, he hit the slow motion button and stared at the screen.

The four figures floated softly to the earth. As they touched down, Tidwell leaned forward to watch their feet and legs. They were landing on uneven ground covered with rocks and small boulders, treacherous footing at best, but they handled it in stride. Their legs were spread and relaxed, molding to the contour of their landing point; then those incredible thigh muscles bunched and flexed, acting like shock absorbers. Their rumps nearly touched the rocks before the momentum was halted, but halted it was.

Tidwell centered his attention on the man who was going to fall. His left foot touched down on a head-sized boulder that rolled away as his weight came to bear. He began to fall to his left, but twisted his torso back to the center line while deliberately buckling his right leg. Just as the awful physics of the situation seemed ready to smash him clumsily into the rocks, he tucked like a diver, curling around the glittering sword, and somersaulted forward, rolling to his feet and continuing as if nothing had happened.

Tidwell shook his head in amazement. Less than a twentieth of a second. And he thought his reflexes were good.

The swordplay he had given up trying to follow. The blades seemed to have a life of their own, thirstily dragging the men from one target to the next. Then the leader turned. He twirled his sword in his left hand and stabbed the point toward his hip. An inch error in any direction would either lose the sword or run the owner through. It snaked into the scabbard like it had eyes.

Tidwell hit the hold button and stared at the figure on the screen. The face was that of an old Oriental, age drawing the skin tight across the face making it appear almost skull-like—Kumo. The old sensei who had been in command before Tidwell and Clancy were hired.

In the entire week they had been reviewing the troops, he had not seen Kumo show any kind of emotion. Not anger, not joy—nothing. But he was a demanding instructor and personally led the men in their training. The cliff was only the third station in a fifteen-station obstacle course Kumo had laid out. The troops ran the obstacle course every morning to loosen up for the rest of the day's training. To loosen up.

Tidwell advanced the tape to the sequence in which the man's arm was broken. As the incident unfolded, he recalled the balance of that episode. The man had finished the obstacle course, broken arm and all. But his speed suffered, and Kumo sent him back to run the course again *before* he reported to the infirmary to have his arm treated.

Yes, Kumo ran a rough school. No one could argue with his results, though. Tidwell had seen things in this last week that he had not previously believed physically possible.

Ejecting the tape cassette, he refiled it, selected another, and fed it into the viewer.

The man on the screen was the physical opposite of Kumo who knelt in the background. Where Kumo was thin to the point of looking frail, this man looked like you could hit him with a truck without doing significant damage. He was short, but wide and muscular, looking for all the world like a miniature fullback, complete with shoulder pads.

He stood blindfolded on a field of hard-packed earth. His pose was relaxed and serene. Suddenly another man appeared at the edge of the screen, sprinting forward with upraised sword. As he neared his stationary target, the sword flashed out in a horizontal cut aimed to decapitate the luckless man. At the last instant before the sword struck, the blindfolded man ducked under the glittering blade and lashed out with a kick that took the running swordsman full in the stomach. The man dropped to the ground, doubled over in agony, as the blindfolded man resumed his original stance.

Another man crept onto the field, apparently trying to drag his fallen comrade back to the sidelines. When he reached the writhing figure, however, instead of attempting to assist him, the new man sprang over him high into the air, launching a flying kick at the man with the blindfold. Again the blinded man countered, this time raising a forearm which caught the attacker's leg and flipped it in the air, dumping him on his head.

At this point, the swordsman, who apparently was not as injured as he had seemed, rolled over and aimed a vicious cut at the defender's legs. The blindfolded man took to the air, leaping over the sword, and drove a heel down into the swordsman's face. The man fell back and lay motionless, bleeding from both nostrils.

Without taking his eyes from the screen, Tidwell raised his voice.

"Hey, Clancy."

His friend sat up on the sofa, scattering folders onto the floor and blinking his eyes in disorientation.

"Yeah, Steve?"

"How do they do that?"

Clancy craned his neck around and peered at the screen. Three men were attacking simultaneously, one with an axe, two with their hands and feet. The blindfolded man parried, blocked, and countered, unruffled by death narrowly missing him at each turn.

"Oh, that's an old martial artist's drill—blindfold workouts. The theory is that if you lost one of your five senses, such as sight, the other four would be heightened to compensate. By working out blindfolded, you heighten the other senses without actually losing one."

"Have you done this drill before?"

Clancy shook his head. He was starting to come into focus again.

"Not personally. I've seen it done a couple of times, but nothing like this. These guys are good, and I mean really good."

"Who is that one, the powerhouse with the blindfold?"

Clancy pawed through his folders.

"Here it is. His name's Aki. I won't read off all the black belts he holds, I can't pronounce half of them. He's one of the originals. One of the founding members of the martial arts cults that formed after that one author tried to get the army to return to the ancient ways, then killed himself when they laughed at him."

Tidwell shook his head.

"How many of the force came out of those cults?"

"About ninety-five percent. It's still incredible to me that the Zaibatsu had the foresight to start sponsoring those groups. That was over twenty years ago."

"Just goes to show what twenty years of training six days a week will do for you. Did you know some of the troops were raised into it by their parents? That they've been training in unarmed and armed combat since they could walk?"

"Yeah, I caught that. Incidentally, did I show you the results from the firing range today?"

"Spare me."

But Clancy was on his feet halfway to his case.

"They were firing Springfields today," he called back over his shoulder. "The old bolt-action jobs. Range at five hundred meters."

Tidwell sighed. These firing range reports were monotonous, but Clancy was a big firearms freak.

"Here we go. These are the worst ten." He waved a stack of photos at Tidwell. On each photo was a man-shaped silhouette target with a small irregularly shaped hole in the center of the chest.

"There isn't a single-shot grouping in there you couldn't cover with a nickel, and these are the worst."

"I assume they're still shooting five-shot groups."

Clancy snorted.

"I don't think Kumo has let them hear of any other kind."

"Firing position?"

"Prone unsupported. Pencil scopes battlefield zeroed at four hundred meters."

Tidwell shook his head.

"I'll tell you, Clancy, man for man I've never seen anything like these guys. It's my studied and considered opinion that any one of them could take both of us one-handed. Even . . ."—he jerked a thumb at the figures on the screen behind them—". . . even blindfolded."

On the screen, a man tried to stand at a distance and stab the blindfolded Aki with a spear, with disastrous results.

Clancy borrowed Tidwell's drink and took a sip.

"And you're still standing by your decision? About extending our entry date to the war by two months?"

"Now look, Clancy . . ."

"I'm not arguing. Just checking."

"They aren't ready yet. They're still a pack of individuals. A highly trained mob is still a mob."

"What's Kumo's reaction? That's his established entry date you're extending."

"He was only thinking about the new 'super-weapons' when he set that date. He's been trained from birth to think of combat as an individual venture."

"Hey, those new weapons are really something, aren't they?"

"Superweapons or not, those men have to learn to function as a team before they'll be ready for the war. They said I would have free rein in choosing men and tactics, and by God, this time I'm not going into battle until they're ready. I don't care if it takes two months or two years."

"But Kumo—"

"Kumo and I work for the same employer and they put *me* in charge. We'll move when *I* say we're ready."

Clancy shrugged his shoulders.

"Just asking, Steve. No need to . . . whoa. Could you back that up?"

He pointed excitedly at the screen. Tidwell obligingly hit the hold button. On the screen, two men were in the process of attacking simultaneously from both sides with swords. Images of Clancy and Tidwell were also on the screen standing on either side of Kumo.

"How far do you want it backed?"

"Back it up to where you interrupt the demonstration."

Tidwell obliged.

The scene began anew. There was an attacker on the screen cautiously circling Aki with a knife. Suddenly Tidwell appeared on the screen, closely followed by Clancy. Until this point they had been standing off-camera, watching the proceedings. Finally Tidwell could contain his feelings of skepticism no longer and stepped forward, silently holding his hand up to halt the action. He signaled the man with the knife to retire from the field, then turned and beckoned two specific men to approach him. With a series of quick flowing motions, he began to explain what he wanted.

"This is the part I want to see. Damn. You know, you're really good, Steve. You know how long it would take me to explain that using gestures? You'll have to coach me on it sometime. You used to fool around with the old Indian sign language a lot, didn't you? Steve?"

No reply came. Clancy tore his eyes away from the screen and shot a glance at Tidwell. Tidwell was sitting and staring at the screen. Every muscle in his body was suddenly tense—not rigid but poised, as if he was about to fight.

"What is it, Steve? Did you see something?"

Without answering, Tidwell stopped the film, reversed it, then started it again.

Again the knifeman circled. Again the two mercenaries appeared on the screen. Tidwell punched the hold button and the action froze.

He rose from his chair and slowly approached the screen. Then he thoughtfully sipped his drink and stared at a point away from the main action. He stared at Kumo. Kumo, the old sensei who never showed emotion. In the split second frozen by the camera, at the instant the two men stepped past him and interrupted the demonstration, in that fleeting moment as he looked at Tidwell's back, Kumo's face was contorted in an expression of raw, naked hatred.

Chapter Nine

Fred dispensed with the waiter's profuse thanks with an airy wave of his hand. He could still vividly remember his high school days working as a busboy, and as a result, habitually overtipped.

"Incredible! You feel it necessary to offer bribes even for the simplest of services."

"Have you ever tried waiting on tables for twelve hours solid, Ivan, old friend?"

"Yes. As a matter of fact, I have. My pay for the entire twelve hours was less than you just gave that man as a tip. But I did not mean to start another argument, my friend. I was merely commenting on the differences between how money is handled here and how it was in my old homeland."

"Well, you're in America now."

"Yes, and as I said, I apologize. I meant no offense.
Please, for once let us end our meeting on a pleasant note."

"Fine by me."

Still maintaining an annoyed air, Fred rose to leave. However, he was puzzling over Ivan's last remark. Strange. It was the first time Ivan had ever apologized for getting under Fred's skin. If anything, he usually enjoyed doing it. In fact, Ivan had been acting strange all evening—no, make that all day.

Fred habitually spent more time studying his enemies than he did his friends, trying to memorize their quirks, their moods, anything that might give him an advantage in a confrontation. Quickly reviewing Ivan's reactions or lack thereof during the entire day, Fred would be willing to bet a month's wages that there was something bothering him. But what?

He paused for a moment to light a cigarette, and was rewarded by having Ivan rise to join him.

"Please, Fred. Might I walk with you for a bit?"

"Sure. I'm heading back to my hotel. Tag along and I'll buy you a drink. It's just across the park."

Ivan fell in step beside him and they left the restaurant in silence. Fred played the waiting game as they crossed the street and started down the sidewalk through the park. The night sounds of the city filtered through the air, giving a feeling of unreality, a persistent counterpoint to the deep shadows of the trees.

"Fred, we have been meeting privately at dinner for two months now. During these unofficial talks, I feel we have grown to know each other, yes?"

"I suppose."

C'mon, you bastard, spit it out. What's in the wind?"

"I have a personal favor to ask of you."

Bingo! Deep in Fred's mind, a bright-eyed fox perked up its ears. If this was what it sounded like, he'd finally have his rival right where he wanted him. Nothing like having a member of the opposition over a barrel.

"What's the problem?"

"It is my daughter. I have recently received word she is alive . . . ah, I am getting ahead of myself. When I escaped . . . when I left my homeland, I was told that both my wife and daughter had been killed. Now word has been smuggled to me that my daughter is alive and living with friends. However, there is danger of the authorities finding her and I wish very badly to have her join me here in America."

"Have you told them at Oil?"

"Yes, but they cannot help me. They say I have not been working for them long enough."

"Bastards!"

"I have saved some money, but it is not enough. They say they can give me a loan in another six months, but I am afraid. My fellow workers will not help me. I am not well liked because of my many promotions. I thought that perhaps . . ."

His voice trailed off into silence.

Fred's mind was racing. He'd help Ivan, of course. If Communications would not spring for the money, he'd do it out of his own pocket. This was too good an opportunity to miss. The big question was what could he get out of Ivan in return? Fred could probably shake him down for one big favor before Oil found out that their number two negotiator had sold out, but if he played it right, one would be plenty.

"Tell you what, Ivan—"

"All right, you two! Hand 'em over!"

The two men spun to face the source of the interruption. A youth was standing on the sidewalk behind them; he must have either followed them or been waiting in the bushes. His voice was firm, but the gun in his hand wavered as he tried to cover the two men.

"C'mon! Give!" The boy's voice cracked.

"Steady fella, we're giving."

Fred reached for his wallet, taking care to move slowly. If the kid had a knife he might have tried taking him, but he had a healthy respect for guns, particularly when they were held by nervous amateurs.

"No!"

All movement froze at the sound of Ivan's voice.

"What'd you say, Mister?"

"Ivan, for God's sake . . ."

"I said, 'No!' "

He began to move toward the mugger.

"All my life I have been ordered around!"

"Stand back!"

"Ivan! Don't!"

Fred's mind was racing. He had to do something quickly.

"You have no right to—"

The gun exploded in a flash of light, the report deafening in the night.

Ivan lurched backward. Shit! Fred threw his wallet at the mugger's face. The boy instinctively flinched away, raising his hands, and Fred was on him.

There was no style or finesse to Fred's attack. He snared the boy's gun hand with one hamlike fist, grabbed his shirt with the other, picked him up, and slammed him to the pavement. The boy arched and let out a muffled scream from the pain of impact. The scream was cut short as Fred hammered him into unconsciousness with two blows from his fist.

Breathing heavily, he pried the gun from the boy's fist, rose, retreated a few steps, then turned to look for Ivan. He was lying where he fell, unmoving, a large pool of blood oozing from beneath his loose-jointed form. Fred scrambled crabwise over to look at him. His eyes were open and unseeing.

Shit! So close! So damn close!

For a moment, Fred was filled with an urge to stand up and kick the unconscious mugger.

You son-of-a-bitch! You've ruined everything!

He was still swearing to himself two and a half hours later when he left the police station. It had taken him almost half an hour to flag down a cop, a glowing testimonial to police efficiency. Now the body had been carted away, the mugger was safely locked up, and Fred was left with nothing.

Shit! Of all the bad breaks! Just when Ivan was about to bust open! Now he'd have to start from scratch with another negotiator. Well, maybe not from scratch. C'mon, Fred. Think. You're supposed to be able to make an advantage out of anything, even a disaster like this. Think!

He ignored the hail of a taxi driver and started the long walk back to his hotel. He covered nearly eight blocks lost in thought, when suddenly an idea stopped him in his tracks. He stood there as he checked and rechecked the plan mentally, then looked around and ran back half a block to a pay phone.

He fumbled for some loose change, then fed a coin into the phone and hurriedly dialed a number.

"Mark? Fred here. I've got a hot assignment for you. . . . I don't give a damn . . . Well, kick her ass out, this is important . . . All right, I want you to get down to the police station and bail out the mugger that just killed Ivan . . . That's right, Ivan Kramitz . . . Yes, he's dead . . . Look, I don't have time to explain now. Get down there and spring that mugger. I don't care how much it costs—spring him! And Mark, this time don't be too careful about covering your tracks . . . That's right. I said don't be . . . right, let them know you work for Communications. . . . Look, I don't have time to explain now. Just do it."

He hung up the phone and sagged against the side of the phone booth. For several minutes he sat there, smiling. It was not a pretty smile.

"Before any business is transacted today, the negotiating team from Oil would like it read into the record that we are attending today's meeting under protest. We are both shocked and disappointed that Communications has insisted on convening today's meeting despite the death last night of one of our teammates. We only hope you will at least have the decency to keep today's business brief so that we might attend the funeral this afternoon."

A low growl of assent rose from the rest of the Oil team.

"We thank the First Negotiator of Oil for his comments. They will be duly noted in the records. The Chair now recognizes the Third Negotiator from Communications."

"Thank you, Mark." Fred rose to face the assemblage.

"May I assure you I will try to keep my proposal as brief as possible.

"Ivan's death last night was a serious blow to the Oil team. We share your grief and will miss him greatly. But, gentlemen, this should serve as another example of the hazards of war!"

There was a sudden stirring in the Oil team.

"Just as you pointed out in your one-for-one proposal that logistics is a real part of military strategy, so is assassination!"

"Are you trying to say you had Ivan killed?"

Fred smiled placidly at the interrupter.

"I have said no such thing. I merely point out that assassination of key personnel is as much or more a part of military tactics as moving boxes of ammo. Because of this, Communications proposes a conditional rider to your one-for-one proposal: that in a similar effort to insure realistic combat, all key personnel of both corporations be required to wear kill-suits at all times and be subject to the same rules of combat as the mercenaries. If we want realism, let's go for realism throughout. If not, we junk both ideas. Gentlemen, the time has come to put up or shut up!"

Chapter Ten

The men and women of the force were kneeling in the traditional student's position, backs straight, hands open, and palms resting down on their thighs. To all appearances they were at ease, listening to the morning's instruction.

This morning, however, the assembly was different. This morning, the raised instructor's platform held a dozen chairs filled by various corporation dignitaries. More importantly, the subject at hand was not instruction, but rather the formal transfer of command from Kumo to Tidwell.

Tidwell was both nervous and bored. He was bored because he was always bored by long speeches, particularly if he was one of the main subjects under discussion. Yet there was still the nervousness born from the anticipation of directly addressing the troops for the first time as their commander.

The speech was in English, as were all the speeches and instructions. One of the prerequisites for the force was a fluent knowledge of English. That didn't make it any the less boring.

He grimaced and looked about the platform again. The corporation officials were sitting in Tweedle-Dee and Tweedle-Dum similarity, blank-faced and attentive. If nothing else in this stint of duty, he was going to try to learn some of the Oriental inscrutability. Depending on the Oriental, they viewed Westerners with distaste or amusement because of the ease with which their emotions could be read in their expressions and actions. The keynote of the Orient was control, and it started with oneself.

Craning his neck slightly, he snuck a glance at Clancy, standing in an easy parade rest behind him. There was the Western equivalent to the Oriental inscrutability: the military man. Back straight, eyes straight ahead, face expressionless. Behind the mask, Clancy's mind would be as busy and opinionated as ever, but from viewing him, Tidwell did not have the faintest idea what he was thinking. In fact, Tidwell realized, he himself was currently the most animated figure on the platform. Suddenly self-conscious, he started to face front again when his eyes fell on Kumo.

Kumo was resplendent in his ceremonial robes. Protruding from his sash, at an unlikely angle to the Western eyes, was a samurai sword. Tidwell had heard that the sword had been in Kumo's family for over fifteen generations.

He held the weapon in almost a religious awe. Its history was longer than Tidwell's family tree, and it seemed to radiate a bloody aura of its own.

Anyone who didn't believe that a weapon absorbed something from the men who used it, from the men it killed, anyone who didn't believe that a weapon couldn't have an identity and personality of its own had never held a weapon with a past.

He suddenly snapped back into focus. The speaker was stepping away from the microphone, looking at him expectantly, as were the others on the platform. Apparently, he had missed his introduction and was "on."

He rose slowly, using the delay to collect his scattered thoughts, and stepped to the edge of the platform, ignoring the microphone to address the force directly. A brief gust of wind rippled the uniforms of his audience, but aside from that, there was no movement or reaction.

"Traditionally, Japan has produced the finest fighting men in the world. The Samurai, the Ninjas, are all legendary for their prowess in battle."

There was no reaction from the force. Mentally he braced himself. Here we go!

"Also, traditionally, they have had the worst armies!"

The force stiffened without moving. Their faces remained immobile.

"The armies were unsuccessful because they fought as individuals, not as a team. As martial artists, you train the muscles of your body, the limbs of your body, to work together, to support each other. It would be unthinkable to attempt to fight if your arms and legs were allowed to move in uncontrolled random motions."

They were with him, grudgingly, seeing where his logic was going.

"Similarly, an army can only be effective if the men and women in it work in cooperation and coordination with each other."

He had made his point. Time to back off a little.

"Different cultures yield different fighting styles. I am not here to argue which style is better, for each style has its time and place. What must be decided is what style is necessary in which situation. In this case, that decision has been made by the executives of the Zaibatsu. As a result of that decision, I have been hired to train and lead you."

Now the crunch.

"You are about to enter a highly specialized war. To successfully fight in this war, you must abandon any ideas you may have of nationalism or glory. You are mercenaries, as I am a mercenary, in the employ of the Zaibatsu complex. As such, you must learn to fight, to think in a way which may be completely foreign to what you have learned in the past. To allow time for this training, the date for our entry into the war has been moved back by two months."

"I disagree, Mr. Tidwell."

The words were soft and quiet, but they carried to every corner of the assemblage. In an instant the air was electric. Kumo!

"I disagree with everything you have said."

There it was! The challenge! The gauntlet! Tidwell turned slowly to face his attacker. Kumo's words were polite and soft as a caress, but the act of interrupting, let alone disagreeing, carried as much emotional impact in the Orient as a Western drill sergeant screaming his head off.

"In combat, the action is too fast for conscious thought. If one had to pause and think about coordination of one's limbs, the battle would be lost before a decision was made. It is for this reason that martial artists train, so that each limb develops eyes of its own, a mind of its own. This enables a fighter to strike like lightning when an opening presents itself. Similarly, we train each man to be a self-contained unit, capable of making decisions and acting as the situation presents itself. This means he will never be hamstrung by slow decisions or a break in communications with his superior. As to your 'specialized war', a trained fighting man should be able to adapt and function in any situation. Your failure to recognize this betrays your ignorance of warfare."

Tidwell shot a glance at the corporate officials. No one moved to interfere or defend. He was on his own. They were going to let the two of them settle it.

"Am I to understand that you are questioning the qualifications of Mr. Clancy and myself?" He tried to keep his voice as calm as Kumo's.

"There is nothing to question. After two weeks here, you presume to be an expert on our force and seek to change it. You expect the force to follow you because the corporation tells them to. This is childish. The only way one may lead fighting men is if he holds their respect. That respect must be earned. It cannot be ordered. So far, all we have for proof is words. If your knowledge of battle is so vastly superior to ours, perhaps you could demonstrate it by defeating one of the force that we might see with our own eyes you are fit to lead us."

Tidwell was thunderstruck. This was unheard of! In paperback novels, leaders would issue blanket challenges to their force to "any man who thinks he can lick me." In life it was never done. Leaders were chosen for their knowledge of strategy and tactics, not their individual fighting prowess. It was doubtful that either Patton or Rommel, or Genghis Khan for that matter, could beat any man in their command in a fistfight. No commander in his right mind would jeopardize his authority by entering into a brawl.

It crossed his mind to refuse the challenge. He had already acknowledged the superior ability of the Japanese in individual combat, contesting only their group tactics. Just as quickly he rejected the thought. No matter how insane it was, he could not refuse this challenge. He was in the Orient. To refuse would be to indicate cowardice, to lose face. He would have to fight this battle and win it.

"Sensei, I have publicly stated that the people of Japan have produced the greatest fighters in history. I will elaborate and say that I have no doubts that the men and women under your instruction equal or surpass those warriors of old in skill. Moreover, I must bow to your superior knowledge of their abilities and attitudes."

Kumo bowed his head slightly, acknowledging the compliment, but his eyes were still wary.

"However, what you tell me is that they must be convinced with action, not words. It has been always a characteristic of man that he can settle differences, pass his experiences from one generation to the next, and develop new ideas and concepts through the use of words. If you are correct in your appraisal of your students, if they are unable to be swayed by words, if the only way their respect can be earned is by action, then they are not men, they are animals."

Kumo's back stiffened.

"This is not surprising because you have trained them like animals."

There was an angry stirring in the ranks.

"Normally, I would stand aside for men and women of such training, for they could defeat me with ease. But you tell me they are animals. As such, I will accept your challenge, Kumo. I will stand and defeat the man or woman of your choice any time, any place, with any weapon, for I am a man, and a man does not fear an animal."

There were scattered angry cries from the ranks. First singly, then as a group, the force rose and stood at the ready position, wordlessly volunteering to champion the force by facing Tidwell.

The mercenary suppressed an impulse to smile at the sensei's predicament. Kumo had obviously planned to face Tidwell himself. In slanting his retort toward the force, Tidwell had successfully forced Kumo into choosing a member from the ranks. A teacher cannot defend his students without implying a lack of confidence in their prowess. If the abilities of a student are challenged, the student must answer the challenge. Terrific. Would you rather face a tiger or a gorilla?

"Mr. Tidwell, your answer is eloquent, if unwise. You are aware that such a contest would be fought to the death?"

Tidwell nodded. He hadn't been, but he was now. Inwardly, he gritted his teeth. Kumo wasn't leaving him any outs.

"Very well. The time will be now, the place here. For weapons, you may have your choice."

Clever bastard! He's waiting to see weapons choice before he picks my opponent.

"I'll fight as I stand."

"I will also allow you to choose your opponent. I have faith in each of my students."

Damn! He'd reversed it. Now if Tidwell didn't choose Kumo for an opponent, it would appear he was probing for a weaker foe.

Tidwell scanned the force slowly, while he pondered the problem. Finally, he made his decision.

He turned to Kumo once more.

"I will face Aki."

There was a quiet murmur of surprise as Aki rose and approached the platform. Obviously Tidwell was not trying to pick a weak opponent.

The powerhouse bounded onto the platform and bowed to Kumo. Kumo addressed him in rapid Japanese, then much to everyone's astonishment, removed his sword and offered it to his student. Aki's glance flickered over Tidwell, then he gave a short bow, shaking his head in refusal. Raising his head in calm pride, he rattled off a quick statement in Japanese, then turned to face Tidwell. Kumo inclined his head, then returned the sword to his sash. He barked a few quick commands, and several men sprang to clear the platform, relocating the dignitaries and their chairs to positions in front of and facing the scene of the upcoming duel.

Tidwell shrugged out of his jacket and Clancy stepped forward to take it.

"Are you out of your bloody mind, Steve?" he murmured under his breath.

"Do you see any options?"

"You could have let me fight him. If Kumo can have a champion, you should be able to have one too."

"Thanks, but I'd rather handle this one myself. Nothing personal."

"Just remember the option next time, if there is a next time."

"C'mon Clancy, what could you do that I can't in a spot like this?"

"For openers, I could blow him away while he's bowing in."

Clancy opened his hand slightly to reveal the derringer he was palming. Tidwell recognized it at once as Clancy's favorite holdout weapon—two shots, loads exploding on impact, accurate to fifty feet in the hands of an expert, and Clancy was an expert.

"Tempting, but it wouldn't impress the troops much."

"But it would keep you alive!"

"Academic. We're committed now."

"Right. Win it!"

Win it. The mercenary's send-off. Tidwell focused his mind on that expression as he took his place facing Aki. At times like this when the chips were down, it meant a lot more than all the good lucks in the world.

Suddenly the solution to the problem occurred to him. Chancy, but worth a try!

"Clancy, give me a pad and pencil."

They appeared magically. No aide is complete without those tools. Tidwell scribbled something quickly on the top sheet, ripped it from the pad, and folded it twice.

"Give this to Mr. Yamada."

Clancy nodded and took the note, stashing the pad and pencil as he went.

Everything was ready now. With relatively few adaptations, a lecture assembly had been converted into an arena. As he was talking to Clancy, Tidwell had been testing the platform surface. It was smooth sanded wood, unvarnished and solid. He considered taking off his boots for better traction, but discarded the idea. He'd rather have the extra weight on his feet for the fight—increased impact and all that.

Kumo sat at the rear center of the platform, overseeing the

proceedings as always. Then Clancy vaulted back onto the platform, his errand complete. Deliberately he strode across the platform and took a position beside Kumo on the side closest Tidwell. Kumo glared, but did not challenge the move.

Tidwell suppressed a smile. Score one for Clancy. This was not a class exercise and Kumo was not an impartial instructor. It was a duel, and the seconds were now in position. One thing was sure—if he ever took a contract to take on the devil, he wanted Clancy guarding his flanks.

But now there was work to be done. For the first time, he focused his attention on Aki, meeting his enemy's gaze directly. Aki was standing at the far end of the platform, relaxed and poised, eyes dead. The eyes showed neither fear nor anger. They simply watched, appraised, analyzed, and gave nothing in return. Tidwell realized that he was looking into a mirror, into the eyes of a killer. He realized it, accepted it, and put it out of his mind. He was ready.

He raised an eyebrow in question. Aki saw and gave a fractional nod of his head, more an acknowledgement than a bow, and the duel began.

Tidwell took one slow step forward and stopped, watching. Aki moved with leisurely grace into a wide, straddle-legged stance, and waited, watching.

Check! Aki was going to force Tidwell into making the opening move. He was putting his faith in his defense, in his ability to weather any attack Tidwell could throw at him and survive to finish the bout before his opponent could recover. However the duel went, it would be over quickly. Once Tidwell committed himself to an attack, it would either succeed or he would be dead.

Tidwell broke the tableau, moving diagonally to his right leisurely, almost sauntering. As he approached the edge of the platform he stopped, studied his opponent, then repeated the process, moving diagonally to the left. Aki stood unmoving, watching.

To an unschooled eye, it would appear almost as if Tidwell were an art connoisseur, viewing a statue from various angles. To the people watching, it was Aki's challenge. He was saying, "Pick your attack, pick your angle. I will stop you and kill you."

Finally Tidwell heaved a visible sigh. The decision was made. He moved slowly to the center of the platform, paused, considering Aki, then placed his hands behind his back and began moving toward him head-on. Theatrically he came, step by step, a study in slow motion. The question now was how close? How close would Aki let him come before launching a counterattack? Could he bait Aki into striking first? Committing first?

Ten feet separated them. Step. Seven feet. Step.

Tidwell's right fist flashed out, whipping wide for a back-knuckle strike to Aki's temple, a killing blow. In the same instant, Aki exploded into action, left arm coming up to block the strike, right fist driving out for a smashing punch to Tidwell's solar plexus. Then in mid-heartbeat, the pattern changed. Tidwell's left hand flashed out and the sun glinted off the blade of a stiletto lancing for the center of Aki's chest. Aki's counter-punch changed and his right arm snapped down to parry the knife-thrust.

Instead of catching Tidwell's forearm, the block came down on the raised knife point as the weapon was pivoted in mid-thrust to meet the counter. The point plunged into the forearm, hitting bone, and Tidwell ripped the arm open, drawing the knife back toward him. As his arm came back, Tidwell jerked his knee up, slamming it into the wounded arm, then straightened the leg, snapping the toe of his boot into the wound for a third hit as Aki jerked backward, splintering the bone and sending his opponent off balance. Aki reeled back in agony, then caught his balance and tried to take a good position, even though his right arm would no longer respond to his will. His eyes glinted hard now, a tiger at bay.

Tidwell bounded backward, away from his injured foe and backpedaled to the far end of the platform. As Aki moved to follow, he pegged the knife into the platform at his feet, dropped to one knee, and held his arms out from his body at shoulder height.

"Aki! Stop!"

Aki paused, puzzled.

"Stop and listen!"

Suspiciously, Aki retreated slowly to the far end of the platform, putting distance between himself and Tidwell, but he listened.

"Mr. Yamada! Will you read aloud the note I passed you before the fight began."

Mr. Yamada rose slowly from his seat with the other company officials, unfolded the note, and read: "I will strike Aki's right forearm two to four times, then try to stop the fight."

He sat down and a murmur rippled through the force.

"The point of the fight was to determine if I was qualified to lead this force in battle. At this point I have shown that not only can I strike your champion repeatedly, but that I can predict his moves in advance. This will be my function as your commander, to guide you against an enemy I know and can predict, giving maximum effectiveness to your skills. Having demonstrated this ability, I wish to end this duel if my opponent agrees. I only hope he embraces the same philosophy I do—that if given a choice, I will not waste lives. I will not kill or sacrifice my men needlessly. That is the way of the martial arts, and the way of the mercenary. Aki! Do you agree with me that the duel is over?"

Their eyes met for a long moment. Then slowly Aki drew himself up and bowed.

Kumo sprang to his feet, his face livid. He barked an order at Aki. Still in the bow, Aki raised his head and looked at Kumo, then at Tidwell, then back at Kumo, and shook his head.

Clancy tensed, his hand going to his waistband. Tidwell caught his eyes and shook his head in a firm negative.

Kumo screamed a phrase in Japanese at Aki, then snatched the sword from his sash and started across the platform at Tidwell.

Tidwell watched coldly as the sensei took three steps toward him, then stood up. As he did, the leg he had been kneeling on flashed forward and kicked the knife like a placekicker going for an extra point. The point snapped off and the knife somersaulted forward, plunging hilt-deep into the chest of the charging swordsman. Kumo stopped, went to one knee, tried to rise, then the sword slipped from his grasp and he fell. For several minutes there was silence. Then Tidwell turned to address his force.

"A great man has died here today. Training is canceled for the rest of the day that we might honor his memory. Assembly will be at 0600 hours tomorrow to receive your new orders. Dismissed."

In silence, the force rose and began to disperse. Tidwell turned to view the body again. Aki was kneeling before his fallen sensei. In silence, Tidwell picked up the sword, removed the scabbard from Kumo's sash and resheathed the weapon. He stared at the body for another moment, then turned and handed the sword to Aki. Their eyes met, then Tidwell bowed and turned away.

"Jesus Christ, Steve. Have you ever used that placekick stunt before? In combat?"

"Three times before. This is the second time it worked."

"I saw it but I still don't believe it. If I ever mouth off about your knives again, you can use one of them on me."

"Yeah, right. Say, can you be sure someone takes care of Aki's arm? I just want to go off and get drunk right now."

"Sure thing, Steve. Oh, someone wants to talk to you."

"Later, huh? I'm not up to it right now."

"It's the straw bosses."

Clancy jerked a thumb toward the row of company officials.

"Oh!"

Tidwell turned and started wearily toward the men because they were his employers and he was a mercenary.

Chapter Eleven

"Willard?"

"Yeah, last night." Eddie Bush was visibly shaken as he lit a cigarette.

"I just got the call from Personnel. They got him in a movie theater."

"I'll tell the troops. Damn! You think they'll be more careful."

"I know what you mean. He wasn't even on the 'kill list.'"

"No, I mean I thought *he'd* be more careful. On the 'kill list' or not, anyone who wears a kill-suit is fair game. They're asking for trouble, all of them. They shouldn't be surprised when it finds them."

"Hell, Pete. I wear a kill-suit. So does half the corporation staff now. It's a style, a fad, a status symbol."

"Well, I don't think that people are taking it seriously enough." Pete ground out his own cigarette viciously.

"Haven't we lost enough people already without playing games with the assassin teams?"

"Most of those were on the first day. It was kind of sudden, you know."

"The hell it was. There were memos and meetings going around for over a month. Did you ever get an accurate count of how many we lost the first day?"

"Seventeen, with six near misses. I guess nobody really stopped to think it through."

"That's what I mean about people not taking it seriously. Who came up with this crackpot scheme anyway?"

Bush made a face.

"As near as I can tell we did, but damned if I know why."

"There's some solid talk going around that it was an under-the-table agreement between the corporation hierarchies to weed out some of the management deadwood."

"The 'forced retirement' bit? Yeah, I've heard that, but I don't believe it. Corporations pull some pretty sleazy moves when it comes to personnel management, but I can't believe they'd sink that low. Three years on half-pay would really be rough. I'm not sure I could take it. Oh well, I suppose it could be worse. They could be using real bullets."

"That's happened, too," Pete retorted.

"It was in the rules at the start. After four shots with the quartz-beams, the assassin can use live ammo. If the players don't turn on their kill-suits, it's their own fault."

"Is yours turned on now?"

Eddie ran a hand inside his jacket to check the controls.

"It sure is."

"But you had to check to be sure."

"Yeah, I see what you mean."

"Besides, I wasn't talking about those kills. I was talking about the others. Did you hear what happened to Brumbolt?"

"Just a few rumors."

"They shot him down. With live ammo and real blood. You know why? Because he went to the theater the same night as a couple execs from his old department. They swear they didn't even know he was going to be there. In fact, they haven't even talked to him since he was 'killed' and went on half-pay, all according to the rules. The assassins who spotted him thought he was trying to pass some notes or something, and cut him down in the parking lot. That's the kind of real-kill I'm talking about."

Eddie pursed his lips in a silent whistle.

"I haven't heard about that. That's weird. It's like . . . like—"

"Like we were in a war—that's what I've been trying to say. The big question is, what are we going to do about it?"

Eddie stiffened, his features hardening into a mask.

"Are we going to get into that again, Pete?"

"You're damn right we are. I mean, we are still on a team to submit recommendations, aren't we?"

"Only until we can be reassigned. The project is dead, Pete."

"But—"

"But nothing! It's dead! Marcus has already submitted his recommendations and they've been accepted. The corporation has already sunk a hunk of money into the new weapons, and they won't be looking for new ways to raise costs."

"Eddie—"

"So we are going to sit down and shut up because I don't want to make an ass of myself backing a set of recommendations that won't be followed."

"That's the part I don't buy. I think we'll be making bigger fools of ourselves after spending all this time and money on our team, we don't come up with anything."

"But the cost—"

"Cost, hell. If there's one thing I've learned in my years with this corporation, it's that there's always money to be had for a good idea."

"And if there's one thing you haven't learned, it's when to keep your mouth shut. If you had, then I'd be answering to you instead of you to mc. In theory you're right, but we're dealing with reality, and like it or not, that's the way it is. Now I'm telling you to back down!"

The two men glared at each other for several moments, then Pete forced a deep breath.

"Tell you what, Eddie. I'll make you a deal—no, hear me out. I've got something in my car that I think will change your mind. If it doesn't, then I'll shut up and go along."

Eddie considered him for a moment.

"All right, bring it in. But I honestly can't think of anything you can come up with that will change my mind."

"You'll have to come with me. It's too bulky to bring in."

"Okay, anything to get this thing settled."

He rose, and the two men headed out into the executive corridor. Stepping onto the conveyor, they rode along in silence for several minutes. Finally Eddie cleared his throat.

"Sorry about blowing up in there, Pete. I guess I just don't understand why you're fighting this so hard. There'll be other assignments."

"For you maybe. Oh, turn here, I'm parked on the street. Rolled in a little late and the exec lot was full."

"Okay, but what was that you were saying?"

"Hmm? Oh! Just that I'm not sure how many more assignments will get thrown my way."

"Is that what's bothering you? Hell, don't worry. From what I can see in the meetings, a lot of the decision makers know who you are. That idea you had for using a dummy terrorist group to explain the shootings was a stroke of genius. It really saved our bacon when it came to dealing with the authorities."

"But it didn't go out with my name on it. Oh, out this door."

"Yeah. That was a bad deal. Well, it didn't go out with my name on it either. But don't worry. The people who count know it was your idea. You'll get other assignments. Say, where's your car?"

"Up the block a bit. Can you honestly say you think I'm going to get another assignment from a corporate VP?"

"Well, maybe not directly, but if I get one, you can bet you'll be one of the cornerstones of the team. That much I can . . ."

The bullet took him in the center of the chest. It was the first time Pete had seen the effects of one of the exploding bullets. Eddie Bush kind of blew up, pieces of his body splashing over the sidewalk. There was no doubt he was dead before he hit the pavement.

Pete waved a hand at the assassin on the roof across the street even though he couldn't see him, then stooped over the body. Moving quickly, he reached inside Eddie's jacket and switched the kill-suit controls to the "off" position. Then he stood and smiled down at the corpse.

Wha'dya know, another terrible accident. And Ed Bush wasn't even on the "kill list." Well, it was a risk he ran, wearing a kill-suit. It was only a matter of time before someone took him up on it. Terrible he had forgotten to turn his suit on.

Still smiling, he turned and ran back into the building to report the horrible incident.

Chapter Twelve

Mausier smiled as he read the latest information request on the board. Someone was trying to find out how their security was breached. A hefty sum was being offered as well as immunity from prosecution.

Obviously this client was not as knowledgeable in the field of industrial espionage as Mausier. He briefly considered not even posting the offer, but then decided to go ahead with it. His field agents needed a good laugh once in a while.

Mausier constantly daydreamed about secret agents crawling through the darkness, picking locks, climbing fences, bribing guards, and taking pictures in the dark with mini-cameras hidden in belt buckles. He daydreamed, but he knew it wasn't real. This client had apparently not learned to differentiate reality from daydreams. Agents didn't climb fences, they walked in through the main gate or the employment office—that is, if they walked in at all. A hefty number of his most successful clients were call girls or waitresses. Most of the information holders would be astounded to learn the grateful little girl they impressed with a one-hundred-dollar tip was actually making three times their annual salary.

Secretaries, janitors, and shipping/receiving clerks were all potential key agents, if they weren't already actively engaged in it. But the field was not limited to the "little people." Many of his clients were high-placed trusted executives who felt that seventy thousand dollars a year wasn't enough to make ends meet. Mausier didn't feel this was strange. In fact, his own years in the corporate world convinced him that many of the white-collar spies were driven to it because of the financial pressures of maintaining a social front equal to or better than their job rating. It was a source of vague amusement to him that many executives turned to industrial espionage to be able to afford to keep up with other executives who were already supplementing their incomes as spies.

There were still a few sneak thief spies in the business, but it was unlikely they would disclose their methods either. It would only mean they would have to work around tighter security on their next job.

His whining client was not likely to get an answer to his information request even though the corporate world was crawling with agents. Mausier smiled. In his opinion after years of watching the business, the most successful agents were auditors.

His smile faded as he turned to his doodle-screen. The project was becoming almost an obsession, claiming increasing portions of his time and concentration. The Brazil workspace was so full he could no longer display all items on the screen simultaneously. He thought he had the answer now, but so much of the pattern still didn't make sense.

The screen flickered and displayed a list of names. These were people employed by the nine corporations who had died recently. He sorted them by corporation, then chronologically. There was a pattern here. On one specific day there had been a surge of deaths in the two corporations listed for the Brazilian location. Within a matter of weeks it had spread to the other names on the list, with the exception of Japan. Japan was a misfit in many ways, but he put it out of his mind temporarily and focused on the others.

He tapped the keys, and a series of articles from newspapers and magazines began to display themselves on the screen. Each would show twice for thirty seconds—first the full article, then the portions Mausier had highlighted for summary display.

He watched them idly as they flashed past. He didn't buy the terrorist group story. In all his reading and study, he could not detect a similar increase in deaths in any corporation outside his list of nine—well, eight. He might have been willing to believe the theory of randomly picked target corporations had he not already been studying them as a unit. As it was, it was too pat to be a coincidence. His eight corporations were the only ones to be randomly picked by a mysterious terrorist group? Bullshit. This was a new development of something that had been going on before.

He interrupted the display to reference an information request from the U.S. government that had gone unanswered for more than a month. They were asking for any and all information about the terrorist group, and offering a price that was well beyond tempting. Nobody answered.

The closest anyone had come to catching a member was one nut with a bomb. Although he swore up and down he was a member of that mystical group, investigation discovered he was working alone with a bomb he had built in his basement. Even the newspapers conceded he was probably a loner who was trying to cash in on the international publicity generated by the hunt for the elusive assassins.

Nobody could get a solid lead no matter what price was offered. That was what gave Mausier his first clue. There was only one time before he had known of when all levels of information hunters, governmental and freelance, had come up empty-handed. That was the aftermath of the Russo-Chinese War, when the C-Block sealed itself up and began buying but never selling information. The only possible explanation was the terrorist group was a front manned by and covered for by the C-Block. After all, wasn't it their inquiries that initially alerted him to the tie-in between the nine—no, eight—corporations?

But there his logic fell apart. Why were they doing it? To infiltrate the corporate structure with their own people? If so, why did they request personnel listings? Wouldn't they know who they were sending in?

He put it out of his mind for the moment and keyed for another display. Japan. During the time period in question, there had only been one death in the Japanese companies under surveillance, and that was of old age.

An article from a martial arts magazine eulogized the passing of an old sensei who had retired from teaching to take over some obscure physical fitness program for Japanese industry. That couldn't possibly tie in with the other items—or could it?

Mausier wished for a moment that someone would put in a request for the coroner's report on the old man's death so he could see if it was actually available, but he shrugged it off as wishful thinking. It never occurred to him to request the information himself. That would be cheating! He'd work with the pieces as they were given to him.

Why had Japan escaped the notice of the assassins? In fact, from watching the information requests, they seemed to have escaped the notice of the other eight corporations. The only one requesting information on them was the C-Block. Were they unrelated to the puzzle, or were they in fact the people behind the assassins?

Mausier shook his head in bewilderment and keyed for another display. An article flashed on the screen. It was an account of the death of a corporate executive, Edward Bush, at the hands of one of the terrorist assassins. This held particular interest for Mausier, as Bush had been one of his clients.

According to the article, the incident had not been unlike a score of others. A long-range sniper working in broad daylight picked him off on the sidewalk in front of his office and escaped without a clue.

The pattern was so repetitious Mausier could almost sing it in his sleep.

He was willing to accept it as an unfortunate coincidence. Bush had been a buying, not a selling client, so it was unlikely that his death was linked in any way to his dealings with Mausier. Still, there was something afoot.

Bush's own corporation had submitted an information request for details surrounding his death. What made it strange was that they had not made any similar requests regarding any of their other executives killed by snipers. Bush had not been particularly high-ranked in the corporation. Why the sudden interest in his demise?

There was still another curious coincidence connected with Bush's death. The C-Block was also requesting details. They hadn't requested details on any of the corporate deaths until now. Clearly there was something strange about the killing, but what? Was it Bush or the manner of his death? If Mausier's theory about the C-Block team of assassins was correct, would they know all about the incident already? Maybe it was the Japanese after all. Those damn Japanese! Where did they fit into it all? Did they fit in at all?

Mausier suddenly became aware of sounds in the outer office and realized his employees were arriving. He hastily turned off his doodle-screen and began composing himself for the day's routine.

As he did, however, he made a mental note to himself. He was going to go out at noon. For years he had seesawed back and forth trying to weigh necessity against childish romanticizing, but now he had made up his mind. He was going to buy a gun. Whatever was going on, the game was being played for high stakes and he was sitting on too much information to ignore the potential danger in his position.

Chapter Thirteen

The cliff was as foreboding as ever; the straw dummies waited passively at the base. Still, Tidwell realized his interest was at a peak as he sat waiting with Clancy for the next group to appear. The two mercenaries were perched on the lip of the cliff, dangling their legs idly, about five meters to the left of the trail.

They came, five of them darting silently from tree to tree like spirits. As they approached the cliff, the leader, a swarthy man in his thirties, held up his hand in a signal. The group froze, and he signaled one of the team forward. Tidwell smiled as a girl in her mid-twenties slung her rifle and dropped to her stomach, sliding forward to peer over the cliff. The leader knew damn well what was down there because he had run the course hundreds of times before, but he was playing it by the book and officially it was a new situation to be scouted.

The girl completed her survey, then slid backward for several meters before she rose to a half-crouch. Her hands flashed in a quick series of signals to the leader. Clancy nudged Tidwell, who smiled again, this time from flattered pleasure. Since he had taken over, the entire force had begun using his habit of sign language. It was a high compliment. The only trouble was that they had become proficient with it and had elaborated on his basic vocabulary to a point where he now sometimes had trouble following the signals as they flashed back and forth.

The leader made his decision. With a few abrupt gestures from him, the other three of the team, two men and a woman, slung their rifles and darted forward, diving full-speed off the cliff to confront their luckless "victims" below. The leader and the scout remained topside.

The two observing mercenaries straightened unconsciously. This was something new. The leader apparently had a new trick up his sleeve.

As his teammates sprinted forward, the leader reached over his shoulder and fished a coil of rope out of his pack. It was a black, lightweight silk line, with heavy knots tied in it every two feet for climbing. He located and grasped one end, tossing the coil to the scout. She caught it and flipped it over the cliff, while the leader secured his end around a small tree with a quick-release knot. This done, he faded back along the trail about ten meters to cover the rear, while the scout unslung her rifle and eased up to the edge of the cliff ready to cover her teammates below.

Clancy punched Tidwell's shoulder delightedly and flashed him a thumbs-up signal. Tidwell nodded in agreement. It was a sweet move. Now the three attackers below had an easy, secure route back out as well as cover fire if anything went wrong.

Tidwell felt like crowing. The reorganization of the force was working better than he would have dared hope. The whole thing had been a ridiculously simple three-step process. First, there had been a questionnaire asking eight questions: Which four people in the force would you most like to team with? Why? Who would you be least willing to team with? Why? Who would you be most willing to follow as a leader? Why? Who would you be least willing to follow as a leader? Why?

The next step was to pass the data through the computers a few times. Two jobs were done simultaneously: first, the five-man teams were established along the lines of preference stated by the individuals, second, the deadwood and misfits were weeded out to be sent back to other jobs in the corporate structure.

The final step was to pull various members of the teams for special accelerated training in the more specialized skills necessary in a fighting unit. He had had to argue with Clancy a little on this point, but had finally won. Clancy had felt the existing specialists should be seeded through the teams to round out the requirements regardless of preference lines, but Tidwell's inescapable logic was that in combat, you're better off with a mediocre machine gunner you trust and can work with than an expert machine gunner you wouldn't turn your back on.

From then on, the teams were inseparable. They bunked together, trained together, went on leave together; in short, they became a family. In fact, several of the teams had formed along family lines with mother, father, and offspring all on the same team, though frequently the leadership went to one of the offspring.

It was a weird, unorthodox way to organize an army, but it was bearing fruit. The teams were tight-knit and smooth running and highly prone to coming up with their own solutions to the tactical problems Tidwell was constantly inventing for them. It was beyond a doubt the finest fighting force Tidwell had ever been associated with.

The attackers were regaining the top of the cliff now. Suddenly, a mischievous idea hit Tidwell. He stood up and wigwagged the team leader. With a few brief gestures he sketched out his orders. The team leader nodded, and began signaling his team. The scout recoiled the rope and tossed it to the team leader. He caught it, stowed it in his pack, surveyed the terrain, and faded back into a bush. Tidwell checked the terrain and nodded to himself. It was a good ambush. He couldn't see any of the team even though he had seen four of them take cover. He hadn't seen where the scout went after she tossed the rope.

Clancy was smiling at him.

"Steve, you're a real son-of-a-bitch."

Tidwell shrugged modestly, and they settled back to wait.

They didn't have to wait long. The next team came into sight, jogging along the trail in a loose group. The leader, a girl in her late teens that Clancy was spending most of his off-hours with, spotted the two sitting on the edge of the cliff. She smiled and waved at them.

They smiled and waved back at her. They were still smiling when the ambush opened up.

The girl and the two men flanking her went down to the first burst of fire. The remaining two members dove smoothly under cover and started returning their fire.

Tidwell stood up.

"All right! Break it up!"

There was an abrupt cease-fire.

"Everybody over here!"

The two teams emerged from their hiding places and sprinted over to the two mercenaries. Tidwell tossed his "activator key" to one of the survivors of the second team who ducked off to "revive" his teammates.

"Okay. First off, ambushers. There's no point in laying an ambush if you're going to spring it too soon. Let 'em come all the way into the trap before you spring it. The way you did it, you're left with two survivors who've got you pinned down with your backs to a cliff!"

The "revived" members of the second team joined the group.

"Now then, victims! Those kill-suits are spoiling you rotten. You're supposed to be moving through disputed terrain. Don't bunch up where one burst can wipe out your whole team."

They were listening intently, soaking up everything he said.

"Okay, we've held up training enough. Report to the firing range after dinner for an extra hour's penalty tour."

The teams laughed as they resumed their training. Sending them to the firing range for a penalty tour was like sending a kid to Disneyland. Ever since the new weapons had arrived, the teams had to be driven away from the ranges. They even had to take head count at meals to be sure teams didn't skip eating to sneak out to the range for extra practice.

The girl leading the second team shot a black look at Clancy as she herded her team off the cliff.

"Now who's the son-of-a-bitch, Clancy old friend? Unless I miss my guess, she's going to have a few words for you tonight."

"Let her scream." Clancy's voice was chilly. "I'd rather see her gunned down here than when we're in live action. I wouldn't be doing her any favors to flash her warnings in training. Let her learn the hard way. Then she'll remember."

Tidwell smiled to himself. Underneath that easygoing nice guy exterior was as cold and hard-nosed a mercenary as he was. Maybe colder.

"Nit-picking aside, Clancy, what do you think?"

"Think? I'll tell you, Steve. I think they're the meanest, most versatile fighting force the world has ever seen, bar none. Like you say, we're nit-picking. They're as ready now as they're ever going to be."

Tidwell felt a tightening in his gut, but he kept it out of his voice.

"I'm glad our opinions concur, Clancy. I just received new orders from Yamada this morning. The jump-off date has been changed. We're moving out next week."

Chapter Fourteen

Judy Simmons languished picturesquely in her chair, gazing deeply into the candle of their now-habitual table in the dimly lit restaurant. In turn, Fred studied her cautiously as he sipped his coffee. She was beyond a doubt one of the most dangerous people he had ever encountered.

The two negotiators were enjoying their traditional meditative silence after dinner, a brief breathing spell before they plunged back into the move and countermove of bargaining over after-dinner drinks.

She was striking, the kind of beauty that turned heads on the street. Yet hidden in that enticing frame was a mind as sharp as a straight razor.

Fred had been frequently frustrated in his dealings with Ivan. The man's stubbornness and steadfast refusal to venture information beyond his instructions had been maddening at times. But his successor this lovely little armful, was a cat of a different color. She would smile coyly and match him argument for argument, innuendo for innuendo, and mousetrap for mousetrap.

After four weeks, their talks were at a firm stalemate, neither showing any real advantage or handicap. The original swarm of jokes from his teammate about his "old man immune to the witch's charms" were slowly giving way to impatient proddings and mumbled accusations of his "deliberately prolonging the meetings." He was by no means immune to her mystique, but neither was he throwing the bout. The iron will and keen perception he had noted in the open meetings was even more prevalent when encountered head-on. No sir! She earned her victories, but she was lovely.

"Fred." The voice jarred him out of his reverie. "Can I talk to you about something? Apart from our usual dueling?"

Fred was mildly startled. Something was up. She was breaking pattern. Over his years of negotiating, he had become an unknowing expert on body language, and her whole being expressed a major change. Where she usually leaned back, maintaining personal distance, stretching occasionally, like a well-fed jungle cat, she was now leaning forward on her elbows, her whole body radiating a concentrated intensity. And her eyes—she was usually expressive. But now, her eyes were distant, either looking at the table in front of her or somewhere past his shoulder. It was almost as if she were embarrassed by what she was about to say. In the entire time he had covertly studied her at the meetings, and in the last four weeks of close personal contact, he had never seen her like this. Whatever was coming, it was coming from someplace besides her negotiator's instructions and guidelines.

"It's about the international currency thing that's come up. You were rather outspoken in the meeting today with your views against it."

"That's right. It's a half-baked idea. The costs for running a system like that would be astronomical. Why, just to safeguard against counterfeiting—"

She interrupted with an annoyed wave of her hand as if she was shooing a bothersome fly.

"I know. I know. I heard you at the meeting today. You make nice speeches, but this time . . . this time I think you're barking up the wrong tree."

"Oh, bullshit! Just because your whiz kids came up with the idea doesn't mean—"

"Will you listen to me! I don't like it either!"

Their eyes locked in angry glares. Silence reigned for a few moments before Fred registered what she had said and his anger gave way to embarrassment.

"Sorry. You didn't say anything at the meeting."

"I know. I couldn't believe it was really happening. It was like a nightmare and I kept waiting to wake up."

She stared at her coffee. Fred waited respectfully for her to regain her composure.

"Fred, you talk about the costs, but have you really thought it through? Have you really stopped to think about what would happen if the corporations got together and issued their own worldwide currency?"

She looked at him directly now, her dark eyes deep, almost pleading, as she continued.

"Money makes the world go 'round, and the governments issue the money. If we start issuing our own money, it might make international business a lot simpler and stabilize costs, but the government won't stand for it. They'll be all over us with everything they've got. And it won't be just one or two governments, it'll be all of them. Every single one of 'em united to tear the corporations down. I wouldn't be surprised if the C-Block didn't deal themselves in too. That's why I'm against it!"

Fred considered her words. "Do you really think that would happen?"

"Do you see anything that would keep it from happening?"

Fred started to sip his coffee, then set it down again.

"All the nations . . . when . . . I'm going to have to think about that one."

He looked at her, and realized she was still staring into space.

"Hey! Judy!" His words were soft and concerned.

She looked at him and he realized her eyes were brimming with tears.

"Hey, this thing really has you scared, doesn't it?"

Instead of answering, she rose and fled to the ladies room.

Fred signaled for the check and pondered the situation. Well, he had always wondered what it would take to crack that controlled exterior. Now he knew.

The waiter swept by, leaving the small black tray with the tab on it in his wake.

Fred stared at it thoughtfully for a full minute, then dug out his wallet and carefully counted out a small stack of bills onto the tray. In a twinkling it disappeared with a small murmur of thanks from the waiter, and he lit a cigarette and settled down to wait.

A few minutes later, Judy appeared, face pale but her makeup intact or repaired.

"Sorry about that, Fred, but I . . ."

"Shall we go now?" He rose casually, as if nothing had happened or been said.

"But what about the check?"

"I took care of it."

"Oh, Fred, it was my turn to pay."

"I took care of it."

"But it's going onto the expense account anyway . . ."

"*I* took care of it."

She blinked at him in sudden realization.

"Oh."

"I'm taking you back to the hotel. You need a nightcap . . . somewhere where there aren't other people around."

Chapter Fifteen

"Spare change? Hey, man, any spare change?"

The youthful panhandlers were inevitable, even in a Brazilian airport. Tidwell strode on, ignoring the boy, but Clancy stopped and started digging in his pocket.

"Come on, Clancy! We've got to beat that mob through Customs."

"Yeah, ain't it a bitch?" the youth joined in. "Do you believe these gooks? It's been like this for almost a week."

Curiosity made Tidwell continue the conversation.

"Any word as to what they're doing?"

"Big tour program. Some Jap company is giving free tours instead of raises this year." He spat on the floor. "Damn cheap bastards. Haven't gotten a dime out of one of them yet."

"Here." Tidwell handed him a dollar. "This'll make up for some of it."

"Hey man, thanks. Say, take your bags to that skinny guy on the end and slip him ten, no hassle!"

The youth drifted off, looking for fresh game.

"Hypocrite!" accused Clancy under his breath. "Since when were you suddenly so generous."

"Since I could write it off on an expense account. That item is going in as a ten-dollar payment for an informant. C'mon, I'll buy you a drink out of the profits."

"Actually, I'd rather loiter around out here and make sure everything goes okay."

"Relax." Tidwell shot a glance down the terminal. "They're doing fine. Damnedest invasion I've ever seen."

At the other end of the terminal, the rest of their infiltration group was gathered, taking pictures and chattering together excitedly. Clancy and Tidwell had arrived by commercial flight half an hour after the charter plane, but the group was still fluttering around getting organized. They were perfect, right down to the overloaded camera bags and the clipboards. Even with his practiced eye, Tidwell could not have distinguished his own crew of cold killers from a hundred other groups of Orientals which frequent the tourist routes of the world.

"Hey! There you are!"

Both men winced. The irritating voice of Harry Beckington was unmistakable. After seven hours of his company on the plane, the mercenaries had not even had to confer before dodging him as they got off the plane. He would have made nice camouflage, but . . .

"Thought I lost you guys with all the slant-eyes in here!"

Their smiles were harder than usual to force.

"Sure are a lot of them," volunteered Clancy gamely.

"You know how they are—first a few, then you're hip-deep in 'em." ·

"That's the way it is, all right," smiled Tidwell.

"C'mon. Let me buy you boys a. . . ."

As he spoke, he gestured toward the bar, and collided with one of the "tour group." He collided with Aki.

There was no reason for Aki to be passing so close, except that there was no reason for him not to. He was returning from the souvenir stand and the group of three men happened to be in his path. One of the forces' instructions for the invasion was to not avoid each other. Nothing is as noticeable to a watchful eye as a group of people studiously ignoring each other. It would have been unnatural for Aki to alter his path, so he simply tried to walk past them, only to run into Beckington's wildly flailing arm.

Aki's arm was still in a sling from his duel with Tidwell, and it suffered the full brunt of the impact. He instinctively bounced back, and stumbled over Beckington's briefcase.

"Watch it, gook! Look what you did!"

Aki was the picture of politeness. He bobbed his head, smiling broadly.

"Please excuse. Most clumsy!"

"Excuse, hell. You're going to pick all that stuff up."

Beckington seized his injured arm angrily, pointing to the scattered papers on the floor.

"For Christ's sake, Beckington," interrupted Tidwell, "the man's got a bad arm."

"Injured, my ass. He's probably smuggling something. How 'bout it, gook? What are you smuggling?"

He shook the injured arm. Small beads of sweat appeared on Aki's forehead, but he kept smiling.

"No smuggle. Please—will pick up paper."

Beckington released him with a shove.

"Well, hurry up!"

"Careful, Beckington, he might know karate," cautioned Clancy.

"Shit! They don't scare me with that chop-chop crap!" snarled Beckington, but he stepped back anyway.

"Here are papers. Please excuse. Very clumsy."

Beckington gestured angrily. Aki set the papers down and retreated toward the other end of the terminal.

"Boy, that really frosts me. I mean, some people think just 'cause they're in another country they can get away with murder."

"Yeah, people like that really burn me, too," said Tidwell drily. The sarcasm was lost.

"Where were we? Oh yeah. I was going to buy you boys a drink. You ready?"

"Actually, we can't."

"Can't—why not?"

"Actually, we're with Alcoholics Anonymous. We're here to open a new branch," interrupted Clancy.

"Alcoholics Anonymous?"

"Yes," said Tidwell blandly. "On the national board, actually."

"But I thought you were drinking on the plane."

"Oh, that," interrupted Clancy. "Actually it was iced tea. We've found that lecturing people while we're traveling just alienates them, so we try to blend with the crowd until we have time to do some real work."

"Have you ever stopped to think what alcohol does to your nervous system? If you can hold on a second we've got some pamphlets here you could read."

Tidwell started rummaging energetically in his flight bag.

"Ah . . . actually I've got to run now. Nice talking with you boys."

He edged backward, started away toward the bar, then turned, smiled, and made a beeline for the men's room.

Tidwell collapsed in laughter.

"Alcoholics . . . Oh Christ, Clancy, where do you come up with those from anyway?"

"Huh? Oh, just a quickie. It got rid of him, didn't it?"

"I'll say. Well, let's go before he comes back."

"Um, can we stall here for a few minutes, Steve?"

Tidwell stopped laughing in mid-breath.

"What is it? Trouble?"

"Nothing definite. Don't want to worry you if it's nothing. Just talk about something for a few minutes."

"Terrific. Remind me to fire you for insubordination. How about that Aki? Do you believe he managed to keep his cool through all that crap?"

"Uh-huh."

"That Beckington is a real shit. If we weren't under contract, I'd like nothing better than realigning his face a little."

"Uh-huh."

"Dammit, that's enough! If you don't tell me what's up, I'll cut your liquor allotment!"

"Well . . . we might have a little problem."

"C'mon, Clancy!"

"You saw where Beckington went?"

"Yeah, into the men's room. So?"

"So, Aki's in there."

"What?"

"Doubled back and ducked in while we were doing the A.A. bit with Beckington. Probably needed to take a painkiller."

"Who else is in there?"

"Just the two of them."

"Christ! You don't think Aki—"

"Not out here in the open, but it must be awfully tempting in there."

The two men studied the ceiling in silence for several moments. Still no one emerged from the men's room. Finally Tidwell heaved a sigh and started for the door. Clancy held up a hand.

"C'mon Steve. Why not let him—"

"Because we can't afford any attention. None at all. All we need is to have them detain all the Orientals in the airport for a police investigation. Now let's go!"

The mercenaries started for the door. Tidwell raised his hand to push his way in, and the door opened.

"Oh, hi boys. How's the 'dry' business? Just do me a favor and don't close down the bars until after I've left the country, know what I mean?"

"Um . . . sure, Harry. Just for you."

"Well, see you around."

He brushed past them and strode toward the bar.

Almost mechanically, the two mercenaries pushed open the door and entered the washroom. Aki looked up inquiringly as he dried his hands on a blow-jet.

"Urn . . . are you okay, Aki?"

"Certainly, Mr. Tidwell. Why do you ask?"

The two men shifted uncomfortably.

"We . . . ah . . . we just thought that after what happened outside . . ."

Aki frowned for a moment, then suddenly smiled with realization.

"Ah! I see. You feared that I might . . . Mr. Tidwell, I am a mercenary under contract. Rest assured I would do nothing to draw needless attention to our force or myself."

With that, the three mercenaries headed out into the terminal to continue the invasion.

Chapter Sixteen

Wolfe! Big bad Wolfe! So he was finally going to talk to Wolfe.

Pete took the corner with an almost military precision. As usual, the executive corridor was empty. Bad for one's image to be caught loitering in the corridor. Without people, all efforts to make the hall seem warm and friendly through the use of pictures, hangings, or statues failed miserably. It always looked like you were on your way to a fallout shelter or a secret underground military installation.

After three days, Wolfe had finally sent for him. Well, Petey boy'd have a word or two for him.

He winced at his own false bravado. Who's kidding whom, Pete? You're scared. No . . . not scared. Nervous. Okay . . . admit it. Drag it out and let's have a look at it.

Something's wrong. Very wrong. Not just that I didn't get the number one spot. Something else. After three weeks as acting head of the section, Wolfe shows up. Wolfe, of all people! Wolfe is notorious as a troubleshooter and axeman here at the corporation. His stay in any job was usually brief and always bloody. So what? I've survived purges before. Yes, but he's been here three days and this will be my first time to see him alone. Usually a second-in-command works close with the new chief, shows him the ropes and points out the rough spots. Panic tactics. Yes . . . that's it. Let me sweat it out for three days, then the mysterious summons and I'll open up like a steamed clam, rat on everybody. That must be what he's doing. Well, it's working!

Okay! You've admitted it. Now take a deep breath and play it with a little style.

Right! Wolfe's door loomed before him. He took a deep breath, raised a knuckle, and tapped twice softly.

One . . . two . . . three heartbeats. Five. The light above the door flashed green. He turned the knob and entered.

Wolfe beamed at him as he rose from the desk. California casual and used-car friendly.

"Come in, Hornsby. It's Pete, isn't it?"

"Yes, sir."

"That's Emil. Please, no formality."

They shook hands and Wolfe waved him into a chair.

"Sorry we haven't gotten together sooner, but we've got quite a problem here."

"That was obvious when they called you in." Pete smiled back at him.

"Oh?" Wolfe seemed both surprised and amused. "How so?"

"Well . . . you . . . that is, you have a bit of a reputation—"

". . . As an axeman?" Wolfe dismissed it with a wave of his hand. "Quite exaggerated, I assure you. A bit annoying, actually. Makes people shy away from me."

"Oh, sorry I mentioned it."

"Quite the contrary, always glad to get a little feedback. Now, where were we?"

"The problem."

"Oh, yes! We have quite a problem. That problem, Pete, is you!"

"Me, sir?" Pete felt his hands starting to fidget.

"Yes. This is the second time you've been passed over for promotion, isn't it?"

"Well . . . yes . . . but I've been moving up. Slow and steady."

"Still, it's not a good sign."

"I've been pretty tied up on this war thing."

"It seems to indicate that you aren't developing as fast as we hoped, or you hoped, for that matter," Wolfe continued as if he hadn't heard.

"But I haven't had a chance to get to know—"

"So we've worked up a plan for your leaving. It involves six months on full pay and another—"

"Now just a damn minute!" Pete was on his feet.

"Sit down, Peter. There's no need to shout."

"If you aren't happy with my performance, there *are* other alternatives, you know! I've been thinking of putting in for a transfer."

"Pete, I'm trying to be pleasant about—"

"What about a transfer!"

"Look, Hornsby!" Wolfe's face was grim. "I've been trying to get you transferred! For a week before I came and for the last three days! Nobody wants you! Now sit down!"

Pete sank back into his chair.

"Now, as I was saying." Wolfe was again the pleasant salesman.

"Why?"

Wolfe pursed his lips for a long moment, then sighed and leaned back.

"Basically because of Eddie Bush."

"What about him?"

"Specifically the circumstances surrounding the way he died so conveniently for you."

"Now look! If you're trying to say—"

"*If* we had any solid proof, Hornsby, we'd turn you over to the authorities and that would be that. As it stands, there are just suspicions, perhaps unfounded, but enough that no one wants you working under them. I don't want you, and no one else wants you."

Pete's eyes fell before his gaze.

"Now then, as I was saying, you'll get six months—"

"How long do I have?"

"Beg your pardon?"

"You know what I mean."

Wolfe sighed. For the first time he looked sympathetic. "There's an armed guard waiting in my reception area to escort you out. Your files and office are being placed under lock and key as we're talking now. If you come back Saturday, a guard will meet you at the gate and escort you to your office where he will watch while you have half an hour to remove your personal effects."

"Has my staff been told?"

"A memo was distributed as you entered my office."

Pete thought for several moments. "Then there's nothing else to say, is there?"

"Well, you could let me tell you about the separation plan we've worked up for you. I think you'll find it more than fair."

"Save it. Send me a letter. Right now, I just want to leave."

"Very well."

Pete rose. "You'll understand, sir, if I don't shake your hand?"

"Frankly," Wolfe's eyes were cold, "I hadn't planned to."

He strode through the common corridors, head high, ahead of his guard. He had a disembodied, unearthly feeling, like he was walking in a dream.

He was screwed! No one would hire him now. Job hunting at his pay level without a job or a recommendation!

C'mon, Pete! You can work it out later. First try to put a little style into the exit.

He forced himself back into focus and began to look around him. Maybe a few casual nods or a wink or a wave at a couple of people on his way out. He suddenly realized he didn't know anyone in the halls. Nobody looked at him. Not that they were avoiding his eyes; they were all busy and their eyes passed over him as unimportant. Just a few curious glances at the guard. He didn't see any of his staff.

Usually there were a few of them around.

The window! One of the office windows overlooked the executive parking lot! They would be watching from the window. Some to wave goodbye, some from morbid curiosity, but they'll be at the window! Okay, Petey boy. We'll show them bastards how Peter Hornsby goes to meet his fate.

He cleared the door, forcing a jaunty air into his walk. He found he couldn't whistle, but decided it didn't matter.

As he reached his car and fumbled for his keys, curiosity forced him to sneak one peek at the window.

No one was watching.

Chapter Seventeen

Mausier winced as the gun under his coat bumped against the edge of the viewscreen with a loud *klunk!* He shot a covert glance around the office, but no one else seemed to notice. He heaved a sigh of relief, but was promptly assailed with additional doubts. More likely the staff had noticed and known what had happened, but chose to ignore it. The fact he was now carrying a gun was common knowledge since the afternoon he had accidentally triggered the clamshell shoulder holster, and the weapon had slid from under his coat to bounce on the floor in front of the whole office. A few had raised their eyebrows in surprise, but the majority of them had merely smiled indulgently. Mausier had secretly writhed in agony under those smiles, as he was writhing now under their tolerant silence. They obviously thought he was silly, a child with a toy gun pretending to be dangerous or endangered. They weren't aware of the potentially explosive and violent situation they were all living in.

Then again, how sure was he? Mausier considered for the hundredth time taking the gun back to the store. It was doing him no apparent good and causing him untold embarrassment. His wife never tired of making little digs about "that thing" when he stripped and cleaned it each night. Even though he weathered her taunts in stoic silence, it was beginning to take its toll on him.

He felt foolish. Who would want to attack him anyway? He wasn't a key figure, in fact, he wasn't a figure at all. He didn't make any decisions, he never even touched the various items of information his office posted and negotiated for. He was a watcher, not a doer. All he had was some wild guesses and theories based on information any number of people could have if they read extensively and thought about what they read. Why should anyone come after him specifically? More importantly, what could he do if they did?

The closest thing to an attack that had happened to him had occurred last week. He had been walking through the parking lot of a shopping center and a panel truck backed into him, knocking him sprawling. The driver could have backed over him as he lay on the pavement. Instead he stopped the truck and leaped out to help Mausier back to his feet, apologizing profusely and offering to buy him a drink. At the time, Mausier's gun was locked in the glove compartment of his car two hundred feet away. He had left it behind for fear of tripping the shoplifter detection devices in the store.

If it had been a real attempt on his life, he would be dead. What could he have done to stop it even if he had had the gun along? Shot the driver when he heard the gears engage? He could hurt a lot of innocent people that way. Besides, the modus operandi was wrong for the assassin teams. They preferred to work from long range with scoped rifles. Okay, if one of those had taken a shot at him, what would he do, assuming, of course, the assassin missed his first shot, which they didn't seem to do very often? Draw his handgun and try to outshoot him? A professional assassin two blocks away with a scoped rifle? Fat chance.

The handgun he carried was a Walther P-38, a nastily efficient, medium-sized automatic. Its double action allowed him to carry it with one round chambered and the hammer down and still have the ability to get off the first round by simply squeezing the trigger without fielding slides or anything. He practiced with it at a local firing range at least once a week until he considered himself a moderate shot. That is, he could put the entire clip into a man-sized target if it was close enough for him to hit it with a thrown rock.

He was comfortably content with his abilities, or had been until one afternoon when he noticed the young man practicing in the lane next to him was outshooting him easily, snapshooting from the hip. "Instinct shooting" the youth had called it, all the while bemoaning how much his abilities had atrophied since he left the service.

No, Mausier had long since abandoned any hopes he might have once entertained about outshooting the pros. Still, he clung tenaciously to the weapon. It was a chance, a slim chance admittedly, but still a chance. Without it, he would have no chance at all.

He glanced at his watch. Another hour and the workday would be over. He was anxious for the staff to leave so he could return to his hobby. There were two new items on the board today he was particularly eager to start digging on.

One was an information request from the oil corporation linked to the Brazilian branch of his pet mystery. The request was so off-the-wall he almost wondered if they were putting it on the board as a confusion tactic. They wanted lists of any people who had left service with the Treasury Department of any country in the free world within the last year. Special bonuses would be paid for leads on people who had been directly involved with the minting of currency.

Moneymakers? What in the world were they up to? What possible mess could they have gotten themselves into that would require money experts above and beyond those already available to the corporate world? Counterfeiting? If so, why didn't they simply turn it over to the governments to run down? Maybe the problem was so widespread that they wanted to hush it up by handling it themselves. Maybe it was so widespread they were afraid of an economic panic if the truth leaked out.

Mausier shook his head. He was groping at straws. He'd have to hold off until he had time to scan the files for additional details or related items. Instead, he turned his thoughts to the other new item.

The C-Block had a new information request on the board. This one concerned the Japanese industries which they had been watching. They were asking for a complete listing of personnel taking the newly offered bonus world tour. If possible, they also wanted details as to timetables and rotation schedules.

Tour groups! His Brazilian workspace was getting overloaded with items. Soon he would either have to rent additional computer time or start weeding it down. Tour groups and moneymakers. This whole puzzle was starting to get out of hand.

Sometimes he wondered if he wasn't imagining it all. One of the hazards in the intelligence profession was getting hold of minor data and blowing it all out of proportion. If one tried hard enough, it was possible to take any three newspaper articles chosen at random and weave them into a conspiracy of national or international proportions.

Take as an example those items about the weapon-design corporations. Suddenly many of the corporations on his list were inquiring about who the arms designers were building what for. It had puzzled him for the longest time until he finally figured it out. They were exploring another possible lead on the assassin teams. If the teams were, in fact, using special weapons, someone was supplying them. Very clever, actually—an angle the governments hadn't thought of checking into yet. Now, if he were the overly suspicious and paranoid type, he could build those inquiries into . . . well, he didn't know what, but he could build it into something.

But tour groups? Where in the world did they tie into the picture? There was one thing which might be worth looking into. If he recalled the small article he had noticed on the Japanese tour correctly, their first stop on the world tour was Brazil. It was the first time he had been able to draw even the vaguest connection between the Japanese crew and the other groups of corporations on his list. It was shaky and probably purely coincidental, but it was still worth looking into.

His thoughts were interrupted by Ms. Witley, who told him a gentleman was in the lobby who wanted to talk to him about selling some information. Mausier was not enthused over the news and briefly considered stalling the visitor until the morning. Only occasionally did walk-ins have anything really worth selling, and they were always incredibly long-winded about the risks they had run to obtain their worthless bit of trivia. Still, there were occasional pieces of gold among the gravel, and he hadn't gotten where he was turning away potential clients.

With that in mind, he instructed Ms. Witley to fetch the man back to his office. When he arrived, Mausier's appraising eye quickly classified him as pure corporation. It was more than the distinctive conservative suit—it was the way he held himself. His shoulders were tense, his smile forced, and his jovial pleasantness almost painful. Definitely corporate, maybe middle management, obviously desperate, probably overestimating the value of his information.

"Nice little layout you've got here." The man took in the screens with a wave of his hand.

Mausier didn't smile. He was determined to keep this brief.

"Ms. Witley said you had some information to sell?"

"Yes, I have some information on the terrorist assassin groups everybody's looking for."

Mausier was suddenly attentive. "What kind of information?"

"Say, do you mind if I smoke?"

"I'd rather you didn't." Mausier nodded at the electronic gear lining the office.

"Thanks," said the man, lighting up. "Now where was I? Oh, yes. I guess I know more about the terrorists than anyone. You see, I'm the one who invented them for the corporations . . ."

Mausier suddenly realized the man was more than slightly drunk. Still, he was intrigued by what he was saying.

"Excuse me, what did you say your name was again?"

"Hornsby, Peter Hornsby."

Chapter Eighteen

"Tell the driver to slow up. It should be right along here somewhere."

"I still haven't seen the buses." Clancy scowled through the dust and bug-caked windshield of the truck.

"Don't worry, they'll be—there they are!"

The buses were rounding the curve ahead, bearing down on them with the leisurely pace characteristic of this country. Tidwell watched the vehicle occupants as they passed, craning his neck to see around the driver. The bus passengers smiled and waved joyously, but Tidwell noticed none of them took pictures.

The mercenaries smiled and waved back.

"The fix is in!" chortled Clancy.

"Did you see any empty seats?"

"One or two. Nothing noticeable."

Good. Look, there it is up ahead."

Beside the road there was a small soft shoulder, one of the few along this hilly, jungled route. Without being told, the driver pulled off the road and stopped. They sat motionless for several long moments, then Aki stepped out of the brush and waved. At the signal, the driver cut the engine and got out of the car. The two mercenaries also piled out of the car, but unlike the driver, who leisurely began taking off his shirt, they strode around to the back of the truck and opened the twin doors. Two men were in the back, men of approximately the same description as and dressed identically to Tidwell and Clancy. They didn't say anything, but strode leisurely to the front of the truck and took the mercenaries' places in the cab. Like the driver, they had been briefed.

The two mercenaries turned their attention to the crates in the back. Aki joined them.

"Are the lookouts in place?"

"Yes, sir."

"You worry too much, Steve," chided Clancy. "We haven't seen another car on this road all day."

"I don't want this messed up by a bunch of gawking tourists."

"So we stop 'em. We've done it before and we've got the team to do it."

"And lose two hours covering up? No thanks."

"I'm going to check the teams. I'll send a couple back to give you a hand here."

He hopped out of the truck and strode down the road, entering the brush at the point where Aki had emerged.

Fifteen feet into the overgrowth was a clearing where the teams were undergoing their metamorphosis. Nine in the clearing, and one in the truck made ten. Two full teams, and the buses had looked full.

The team members were in various stages of dress and undress. One of the first things lost when the teams were formed was any vague vestige of modesty. The clothes had been cunningly designed and tailored. Linings were ripped from jackets and pants, false hems were removed, and the familiar kill-suits began to come into view.

Clancy arrived carrying the first case. He jerked his head and two already-clothed team members darted back toward the road. Setting the carton down, Clancy slit open the sealing tape with his pocket knife. He folded the flaps back, revealing a case of toy robots.

Easing them out onto the ground, he opened the false bottom where the swamp boots were kept. These were not new boots. They were the member's own broken-in boots. Clancy grabbed his pair and returned to a corner of the clearing to convert his clothes. One by one, the members claimed their boots and a robot and stooped to finish dressing.

Tidwell had worn his boots to speed the changing process. He whistled low and gestured, and a team member tossed him a robot. He caught it and opened the lid on its head in a practiced motion. Reaching in carefully, he removed the activator unit for his kill-suit and checked it carefully. Satisfied, he plugged it into his suit and rose to check the rest of the progress, resealing the lid on the robot and stacking it by the carton as he went.

Conversion was in full swing as more cartons arrived. The shoulder straps came off the camera gadget bags, separated, and were reinserted to form the backpacks. Fashionable belts with gaudy tooling were reversed to reveal a uniform black leather with accessory loops for weapons and ammunition.

Tidwell particularly wanted to check the weapons assembly. Packing material from the toy cartons was scooped into plastic bags, moistened down with a fluid from the bottles in the camera bags, and the resulting paste pressed into molds previously covered by the boots to form the rifle stocks. The camera tripods were dismounted, the telescoping legs separated for various purposes. First, the rounds of live ammo were emptied out and distributed. Tidwell smiled grimly at this. All the forces' weapons were "convertibles"—that is, they were basically quartz-crystal weapons, but were also rigged to fire live ammo if the other forces tried to disclaim their entry into the war.

The larger section of the legs separated into three parts to form the barrels for both the flare pistols and the short double-barreled shotguns so deadly in close fighting. The middle sections were fitted with handles and a firing mechanism to serve as launchers for the mini-grenades which up to now had been carried in the thirty-five-millimeter-film canisters hung from the pack straps. The smallest diameter section was used for the rifle barrel, fitted with a fountain pen telescopic sight. The firing mechanisms were cannibalized from the cameras and various toys which emerged and were reinserted in the cartons.

One carton only was not refilled with its original contents. This carton was filled with rubber daggers and swords—samurai swords.

These were disbursed to the members, who used their fingernails to slice through and peel back the rubber coating to reveal the actual weapons, glittering and eager in the sun. These were not rigged for use on kill-suits.

The label on the empty box was pulled back to reveal another label declaring the contents camera parts, and the skeletons of the cannibalized cameras were loaded in, packed with the shreds of the outer clothing now torn to unrecognizable pieces.

The cartons were resealed and reloaded, and the truck was again sent along its way with a driver, two passengers, and a load of working toys and camera gear.

Tidwell watched it depart and smiled grimly. They were ready.

"Call in the lookouts, Clancy. We've got a long hike ahead of us."

"What's with Aki?"

The Oriental was running toward them waving excitedly.

"Sir! Mr. Yamada is on the radio."

"Yamada?"

"This could be trouble, Steve."

They returned hurriedly to the clearing where the team was gathered around the radio operator. Tidwell grabbed the mike.

"Tidwell here."

"Mr. Tidwell." Yamada's voice came through without static. "You are to proceed to the rendezvous point to meet with the other teams at all haste. Once there, do not, I repeat, do not carry out any action against the enemy until you have received further word from me."

Tidwell frowned, but kept his voice respectful.

"Message received. Might I ask why?"

"You are not to move against the enemy until we have determined who the enemy is."

"What the hell—"

"Shut up, Clancy. Please clarify, Mr. Yamada."

"At the moment there is a cease-fire in effect on the war. The government of the United States has chosen to intervene."

Chapter Nineteen

CORPORATION WARS CHARGED

A federal grand jury was appointed today to investigate alleged involvement of several major corporations in open warfare with each other. The corporations have refused to comment on charges that they have been maintaining armies of mercenaries on their payrolls for the express purpose of waging war on each other. Included on the list of corporations charged were several major oil conglomerates as well as communications and fishing concerns. The repercussions may he international as some of the corporations involved (continued on p. 28)

CORPORATIONS DEFY ORDERS

In a joint press release issued this afternoon, the corporations under investigation for involvement in the alleged corporate wars flatly refused to comply with government directives to cease all hostilities toward each other of a warlike nature and refrain from any future activities. They openly challenge the government's authority to intervene in these conflicts, pointing out that the wars are not currently being conducted within the boundaries of the U.S. or its territories. They have asked the media to relay to the American people their countercharges that the government is trying to pressure them into submission by threatening to move against the corporations' U.S. holdings. They refer to those threats as "blatant extortion" being carried on in the name of justice, pointing out the widespread chaos which would be caused if their services to the nation were interrupted, (continued on p. 18)

CORPORATE ASSASSIN TEAMS CHARGED

In the wake of yesterday's television broadcasts in which the corporations explained the "bloodless war" concept they claim they have been practicing, new charges have been raised that they have for some time been employing teams of professional assassins to stalk rival executives in the streets and offices of America. Several instances were cited of actual deaths incurred as a result of this practice, both among the executives and innocent bystanders. While not commenting on these charges, the corporations bitterly denied any connection with the forcible abduction yesterday of state's witness Peter Hornsby, whose information first brought the corporate wars to the government's attention. There is still no clue in that abduction, which left two U.S. Marshalls dead and (continued on p. 6)

STRIKER PREDICTS WAR

Simon Striker, noted political analyst of the long silent C-Block, has warned that if the new armed might of the corporations is not checked by the governments of the free world, it is highly probable that the C-Block will take direct action. "Such a threat could not be ignored by the party (continued on p. 14)

ECONOMIST TO SPEAK TONIGHT

Dr. Kearns, Dean of the School of Economics at the Massachusetts Institute of Technology, will speak here tonight as part of his nationwide tour soliciting support for the controversial corporate actions recently discovered. It is Dr. Kearns' contention that the corporations' proposed international currency would bring much needed stability to the world's monetary situation. His talk will begin at 8:00 P.M. IN AUDITORIUM A OF THE ECONOMICS BUILDING. ADMISSION IS FREE TO THE PUBLIC.

AFRICANS JOIN CORPORATE OPPOSITION

The League of African Nations added their support to the rapidly growing list of countries seeking to control the multinational corporations. With the addition of these new allies, virtually all major nations of the free world are united in their opposition to the combined corporate powers. Plans are currently being formulated for a united armed intervention if the corporations continue to defy (continued on p. 12)

WORLDWIDE PROTESTS SCHEDULED

Protest demonstrations are scheduled for noon tomorrow in every major city across the globe as citizen groups from all walks of life band together to voice their displeasure at the proposed governmental armed forces intervention in the corporate wars. War is perhaps the least popular endeavor governments embark on, and it is usually sold to the populace as a step necessary to ensure national security, a reason which many feel does not apply in this situation. Groups not usually prone to voicing protest have joined the movement, including several policemen's unions and civil servant organizations. Government officials (continued on p. 8)

COURT MARTIALS THREATENED

Armed Forces officials announced today that any military personnel taking part in the planned demonstrations will be arrested and tried for taking part in a political rally, whether or not they are in uniform.

GOVERNMENT-CORPORATE TALKS SUSPENDED

Negotiation sessions seeking peaceful settlement between the combined corporations and the united free world governments came to an abrupt halt today when several government negotiators walked out of the sessions. Informed sources say that the eruption occurred as a result of an appeal on the part of the corporations to the governments to "(rail off a situation involving needless bloodshed which the government troops could not hope to win." It is believed that what they were alluding to where their alleged "super-weapons" which the governments continue to discount. "A weapon is only as good as the man behind it," a high-ranked U.S. Army officer is quoted as saying. "And we have the best troops in the world." With scant hours remaining before the deadline (continued on p. 7)

Chapter Twenty

Lieutenant Worthington, U.S. Army, was relieved as the convoy pulled into the outskirts of town. He only wished his shoulders would relax. They were still tense to the point of aching. He tried to listen to the voices of the enlisted men riding in the back of the truck as they joked and sang, but shrugged it off in irritation.

The bloody fools. Didn't they know they had been in danger for the last hour? They were here to fight mercenaries, hardened professional killers. There had been at least a dozen places along the road through the jungle that seemed to be designed for an ambush, but the men chatted and laughed, seemingly oblivious to the fact the rifles on their laps were empty.

The lieutenant shook his head. That was one Army policy to which he took violent exception. He knew that only issuing ammunition when the troops were moving into a combat zone reduced accidents and fatal arguments, but dammit, for all intents and purposes, the whole country was a combat zone. It was fine and dandy to make policies when you were sitting safe and secure at the Pentagon desk looking at charts and statistics, but it wasn't reassuring when you were riding through potential ambush country with an empty weapon.

He shot a guilty sidelong glance at the driver. He wondered if the driver had noticed that Worthington had a live clip in his pistol. Probably not. He had smuggled it along and switched the clips in the john before they got on the trucks. Hell, even if he had noticed, he probably wouldn't report him. He was probably glad that someone in the truck had a loaded weapon along.

They were in town now. The soldiers in back were whooping and shouting crude comments at the women on the sidewalk. Worthington glanced out the window, idly studying the buildings as they rolled past. Suddenly he stiffened.

There, at a table of a sidewalk cafe, were two mercenaries in the now-famous kill-suits leisurely sipping drinks and chatting with two other men in civilian dress. The lieutenant reacted instantly.

"Stop the truck!"

"But sir—"

"Stop the truck, dammit!"

Worthington was out of the truck even before it screeched to a halt, fumbling his pistol from its holster. He ignored the angry shouts behind him as the men in back were tossed about by the sudden braking action, and leveled his pistol at the mercenaries.

"Don't move, either of you!"

The men seemed not to hear him, continuing with their conversation.

"I said, don't move!"

Still they ignored him. Worthington was starting to feel foolish, aware of the driver peering out the door behind him. He was about to repeat himself when one of the mercenaries noticed him. He tapped the other one on the arm, and the whole table craned their necks to look at the figure by the truck.

"You are to consider yourselves my prisoners. Put your hands on your head and face the wall!"

They listened to him, heads cocked in alert interest. When he was done, one of the mercenaries replied with a rude gesture of international significance. The others at the table rocked with laughter, then they returned to their conversation.

Worthington suddenly found himself ignored again. Reason vanished in a wave of anger and humiliation. Those bastards!

The gun barked and roared in his hand, startling him back to his senses. He had not intended to fire. His hand must have tightened nervously and . . .

Wait a minute! Where were the mercenaries? He shot a nervous glance around. The table was deserted, but he could see the two men in civilian clothes lying on the floor covering their heads with their arms. Neither seemed to be injured. Thank God for that! There would have been hell to pay if he had shot a civilian. But where were the mercenaries?

The men were starting to pile out of the truck behind him, clamoring to know what was going on. One thing was sure—he couldn't go hunting mercenaries with a platoon of men with empty rifles.

Suddenly a voice rang out from the far side of the street.

"Anybody hurt over there?"

"Clean miss!" rang out another voice from the darkened depths of the cafe.

The lieutenant squinted, but couldn't make out anyone.

"Are they wearing kill-suits?" came a third voice from farther down the street.

"As a matter of fact, they aren't!" shouted another voice from the alley alongside the cafe.

"That was live ammo?"

"I believe it was."

The men by the truck were milling about, craning their necks at the unseen voices. Worthington suddenly realized he was sweating.

"You hear that, boys? Live ammo!"

"Fine by us!"

The lieutenant opened his mouth to shout something, anything, but it was too late. His voice was drowned out by the first ragged barrage. He had time to register with horror that it was not even a solid hail of bullets that swept their convoy. It was a vicious barrage of snipers, masked marksmen. One bullet, one soldier. Then a grenade went off under the truck next to him and he stopped registering things.

જી જી જી

There was no doubt in anyone's mind as to the unfortunate nature of the incident. For one thing, one of the men in civilian clothes sharing a drink with the mercenaries was an Italian officer with the Combined Government Troops who corroborated the corporations' claim the action was in response to an unprovoked attack by the convoy. The fourth man was a civilian, a reporter with an international news service. His syndicated account of the affair heaped more fuel on an already raging fire of protest on the home fronts against the troops, intervention in the corporate wars.

Even so, the corporations issued a formal note of apology to the government forces for the massacre. They further suggested that the government troops be more carefully instructed as to the niceties of off-hours behavior to avoid similar incidents in the future.

An angry flurry of memos did the rounds of the government forces trying vainly to find someone responsible for issuing the live ammo.

The mayor of the town was more direct and to the point. He withdrew the permission for the American troops to be quartered in the town, forcing them to bivouac outside the city limits. Further, he signed into law an ordinance forbidding the Americans from coming into town with any form of firearm, loaded or not, on their person.

This ordinance was rigidly enforced, and American soldiers in town were constantly subject to being stopped and searched by the local constable, to the delight of the mercenaries who frequently swaggered about with loaded firearms worn openly on their hips.

Had Lieutenant Worthington not been killed in the original incident, he would have doubtless been done in by his own men—if not by the troops under him, then definitely by his superiors.

The sniper raised his head a moment to check the scene below before settling in behind the sights of his rifle. The layout was as it had been described to him.

The speaker stood at a microphone on a raised wooden platform in the square below him. The building behind him was a perfect backdrop. With the soft hollow-point bullets he was using, there would be no ricochets to endanger innocent bystanders in the small crowd which had assembled.

Again he lowered his head behind the scope and prepared for his shot. Suddenly, there was the sound of a *tunggg* and he felt the rifle vibrate slightly. He snapped his head upright and blinked in disbelief at what he saw. The barrel of his rifle was gone, sheared cleanly away by some unseen force.

He rolled over to look behind him and froze. Three men stood on the roof behind him. He hadn't heard them approach. Two were ordinary-looking, perhaps in better shape than the average person. The third was Oriental. It was the last man who commanded the sniper's attention. This was because of the long sword, bright in the sun, which the man was holding an inch in front of the sniper's throat.

The man behind the Oriental spoke.

"Hi guy! We've been expecting you."

The speaker was becoming redundant. The crowd was getting a little restless. Why did the man insist on repeating himself for the third and fourth times, not even bothering to change his phrasing much?

Suddenly there was a stir at the outer edge of the crowd. Four men were approaching the podium with a purposeful stride—well, three men shoving a fourth as they came. They bounded onto the platform, one taking over the microphone over the speaker's protests.

"Sorry, Senator, but part of the political tradition is allowing equal time to opposing points of view."

He turned to the crowd.

"Good afternoon, ladies and gentlemen. You've been very patient with the last speaker, so I'll try to keep this brief. I represent the corporations the Senator here has been attacking so vehemently."

The crowd stirred slightly, but remained in place, their curiosity piqued.

"Now, you may be impressed with the Senator's courage, attacking us so often publicly, as he has been doing lately, when it's known we have teams of assassins roaming the streets. We were impressed too. We were also a bit curious. It seemed to us he was almost inviting an assassination attempt. However, we ignored him, trusting the judgment of the general public to see him as the loudmouthed slanderer he is."

The Senator started forward angrily, but the man at the mike froze him with a glare.

"Then he changed. He switched from his pattern of half-truths and distortions that are a politician's stock in trade, and moved into the realm of outright lies. This worried us a bit. It occurred to us that if someone did take a shot at him, it would be blamed on us and give credence to all his lies. Because of this, we've been keeping a force of men on hand to guard him whenever he speaks to make sure nothing happens to him."

He paused and nodded to one of his colleagues. The man put his fingers in his mouth and whistled shrilly.

Immediately on the rooftops and in the windows of the buildings surrounding the square, groups of men and women stepped into view. They were all dressed in civilian clothes, but the timeliness of their appearance, as well as the uniform coldness with which they stared down at the crowd, left no doubt that they were all part of the same team.

The man whistled again, and the figures disappeared. The man at the mike continued.

"So we kept watching the Senator, and finally today we caught something. This gentleman has a rather interesting story to tell."

The sniper was suddenly thrust forward.

"What were you doing here today?"

"I want a lawyer. You can't . . ."

The Oriental twitched. His fist was a blur as it flashed forward to strike the sniper's arm. The man screamed, but through it the crowd heard the bone break.

"What were you doing here today?" The questioner's voice was calm, as if nothing had happened.

"I . . ."

"Louder!"

"I was supposed to shoot at the Senator."

"Were you supposed to hit him?"

"No." The man was swaying slightly from the pain in his arm.

"Who hired you?"

The man shook his head. The Oriental's fist lashed out again.

"The Senator!" The man screamed.

A murmur ran through the crowd. The Senator stepped hurriedly to the front of the platform.

"It's a lie!" he screamed. "They're trying to discredit me. They're faking it. That's one of their own men they're hitting. It's a fake."

The man with the microphone ignored him. Instead he pointed to a policeman in the crowd.

"Officer! There's usually a standing order about guarding political candidates. Why wasn't there anyone from the police watching those rooftops?"

The officer cupped his hands to shout back.

"The Senator insisted on minimum guards. He pulled rank on the Chief."

The crowd stared at the Senator, who shrank back before their gaze. The man with the mike continued.

"One of the Senator's claims is that the corporations would do away with free speech. I feel we have proved this afternoon that the statement is a lie. However, our businesses, like any businesses, depend on public support, and we will move to protect it. As you all know, there's a war on."

He turned to glare at the Senator.

"It is my personal opinion that we should make war on the war-makers. Our targets should be the people who send others out to fight. However, that is only my personal opinion. The only targets in my jurisdiction are front-line soldiers."

He looked out over the crowd again.

"Are there any reporters here? Good. When this man took money to discredit the corporations, he became a mercenary, the same as us. As such, he falls under the rules of the war. I would appreciate it if you would print this story as a warning to any other two-bit punks that think it would be a good idea to pose as a corporate mercenary."

He nodded to his colleagues on the platform. One of the men gave the sniper a violent shove that sent him sprawling off the platform, drew a pistol from under his jacket, and shot him.

The policeman was suspended for allowing the mercenaries to leave unchallenged, a suspension that caused a major walk-off on the police force. The Senator was defeated in the next election.

The young Oriental couple ceased their conversation abruptly when they saw the group of soldiers, at least a dozen, on the sidewalk ahead of them. Without even consulting each other they crossed the street to avoid the potential trouble. Unfortunately, the soldiers had also spotted them and also crossed the street to block their progress. The couple turned to retrace their steps, but the soldiers, shouting now, ran to catch them.

Viewed up close, it was clear the men had been drinking. They pinned the couple in a half-circle, backing them against a wall, where the two politely inquired as to what the soldiers wanted. The soldiers admitted it was the lady who was the reason for their attention and invited her to accompany them as they continued on their spree. The lady politely declined, pointing out that she already had an escort. The soldiers waxed eloquent, pointing out the numerous and obvious shortcomings of the lady's escort, physically and probably financially. They allowed as how the fourteen of them would be better able to protect the lady from the numerous gentlemen of dubious intent she was bound to encounter on the street. Furthermore, they pointed out, even though their finances were admittedly depleted by their drinking, by pooling their money they could doubtless top any price her current escort had offered for her favors.

At this, her escort started forward to lodge a protest, but she laid a gentle restraining hand on his arm and stepped forward smiling. She pointed out that the soldiers were perhaps mistaken in several of their assumptions about the situation at hand. First, they were apparently under the impression that she was a call girl, when in truth she was gainfully employed by the corporate forces. Second, her escort for the evening was not a paying date, but rather her brother. Finally, she pointed out that while she thanked them for their concern and their offer, she was more than capable of taking care of herself, thank you.

By the time she was done explaining this last point, the soldiers had become rearranged. Their formation was no longer in a half-circle, but rather scattered loosely for several yards along the street. Also, their position in that formation was horizontal rather than vertical.

Her explanation complete, the lady took her brother's arm and they continued on their way. As they walked, one of the soldiers groaned and tried to rise. She drove the high heel of her shoe into his forehead without breaking stride.

Julian rolled down his window as the service station attendant came around to the side of his car.

"Fill it up with premium."

The attendant peered into the back seat of the car.

"Who do you work for, sir?"

"Salesman for a tool and die company."

"Got any company ID?"

"No, it's a small outfit. Could you fill it up—I'm in a hurry."

"Could you let me see a business card or your samples? If you're a salesman . . ."

"All right, all right. I'll admit it. I work for the government. But . . ."

The attendant's face froze into a mask.

"Sorry, sir." He started to turn away.

"Hey, wait a minute!" Julian sprang out of the car and hurried to catch up with the retreating figure. "C'mon, give me a break. I'm a crummy clerk. It's not like I had any say in the decisions."

"Sorry, sir, but . . ."

"It's not like I'm on official business. I'm trying to get to my sister's wedding."

The attendant hesitated.

"Look, I'd like to help you, but if the home office found out we sold gas to a government employee, they'd pull our franchise."

"Nobody would have to know. Just look the other way for a few minutes and I'll pump it myself."

The man shook his head.

"Sorry, I can't risk it."

"I'll give you fifty dollars for half a tank . . ."

But the attendant was gone.

Julian heaved a sigh and got back into his car. Once he left the station, though, his hangdog mask slipped away. Things were going well with the fuel boycott. It had been three weeks since he had had to report a station for breaking the rules. He checked his list for the location of the next station to check out.

The mercenary was wearing a jungle camouflage kill-suit. The hammock he was sprawled in was also jungle-camouflaged, as was the floppy brimmed hat currently obscuring his face as a sunscreen. He was snoring softly, seemingly oblivious to the insects buzzing around him.

"Hey Sarge!"

The slumbering figure didn't move.

"Hey Sarge!" the young private repeated without coming closer. Even though he was new, he wasn't dumb enough to try to wake the sleeping mercenary by shaking him.

"What is it, Turner?" His voice had the tolerant tone of one dealing with a whining child.

"The tank. You know, the one the detectors have been tracking for the last five hours? You said to wake you up if it got within five hundred meters. Well, it's here."

"Okay, you woke me up. Now let me go back to sleep. I'm still a little rocky from going into town last night."

The private fidgeted.

"But aren't we going to do anything?"

"Why should we? They'll never find us. Believe in your infrared screens, my son, believe."

He was starting to drift off to sleep again. The private persisted.

"But Sarge! I . . . uh . . . well, I thought we might . . . well, my performance review's coming up next week."

"Qualifying, huh? Well, don't worry. I'll give you my recommendation."

"I know, but I thought . . . well, you know how much more they notice your record if you've seen combat."

The sergeant sighed.

"All right. Is it rigged for quartz-beams?"

"The scanners say no."

"Is Betsy tracking it?"

"Seems to be. Shall I—"

"Don't bother, I'll get it."

Without raising his hat to look, the sergeant extended a leg off the hammock. The far end of his hammock was anchored on a complex mass of machinery, also covered with camouflaging. His questing toe found the firing button, which he prodded firmly. The machine hummed to life, and from its depths a beam darted out to be answered by the chill whump of an explosion in the distance.

The private was impressed.

"Wow, hey, thanks, Sarge."

"Don't mention it, kid."

"Say, uh, Sarge?"

"What is it, Turner?"

"Shouldn't we do something about the infantry support?"

"Are they coming this way?"

"No, it looks like they're headed back to camp, but shouldn't we—"

"Look, kid." The sergeant was drifting off again. "Lemme give you a little advice about those performance reviews. You don't want to load too much stuff onto 'em. The personnel folk might get the idea it's too easy."

This evening, the news on the corporate wars was the news itself. It seemed some underling at the FCC had appeared on a talk show and criticized the lack of impartiality shown by the media in their reporting on the corporate wars.

News commentators all across the globe pounced on this item as if they had never had anything to talk about before. They talked about freedom of speech. They talked about attempted governmental control of the media. They talked about how even public service corporations like the media were not safe from the clumsy iron fist of government intervention.

But one and all, they angrily defended their coverage of the corporate wars. The reason, they said, that there were so few reports viewing the government troop efforts in a favorable light was that there was little if anything favorable to be said for their unbroken record of failures. This was followed by a capsule summary of the wars since the governments stepped in. Some television channels did a half-hour special on the ineptitude of the government efforts. Some newspapers ran an entire supplement, some bitter, some sarcastic, but all pointing out the dismal incompetence displayed by the governments.

The man from the FCC was dismissed from his post.

The blood-warm waters of the Brazilian river were a welcome change from the deadly iciness of the Atlantic. The two frogmen, nearly invisible in their camouflaged wet kill-suits and bubbleless rebreather units, were extremely happy with the new loan labor program between the corporate mercenaries.

One of the men spotted a turtle and tapped the other's arm, gesturing for him to circle around and assist in its capture. His partner shook his head. This might have the trappings of a vacation, but they were still working. They were here on assignment and they had a job to do. The two men settled back in the weeds on the river bottom and waited.

It was oven hot in the armor-encased boat. The Greek officer in command mopped his brow and spoke in angry undertones to the men with him in the craft. It was hot, but this time there would be no mistakes. He peered out the gunslit at the passing shore as the boat whispered soundlessly upstream.

This time they had the bastards cold. He had the best men and the latest equipment on this mission, and a confirmed target to work with. This time it would be the laughing mercenaries who fell.

"Hello the boats?"

The men froze and looked at each other as the amplified voice echoed over the river.

"Yoo-hoo! We know you're in there."

The officer signaled frantically. One of his men took over the controls of the automount machine gun and peered into the periscope. The officer put his mouth near the gunslit, taking care to stand to one side of view.

"What do you want?"

"Before you guys start blasting away, you should know we have some people from the world press out here with us."

The officer clenched his fist in frustration. He shot a glance at his infrared sonar man who shrugged helplessly; there was no way he could sort out which blips were soldiers and which were reporters.

"We were just wondering," the voice continued "if you were willing to be captured or if we're going to have to kill you?"

The officer could see it all now. The lead on the target had been bait for a trap. The mercenaries were going to win again. Well, not this time. This boat had the latest armor and weaponry. They weren't going to surrender without a fight.

"You go to hell!" he screamed and shut the gunslit.

The mercenary on the shore turned to the reporters and shrugged. "You'd better get your heads down."

With that, he triggered the remote control detonator switch on his control box, and the frogmen-planted charges removed the three boats from the scene.

The mercenary doubled over, gasping from the agony of his wounds. The dark African sky growled a response as lightning danced in the distance. He glanced up at it through a pink veil of pain. Damn Africa! He should have never agreed to this transfer.

He gripped his knife again and resumed his task. Moving with the exaggerated precision of a drunk, he cut another square of sod from the ground and set it neatly next to the others.

Stupid. Okay, so he had gotten lost. It happens. But damn it, it wasn't his kind of terrain. He sank the knife viciously into the ground and paused as a wave of pain washed over him from the sudden effort.

But walking into an enemy patrol. That was unforgivably careless, but he had been so relieved to hear voices.

He glanced at the sky again. He was running out of time. He picked up his rifle and started scraping up handfuls of dirt from the cleared area. Well, at least he got 'em. He was still one of the best in the world at close-in, fast pistol work, but there had been so many.

He sagged forward again as pain flooded his mind. He was wounded in at least four places in his chest cavity alone. Badly wounded. He hadn't looked to see how badly for fear he would simply give up and stop moving.

He eased himself forward until he was sitting in the shallow depression, legs straight in front of him. Laying his rifle beside him, he began lifting the pieces of sod and placing them on his feet and legs, forming a solid carpet again.

His head swam with pain. When he had gotten lost, his chances of survival had been low. Now they were zero.

But he had gotten them all. He clung to that as he worked, lying down now and covering his bloody chest.

And by God, they weren't going to have the satisfaction of finding his body. The coming rain would wash away his trail of blood and weld the sod together again. If they ever claimed a mercenary kill, it was going to be because they earned it and not because he had been stupid enough to get lost.

The rain was starting to fall as he lifted the last piece of sod in place over his face and shoulders.

Chapter Twenty-one

Tidwell trudged through the darkness trying to ignore the feeling of nakedness he had without a rifle. He grinned to himself. This was a wacky idea, but if it worked it would be beautiful.

"Okay, Steve, you're there!" Clancy's voice came to him through his earplug. "If you take another fifteen steps, you'll kick one."

He halted his forward progress, and covertly studied the underbrush as he fished out a cigarette. He stalled a few more seconds fumbling for a match, then grudgingly lit up. These guys are good. He slowly exhaled a long plume of smoke.

"You can come out, gentlemen. All I want to do is talk."

His voice seemed incredibly loud in the darkness, even to him. He waited a few moments. The night was still.

"Look, I don't have a white flag with me, so I'm pinpointing my position with a cigarette instead. I'd like to talk to your ranking officer or noncom."

There was still no response. If he didn't have absolute faith in his back-up, he would feel silly standing there talking to himself.

"I'd love to stand here all night, but the bugs are getting bad. Look, we know you're here. We've been tracking you through our scopes for over an hour now. If we wanted you dead, you'd be dead. If it will convince you, there are twenty of you and we know your positions.

Now does that convince you or do I have to bounce a rock off a couple of you?"

He paused again. Suddenly, there was a soldier standing ten feet from him. He hadn't seen him stand up or step out of the bushes; it was as if he had sprung from the earth itself.

"It's about time. Want a smoke?"

"You wanted to talk, so talk."

The man sounded annoyed. Tidwell grinned to himself—probably upset that his crack team had been discovered.

"I've got a message for you. We're asking you once politely to withdraw your men."

"Give me one good reason why we should pull out, wise guy?"

"I can give you a list. First off, we found you. Right off the bat that should tell you your hotshots aren't as good as you'd like to think they are. Now, don't get me wrong, they're good—some of the best I've seen in a government force. But you're outclassed, friend. Our troops have been at this game since the time they could walk. Stack that up against your five years' service and you've got some idea where you stand in this war. A poor third in a two-sided fight!"

"That's your story."

"Let me spell it out for you. You're the advance scout of a company of light infantry that's bivouacked about fifteen miles back. They've been out here blundering around for over two weeks and I'm the first person you've seen to put your sights on. During that time, we've penetrated your defense at will, putting BANG signs on your ammo dump, green dye in your drinking water, Mickey Mouse Club badges on your tents while you're sleeping at night. The fact that you and your force aren't dead isn't because we've never had the chance."

"You're the guys who have been doing all that?"

"You want to know how many of us there are? Five, and two of us are women. A five-member team is all that it takes to keep a company of you bozos running in circles for half a month."

"So how come you haven't attacked?"

"Why? We don't want to fight you clowns. None of the corporation mercenaries do. We just want you to clear the hell out and leave us alone. Why are you out here anyway?"

"Well . . . supposedly we're trying to keep you from destroying the world economy."

"Bullshit. You wouldn't know a world economy if it bit you on the leg. Hell, man, the corporations have *been* the world economy for over half a century now."

"So you want us to pull back to camp?"

"No, we want you to pull out completely. The whole damn company—tell your CO we said so."

"And that's supposed to convince him?"

"No, but this might." Tidwell pulled a bulky envelope from inside his shirt and pitched it to the soldier who caught it deftly.

"What is it?"

"Well, you can't see them in this light, but it's a batch of pictures of your CO."

"And that's supposed to convince him?"

"They might. They were taken through a rifle scope. The cross hairs show up just swell."

"We'll show them to him. We were about to pull back anyway."

"Oh, just one more thing. If you could tell your men to leave their rifles behind when they go."

"What!"

"You can come back tomorrow and pick them up, but we want to be sure you pass the message to your CO, and showing up without your rifles will make sure you don't forget to talk to him."

"Tell you what, fella. Why don't you come along and tell him personally. We're supposed to be looking for prisoners to interrogate and I guess you'll do just fine!"

"You know, I get the distinct impression you think I'm bluffing. Very well; which impresses you more—distance work or close quarters?"

"What?"

"Never mind, we'll give you a quick demo of each. Um, tell your men to ease off their triggers. There's going to be some noise, quite harmless of course, but I wouldn't want to see you all get wiped out because someone flinched off a shot."

"What are you talking . . .?"

The night was rent by two ear-splitting explosions, one to their left, one to their right. Two full heartbeats behind the blast came the unmistakable twin flat cracks of the rifle reports.

"In case you're wondering, those shots were squeezed off by my partner—the one I was telling you about who is two miles back. He's firing the mercury-tipped bullets you've heard about. Nasty things. Blow a man open like a ripe melon."

"Jesus Christ!"

"But you're a sneaky-pete type, so you'll probably be more impressed by night movement. Hang onto yourself, sonny."

A shotgun blast went off into the air halfway between the two men, and one of Tidwell's teammates sat up from where he had been lying prone in the calf-high undergrowth.

"Now then, little man," Tidwell's voice was hard, "let's not hear any more crap about taking prisoners. I suggest you take your underpaid boy scouts and get the hell out of our jungle before we start playing rough."

Tidwell was in the blackout tent scanning the radio transcripts when Clancy burst through the double-flap entrance.

"Worked like a charm. They didn't stop until they got back to their camp. If they didn't wet their pants when that shotgun went off, it's only 'cause they haven't had anything to drink for twenty-four hours."

"Speaking of drinks, help yourself."

"Thanks," beamed Clancy, pouring himself a dollop of Irish. "What a crazy way to fight a war. I wonder who came up with this idea?"

" 'The object of war is not to destroy the enemy, but rather to destroy his will to resist.' Von Clausewitz, *On War*. The idea goes way back, Clancy. We're just carrying it out to the nth degree. Have you seen the latest?"

"What? The bit about our robot planes dropping sacks of flour on the steps of the White House?"

"No, the release about the high-altitude reconnaissance planes."

"What's the gist of it?"

"Basically the corporations sent a memo to the governments and the press citing the exact times high-altitude reconnaissance planes had flown over the zone in the last week. They pointed out that we were tracking them easily while our own troops were protected from the infrared snoop by jamming screens, and would they kindly refrain from sending them out or we would be forced to start downing them to eliminate the nuisance."

"Can we do it?"

"I don't think our force has anything that could, but that doesn't mean *someone* on the corporate team doesn't have a gimmick. Remember last month when the governments called a corporate bluff and we blew up one of their destroyers offshore?"

"Yeah. You know, that kind of gets me down, though—all the gimmick warfare. It takes the personal touch out of things."

"How about the 'gunsight' photos? You can't get much more personal than that. I bet a lot of governmental big mouths changed their tune when they saw themselves in the cross hairs."

"Tell me honestly, Steve—do you think we're going to win?"

"I don't see how it can go any other way. There's no way they can catch us short of saturation bombing or nukes, and public opinion is too much against them.

Hell, they're having a hard time with the pressures folks are putting on over this united effort. A third of the governments have already had to pull their troops. It's only a matter of time before the rest of them have to bail out."

"What then?"

"What do you mean?"

"Just that. Okay, the governments pull their troops out, effectively admitting they don't have the military power to police the corporations. What then?"

Chapter Twenty-two

The crowds of curiosity seekers threatened to choke off the street and probably would have if not physically restrained by the lines of armed government troops holding them at bay in the shadow of the poshest hotel in Rio de Janeiro. Even so, a sizeable crowd gathered around the limousines as they drew to a halt at the curb and had to be cleared back by the bodyguards who emerged from the autos first.

This smaller mob were members of the press who passed unhindered through the lines of troops with a wave of a media card. The troops were under strict orders not to affront the press, who had been adding volume to the already thunderous chorus of public protest against the governments' actions. Even the papers who had earlier supported the governments were now scathingly critical of the armed forces' ineffectiveness and inability to deal with the corporations. The governments did not need any more bad press.

Three men emerged from the limousines and headed for the door of the hotel. At their appearance, the reporters surged forward again and the men stopped, apparently consenting to giving a brief statement.

Several stories up, in a window of the hotel across the street from the activity, a machine was tracking the movements of the three men. Deeper in the room, well out of sight of the window, a small group of uniformed technicians were feverishly processing the data being collected by the combination closed-circuit television-shotgun mike. Their work was being closely supervised by a nervous officer.

"Are you sure, Corporal?"

"Positive, sir. Identification is confirmed on all three targets. A/V tapes and voice prints all match."

The officer squinted at the three figures in the monitor screen.

"Becker for Communications, Wilson for Oil, and Yamada for the Zaibatsu. They actually took the bait." He nudged the corporal.

"Look at them, soldier. Those three fat cats are responsible for the drubbing we've been taking for the last six months. They don't look like much, do they?"

"Some of the men are saying it doesn't take much, sir," replied the corporal flatly, not looking at the screen.

"Is that a fact? Well now it's our turn. Get Command on the phone and tell them the three little pigs are in the briar patch."

"Can I speak to you a moment, Captain?"

"Certainly, Lieutenant, but it'll have to be quick."

The lieutenant stepped into his CO's office and stood before the desk, fidgeting slightly.

"Well, sir, I think we've got a morale problem on our hands."

"We've had a morale problem for months, Larry. Why should today be any different?"

"It's the executions, sir. There's a lot of bad talk going around the men."

"Were they informed the men executed were infiltrators? Spies for the corporations who've been selling us all out for months?"

"Yes, sir. But . . . well . . . it's the suddenness of it all. This morning they had breakfast with those guys. Then all of a sudden . . . well, a lot of the men think they should have gotten a trial is all."

"Lieutenant, it's been explained—the corporation men have communication devices like we've never seen. They could have had something built into their boots or woven in their uniforms. If we took the time to observe formalities, they could have gotten word out. We couldn't take that chance."

"Well, the men think that without a trial it could have been any one of them. Now they've got the feeling that at any moment they could be pulled out of line and shot without any chance to defend themselves against the charges."

"Damn it, Larry, we know those men were spies. We ran everybody through the computers. Their finances, their families' finances—everybody got checked. You, me, everybody. Those men were on the corporations' payroll, either directly or through a front. We haven't been able to move without those guys tipping the enemy. I don't like it either, but that's the way we had to do it."

"Okay, Captain, I'll try to tell them . . ."

"Wait a minute, Lieutenant Booth. There's more. I just got the call from HQ. Alert the men to be ready to move out in fifteen minutes. We're mounting an offensive."

"An off . . . but sir, what about the cease-fire?"

The captain leaned back.

"It's all tied in together, Lieutenant. We've got their commanders tied up at the conference tables and their spies are dead. For the first time in this war, we've got a chance to catch those damn mercenaries napping."

"But—"

"Lieutenant, we don't have time to argue. This is coordinated with all the other forces. Our troops are making a worldwide push to try to finish the war in one fell swoop. Now alert the men!"

Wilson was clenching and unclenching his fists nervously out of sight under the table. It was clear to Yamada that the Oiler wanted to speak, but it had been agreed in advance that Yamada would do the talking and Wilson held his peace. As a solid front, the three men sat staring levelly down the table at government representatives facing them, ignoring the guns leveled at them by the guards.

"We cannot help but notice, gentlemen, that there are no civilians in your number." Yamada's voice was, as always, patiently polite.

"Are your governments sanctioning your action or is this a purely military decision?"

The American officer who seemed to be doing the talking for

the government forces smiled wickedly as he mimicked Yamada's speech.

"The military is, as always, carrying out the orders of our governments. You may therefore assume that this is the governments' official stance on negotiating a truce with the corporations."

"Then perhaps you could clarify for us what exactly it is you mean when you say we are under arrest?"

"It means you are detained, incommunicado, bagged. It means that we're sick of being blackmailed. We don't bargain with extortionists; we arrest them. When the corporations pull their troops out, we let you go. Until then, you sit here and rot. Only one thing— you don't get a phone call. Your troops will just have to get along without your golden tones."

Even though he kept his face impassive, Yamada's thoughts turned to the transmitter in his belt. By now the news of their arrest would be en route to the home offices . . . and to the mercenaries.

"Your usual, gentlemen?"

The petite waitress smiled fetchingly.

"Only if you'll join us, Tamia," leered the older of the three men seated at the table, beckoning to her.

The girl rolled her eyes in exasperated horror.

"Oh, nooo! If the boss saw me . . ." She rolled her eyes again. "I'd lose my job like that." She clicked her fingers. "Then where would I work?"

"You could come and live with me."

"Oh!" She giggled and laid a hand on his shoulder. "You're terrible!"

One of the other men leaned forward conspiratorially as she disappeared through the beaded curtains into the kitchen.

"Sir, I don't think it's wise to—"

"Relax, Captain." The older man waved him silent.

"That's why we're in our civvies—so we don't have to keep looking over our shoulders all the time. Nobody recognizes us out of uniform. I've been flirting with that little number for over a month now. Sooner or later she's bound to give in."

"But sir—"

"If anything was going to happen, it would have by now. Look, she doesn't even know my name, so relax."

But Tamia knew his name, and a good deal more. General Thomas Dunn was the main reason she was working at this shabby restaurant, an assignment that ended this evening when she received a phone call. The general stopped here nightly for a bowl of won ton soup, and tonight there would be a special surprise in it. Tonight she would include the special noodles she had been carrying for a month.

Actually, the basis for the idea was Eskimo, not Japanese, but the Japanese were never a group to ignore a good idea just because someone else thought of it first. The Eskimos would kill polar bears by freezing coiled slivers of bone inside a snowball flavored with seal blubber and leaving it on the ice floes. A bear would eat the snowball, and his body heat would melt the snow, releasing the bone sliver to tear at his insides.

The Japanese had improved on the concept. Instead of bone slivers, they were using a substance more like ground glass, guaranteed to cause a painful and irreversible death. In addition, they added a special touch of subtlety especially for the general. Instead of ice and seal blubber, they imbedded their lethal surprise in a special gel. Tamia would serve the general and his aides out of the same large bowl openly at the table. The gel would pass completely through the human digestive tract without dissolving. In fact, it would only dissolve if it came into contact with alcohol.

The files on the government forces were very complete. Of the three men at the table, only the general drank. In fact, he always had at least one nightcap before retiring for the evening.

After his death, his aides could and would tell the medic that they had shared the general's soup without any noticeable side effects, averting suspicion from the small restaurant and from Tamia.

Tamia scowled as she went about her task. While it was true she was successfully completing her mission and it would look good on her performance review, she wished she was in the field with the rest of her team. That's where the challenging work was.

෯෯ ෯෯ ෯෯

Lieutenant Booth was nervous. So far their "big offensive" had been no different from a hundred other fruitless missions they had been on. All their infrared and sonic scans had yielded nothing. They were sweeping back and forth looking for one of the laser cannons reported to be in their vicinity. In theory, if they could knock out the cannon and if the other forces were equally successful, the government troops could regain air supremacy.

That was the theory. In actuality, they were finding nothing to fight. It was the lieutenant's guess that this mission would end up like all the others—a big bust. The only difference was that their radios were acting up again. They had lost contact both with headquarters and with their flanking company.

This was nothing new. It wasn't the first time they had had trouble with their radios in the field. As such, the captain just kept the company plodding on, but it made Booth nervous. To him it meant their much valued technology was unreliable. If the radios could malfunction, so could the scanners!

". . . And I repeat, gentlemen, the troops employed by the corporations have not been fighting at their full capacity."

"Frankly, Mr. Yamada, I find that a little hard to swallow."

Yamada sighed slightly.

"For proof, I would offer two examples. First, it is not in the corporations' best interests to indulge in the bloodbath form of warfare the governments' forces seem to favor. We make a living by selling our products to consumers, to the public. If we inflict heavy casualties on you, it hurts us in the marketplace. Currently, public sympathy, as well as the sympathy of many of your own troops, is with the corporations. We will not jeopardize this by making martyrs out of the forces opposing us. All we have to do is wait until public opinion forces your governments to withdraw from the conflict."

The military men in the room maintained a thoughtful silence as Yamada pursued his point.

"Think back, gentlemen. Our troops have spent exceptional time and effort evading your forces. When they have fought, it has always been to discourage rather than to destroy. In every situation, your troops were called upon to surrender or withdraw before our men opened fire."

The American officer was scowling.

"You mentioned two points of proof, Mr. Yamada. What's the other one?"

"There may be those who would question our capacities, whether we have the ability to inflict more damage than we have. To prove this ability, you need only to try to phone your commanding officers. I say specifically to phone because by now we will have jammed or disrupted all your radio communications. As soon as you placed us under arrest, an order went out to some very specialized soldiers in our employment. All officers in your forces above the rank of lieutenant colonel have been assassinated. Your forces, already demoralized, are now without communications or leaders."

Lieutenant Booth could scarcely contain his excitement as he waited for confirmation on the smoke flare coordinates.

"I've got it, Lieutenant! Right on the button! They're clear!"

"Open fire! Level the entire target area."

The shells were hitting before he stopped talking as his mortar teams eagerly pumped round after round into the designated target area.

At last! After six months—contact! He watched gleefully as explosion after explosion rocked the area. Luckily they picked up that transmission from B Company. The way the radios had been acting up they could have missed it completely. Probably some new jamming device the mercenaries were using. Well, it was nice to know they had trouble with their gear too.

"Keep it up, men!"

B Company was under fire from the mercenaries. If the radio signal hadn't come through the bastards could have chopped up the government troops one company at a time, but now their plan had backfired. B Company's position was marked by the smoke flare, and for the first time the mortar teams knew where the mercenaries were.

"Lieutenant Booth! Cease fire! Cease fire!"

The lieutenant turned to see a soldier running toward him waving his arms.

"Cease fire!" he barked at his men, and the cry was echoed down the line.

The sergeant who had hailed him ran up, ashen-faced and out of breath.

"What is it, Sergeant?" Booth was aware of the nearby teams listening in curiously.

"Lieutenant, that's not . . . we saw them . . . it's not . . ."

"Spit it out, Sergeant!"

"It's not the mercenaries. We're shelling our own troops!"

"What?"

"Sommers climbed a tree with binoculars to watch the show! Those are our men down there!"

"But the smoke flare—"

Realization struck him like a slap in the face. It was the mercenaries. They had given him a fake radio call and a fake smoke flare.

He suddenly was aware of his men moving. They were abandoning their equipment and walking back toward the base. Their eyes were glazed and some of them were crying. He knew he should call to them, order them, console them. He knew that he should, but he couldn't.

". . . Now look, Yamada. We're through playing around. You've got fifteen minutes to make up your mind. Either you and your playmates call off your dogs or we'll have a few assassinations of our own here and now!"

Yamada considered them levelly.

"Gentlemen, you seem to have missed the point completely. First, holding us hostage will gain you nothing. Terrorist groups have been kidnapping corporation executives for over twenty-five years now, asking either for money or special considerations. In all that time, the corporations' policy for dealing with them has not changed. We don't make deals, and the executive threatened is on his own."

He crossed his arms and continued.

"Secondly, you assume that you can threaten us into selling out our forces in exchange for our lives. We are as dedicated to our cause as any soldier and as such, are ready to sacrifice our lives if need be. I do not expect you gentlemen to believe this on the strength of my words—it must be demonstrated."

He raised his right hand and pointed to his left bicep.

"In the lining of my coat was an ampule of poison. As I crossed my arms, I injected it into my bloodstream. I am neither afraid to die nor am I willing to serve as your hostage."

He blinked as if trying to clear his focus.

"Mr. Becker, I fear you will have to . . ."

His face hit the table, but he didn't feel it. The other two corporation men did not look at his body, but continued staring down the table at the military men who were sitting in stunned silence.

"I feel Mr. Yamada has stated our position adequately," Becker intoned. "And I for one do not feel like continuing this discussion."

He rose, Wilson following suit.

"We're leaving now, gentlemen. Shoot if you feel it will do any good."

Chapter Twenty-three

"This still seems strange."

"What does?" Judy turned from gazing out the taxi window to direct her attention to him.

"Dictating terms to the government. It's weird. I mean, as long as I've been working, the corporations have bitched about government controls and chafed under the rules. Sometimes we bought our way into some favorable legislation and sometimes we just moved our operations to a more favorable climate. But just telling them . . . that's weird."

"Look at it like the Magna Carta."

"The which?"

"History . . . medieval Europe. A bunch of the lorded barons, the fat cats of the era, got together and forced the king to sign a document giving them a voice in government."

"Is that what we're doing?"

"In a manner of speaking. Look, love, any system of government involves voluntary acceptance of that authority. Once the populace decides they don't want to play along, the Lord High Muckity-Mucks are out of luck."

"Except in a communist police state."

"Including a communist police state. If the people aren't happy or at least content, they're going to take things into their own hands and trample you."

"But if anyone mouths off you can just take them out and shoot them."

"If enough people are upset, you're in trouble. You can't shoot them all. And who's going to do the shooting? If things are out of hand, odds are the military won't follow your lead either."

"It still seems unnatural."

"It's the most natural thing in the world. Ignore governments for a minute. Look at any power structure. Look at the beginning of the unions. The fat cats had all the cards. It was their football. But when conditions got bad enough, the workers damn well dealt themselves in whether the fat cats liked it or not."

"But the unions are only a minor power now."

"Right, because they're no longer necessary. Business finally wised up to the fact that keeping the workers happy is the key to success. The conditions that caused the unions to form and justified their existence disappeared, and people started wondering what they were paying their dues for. Just like the corporations are asking what they're paying taxes for. You can't force a loyalty to any system. It's either there or it isn't. Inertia maintains the status quo, but once the tide turns there is no stopping it."

"You make this sound like a takeover."

"Effectively it is. The only reason the governments still exist today is because they do a lot of scut work the corporations don't want to dirty their hands with. But anything we want, we've got. They tried to assert their authority and proved that they don't have any."

"So where do we go from here?"

"We go in there." She pointed through the window at the large steel and glass building as the taxi pulled over to the curb. "As delegates to the First United Negotiations Council, the most powerful assemblage the free world has ever seen—every major corporation and industrial group gathered to decide how we want the world to run."

As they started up the stairs, she drew close to him.

"Stay close to me, huh?"

"Nervous? After that talk in the car, I thought you were ready to take on anyone in the council."

"It's not the council, it's them."

She nodded at the mercenaries lounging around the lobby, their hard eyes betraying the casual manner with which they checked the delegates' ID's.

"Them? C'mon, sweetheart, those are our heroes; without them, where would we be now?"

"I still don't like them, they're animals."

She quickened her step, and Fred had to hurry to keep up.

"How about that?"

"What?" Tidwell drifted over to the mezzanine railing to see what Clancy was ogling.

"That little bit of fluff with the old geezer—rough life, huh?"

"Nice to know what our fighting is for, isn't it—so some fat cat can bring his chippie along to meetings with him."

"Don't short sell them, Steve. They fight as hard as we do. Just in different ways."

"I suppose." Tidwell turned away and lit another cigarette, leaning back against the railing.

"What's eating you today, Steve? You seem kinda on edge?"

"I dunno. I keep getting the feeling something's about to happen."

"What?"

"I dunno. Maybe it's just nerves. I'm not used to just standing around."

"Just the wind down after being in the field so long. You'll get over it."

They stood in silence for a few moments. Then Tidwell eased off the railing, and ground out his cigarette in an ashtray.

"Clancy, what do you know about samurai?"

"Not much. They were badass fighters as individuals, but not much as an army."

"Do you know what happened to them?"

"No. Outmoded when gunpowder came in, I guess."

"Wrong—they got done in by a change in the system."

"How's that?"

"Well, they were professional bodyguards when Japan was essentially a bunch of small countries each lorded over by a warlord. Anyone who was wealthy and landed maintained a brace of samurai to keep his neighbors from taking it all away from him. The constant raiding and feuds kept them busy for quite a few generations. Then the country became united under one emperor who extended his protection over the whole shebang. All of a sudden the samurai were unnecessary and expensive, the clans were disbanded, and they were reduced to beggars and outlaws."

"And you're worried about that happening to us?"

"It's a possibility."

"There are other options."

"Such as?"

"Well, for openers . . ."

"Wait a minute." Tidwell was suddenly alert and moving along the railing. A group of some twenty mercenaries had just entered and were standing just inside the glass doors.

"Who are those men?" Tidwell leaned on the railing and craned his neck, trying to see a familiar face in the group.

"They're our relief."

"Relief? What relief? We're supposed to be on guard for another . . ." He stopped abruptly.

Clancy was holding his favorite derringer leveled at him, the bore immense when viewed from the front.

"What's this?"

"It'll all be clear in a few minutes. In the meantime, just take my word that those men are here with peaceful intentions."

"Who are they?"

"Some of the guys from my old outfit."

"Your old outfit? You mean during . . ."

"During the Russo-Chinese War, right. The C-Block is about to break their communications silence, and we're delivering the message."

"Since when did you work for the C-Block?"

"Never stopped."

"I see. Well, now what?"

"Now you tell the guards they're relieved. Tell 'em it's bonus time-off or something, but make it sound natural. My men have been briefed on you and your team and will be watching for anything out of line."

"I thought you said this was peaceful."

"It is, but we don't want anyone going off half-cocked before we have our say."

"So all I have to do is dismiss the men."

"Right. But stick around. I think you'll find this kinda interesting."

"Wouldn't miss it for the world."

If Fred had not been already bored with the opening comments from the chairman pro tem, he probably would not have noticed the mercenaries entering the auditorium, but curiosity made him watch first leisurely, then with growing interest as the patterns formed. Four of them spreading quietly along the back walkway. Three more appearing in the balcony. Fred straightened slightly. Were the two by the door holding weapons on the stone-faced mercenary leaning against the back wall?

Something was up. What was it? Had an assassin been infiltrated into the meeting? A bomb threat?

Fred's eyes scanned the assemblage uneasily. His eyes met those of the stone-faced mercenary in the back who arched one eyebrow in surprise, then slowly and solemnly winked at him.

What was up? Oh, well, they'd know soon enough. One of the mercenaries flanked by two others was approaching the podium. The chairman noted their approach and interrupted his speech. He stepped down and spoke briefly with the center mercenary. The delegates took advantage of the interruption to converse and shift back and forth. Fred watched the conversation. It seemed to be growing more heated. Suddenly the chairman broke away shaking his head angrily and started back for the podium. The mercenary he had been talking to gestured to one of his flankers. The man stepped in behind the chairman and chopped him across the back of the neck with his hand. The chairman crumpled to the floor.

Jesus Christ! What was going on? The delegates recoiled in horror as the mercenary dragged the chairman to a vacant seat where they deposited him in an unceremonious heap, then turned to face the assemblage. As their apparent leader took over the podium, the audience sank into silence.

"Well, folks, it looks like I'm going to have to do this without an introduction."

He paused as if expecting a laugh. There was only silence as the delegates watched him coldly.

"Some of you may recognize me as one of your mercenaries. We have a proposal to put before the council and—"

"What the hell is this?"

A voice rang out from the audience, which was quickly echoed by several other indignant delegates. Clancy raised his hand, and suddenly the other mercenaries were moving into position along the edge of the room, drawing their weapons as they went. The assemblage suddenly submerged into silence once more.

"I do apologize for the unorthodox nature of this presentation, but I'll have to ask that you hear me out before any questions are raised. What is more, I'll have to ask you to listen quietly and not make any sudden outbursts or movements. The boys are a little jumpy and we wouldn't want them to think you were getting hostile when you really weren't."

Fred shot a glance back at the stern-faced mercenary who shrugged as if to say he didn't know what was happening either.

"Now, as I was starting to say, we are a coalition of mercenaries. Our current employers are the people you refer to as the C-Block."

Fred felt his flesh turn cold. Commies! They were being held at gunpoint by a pack of Commies!

"We are relaying a proposal to you from our employers. What we are offering you is a lasting world peace. Now let me elaborate on that before everyone panics. In the past, when someone offers world peace, it's usually on their terms. 'Do things my way and nobody will get hurt!' Well, this isn't what we're saying. We aren't saying the free world should convert to communism, or that the Communists should go imperialistic. We are proposing a method by which both ideals can be left free to pattern their lives according to the dictates of their conscience and traditions."

Neat trick if you can do it. Fred was nonetheless interested.

"One of the purposes of this Council is to determine how much support you feel you should give the governments in the way of taxes. Part and parcel with this is an appraisal of how much they really need. We would suggest that the governments of the world can cut a major portion of their expense by disbanding their armed forces."

A murmur rippled through the delegates which quickly subsided as they remembered they were under the guns.

"What we propose to replace the multitude of individual armies with is one worldwide army of hard-core professionals, mercenaries if you will, paid equally by the corporations and the C-Block. It would be their job to maintain world peace, moving to block any country or group who attempted a forceful infringement on their neighbors. This was tried unsuccessfully once by the United Nations. It failed for two reasons. First, the nations still kept their armed forces, giving them a capacity for attacking each other, and second, the UN forces were not given adequate power to do their job. May I assure the assemblage that if we say we will stop a conflict, it will be stopped."

He smiled grimly at them. Not a person in the room doubted him.

"Now, there are several automatic objections which would be raised to such a force. The most obvious is the fear of a military takeover. In reply, I would point out that right now we could kill everyone in this room. The question is why? Any such army which abused its power would rapidly be confronted by several things. The first would be an armed uprising of the general populace. If every time we killed someone, five other people got upset and we had to kill them, eventually there would be no one left in the world but soldiers. We are not that kind of madmen. By definition, we are soldiers, not farmers or storekeepers. We are dependent on you for our livelihood. You don't kill the goose that lays the golden egg, and a sane man doesn't shoot his boss."

He paused. There was a thoughtful silence in the room.

"It might be pointed out that we have been operating in the C-Block for a number of years now in this capacity. They needed all available manpower for their rebuilding, so they cannibalized the army and turned the job of security over to us. It was a desperate move, but it's worked. The arrangement has proven beneficial to all concerned. I might add that to date there have been no attempted military takeovers. The only lingering fear is of a takeover attempt from outside the C-Block, which is why we are here. We offer you a cheap and lasting peace by subscribing to our services. There is no threat of invasion if there is no armed, organized invasion force."

His words hung in the air. Fred found himself trying to imagine a world without a threat of war.

"There is another, less pleasant objection which might be raised to this plan. I'm sure that as businessmen, it has occurred to you. War is good business. It can provide a vital shot in the arm to a sagging economy. Do we really want to eliminate war?

"Before I answer that question, let me point out another problem. How do we keep in training? If we are successful, if war becomes obsolete, if there is no enemy for us to train for, what is to keep us from becoming fat, lazy, and useless leeches?"

He smiled at the room.

"You in this room have given us an answer to both problems. For the last two years in the C-Block, we have been using your kill-suits in our training. Our main purpose was to provide hard training for our troops, but it had a surprising side product. Military maneuvers in kill-suits have emerged as a spectator sport of astounding popularity. We have developed various categories of competition and regular teams have formed, each with their followers and fans. Apparently, once the populace becomes accustomed to the fact that no real injuries or deaths are incurred, they find it far more enjoyable than movies or television. Certain of our mercenaries have become minor celebrities and occasionally have to be guarded from autograph-seeking fans."

There was a low buzz of conversation going as he continued.

"Now this means that not only does the military industry continue, but that there is an unexpected windfall of a new spectator sport. I am sure I do not have to elaborate for this assemblage the profits latent in proper handling of a spectator sport."

This time he actually got a low ripple of laughter in response to his joke. Even Fred found himself chortling. *Don't teach your grandmother to steal sheep, sonny.*

"Well, I feel I have used up enough of your time on the proposal. I'd ask that you discuss it among yourselves and with your superiors. We will be back in a week, at which time we will be ready to answer any and all questions you might have. I would like to apologize for the tactic of holding you at gunpoint, but we were not certain what your initial reaction would be to our appearance. I will pay you the compliment of telling you the guns are loaded. We are more than slightly afraid of you. You are dangerous men. Thank you."

He stepped down from the podium and started for the door, gathering his men as he went.

Gutsy bastard! thought Fred, and started to clap. Others picked it up, and by the time the mercenaries reached the door, the applause was thunderous. They paused, waved, and left.

"Sorry I couldn't tell you sooner, Steve, but orders are orders."

"No problem."

"I want to tell you I rate drawing down on you as one of the nerviest things I've done in my life. Oh, I have a contract offer for you from the coalition."

"Kind of hoped you would. Come on, I'll buy you a drink."

"Hey, thanks. I need one after that."

They walked on in silence for a while. Finally Tidwell broke the reverie.

"Autograph-seeking fans?"

"Hey, wait till it happens to you. It's spooky."

They both laughed.

"Say, tell me, Clancy—what's it like working for the C-Block?"

"Do you want the truth? I couldn't say this back there for fear of being torn apart, but there's no difference. Call it the United Board of Directors or the Party. A fat cat string-puller is a fat cat string-puller, and anyone in a position of power without controls has the same problems. The phrasing is different, but they both say the same thing. Keep the workers happy with an illusion of having some say so they don't tear us out of our cushy pigeonholes. That's what makes our job so easy. People are people. They shy away from violence and stuff their faces with free candy whenever they can. And nobody but nobody acknowledges their base drives like greed. We do, so we have the world by the short and curlys."

Tidwell waved a hand.

"That's too heavy for me. Speaking of base drives, I still want that drink. Where are we going?"

"Aki's found a little Japanese restaurant that serves a good Irish whiskey. The whole crew hangs out there."

"You're on. Autograph-seeking fans, huh?"

The two mercenaries walked on, laughing, oblivious to the curious and indignant stares directed at them.

Chapter Twenty-four

Thomas Mausier was extremely busy. Ever since the C-Block's curtain of silence had been lifted, his business had almost tripled. All the questions that had backlogged so long without answers were suddenly live again. His agents were having a field day.

The biggest problem confronting Mausier currently was determining if this was merely a wave that would die back down to normal levels, or if he should expand his operations to handle the new volume. He had already had to add a second shift just to process the items pouring in 'round the clock, and he hadn't had time to pursue his hobby in nearly a month. Not bad for a little business he had started to escape the gray flannel rat race.

At one point he had been worried about his business collapsing in the wake of the new order, but he should have known better. Information doesn't answer questions, it raises new ones. As long as there was money and people at stake, he'd be in business.

The light on the closed circuit television screen on his desk glowed to life, and he keyed it on.

"Yes, Ms. Witley?"

"Two men in the outer office to see you. They say it's important."

As she spoke, she subtly manipulated the controls and the two men appeared in a split-screen effect.

They looked like corporate types, and their visit was

uncomfortably close to lunch. Then he remembered his first visit from Hornsby.

"Bring them back."

A few moments later, they appeared. Ms. Witley did a quick round of introductions and left. Mausier slyly tripped the videotape recorders as he shook their hands. He'd gotten into the habit of taping all of his private conferences for later review.

"Now then Mr. Stills, Mr. Weaver. Are you buying or selling?"

They looked at him blankly. He felt a spark of annoyance.

"Buying or selling . . . ?"

"Information. I assume that's why you're here. We don't deal in anything else."

"Oh! No! I'm afraid you've got the wrong idea about why we're here. You see, Mr. Weaver and myself are here representing the United Board of Corporations."

Mausier suddenly thought of his gun. It was at home, hanging in the bedroom closet. He hadn't worn it in weeks.

"I don't understand, gentlemen. Is there some kind of complaint . . ."

"No, no. Quite the contrary." Stills' smile was pleasant and reassuring. "There's a matter we'd like to discuss with you that we feel is of mutual benefit. We were hoping you'd let us buy you lunch and we could talk at leisure."

Mausier didn't return his smile.

"I'm in the habit of working through lunch. One of the disadvantages of working for yourself is that, unlike the corporations, there *is* such a thing as an indispensable man. In this business it's me. Now if you could state your business, I am rather a busy man."

The two men exchanged glances and shrugged without moving their shoulders.

"Very well. We are authorized by the Board to speak to you about selling out—that is, the corporations are interested in acquiring your business."

Mausier was stunned. For a moment he was unable to speak.

"Frankly, I think the first way you phrased it was more accurate," he blurted out at last.

Weaver smiled, but Stills held up a restraining hand.

"Seriously, I phrased that rather poorly. Let me try again. You see, the Board has been investigating your operation for some time. The more they find, the more impressed they are."

Mausier inclined his head slightly at the compliment.

"Originally, the plan was to build a similar operation for the Board's use. As it turned out, the more they looked into it, the more they realized the difficulties of duplicating your setup. Just building the network of agents you have would take time, and during that time, important things could happen."

He paused to light a cigarette. Mausier glanced at his equipment but said nothing.

"So anyway, they decided the most efficient way to approach the problem was to simply acquire your setup and put it to work for them."

"There's one major drawback to that plan," Mausier interrupted. "I'm not interested in selling."

Again Stills held up his hand.

"Now, don't jump to conclusions, Mr. Mausier. I don't think you completely understand what we're proposing. You'd still be in control of the operation. You'd still be carried on the payroll at a hefty salary in addition, of course, to the acquisitions price, which I'll admit I feel is exorbitant. We wouldn't be taking anything away from you; in fact, we're anticipating—we're expecting the operation will expand. With proper pressure, all the corporations will deal through you for information. The way it's looking, you could end up as one of the most powerful men in the corporate world."

This time it was Mausier who interrupted, rising to his feet and leaning across his desk.

"And I don't think *you* understand, gentlemen. I don't want to be one of the most powerful men in the corporate world. I don't want to expand my operation. And I don't want to sell my business!"

He was getting excited and losing control, but for once he didn't care.

"I spent enough time in your corporate world to know the one thing I wanted from it was out. I don't like brown-nosing, I don't like operating plans, I don't like performance reviews, I don't like benefits packages, I don't like pointless meetings, I don't like employee newspapers, I don't like office gossip, and I don't like being expendable. In short, gentlemen, I don't like corporations. That's why I started this business. To run it, I work harder than both of you put together and probably make less. But there's one thing I am that I'll bet neither of you has the vaguest conception of—I'm happy. You can't tax it, but it means a lot to me. Do I make myself quite clear?"

The two men languished in their chairs, apparently unmoved by his tirade.

"I don't think you understand, Mausier," said Stills softly. "We weren't asking you."

Mausier suddenly felt cold. He sank slowly back into his chair as Stills continued.

"Now, we're being nice and giving you an honest deal, but don't kid yourself about having a choice. In case you haven't been following the news, the corporations are running things now. When they say 'jump,' you don't say 'how high?' You say, 'Can I come down now?' That's the way it is whether you like it or not."

Mausier felt weak. "And if I don't jump?" he asked quietly.

Stills grimaced. "Now that would be unpleasant for everybody."

Mausier raised his eyes to look at them. "Are you saying they'd actually kill me?"

Stills actually looked surprised. "Kill you? Hell, man, you read too many spy novels!"

Weaver spoke for the first time.

"Look around you, Mr. Mausier. You're running a very delicate operation here. What happens to it if the phone company refused you service? Or if the people who manufacture all the gadgetry either recall it or refuse to service it? The Zaibatsu have been monitoring your scramblers for years. Suppose they publish a notice in all newspapers that in one week they'll publish a list of names of all agents still on your list of clients? Now, I don't like threats, Mr. Mausier, but if we wanted to we could shut you down overnight."

Mausier sagged in his chair. The two corporate men waited in respectful silence for him to recover his composure.

"Where do we go from here?"

Stills stood up.

"I've got to report in. Weaver here will stay with you as your new assistant to start learning the ropes. Policy says that all key personnel are supposed to have understudies."

He started for the door.

"Stills!"

Mausier's voice stopped him with his hand on the knob.

"Is this the way it's going to be?"

Stills shrugged and smiled and left without answering.

The room lapsed into silence as Mausier sat staring into space. Suddenly, he felt a hand on his shoulder. It was Weaver.

"Cheer up, Mr. Mausier." His voice was sympathetic. "It could be worse. You're a valuable man. Just play ball and they'll take care of you. You know, 'go along, get along.'"

Mausier didn't respond. He just kept thinking about the gun in his bedroom closet.

The Bug Wars

"Reminder"
by Buck Coulson

The stardrive was discovered on a planet in Centaurus,
By a race that built their cities when the Earth was burning gas.
They swept across the starlanes in the dawning of creation,
And a million years of empire came to pass.

Their successors were a swarm of mighty insects from Orion.
They did not have the stardrive, but they did not ever die.
They smashed a dying empire and then settled down to rule it,
And another million years or so went by.

The Insects were supplanted when the drive was rediscovered.
They could not stop rebellion when they could not catch their foes.
And the Tzen became the rulers. They were reptiles from Arcturus,
And they worshipped the dark swamps from which they rose.

But the Tzen were few in number and the universe is mighty,
And they felt their domination slip away between their claws.
Others fought for domination and the universe was chaos,
While on Earth a creature shaped flint with its paws.

Now the first ones are forgotten and the Insects but a memory,
And the creature called Man stands upon the threshold of his fame.
But remember, puny Earthlings, there were others here before you,
And still others who will follow in your flame

Book One

Chapter One

I became awake. Reflexively, with the return of consciousness, I looked to my weapons. I felt them there in the darkness, strapped to my body and attached to the panel close over my head. I felt them, and relaxed slightly, moving on to other levels of consciousness. I have my weapons, I am alive, I am a Tzen, I am duty-bound, I am Rahm.

Having recalled I am a Tzen, it did not surprise me that I thought of my duty before even thinking of my name. It is part of the character of the Tzen to always think of the species and the Empire before thinking of themselves, particularly the Warrior caste, of which I was one. It has occasionally been suggested, privately of course, that some of the other castes, particularly the Scientists, think of the individual before they think of the species, but I do not believe this. A Tzen is a Tzen.

I flexed my talons. Yes, my body was functioning efficiently. I was ready to venture forth. There had been no sound of alarm or noises of battle, but I still was cautious as I pressed the release lever of my shelf with my tail. The door slid down a fraction of an inch and stopped as I scanned the chamber through the slit.

The chamber was dimly lit, closely approximating moonlight. The air was warm—not hot, but warm and humid, the temperature of night in the Black Swamps. We were not being awakened for relaxation and food replenishment. We were being awakened to hunt. We were preparing for combat.

Without further meditation, I slid the door the rest of the way open and started to slide from my shelf, then paused. Another Tzen was moving along the walkway I was about to step out on. I waited for him to pass before standing forth and securing my weapons.

The fact that I outranked him, in fact was his immediate superior on this mission, was irrelevant. My waiting was not even a matter of courtesy, it was logical. The walkway was too narrow for two to pass, and he was moving on it first.

We exchanged neither salutes nor nods of recognition as he passed, his tail rasping briefly on the walkway. His ten-foot bulk, large even for a Tzen, was easy to recognize in the semi-darkness. He was Zur, my second-in-command for this mission. I respected him for his abilities, as he respected me for mine. I felt no desire to wish him luck or a need to give him last-minute instructions. He was a Tzen.

He, like the rest of my flight team, had performed efficiently in practice, and I had no reason to expect they would perform otherwise in actual combat. If he or any of the others seemed lax or panicky in battle, and if that shortcoming endangered me or the mission, I would kill them.

The walkway was clear now, and I moved along it to the junction between the shelf-wall and the engine-ward flex-well. For a moment, I was thankful for my rank. As flight team Commander, my flyer was positioned closest to the floor, which spared me climbing up the curved wall. Not that I would mind the climb, but since flyer training began, I had discovered I was mildly acrophobic. It didn't bother me once I was flying, but I disliked hanging suspended in midair.

I didn't spend a great deal of time checking over the flyer. That was the Technicians' job. I knew enough about the flyers to pilot them and effect minor repairs, but machines were the Technicians' field of expertise as weapons are mine, and anything they missed on their check would be too subtle for me to detect.

Instead, I occupied my time securing my personal weapons in the flyer, a job no Technician could do. I do not mean to imply by this that the Technicians are lacking in fighting skill. They are Tzen, and I would willingly match any Tzen of any caste on a one-for-one basis against any other intelligent being in the universe. But I am of the Warrior caste, the fighting elite of a species of fighters, and I secure my own weapons.

In truth, it was doubtful they would be necessary on this mission; still, it heartened me to have them close at hand. Like so many others, I had not yet completely acclimated myself to the new technology that had been so suddenly thrust upon us. The hand weapons were a link with the past, with our heritage, with the Black Swamps. Even the High Command did not object to the practice of carrying hand weapons on a mission. They merely limited the total weight of personal gear carried by a Warrior in his flyer. Nobody comes between a Tzen and his weapons, not even another Tzen.

Content with my inspection, I eased myself into the flyer and settled into the gel-cushion. With a sigh, the flyer sealed itself. I waited, knowing that as my flyer sealed, a ready light had appeared on the pilot's board; and that as soon as all the lights from this chamber were lit, we would be ready to proceed with the mission.

Unlike the colony ships, transports such as the one we were currently chambered in were stark and bare in their interiors, devoid of anything not absolutely vital to the mission. This left me with little to meditate on as I waited. Almost against my wishes, my thoughts turned toward the mission we were about to embark upon. My reluctance to think about the mission did not spring from a reluctance to fight or a fear for my personal safety. I am a Tzen. However, I personally find the concept of genocide distasteful.

Finally the flex-walls, both the one my flyer was affixed to and the one across the chamber, trembled and began to move. The mission was about to begin. Slowly they straightened, changing the parabola-cross-sectioned shape of the room into a high, narrow rectangle. The flyers on my wall were now neatly interspaced with those on the far wall. The net result was to stack us like bombs in a rack, poised and ready to drop.

As our flight team made their final preparations, we knew that the chambers on either side of us would be spreading their walls, taking advantage of the space vacated by our walls to ease the loading of its flyers. As I have said, there is no wasted space on a transport.

The floor of the chamber opened beneath me. As the bottom flyer in the stack, I had an unobstructed view of the depths below. I experienced a moment of vertigo as I looked down at the patch of darkness. We are not an aerial species.

Then I was in a free-fall. There was no jerk of release; I was just suddenly falling. Although I normally avoid stating opinions as fact, this is not a pleasant sensation.

As we had been warned during our briefings, the Battle Plan called for a night attack. This was tactically sound, since the Enemy are day-hunters, while we Tzen are accustomed to working at night. It gave us an immeasurable advantage in the impending fight. It also meant that the planet-face we were plummeting toward was dark, giving no clue of terrain features.

Crosswinds buffeted my flyer as I fell, but I was not concerned. Crosswinds, like atmospheric pressures and weather conditions, would have been taken into consideration by the pilot when he'd dropped us. In their own way, the pilots were specialists as highly trained as the Warriors.

The tingle in the footplate told me my flyer was in the outer fringe of one of the power sources dropped by scout ships. Still I fell. Now I could make out a few features of the terrain below. Far off to my left was a large body of water, below was some type of mountain range, while off to my right stretched an immense forest. Obviously it was a highly inhabitable planet. No wonder the Enemy had picked it as one of the spots to settle in. No wonder we had to take it away from them.

The tingle in the footplate was noticeably stronger now, but I continued to fall. I allowed myself to ponder the possibility of an auto-pilot malfunction, but dismissed the thought. The programs were so simple as to be essentially infallible, and thus far, I did not have sufficient cause to assume malfunction.

As if to confirm my conclusions, the auto-pilot chose that instant to react to the ground rushing towards us from below. With a soft pop, the mighty flexi-steel bat wings that had been folded against the flyer's sides unfurled, catching the rushing air and slamming the craft from a dive into a soaring glide. The sudden declaration forced me deep into the gel-cushion and narrowed my eyes.

A jab of pressure with both my heels on the footplate took the flyer out of auto-pilot and gave me full control. I allowed the flyer to glide forward for a few moments, then arrested its progress, hovering it in place with subtle play on the footplate. It was a moderately delicate process, but we had been trained by long hours of practice to be able to accomplish this almost without thinking, as we had trained in all facets of handling the flyers. The flyers were to be an extension of our bodies, requiring no more thought for operation than the operation of our legs. It was an advanced form of transport, nothing more. Our minds were to be focused on the mission, on the Enemy.

As I waited, I surveyed the immediate terrain, using both my normal vision and the flyer's sonic sensor screens. I was not overly fond of the latter, but their use was essential when operating a flyer. There would be times, particularly flying in the dark, when we would be traveling at speeds requiring warning of approaching obstacles well in advance of the range at which our normal night vision was effective.

I was hovering over a river valley, the rising thermals making the job of hovering an easy one. Ahead and to the right was the beginning of the vast forest range I had noted from the air. Obviously the pilot had been accurate in his drop calculations.

"Ready, Rahm."

It was Zur's voice telepathed into my mind. I did not look back. I didn't need to. His signal told me all I needed to know, that the team was in position behind me, each flyer in place in our tetrahedron formation, hovering and impatient to begin.

I telepathed my order to the formation.

"Power on one . . . Ready . . . Three . . . Two . . . One!"

As I sent the final signal, I trod down solidly on the footplate and felt the surge of power as the engine cut in. There was no roar, not even a whisper of sound. This was one of the advantageous features of this new propulsion system. The sparkling engines were noiseless, giving deadly support to our favored surprise attack tactics. The race that had developed the engine were fond of using it for noiseless factories and elevators. As a Warrior race, we had other uses for it.

Our formation darted forward through the dark on the first assault of the new war.

Chapter Two

Faintly in the darkness, we could see other formations paralleling our course. Somewhere behind us were four other waves, constituting the balance of our Division. One hundred formations, six hundred flyers pitted against an enemy numbering in the hundreds of thousands. Still, we were not overly concerned with the outcome. Our flyers gave us superior speed and maneuvering ability in the air. Our weapons were more than adequate to deal with the enemy. Given superior maneuverability and weapons, we would have an edge in any fight, regardless of the odds. Our military history had proven this to be true time and time again. Then there was the fact we were Tzen. I would trust in the fighting-born—and-trained of the Tzen over any Insect's blind hive instinct. We would win this War. We would win it because we had to.

We had reached the trees now, our formation flying low and straight without seeking targets. The trees dwarfed our craft with their size. Their trunks were over thirty feet in diameter, and stretched up almost out of sight in the darkness. Our zone was some distance ahead. If the transport had timed its drops properly and if everyone maintained the planned courses and speeds, the attack should be launched in all zones simultaneously, just as our Division's attack was tuned to coincide with the attacks of the other divisions taking part in the assault on this planet. In theory this would keep the Enemy from massing against us.

I could see the dark masses of the nests high in the trees as we sped silently on. I strained my eyes trying to get a good look at the Enemy, but could make out nothing beyond general seething blobs. They were sleeping, gathered in great masses covering the nests, apparently unsuspecting of the shadows of death flitting through their stronghold. This was not surprising. They and their allies had ruled the stars virtually uncontested for over a million years. We Tzen had taken great pains to mask our existence, much less our development, until we were ready to enter into combat. Now we were ready for combat, and the Enemy would know us—if any survived, that is.

Still, I wished I could get a better look at them. It was difficult for me to accept the concept of a wasplike creature with a twenty-to-thirty-foot wingspan. Studying drawings and tri-D projections was helpful, but nothing could serve as well as actually seeing a live enemy.

Though confident, I was uneasy. I would have preferred to have the first encounter with the Enemy on solid ground, or better still, on the semi-aquatic terrain we were accustomed to battling on. I was uneasy about having our first encounter as an aerial fight against an aerial species. For all our practice with the new flyers, the air was not our element. I wished the initial battle did not hinge on our ability *to* outfly creatures born with wings. It made me uneasy. I did not contest the logic behind the decision. It would be disastrous to enter into ground maneuvers while the Enemy still retained air supremacy. But it did make me uneasy.

Suddenly something struck the side of my flyer too quickly to be avoided. It clung to the Plexiglas, scrabbling and rasping, seeking entrance. It took a great deal of effort to keep my attention focused forward, to avoid flying into something, with the creature raging at the edge of my peripheral vision less than a foot from my head. I had a quick impression of multifaceted metallic eyes glaring at me and darting mandibles gnashing on the transparent bubble; then I rolled the flyer and it was gone. There was a quiet burst of sound behind me like a sudden release of compressed air, and I knew that Zur had finished off the interloper. I shot a sideways glance at the spot on the canopy where the creature had clung briefly before being shaken off. There were deep gouges in the bubble from the Enemy's efforts, and a few spots where the creature's saliva had begun to eat through.'

I was pleased. The brief encounter had prepared me for battle far more than any mental exercise I could have devised. New energy coursed through my veins, adding that all-important extra split second of speed to my reflexes. Instead of developing it in the first pass, I would now be entering the conflict in a controlled battle frenzy.

For the first time I began to entertain hopes of emerging from the battle alive.

Then we were at our target zone. At my signal the formation expanded, each Tzen increasing the distance between his flyer and his teammate's. Then, as a unit, we climbed toward the treetops and the Bug War began.

The combat, like any combat, soon became too fast-paced for conscious thought. We had trained with our flyers and weapons until they were a part of us, and their use was as unthinking as flexing our talons. Our minds and senses were focused on the Enemy and the terrain.

Thoughts became a flashing kaleidoscope of quick impressions and hazily remembered instructions. Use the cold-burn rays as much as possible . . . less effective than the hot-beams, but they'll damage the forest less . . . we'll want to settle here someday. . . . Swarm massing to block flight path . . . burn your way through . . . don't wander more than five degrees from your base course . . . sweep three nests simultaneously with a wide beam . . . if you wander you'll end up in a teammate's line of fire . . . turn ninety degrees . . . turn right, always right . . . Kor is on your right . . . don't trust her for a left turn . . . avoid the tree trunk and burn the nests as your weapon bears . . . Enemy on the wing tip . . . roll . . . burn the nests . . . don't wander from base course . . .

We were working our zone in a broken sweep pattern. A straight geometric pattern would have been easier to remember and more certain for a complete sweep. It also would have been predictable. If we tried to use a geometric sweep, by the third pass the Enemy would be massed and waiting for us. So we continued our twisted, seemingly random pattern, crossing and recrossing our own path, frequently burning our way through swarms of the Enemy flying across our path in pursuit.

. . . Turn to the right . . . burn the nests . . . cold-beam rays only . . .

We were constantly flirting with disaster. Our flyers could outdistance the lumbering Enemy; but if we used our speed, dodging trees required most of our attention, and we ran the risk of missing nests. If we slowed our speed to an easy pace for sweeping, the Enemy could either overtake us or move to intercept. So we flirted with death, sometimes plunging recklessly ahead, sometimes rolling as we turned to free our flyers of the Enemy clinging to the wings, threatening to drag us to the ground with the sheer mass of their numbers.

. . . Avoid the trees . . . burn through a swarm . . . turn to the right . . . burn the nests . . . roll . . .

One thing bothered me. The mission was going too smoothly. I received no sign-off and visually confirmed on the passes when I was bringing up the rear. All our flyers were still with us. We had not lost any team members. If the other divisions were experiencing similar success, there could be difficulties when we headed back.

. . . Don't wander . . . roll . . . turn to the right . . . burn the nests . . .

We were near completing the sweep of our zone. I was concerned about the north border, however. The team zones overlapped to ensure no "live" pockets were accidentally overlooked. This meant careful timing between the teams was necessary to be sure two teams didn't sweep the same region at the same time and accidentally fly into each other. It was a bothersome but effective system; however, something was wrong. We seemed to be the only ones working the region by the north border, and when we turned, we could see nests remaining beyond our zone.

Something was very wrong with the flight team to our north. The end of our sweep was upon us, and I had to make a decision fast. This was not particularly difficult, as there was really only one course of action to be followed. We could not risk leaving unburned nests behind. This was a genocide war. If we left any eggs behind, we would have to come back later and fight this action all over again, but this time against an Enemy that was prepared and waiting for us. We couldn't leave those nests behind.

As we completed our sweep, I signaled the formation to return to the north border. This undoubtedly caused some consternation in my team, but they were Tzen, and they followed without complaint as I led the formation in a turn to the left. In this situation, a turn to the left was safe. I didn't have to worry about Kor, as long as we were moving, to prolong contact with the Enemy.

The fighting became more difficult as we made our supplemental sweep. This was only to be expected. Not having had an opportunity to work out a coordinated random pattern, we were forced to work a simple back-and-forth geometric pattern. As it has been noted before, geometric patterns are suicidal.

We had reached a point where we were spending as much time burning swarms of the Enemy as we were burning nests when the long-awaited call was beamed into my mind. When we crossed into another flight team's zone we turned on the trespass beacons in our craft to alert the assigned team of our presence, and we were finally getting a response.

"I have a fix on your beacons," came the thought. "While I appreciate the assistance in covering this zone, I can now complete assignment without additional support. You may return to rendezvous point."

I noted her use of the word "I" instead of "we."

"What is your condition?" I queried.

"Five flyers lost. My own canopy is breached. It is therefore impossible for me to meet pickup ship. However, I can complete the mission. Feel free to return to rendezvous point."

What occurred to me was the difficulty our six flyers had had sweeping this zone, giving rise to the question of the lone flyer's ability to finish the job.

I rejected the thought. She was a Tzen. If she said she could complete the mission, she could complete it.

"Return to rendezvous!" I beamed to my team and slammed my flyer into a steep climb out of the trees.

I experienced a moment of worry about Kor, but it appeared to be without basis. As we broke out into the predawn light, she was in her appointed position in the formation.

I did not ponder the nobility of the Tzen who sent us on, staying to fight alone. Among the Tzen, this was not exceptionally heroic. Rather, it was our expected performance of duty.

The sky was empty of other flight teams as we streaked toward the rendezvous point. This was not surprising, as our supplemental sweep had taken us extra time. The other units were probably already at the rendezvous point.

Far below I noticed a portion of the forest blazing. Apparently someone had been careless with the use of his hot-beam. I studied it as we flashed overhead. It was in a relatively small portion of the forest, set off from the main mass by a river. Hopefully the river would halt the fire's march. After all this trouble to keep the forest intact, it would be disappointing to see it all lost because of one flyer's carelessness.

We were almost at the pickup point, and our formation was climbing steadily to gain the necessary altitude. We could see the transport now, and as we drew closer, the small cloud of flyers waiting their turn in a holding pattern.

I tried to ignore the implications of this as our team joined the holding pattern. Either we weren't the only ones who had had our mission delayed, or . . .

I forced the thought from my mind. It was almost our turn for entry. I led my team away from the ship in a long circle, allowing maneuvering room for the members to rearrange the formation from a tetrahedron to a single file. Ready now, we turned our line toward the ship, setting a bearing for the open pickup port.

The port was closed. As we watched, the transport broke orbit and began to move away, gaining speed as it went.

Chapter Three

One of the most difficult phases in planning a military campaign is deciding an "Anticipated Casualty Rate." Interstellar combat has made this phase even more crucial. You estimate the number of warriors required to complete the mission after casualties. You then calculate your transportation and supply needs based on that number. If you underestimate your casualties, you run the risk of losing the battle. Overestimate and you are in danger of losing your entire force if your supplies or fuel run out while you're still in space.

The High Command had arrived at a solution to this problem: They calculated the number of anticipated casualties and then stuck to it. They might suffer more casualties than planned, but never less. They planned for returning a specific number of troops to the colony ship, and when that number was on board the transport, they simply shut the doors. Anyone still outside was then considered a casualty.

Apparently this is what had happened to us.

As this was our first confrontation with the Insects, the High Command had had no data on which to base their casualty estimates, so they had estimated high. This ensured the mission would be completed. This also meant we were shut out.

This did not mean simply diverting to another transport. If there had been extra space available in another ship, we would have been directed to it. We hadn't. There was no more space. As far as the High Command was concerned, we were now officially dead.

I found my position curious, the live commander of a live "dead" flight team. What does one do after one is dead? I decided the crisis was of a magnitude to warrant getting the thoughts of the team.

"Confer!" I beamed to the formation at large. I expected a few moments' silence while they collected their thoughts, but Kor's answer was almost immediate.

"If we're dead, the obvious course is to take additional legions of the Enemy to the Black Swamps with us. We may have gotten all the eggs and queens on the formal raid, but there are still a large number of workers we can destroy before the power sources burn out."

"Ahk here, Rahm. Should we accept so readily that we're dead? There is always a chance of a missed transmission from the transport. I would suggest we use whatever power remains to sweep for another transport. If we cannot find one, then we can decide a course of action."

"May I remind the team," came Ssah's voice, "that dead or not, Rahm is still in command. As Commander, it is his duty, difficult though it may be, to decide our course of action, not waste our time in idle debate."

"Mahz confirms Ssah's contention!"

I was about to reply to this implication of my shirking of duty, when Zur's quiet voice interrupted.

"If I may, Commander, there is no need for us to die. However, if the Black Swamp calls us home, there is much we can do for the Empire first."

His assertion intrigued me. "Explain, Zur."

"There is another species of the Coalition of Insects present on this planet. This means the fleets will be back. If we can survive long enough, we can rejoin the Empire at that time. Even if we do not survive until rendezvous, we may be able to gather information on the Enemy to leave for the Empire's use."

His advice was timely and meritorious. If there was a chance we could still be of use to the Empire, there was nothing further to discuss.

"On my lead!" I beamed at the team and wheeled toward the planet surface. Behind me, the flyers broke from the circling holding pattern we had maintained for our conference to form the tetrahedron behind me. We were again Tzen with a purpose.

Time was of the essence now. The ground-based power sources for our flyers were not long-lived. They should have output beyond the forecast time of the mission to allow extra flyers to find secondary transports if available, but as we had cause to know, casualties had been light. That meant additional drain on the power sources. We had no way of knowing how much time was left before our engines would die.

"As we reach low altitude, scatter and search individually. We want a large, deep cave in the low mountain range, not more than five hundred meters from a water source, preferably with an overhanging ledge. Avoid the forests and high-altitude flying at all costs."

As Kor had pointed out, there were still worker Wasps about. It would not pay to have them discover the presence of lingering Tzen to vent their vengeance on.

"Commander, may I suggest—"

"You may not, Ssah! As you pointed out, this is my decision to make and I have made it. You have your orders."

The team scattered, each taking a sextant to canvass. Our flyers skimmed low over the rolling foothills, racing to find refuge before our time ran out. Each pass through my sextant took longer as the search pattern widened. I began to grow concerned. The pattern might spread too far without success, and then we would be in danger of being unable to regroup our flyers if the power source stopped.

I banked the flyer into another turn and started back through my sextant, alert for any sign of a cave such as we were seeking. In another few sweeps I would have to break off the search and try another plan. If we flew too far apart, we would be unable to contact each other telepathically.

"Commander! I have a cave."

"Message confirmed, Ssah. Is it large enough to get our flyers into?"

"I have already flown in and back out again successfully. It will suit our purposes."

Not for the first time I noted Ssah's tendency for unnecessarily reckless action. However, this was not the time to go into it at length.

"Team confirm and home on Ssah's beacon."

"Mahz confirms."

"Ahk confirms."

"Zur confirms."

I waited for a few moments. Kor did not confirm.

"Zur, Mahz, you are closest to Kor's sextant. Relay message or confirmation."

"I have her confirmation, Commander," came Mahz's reply.

With the order acknowledged throughout the team, I wheeled my flyer over and made for Ssah's beacon. Traveling at maxspeed, I soon had the cave in sight. The opening was low, with only a little over ten feet clearance, but more than wide enough to accommodate the flyer's wingspan. I saw two of the team, Ahk and Mahz, dart their flyers into the cave's mouth as I began my approach.

I cut power and leveled my glide two feet off the ground, I had to assume the cave was deep enough that I wouldn't have to worry about plowing into the flyers ahead of me. If it was not, the others would have warned me.

The entrance loomed before me; then I was through. The sudden change from early morning light to the utter blackness of the cave temporarily robbed me of vision. My sonic sensor screens, however, told me I had flown through an opening at the top of a wide cavern, about forty feet deep. I could make out the other flyers, four of them, grounded at the bottom of the cavern. I steered for them, wondering who the missing flyer was. I prepared for landing, taking a deep breath and exhaling it slowly. Even though my current glide speed felt slow compared to my earlier power-flight, the ground was coming up fast, and our flyers were not adapted for ground landings. My flyer touched down, jarring me with the impact, and slid along the cavern floor, the bubble making painful sounds against the rock. I ignored it.

"Who's missing?" I queried before my flyer had ground to a complete halt.

"Kor."

This could mean trouble.

"Mahz! Are you sure she confirmed . . .?"

"Here she is now, Commander."

My eyes were becoming accustomed to the darkness now. I could make out the shape of Kor's swooping silently down on us from the mouth of the cave.

I was burning with questions, but held them in check. You do not distract someone with questions while they're trying to crash-land a flyer.

Finally she touched it down, the flyer coming to a halt a few feet from the others. By this time we were all out of flyers and waiting for her.

"Kor! Explain your delay."

I was aware my head was sinking dangerously close to the flat position of extreme anger. Apparently she noticed it, for as she rose from her flyer, her head position denoted both anger and defense.

"I encountered the Enemy, Commander. There were three—"

"Did they see you?"

"Yes, but I destroyed all three of them and swept the immediate area for any others, that's why I was—"

"Zur!" I diverted my attention to my second-in-command, who had approached behind Kor as we spoke, his massive ten-foot height dwarfing her six-foot stature.

"Yes, Commander?"

"Is there any evidence known of telepathic powers in the Enemy?"

"None known, but it is not beyond speculation. Many of the lower orders of insects are known to communicate telepathically."

I turned from them abruptly.

"Ssah! Check your indicators. Is the power source still broadcasting?"

"Yes, Commander."

"Then you and Mahz pivot your flyers around and use the hot-beams to seal the cave."

I turned back to Kor, my tail lashing angrily despite my efforts to control it.

"Kor, I have a direct order for you. Even though you are without question the most efficient fighter on the team, I will not have the unit's safety jeopardized by independent action. In the future, if you contact the Enemy, you are to so inform the team immediately. If you do not, it will be considered a direct breach of orders."

There was a rumbling crash, and the meager light in the cavern disappeared. The cave was sealed. I turned and raised my voice in the darkness.

"Now use your narrow beams to open a tunnel to the surface. I want it to be just large enough to allow us passage one at a time on all fours."

There was a moment of silence.

"That will be impossible, Commander."

"Explain."

"The power-source has just stopped broadcasting."

Chapter Four

We were effectively buried alive. I considered the problem carefully.

"Did anyone bring a glow-bulb in their personal gear?"

"I did, Commander." Ahk's voice came out of the blackness.

"I feel it would be in the team's best interests if you lit it now."

"Agreed. It is still in my flyer, so if I could get a sound fix from either of the two who were at the flyers when the cave was sealed—"

"Ssah here. Your flyer is about four feet to my left. Would you like me to keep talking to serve as a beacon, or do you have the location?"

"I have it. I'll fetch the bulb now, Commander."

I heard a faint scratching as he moved past me. Even though nothing could be seen in this total absence of light, I knew clearly enough what he was doing to visualize it in my mind's eye. He was edging slowly sideways across the cavern, one hand sweeping the area in front of his head and shoulders, his tail probing for obstacles in the path of his feet and legs. It was not the first time Tzen had had to operate in a total absence of light. The probability of his stumbling was practically nonexistent.

"Ssah! When you scouted the cave, did you have an opportunity to give it a full scan with your sonic screen?"

"I did, Commander."

"Are there any other openings to the outside of any size?"

"None."

A pinpoint of light appeared, widening to disclose the entire small glowing ball as Ahk twisted the glow-bulb to its fullest setting. The light revealed the rest of the team standing around the cavern. They had remained motionless in the darkness to avoid blundering into Ahk's path, but now that a light source had been reestablished, they became animated again.

"Where would you like the light, Commander?"

"Just set it on top of your flyer for now."

My eyes were rapidly adapting to the dim light. Features of the cavern were becoming visible again. I was impressed with the glow-bulbs and made a mental note to include one in my personal gear in the future. Though the visibility was improving, I was pleased that Ssah had used her sonics to check the chamber. It would have taken a great deal of time to perform a close visual check for other openings, whereas the sonics had provided us with the same data in a matter of seconds. It was an efficient use of available equipment.

"My preliminary scouting also showed no other life, plant or animal, in the cavern."

This added bit of data from Ssah was needless. I had assumed that had there been other life, she would have told me in her initial report, particularly in Enemy-held terrain. I was not sure if this was another display of her tendency to overassert herself, or if it was a subtle implication that she felt my earlier question about the sonic scan was also needless. However, there were other, more pressing problems to be dealt with.

I surveyed the cavern again, gauging distances and performing a few mental calculations. No, oxygen supply should not be a problem. There would be no need to put the team in Deep Sleep while the work progressed.

I moved to my own flyer.

"Zur!"

He appeared at my side. I extracted a hand-burner from my personal weapon stock and handed it to him. He examined it swiftly. Not many Tzen used the hand-burners. They were still new and relatively untested in combat, so preference was usually given to the old hand weapons or their recent modified relatives. I had not really intended to use the burner when I chose my weapons, but brought it along to accustom myself to having it ready at hand. Our unexpected situation of being stranded had elevated its importance, and I had been mentally making plans as how to best utilize its devastating capacities. The abrupt demise of the major power-source cut that planning short. The hand-burner's compact independent power-source now had an immediate demand to answer.

"Take this and get the tunnel established. Work by hand as much as possible, but feel free to use it as necessary."

Without further question he turned and strode across the cavern to begin the climb to the recent rubble of the cave-in. I considered the problem solved. Freed of that situation, I turned to the remaining team members.

"I will summarize our situation. We are stranded for an indefinite period on an Enemy-held planet with no support other than each other and whatever equipment and weapons we brought with us. There are two objectives which will guide our actions. First, we must attempt to gather whatever information we can on the Enemy to assist the Empire in its efforts to overthrow their influence. Second, we must survive in order to rejoin the Empire when the fleets return. These objectives are potentially contradictory. As such, when we finish speaking here I will meet with the team members individually to hear their opinions and advice as to how these goals can be best pursued. Questions?"

"Question, Commander."

"Yes, Ssah."

"Why is this to be handled in private conference rather than open discussion?"

I fixed her with my gaze. "In a prolonged survival situation such as this, it will be necessary for me as Commander to have a knowledge of each team member's opinions, attitudes, and priorities beyond those required to lead a formation in a raid. Much of this information is of a highly personal nature, including what they think of me, what I think of them, and what they think of their fellow teammates. This is data which is not only unnecessary, it is undesirable for it to become general knowledge, therefore warranting private conferences. I trust you will remember that when and if you become a flight team Commander."

Her head flattened slightly at the rebuff, but she remained silent.

"Any other questions?"

There were none. I rose and started for the far end of the cavern.

"Ahk! I would speak with you first. The rest of the team is to secure their personal gear from the flyers."

Ahk was the only member of the team senior to me in both years and combat experience. Both his combat record and my personal impressions of him, however, could best be described as bland. I was anxious to obtain further data.

We sought and found comfortable places to squat and settled in before I began the conference.

"Ahk, even though I know little about you, your years of experience cannot be overlooked. I will doubtless be turning to you often for counsel and advice. I cannot help but wonder, however, with your record, why you are not of higher rank. Would you clarify this for me?"

"My slow advancement in rank is a direct result of my characteristic trait of habitual caution," he stated without hesitation. "This is born of seeing too many losses in combat from overzealous and reckless action. My conservatism excludes the type of noteworthy action which attracts promotion. What is more, my feelings are heightened with each battle I participate in, thus making the probability of promotion even more remote. I realize this, and accept it. However, do not mistake my caution for cowardice. Many have gone to the Black Swamps from the dueling ground who chose to label it thus. My abilities as a Warrior are well above average, and I can be relied upon to complete any assignment undertaken."

He shifted position, looking at me more directly. "As for my opinion of you as a Commander, I find you more than acceptable. Even though you occasionally take risks I would avoid if left to my own devices, you carry them off with a firmness of resolve and a sense of control which eliminates needless danger. I will have no reservations in following your lead."

"What would be your recommendations for undertaking the task before us, Ahk?"

"I would recommend Deep Sleep for the majority of the team, Deep Sleep with varying wake times in event of something happening to the functioning team members. This would maximize our chances of having some of the team survive to rejoin the Empire. The fewer members left functioning, the less foraging for supplies will have to be done, and therefore the less chance of discovery by the Enemy. The functioning members could then guard those in Deep Sleep as well as scout the Enemy for additional information."

I inclined my head slightly toward the ceiling as I replied.

"Your recommendations will be taken under consideration. However, I will tell you I do not agree with your conclusions. Deep Sleep enabled our species to survive when times were lean, but I do not feel it should be resorted to here. The Longevity Serums developed by the Scientist caste virtually ensure that a Tzen will live until killed. With the overwhelming number of the Enemy present on this planet, I feel the best tactic to ensure against our being killed is to keep as many of the team conscious as possible and thereby maximize the fighting strength available at any given time."

He listened without rancor. He had his opinions, and I had mine. There was no question of who was right or wrong. I was the team Commander, and my orders would be followed.

"Also, would you provide a list of weapons in your personal arsenal at this time?"

"My weapons consist of a bandoleer of two dozen spring-javelins, a flexi-steel whip, an acid spray belt, a telescoping knife, and dueling sticks."

"What weapons, if any, would you be willing to make available for team use?"

He thought for a few moments. "Any and all of them with the exception of the dueling sticks. This is, of course, assuming I would not be left weaponless, that something would either be left me or issued to replace the weapons taken."

This was acceptable to me.

"One more question, Ahk. What are your opinions of your individual teammates?"

His answer was brisk. Apparently he had given prior thought to this question.

"Zur is a highly efficient and terrifyingly fierce fighter. However, at times I fear he thinks too much. Sometimes I give pause to wonder if his heart is truly in the Warrior caste. While he performs his duties easily and well, they do not seem to give him any pleasure or pride of accomplishment."

He cocked his head in minor puzzlement. "Kor is perhaps the finest fighter I have ever encountered. Of the entire team she is the one I would be least eager to face on the dueling-ground. Her reflexes and combat instincts are nearly beyond belief. I must admit to a certain unease around her, though. At first I thought it was envy of her talents, but it goes beyond that. I think she takes more pleasure in killing than she should. That is, I feel more confident of victory with her on my side, but I would not wish to be the one to order her to stop."

He paused thoughtfully for several moments, then bobbed his head in indecision. "Mahz I have no opinion of. He seems capable enough, but is completely under the influence of Ssah. As things are now, he is an extension of her will. I would have to observe him in her absence before I could form an opinion."

His head sank to a dangerously low position. I have seen Tzen issue challenges for personal duels with heads held higher.

"Ssah is dangerous. If you were to adopt my suggestion for Deep Sleep, I would propose her as one of the members to be rendered nonfunctional. Her presence is a threat to the survival of the entire team. Where you, Rahm, take calculated risks, she indulges in recklessness. Recklessness is dangerous in any combat situation, but in our current predicament it is disastrous. What is more, she has taken to habitually challenging your authority and decisions. It is my opinion that there will be trouble if she remains functional with the team."

"Very well, Ahk. That answers my questions. If you have no further questions or opinions, pass the word for Kor. I would speak with her next."

Kor was an enigma. She was small, a full foot below the six-foot minimum height requirement for the Warrior caste. As had been noted, however, her phenomenal aptitude for combat had earned her a waiver from the height requirement for entrance. She would doubtless be bred in an attempt to pass her traits on to the next batch of Warriors, providing . . . providing she proved to be reliable in actual combat. It was this question that was foremost in my mind as she appeared for her conference.

"Kor, I will not belabor my opinion of your abilities. They are superior and an asset to any fighting team. But aside from that, it cannot be ignored that this is your first combat mission for the Empire and your reliability under fire is therefore untested. As you, like Ssah, are part of a new wave of Warriors that received initial training under the new technology rather than being re-trained from the old ways like the rest of the team, your performance is under constant scrutiny by me and by the High Command."

I paused to allow her to react or reply. She didn't.

"It has been noted that you display an exceptional enthusiasm for battle. This has given rise to several questions, of which two require immediate consideration. First, is this enthusiasm an individual characteristic or is it a pattern of the entire new wave which the rest of us should grow accustomed to? Secondly, will this enthusiasm interfere with your ability to obey orders in a precise and efficient manner?"

She withdrew her head slightly, narrowing her eyes thoughtfully. I didn't rush her, as the questions required deep thought and judgmental weighings. There was a soft thumping as the tip of her tail twitched, impacting the floor of the cavern.

"Upon serious reflection, it is my belief that the enthusiasm with which I enter into combat is an individual rather than a new-wave characteristic. To anticipate your next question or perhaps a question you would leave unasked, yes, I enjoy fighting. It is something I do well and efficiently. Most of my current status I owe to my fighting abilities, and my applying them is the only way I can serve the Empire. When I am not fighting I feel parasitic and useless. However, I am quick to acknowledge my lack of experience and not only will obey, but I actually appreciate the guidance I receive from seasoned officers."

She cocked her head quizzically at me. "I have a question, Rahm. During our strafing run, I noticed a tendency on your part to pattern our sweep such that we would always turn to the right. Was this merely coincidental, or was it in fact a display of your concern for having me posted to your right?"

"It was not coincidental," I admitted. "I experienced some unease when speculating upon your willingness to break off an engagement on command. It occurred to me that if you did feel any resentment at being ordered to stop fighting, it could easily become focused on the Tzen issuing the order, in this case myself. If that occurred, I did not wish to perform a maneuver which would require your weapons to align, even briefly, with my flyer as you turned. As a Commander, I had to acknowledge the possibility, and lacking any basis to calculate probability, felt it necessary to take those preventive precautions. In part it was due to the realization that with your degree of skill, if you chose to attack me, I would probably be unable to defend myself."

She listened without any sign of irritation.

"Understood, Rahm. But I would assure you your apprehension is needless. As I have said, I feel no resentment when receiving instruction from a veteran Warrior such as yourself. In addition, I have noted in myself a marked resistance to using my powers against other Tzen. I feel I have been trained to fight the Enemy, and that fighting each other is a misuse of that training. You may notice from my record that I have never fought a duel. My well-known abilities lessen the probability of being challenged, and my feelings about fighting another Tzen forbid me issuing a challenge regardless of provocation."

"What are your opinions of the others on the team?" I asked.

"I have none. They are Tzen and they do their share of the fighting. Beyond that I do not concern myself with their thoughts or motivations. As for yourself, my feelings are much the same. I am neither enthused nor disheartened by your performance as Commander. You perform your duties efficiently, and none can ask more of a Tzen than that."

"Do you have any suggestions for our plan of action on this planet?"

"As I have said, I readily acknowledge the superior experience in planning present on this team. However, as I am requested to express my opinions, I would recommend moving out into the open. We should seal the cave with the flyers inside and adopt a mobile format for our existence. A fixed location, particularly one with only one exit, is vulnerable. A wandering pattern in the open would allow us more flexibility for flight or counterattack, depending upon the specific situation."

"Would you list the weapons in your personal arsenal at this time?"

"I have a set of the weighted, spiked hand armor; a wedge-sword; an alter-mace; three steel balls, two and a half inches in diameter; two long knives and one short; and dueling sticks."

"What weapons, if any, would you be willing to make available for team use?"

She hesitated. "I would be willing to surrender any of them, but would prefer not to. As you have noted, I am exceptionally effective in combat. This is because I have spent much time practicing with these specific weapons in a particular array. I can switch weapons in midcombat without motion loss because I do not have to pause to think. I fear that would be lost if I had to readjust my style. The only weapons I would release without hesitation would be the alter-mace and the dueling sticks. The alter-mace is my newest addition, and I am not yet at home with its use. The dueling sticks . . . well . . . I've already explained my willingness to part with them."

"That answers all my questions, Kor. Unless you have any additional questions, pass the word for Mahz."

She rose to leave, then hesitated. "No further questions, Commander, but I do have an amendment to an earlier statement."

"What is it?"

"I said I had no opinions on my teammates. Upon reflection I must change that. When you mentioned that Ssah and I were of the same new-wave of Warriors, I experienced a rush of irritation and suppressed an impulse to request that you not classify her and me together. I realize now that is to some degree an attitude or opinion on my part. I cannot define it clearly or give adequate reasons, but I would rather not associate with her if given a choice."

She left to fetch Mahz. I was looking forward to my conference with Mahz. Like Ahk, I was having difficulty forming an opinion of him when he was so much in Ssah's shadow.

"Make yourself comfortable, Mahz. There is much I would—"

"I'd rather stand, Commander, and if you'll allow me to express myself first, I feel we can keep this conference brief and to the point."

"Proceed."

"Before we occupy considerable time discussing my opinion of you and the rest of the team, I would state that I do not feel those opinions matter."

He hastened on before I could interrupt. "Not that I am suggesting you would not give proper consideration to my thoughts; rather that I do not. You see, early in my career, I constantly monitored and assessed my abilities, far closer than my trainers did. In doing so, I was forced to admit I had no exceptional qualities. Not that I am incompetent or incapable, just not exceptional. I do not possess the phenomenal fighting ability that Kor does, nor the flair for leadership and tactics that you and Ssah have. As such, I decided that if I was to rise in rank and power, the best asset I could offer would be service, to pick a rising Tzen and serve him or her faithfully as an aide, helping them to advance and advancing with them."

He paused to look at me directly. "The Tzen I have chosen to support is Ssah. In that choice, my own opinions pale to insignificance. What she supports, I support. What she opposes, I oppose."

"Why have you chosen Ssah?"

"And not yourself? I have no objections to you, Rahm. That is not what swayed my choice. Several factors came into account in making my decision. She is new, while you are an acknowledged veteran. While you have already established working relationships with several Tzen such as Zur and Ahk, she has none. This makes it easier for me to establish myself at her sword hand. If I were to be offered a second-in-command position with an established officer, it would have happened by now, and it hasn't. Consequently, I choose to focus my efforts with a younger, newer Tzen. She has a tendency toward reckless, independent action. If she learns caution, these exploits are apt to attract the attention of the High Council, and she, and therefore I, will rise in rank. If she does not learn caution and is killed, then perhaps my loyal service will have been noted, and I will be requested to attach my services to another ambitious Tzen, and the process will start anew."

I considered this for a few moments.

"Have you considered the dangers inherent in submerging your will completely in favor of another's?"

"I have not completely submerged my will, Rahm. If Ssah should undertake a course which in my opinion is not in the best interests of the Empire, I will speak up or move to block her. I am an ambitious Tzen, but am still a Tzen."

"What weapons do you have in your personal arsenal at this time?"

"A wedge-sword, a whip sword, a telescoping thrusting spear, long knife, and dueling sticks."

"What weapons, if any, are you willing to place at the disposal of the team?"

He didn't hesitate. "I will have to think that over and consult with Ssah before giving you my reply."

"That answers my questions. Unless you have any further questions, pass the word for . . ."

I hesitated in midsentence. Zur's massive bulk had just appeared in the gloom of the cavern. I waved Mahz away and beckoned Zur to report to me.

"Is the tunnel complete?"

"Yes. I left Ahk posted at the mouth as lookout and came back to report to you."

He handed me back my hand-burner. I glanced at the charge indicator: less than a quarter-charge remaining! That wasn't good.

"Shall we have our conference now, Rahm?"

I considered it. I knew my second-in-command better than I knew any of the other team members. However, when we talked, there would be much to plan and discuss. "Not yet, Zur. For now, pass the word for Ssah."

Chapter Five

Flattened against the tree trunk some ten meters in the air, I slowly surveyed the terrain. The trunk swayed gently in a gust of wind, and I swayed with it. This did not worry me. Swaying trees are a natural movement and do not attract even a watchful eye. However, my turning my head to look about would not be a natural movement, so I did it extremely cautiously. Even if I could be detected through the foliage, my silhouette was altered enough by the tree trunk so as not to arouse suspicion. As such, only my head movement would betray my position. Due to our eyes being mounted on the sides of our heads, the peripheral vision of a Tzen is extremely wide, requiring less than a six-inch movement to scan a full 360-degree field. I took almost a quarter hour to move my head the necessary six inches.

Still nothing.

Aside from random movement of lesser life forms in the meadow ahead of us and at the edge of the river behind us, there was no activity. Still our ambush waited.

Zur, Ahk, and Kor were with me in the ambush. They were well hidden on the ground. I did not worry about their being discovered. They were Tzen, and Tzen don't move when waiting in ambush.

I knew our techniques of concealment were effective against the

Leapers. We had been observing them for over a month now without being discovered. A few hours ago a Leaper came down to the river to drink. It came to the far side of the river, exempting it from our ambush, but had not detected us, though it was within a dozen meters of our position. I was not worried about our ambush being discovered.

Nor was I worried about finding a victim. Our site had not been chosen at random. The tree trunk I clung to overhung the only major break in the strand of trees that lined the river for several miles. We had observed that the Leapers tended to avoid entering tree cover, possibly due to a habitual adherence to a coexistence pact with the now nearly defunct Wasps. Whatever the reason, this opening was the main thoroughfare between the hunting ground of the meadow and the water source of the river. A victim would be along eventually.

I was in an exposed position serving as spotter and ready to provide cover fire if needed. Even partially charged, my hand-burner would give us a definite edge if plans went awry.

Thinking of my hand-burner turned my thoughts once more toward my conference with Ssah. For the hundredth time I went over the details in my mind.

The conference had not gone well. Ssah was one of my offspring. She was probably unaware of this. I had not mentioned it to her; it would have made no difference to her thinking as it had made no difference to mine. I had simply noted it as a point of interest in her genetic record when going over her personnel file prior to the mission.

The mating with her Mother had been an experiment by the High Command. Her Mother was a bit of a misfit, a Scientist who was more imaginative than inquisitive. At the time of our mating, my leadership potential was already being rated as well above average, but it was noted that my methods were strongly influenced by earlier precedence, that I lacked inventiveness . . . imagination if you will. It is my guess this crossbreeding between Warrior and Scientist, particularly considering the individuals concerned, was an effort to produce a more imaginative leader for the Warrior caste.

Some experiments are more successful than others. In Ssah, they had produced a Warrior leader who was unrestrained by the traditions and concerns of the caste. She was the only result of that mating I had encountered to date, but if she was anything like the others, the entire hatching should have been destroyed after the first round of tests.

"Ssah, I disapprove strongly of many of your methods and attitudes. Tactics such as flying into the cavern before reporting its location to the rest of the team jeopardized our survival. Had you crashed your flyer or been attacked in the interior, we would have been left unaware of the situation, and an entire sextant would have gone unscanned."

She met my gaze with indifferent neutrality as I continued.

"Then there is your habit of questioning my orders. It is every Warrior's right to question the orders of a superior, but I feel that many of the objections you raise are pointless. They frequently either repeat questions covered in earlier discussions or briefings, or are of a rhetorical nature seeming to be designed with no other intent than to goad me. Before I can work with you comfortably I will require further clarification on your logic and motivations."

She faced me levelly as she replied. "My actions are easily understood if you understand my one basic premise. I feel that I should be leading this team instead of you."

I felt my head lowering against my will as I answered.

"The High Command commissioned me and appointed me as Commander of—"

"I know," she interrupted. "I do not expect you to relinquish command, as I would not were I in your position. I recognize this logically. However, I also recognize my own feelings on the matter. I do not attempt to justify them, but merely state them as a cause for my behavior."

I had regained control of myself, and my reply was level.

"Do you also acknowledge the danger to the team potential in your attitude?"

"Of course, that is why I would strongly urge that you follow my proposed plan of action in this mini-campaign."

Though still affected by her audacity, I was nonetheless curious to hear her plan and settled back to listen.

"Realizing the friction that would doubtless result from having a running power struggle within the team, I would propose that we scatter the team, divide it into three two-Tzen teams. In addition to relieving the pressures of our current situation, there are several other advantages inherent in this plan. First, it would lessen the chances of the entire team's being wiped out in one chance encounter with the Enemy. Thus, there would be a higher probability of at least some of us surviving to pass the gathered information on to the Empire. Second, with three teams working independently, we could gather more information than any single unit. Third . . ."

She hesitated and glanced back toward the cavern, then continued in a conspiratorial voice.

"Third, it would allow us to rid ourselves of some of the less desirable elements on the team."

My head wanted to lower again, but I kept it level.

"Explain your last comment."

"The composition of the teams should be clear, even to you. Mahz is a good Warrior, and his loyalty to me is undeniable. He and I would form one team. You are a capable Commander. Understand my earlier comments were not meant to deride your abilities, but rather to say I felt mine were better. Zur is slow, but his strength makes up for any lack of speed. The two of you would make a team with a better-than-average chance of survival."

She hesitated again.

"And Kor and Ahk? What about them?"

"Kor is bloodthirsty, and Ahk is a coward. If they don't kill each other off, the Enemy will."

I abandoned my hope of control.

"You claim you want to lead the team, yet at the same time you tell me you would willingly try to kill off one-third of the members?"

"Rahm, you and I both know a good small team has as much or better chance of survival as a large sloppy team."

"Do you have the vaguest conception of what we are facing on this planet, Ssah? The Enemy doesn't count its strength in troops, they count it in swarms. Swarms! Against that we have six Tzen. Six! And you want to divide our strength? Divide it and cut our numbers to four!"

I caught myself and forced my head and voice level, though both had a dangerous tilt.

"I reject your proposal, Ssah. It is my opinion that the six of us should remain together as a single unit to maximize our strength and firepower. As an example of how desperate I feel the situation is, at this time I even consider your presence an asset!"

"If those are your opinions—"

"Those are my orders!"

She rose to leave. "If there are no further questions—"

"There are! Would you list your weapons in your personal possession at this time?"

"Certainly. I have a half-dozen spring-javelins, an acid spray belt, two wedge-swords, a long knife, and, of course, dueling sticks."

"What, if any, weapons are you willing to place at the disposal of the team?"

"Neither Mahz's nor my weapons are to be used by another team member. We selected our weapons for ourselves. I trust the other team members had the sense to do the same. We withhold our weapons for personal use."

"That is your prerogative if you choose to exercise it. That answers all my questions. If you have no additional questions, pass the word for Zur. I would speak with him next."

She started to turn away, then turned once again to face me.

"Commander, there is one weapon I neglected to list with my arsenal." She met my eyes coldly and levelly. "I also have a fully charged hand-burner, identical to the one you loaned Zur to burn a tunnel with."

So here we were. Ssah with her fully charged hand-burner, backed by Mahz, was guarding the cave and the flyers, while I clung to a tree trunk covering the balance of the team with my meager quarter charge.

Suddenly there was a flicker of movement a hundred meters into the meadow. A Leaper! It moved out of the brush into the open, hesitated for a few moments, then made a twelve-foot leap in our direction and hesitated again.

I studied it narrowly. It was relatively small, scarcely six feet long. This probably meant it was still young. Good. If our guesses were correct, its exoskeleton would be softer than that of a full adult.

I watched it as it leaped in our direction again and paused once more. Either it was hunting or it was being exceptionally wary.

Even though we had been observing them for over a month, I still had a horrified fascination with the nightmarish lethalness of its appearance. Its hind legs were twice the size of the other four, giving it incredible power on its leaps. The middle legs were primarily for walking and balance, but the forelegs . . . the forelegs were awesome. They had developed into slender pincers, saw-toothed on the inside and lightning fast. We weren't sure if they were poisoned or not; that was part of our mission today. More likely they were designed to grasp and hold a victim for the terrible mandibles. The Leaper's jaws were also enlarged pincers, razor-edged and saw-toothed and three times the size of the pincer forelegs. I had once seen a Leaper tear a four-footed warm-blooded creature in half with its jaws, which was one reason we didn't know if the forelegs were poisonous. Once a victim was dragged within reach of those jaws it didn't survive long enough for us to tell if it died of poison or not. Hopefully we would have the answer to that and other questions soon. Zur wanted a specimen to dissect, and we were here to get one for him.

The Leaper moved toward us again. It was definitely coming to the river and would pass through our ambush. I ignored it and began scanning the meadow behind it. There was no sign of other Leapers about.

I beamed a warning to the waiting ambushers.

"Get ready."

Although there was no betraying movement, I knew the teammates were readying themselves. Prolonged stillness tends to lock and cramp the joints. They would be alternately tensing and relaxing their muscles, restoring circulation so that they could spring to the attack without loss of time or motion.

There was still no sign of other Leapers on the meadow. This would tend to confirm our observations and disprove the current Empire theory. According to Zur's briefing, the Empire was aware of the occasional solitary Leaper, but chose to interpret it as an outlying scout for one of the major packs. It was our conclusion from prolonged firsthand observation that in actuality, most of the loners were just that loners, unattached to any pack.

The Leaper was almost on our position now, and it switched to its short-distance crawling walk, a curious waddling procedure.

"Get ready," I beamed for a second time and scanned the meadow again. Still nothing. The Leaper passed under my tree trunk and approached the river bank.

"Now!"

Ahk seemed to rise up out of the ground to the Leaper's right. He drew back his arm and the spring-javelin snapped open, the two halves telescoping out from the center handgrip and locking in place.

The Leaper saw him instantly and froze. It seemed both startled at his sudden appearance and torn by indecision as to whether to attack or flee. Then it saw Zur and Kor leaping from cover on its left, and its decision was made. It gathered its mighty hind legs for a desperate leap, but it was too late.

Ahk's arm flashed forward, and the spring-javelin darted out. It pierced the Leaper's thorax and passed through into the ground, effectively pinning it in place. A high-pitched squeal rent the air, like a prolonged shriek. I quickly scanned the meadow again. Still no other Leapers in sight.

I started to call down to silence the beast, but saw my advice was unnecessary.

Zur stepped up to the pinned Leaper, hesitated for a moment to gauge its wild thrashing, then raised his wedge-sword. He darted forward with an agility surprising in one of his bulk, swayed past the snapping mandibles, and struck with all the power in his massive arm. In the same movement he ducked under one of the groping pincered forelegs and rolled clear, coming to his feet with his sword raised again in the ready position.

His guard was reflexive, but unnecessary. The sword stroke had split the creature's head open, killing it even though its limbs continued to thrash and grope with stubborn life. Without guidance, though, its death throes were blind and easily avoided. Most important, the creature's alarm signal had been silenced by the blow.

I scanned the meadow once more. There was no sign of Leapers moving to support their fallen member. We had guessed correctly! Our victim was a loner. We had gambled and won. As a prize, we had a specimen for dissection.

Then we saw the Wasps.

Chapter Six

When we made our initial strafing run on the Wasps, our targets were the queens and the nests. The battle plan had not included eliminating the workers. As it was our first attack of the Bug Wars, High Command had deemed such an action a pointless risk of Warriors and equipment. Without eggs hatching or new eggs being laid, there would be no replenishment of the worker population as the existing workers reached the end of their life span. Thus, by the time the fleets returned to attack the Leapers, there would be no opposition from the Wasps.

This philosophy was fine for the fleets, but we were still on the planet, and so were the worker Wasps. Even though the initial attack had made a sizable dent in their numbers and still more had perished in the month we had been there, there was still an overwhelming number left.

They were constantly patrolling the airways, singly or in small groups, though we weren't sure why. They were there and that was all that really mattered. We had experienced no difficulty in avoiding them . . . until now.

There were three of them, apparently alerted by the death shrieks of the ambushed Leaper. The first warning we had of their presence was when they dropped from the treetops some seventy-five meters distant in the tree line. They approached us in a slow, heavy drone not more than a dozen feet off the ground. Caught in the open, Ahk, Zur, and Kor had no hope of escaping detection. With cold calculation they shifted weapons in preparation for battle. I was uncertain if I had been detected in my lofty perch. I remained motionless, and the other team members did nothing to betray my presence.

The Wasps seemed to be in no hurry to press the attack. As they neared our position, instead of swooping to the attack, they rose lazily to the treetops once more. They touched down in the higher branches and rested there, staring down at us and fidgeting nervously among each other.

I might have been able to burn the three of them where they were, but I was loath to further deplete the energy source if the situation could be handled with the hand weapons. Then, too, the day would come when the hand-burners would be fully discharged and we would have to rely upon the hand weapons entirely. It would be best to begin practicing for that day now, when the cover fire of the hand-blasters was still available.

"Confirm count of three Enemy, Commander," came Zur's telepathed message.

"Confirmed. No indication of additional Wasps or Leapers in the immediate area."

The two forces considered each other warily. This would be the first actual confrontation between the Coalition of Insects and the Tzen Empire. Surprise attacks such as the original strafing mission or our ambushing the solitary Leaper were deliberately planned to favor the attacker and play into the defenders' weakness. Now, for the first time, individuals of a roughly even number were squaring off for head-on combat, each side with an equal degree of preparedness or non-preparedness, as the case may be.

Although we had seen hundreds, even thousands of Wasps when we were strafing the nests, it was quite a different thing to face the Enemy from a short distance when they were awake, alert, and ready to fight instead of viewing them from inside a flyer's canopy as they buzzed around groggy and confused.

They continued to stare down at us with those dead metallic eyes, occasionally shifting position and touching antennae as if in conference. Their bodies were a glossy ten feet in length, and in flight their wings spanned over twenty feet, presenting a formidable and not particularly vulnerable target.

My teammates were not idle. With a cold calmness, they warily made their preparations for battle. Ahk had opened half a dozen of his spring-javelins after first retreating to a position near the base of one of the towering trees. Grasping his flexi-steel whip in one hand, he began sticking the javelins in the ground around him, forcing one end deep into the soil. At first I thought he was attempting to prepare by having a ready supply of missiles close at hand, a tactic that seemed unwise to me considering the extremely tough exoskeleton of the Wasps. Then he turned and drove two of the javelins into the tree trunk behind him, leaving them to jut into the air at an unlikely angle, and I saw his plan. He was erecting a maze of sharp spikes between himself and the Enemy—negating any chance of being taken by a sudden rush. It seemed there was still much I could learn from this campaign-scarred veteran.

Zur stood alone in the open about a dozen meters from Ahk. In his hands he held the long-shafted alter-mace that had originally been part of Kor's arsenal. He stood in almost lazy stillness, the rigid shaft gripped in his hands; but his eyes never left the Wasps. They would find him no easy target. A ten-foot Tzen with an alter-mace is an opponent to be reckoned with.

Another dozen meters from Zur, completing the triangle, was Kor. She was waiting near, but not taking cover from, a slightly sloping tree trunk. The heavy spiked hand-armor glittered at the end of her arms, but she didn't seem to notice the weight, tossing one of her steel balls back and forth from hand to hand as she watched the Wasps.

"Commander!" It was Kor's voice that was beamed into my mind.

"Yes, Kor?"

"Request permission to commence combat."

"Granted."

I gave permission not so much out of impatience as curiosity to see what action she had planned. I didn't have long to wait.

Slowly at first, then smoothly accelerating, she began to turn and rotate like a warmblood chasing its tail. Her own tail, however, rose slowly until it was pointed straight up; then with a sudden whiplike action she bent double and hurtled the steel ball at the Wasps, levering her tail down as she did for added power and balance.

I would have thought the distance too great to throw one of the steel balls with any accuracy, much less with any power, and apparently so had the Wasps. As if to prove my assumptions wrong, the ball flashed past me as if fired from a power sling and smashed into one Wasp's thorax with an audible *crack!*

The impact knocked the Wasp from its perch, but it caught itself in midair, apparently unhurt, and hovered there, soon to be joined by the other two. They hung in the air for several long moments, and I thought they were going to alight again. Then, without warning, they attacked.

To be accurate, two of them attacked, descending unhurriedly toward my teammates on the ground. The third rose and began to fly away, assumedly to bring others. I tracked the messenger with my hand-burner, not daring to fire until battle had been joined. The two attackers passed by my lofty perch, and I decided I could wait no longer. I triggered the burner and watched the messenger flame and fall. Then I turned my attention to the scene below.

The two attacking Wasps were centering on one target—Kor. For a moment I lost sight of her as my line of vision was obscured by the descending attackers, though I could see Zur and Ahk leaving their chosen positions and moving to assist their teammate. Then Kor was in sight again, moving fast, rolling sideways along the ground. Apparently she had waited until the last possible instant, waited until the Wasps' trailing forelegs were about to close on her, then evaded by dive rolling under them, passing dangerously close to their acid poisoned stings.

The Wasps hesitated, seemingly confused by the sudden movement of their target. Intelligent beings shouldn't hesitate when fighting Tzen. The split-second stabilization of his target was all the opening Ahk needed. The flexi-steel whip lashed out, striking the Wasp nearest him just behind the head, severing it from the body.

Still functioning, but without guidance, the headless body veered sideways, crashing into its partner. The second Wasp wobbled in midair from the impact and tried to steer away. Again, the maneuver came too late.

Zur was behind it, swinging the alter-mace. He had changed its setting at some point, and the once rigid shaft was now as limp and flexible as a rope, adding incredible whipping velocity to the already awesome power of his arms.

The blow struck the Wasp in the abdomen, spinning it around and bringing it crashing to the ground. The beast apparently realized its vulnerable position immediately and again tried to take to the air, again in vain.

Kor's dive roll had taken her to the base of the sloping tree trunk. As she regained her feet, she sprang onto the trunk, clawed her way several yards up it, and launched herself at the rising insect.

She landed on its back, her weight and impact driving it back to the ground, and she clung there, one arm wrapped around the beast's neck; her free hand, weighted with armor and clutching another steel ball, rose and fell repeatedly as she smashed at the Wasp's head. The insect thrashed and writhed on the ground, dragging Kor back and forth as she clung stubbornly to her precarious handhold. The beast was bent almost double now, desperately probing with its sting to find its tormentor.

That I could do something about. Ahk wasn't the only one with spring-javelins. I clung to the tree trunk with one hand, my feet, and my tail, as I leaned out, opened the javelin, and hurtled it downward. My aim was true. The javelin struck the Wasp's abdomen, spinning it to the ground and ending the threat of the sting.

"Kor!" I called. "Break off the attack. It's dead!"

And it was. Reflex was keeping its limbs moving, but Kor's pummeling had caved in the beast's head.

"Acknowledged, Commander."

She sprang clear of the Wasp's death throes and stood waiting.

I scanned the meadow once more, but there was still no activity. I began to descend the tree trunk cautiously. Leaping wildly into thin air was fine for hatchlings like Kor, but I had too much respect for my own vulnerability to risk injury needlessly. Besides, as I have said, I'm slightly acrophobic.

I will admit to a certain feeling of contentment as I descended, however. We had our specimen Leaper for Zur to dissect, and I was no longer as worried about the team's ability under fire.

Chapter Seven

The team was enjoying a brief period of rest. We were secure in our cavern with Mahz guarding the entrance, and, more importantly, we had eaten.

We had made several adaptations to the cavern in the month since our arrival. One of these was the addition of a series of crude pits, pens, and cages in which we kept small warm-bloods as a ready food source. While we can consume dead meat, we prefer it live. What is more, it proved to be easier to maintain livestock than devise a means of keeping the meat from spoiling if we killed them upon capture.

However, the situation posed more problems than simply maintaining a ready food source. Like other reptiles, Tzen tend to be sleepy and sluggish immediately after a heavy meal, a condition we could not afford now. We were not on a secure colony ship or transport where we could sharpen ourselves for combat by long periods without food, then glut ourselves after the battle and sleep it off while others took our place on the battle line. We were in a situation where we needed each Warrior at peak efficiency all the time. As such, instead of following our usual feeding pattern, we were forced to eat often and lightly, therefore obtaining minimal recovery time. This was particularly hard on Kor. Her small frame and high energy output left her constantly hungry. She would always have to cut short her feeding before her hunger was completely satisfied. As a result, she was beginning to grow irritable, a condition I would have to find a solution for if the team was to continue to function smoothly.

Unlike the rest of us, Zur had chosen not to eat following our battle with the Wasps. Instead, he busied himself at the rear of the cavern, working by torchlight to dissect the body of the Leaper we had killed.

As I rested, I watched his deft motions as he cut and probed at the corpse, pausing occasionally to murmur notes into his wrist recorder. It was good to see him in his element once more.

Zur was a misfit on the team, indeed in the Warrior caste. Unlike the rest of us, he was not raised and trained as a Warrior. His background was as a Scientist, and it was only after failing to meet the standards of the Scientists' caste that he had become a Warrior, largely owing to his imposing stature.

This constantly set him apart from the rest of the team, even though they knew nothing of his background. He fought well and efficiently, and they were glad to have him as a teammate, but there were periodic occurrences and utterances that clearly marked him as non-Warrior-raised.

One example of this was my conference with him immediately following our arrival on this planet. Even aware of his background, I was shocked to discover he was without a personal arsenal. Well, to be accurate, he was not completely unarmed. He was still a Tzen. But his armament consisted of only a long knife and a wrist dart-thrower and a supply of acid and tranquilizer darts. For a Warrior he was naked!

Instead of weapons, he had used his weight allotment to bring along an assortment of information discs and blank discs for recording.

"Knowledge is my weapon, Commander," he had informed me.

I will not argue the relative value of knowledge, particularly with a Scientist. Further, I will acknowledge the discs he brought both increased our odds of survival and gave us a means of ensuring whatever data we gathered would be passed on to the Empire. However, I will also state as a Tzen and a member of the Warrior caste that I felt much more optimistic about our odds of survival after I issued him a wedge-sword and an alter-mace!

Watching him work and recalling our conference, I found my thoughts wandering back to when Zur and I first met. Normally, I would not waste time in idle reminiscence, but I had recently eaten and I let my mind wander back—back to the conference when I first met Zur, and, for me, the Bug Wars began.

I was awakened prematurely from Deep Sleep, a sign in itself that something was amiss. There were other Warriors moving about, but too few for it to be an attack or even preparation for a campaign. However, I was a Warrior, not a Scientist, and curiosity was not one of my major motivating drives. As such, I simply followed my orders and reported to the designated conference room.

The Tzen waiting for me was of gigantic proportions. I recall wondering at the time why he was a Scientist rather than a Warrior. We could put the strength to good use. He motioned for me to join him at the viewing table in the middle of the room.

"Rahm, the Scientists' caste has received authorization to waken you as one of several experts to aid us in seeking a solution to a puzzle confronting us. First, will you confirm the service record—that you have fought in several campaigns against other intelligent life forms, and in at least one case, a culture whose technology was more advanced than our own?"

"Confirmed."

"Realizing this, we would like your military analysis and opinion on a recent discovery."

Reaching down, he pressed the levers to activate the viewing table. The picture of a city sprung into view. A magnificent city, far advanced of anything I had ever seen before. It was in a state of total ruin.

"An exploratory expedition discovered this city in the northern reaches of the Black Swamps. Its builders obviously possessed a technology far superior to anything we have ever imagined, much less hoped to achieve. Could you give us your opinion on it?"

As he spoke, the scene was slowly changing, now playing across the faces of the structures, now moving into the interiors. I watched the table for several moments before speaking.

"While these scenes are interesting from a technical viewpoint, if I am to give a military analysis of the ruin, I must view those aspects of the city I am most familiar with. Could I see the defense installations, the armories, and the barracks?"

"There are none."

I considered this answer. Then I reviewed my question. Occasionally there are communication difficulties encountered in cross-caste conversation. In this case, however, the question was too simple to have been misunderstood, yet the answer was incredible.

"None at all?"

"It has been checked and rechecked. There is absolutely no evidence anywhere in the city of anything which was designed for violence. While there are items which could be used in a crude, makeshift manner, there is no trace of any weapons or armed force commensurate with the level of technology shown throughout the city."

I continued to study the ruin. After several thoughtful moments, I was ready.

"It is obvious that the city and probably its inhabitants were destroyed in an attack. There is evidence in the ruins of attack from above and below as well as at a ground level. This indicates an organized, concerted attack controlled by intelligence. If there is no local weapons technology, it was not the result of a civil war, but rather the attack of an outside force."

I paused and watched the table for a few more moments.

"The extent of the damage would indicate a mechanized attack; however, there are signs that this assumption would not explain. Here is a building with the front partially ripped off. I say specifically ripped off rather than blown off. Notice the machinery in the interior of this room remains undisturbed, which would indicate the absence of an explosion. The portion of machinery toward the front, apparently of similar design and material as that in the rear, has been sheared off even with the breach in the wall. From this I would conclude that the limited extent of the damage is due not to the nature of the machinery, but rather the limited, nonexplosive, nonchemical nature of the attack."

I took over control of the table to enlarge a specific portion of the view.

"The key thing to note is the nature of the breach. As I said, the fact that this portion of the wall was ripped out would indicate a mechanical attack, yet the scars on the wall resemble those marks left by the jaws of a beast rather than a machine."

I raised my head to address him directly.

"My conclusions from what I have observed would then be that a city built and operated by beings of advanced technological knowledge but no concept of violence was attacked and destroyed by a group of intelligent beings who were either in the form of, or built their war machines in the form of, giant, powerful beasts. To extrapolate on that conclusion, such an attacking force is, first, extremely powerful, and second, willing and able to use that power ruthlessly against a culture which was not threatening them. Such a force could constitute a serious threat to the existence of our Empire. It would therefore be my military recommendation that Top Priority be given to averting any possibility of attack by such a force, specifically by hunting it down and destroying it completely."

My analysis and recommendation did not seem to surprise him.

"Your opinions are noted and logged, Rahm. Your analysis coincides with the preliminary analysis submitted to the High Command. The probability of a Major War is high enough that you are asked to stop at the breeding chambers before returning to your sleep. As always, time is the key factor. Let us hope the Enemy grants us enough time to gather and analyze information and to prepare our Armies before battle is joined."

I turned to go, as the business at hand seemed to have been completed, but he raised a restraining hand.

"Before you go, Rahm, there is one additional point I would like to discuss with you. As it is of a personal nature, quite apart from the official orders bringing you here, you're not required to remain."

I was in no hurry; besides which, this massive scientist had piqued even my lax curiosity. Personal conversations were rare between Tzen; between castes, practically unheard of. I gestured for him to continue.

"As my part in this current survey of analyses and opinions, I have interviewed many of the Warrior caste. Curiosity has prompted me to look into their military records in an effort to determine why these specific Warriors were chosen to be polled. From what I have found in your and other records, confirmed by having met you personally, I have extrapolated that you will soon be advanced in rank. Should that come to pass, I would request that I be allowed to serve under you in the upcoming war."

His position took me aback, though I tried not to show it. Intercaste pride is such that one makes an extra effort to not be unsettled by a member of another caste.

"As your request hinges on the accuracy of your extrapolation, I would inquire as to the progression of your logic before replying."

"In any war, additional officers are needed. The High Command invariably reviews the records of combat veterans before considering any new Warriors for appointment. Not only is your service record exemplary, it displays many of the specific traits the High Command looks for in its officers. Realizing this, it is only logical that the probability is high that you will receive your appointment prior to the impending war."

"And what do you envision these officers' traits to be?"

"The major one is careful attention to those around them, a conscious plotting of attitudes and behavior patterns and the extrapolation of future behavior. In this regard, they are not unlike the Scientists' caste, which is why I am able to note the process so accurately."

"However, I fear you are drawing the wrong conclusions," I corrected him. "That particular trait is common among the officers because it is common among all veteran Warriors. It is contributory to our survival to be aware of our teammates."

He rose and began to pace as he replied.

"But all Warriors do not measure each other on the same scale. This is because they are putting the resulting data to different uses. It is difficult for me to explain to you, Rahm, because it is such a fine line you have crossed that you assume that others have done the same. Consider it in this way: others view each other with a positive-negative judgment. That is, as they look at another Warrior, they ask themselves,

Is this Warrior efficient or not? Will he be dangerous to me if I accept a post next to him on the battle line? You and others like you who are either officers or officer material do not make positive-negative judgments. You observe another's strengths and weaknesses and adjust your actions accordingly. If you were currently in an officer position, it would mean that rather than rejecting a Warrior from service under you, that you would simply place him in a position on the team which would utilize his strengths and guard his weaknesses. That is what the High Command is looking for, officers who take what's given them for personnel and make it work, not Warriors who would waste everyone's time picking and choosing, looking for a perfect team."

I needed time to think that premise through, for both its accuracy and its applicability to me, so I changed to another line of questioning.

"Returning to your own situation, why would a Scientist want to go along to the Wars, or more specifically, why would an officer want to take the burden of accepting a Scientist on his team?"

"I did not express myself clearly. I do not wish to serve under you as a Scientist, but as a Warrior. My progress in the Scientist caste has slowed to immobility, and my superiors have suggested to me with increasing frequency that I could perhaps better serve the Empire in another caste. If this is to be the case, my personal choice for an alternate career is the Warrior caste."

Though I tried to suppress my outrage at the implications in his statement, my next question came out more terse than I would have liked.

"Then you feel that the Warrior's path is easier to follow than the Scientist's?"

"For me it is. Do not misunderstand me. I am not attempting to depreciate the difficulty of the Warriors' caste. However, for me fighting has always been easy, too easy. That's why I entered the Scientists' caste. With my build, it was no great achievement to run faster or hit harder than the others in training. It required no effort, so I had no feeling of serving the Empire. Having failed as a Scientist, however, it is time for me to swallow my personal feelings and preferences and serve the Empire in the capacity I am most suited for, specifically as a Warrior."

"So you turn to me with my lack of positive-negative judgment, expecting me to somehow make special allowances for you?"

"Not at all. I expect to carry my full weight as a team member. However, I would hope to find a commander who did not hold my non-Warrior background against me, but rather would use my supplemental knowledge and abilities to best advantage. I ask no more than any Tzen, and that is the chance to be efficient, to make maximum use of all my abilities."

I was finding his logic difficult to grasp.

"But by your definition any officer would do this. Why make this request specifically to me?" I asked.

"In theory that is the case. In actuality the lack of positive-negative judgment frequently only applies within the Warrior caste. Many of your fellow Warriors, while cognizant of the value of the other castes and therefore rendering proper respect, maintain an aloof, patronizing, almost disdainful air when dealing with those outside their own caste. Not that this trait is exclusive to the Warriors; the other castes also display it, including the Scientists. I find it particularly distressing in Warriors because that is the caste I wish to enter. I have not sensed that disdain in my talk with you and as such have requested service under you. Not because I expect special consideration, but because I expect you would use me as fully as you would use any of your caste-raised Warriors."

I thought about his proposal for several moments, then turned to go.

"Your proposal is not disagreeable to me. If the predicted promotion indeed comes to pass, I will accept your service."

I paused in the doorway.

"What is your name, Scientist?"

"Zur," he replied.

Zur it was, and his service has proved to be as true as his prediction of my promotion. Not only had he not given me any cause to regret my choice, his abilities had prompted me to name him my second-in-command, a move none of the other teammates seemed displeased with, even Ssah.

"Commander!" Zur's voice interrupted my reverie.

"What is it, Zur?"

"Could you come here for a moment? I have discovered something in my dissection you should be made aware of."

So much for after-eating relaxation. I rose and moved to join him.

Chapter Eight

The onslaught of cold weather brought a period of inactivity to the team. I ordered the majority of them to go into Deep Sleep until the advent of spring. Even though our standard survival kits contained drugs by which we could counteract our bodies' natural reactions to extreme temperatures, I saw no need to use them. Activity among the Leapers had ceased as they either moved to hibernate or expired in the encroaching cold. As there was no data to be gathered in their absence, and as we lacked both the personnel and the equipment to exterminate them as they slept, it was only logical that we take advantage of the slack time for some much-needed rest.

Zur and I remained awake longer than the others. Kor also maintained consciousness, but that was as first watch on the tunnel entrance. Zur and I were conferring, both to organize and analyze the data we had accumulated so far on the Leapers, and to increase my own knowledge of the data already accumulated by the Empire.

I make no apologies for the limited information I possessed when originally undertaking this mission. There had been much to learn and relatively little time to learn it in. Following the discovery of the mined city and the subsequent inference of the existence of the Coalition of Insects, the full might of the Empire's Scientist and

Technician castes had swung into action as the Warriors slept. Every effort had been expended to decipher the language of Builders—or the First Ones, as they came to be referred to—and in turn, in using that language as a key to unlock the secrets of their history and technology. This process was not new to us. As has been noted, it was not the first time the Tzen had encountered an intelligent, technically advanced race.

Investigating the First Ones brought an incredible wealth of new information into the coffers of the Tzen. It is difficult to determine which was more fantastic to us—their technology, which allowed them to travel and colonize the Starlanes, or the fact that they had no concept of War or violence. Realizing the latter, however, we found it easy to see how they came to the abrupt end that they did.

Even before pushing out into the reaches of space, simply from our race's history in the Black Swamp of our home Planet, the Tzen have learned a basic principle of survival: not to take anything, not to build anything, unless you can defend it. Whatever you have, whether it be a source for water or the blood in your veins, there is bound to be someone or something else that wants it, and the only thing stopping the Enemy from taking it is you.

The First Ones apparently never learned this lesson. Whether they thought that nothing wanted what they had, or that others would be content with sharing, was never determined. However, when they first encountered the Insects and detected intelligence, the First Ones attempted to share their knowledge with them. They taught the Insects about the Starlanes and the vast number of inhabitable worlds in the universe to demonstrate that there was no need for territorial-food wars. They even showed the Insects how to operate some of the cruder interstellar transports to make these new worlds available to them.

The Insects worked on a much simpler logic process. Being a population-sensitive culture, they felt there would never be enough worlds for everyone. Realizing this, they could only view the First Ones as potential competitors for the inhabitable worlds. Following this logic, they used the ships the First Ones gave them along with the knowledge of the locations of the other colonies and launched an attack, an attack that brought the First Ones and their culture to an abrupt end. Then, having eliminated the known competition, the Insects pulled back to their home system, expanding out slowly as the population pressures dictated. This process had continued uninterrupted until the rise of the Tzen.

The First Ones were the Technicians, and the Insects the first Conquerors, but the Tzen were the first Warriors. Our victories had never hinged on the helplessness of our opponents. Therefore, unlike the Insects, we did not shun the technology left behind by the First Ones. Although they had not developed any instruments of War, many of their inventions and discoveries were readily adaptable to that purpose.

Having long since realized that any discovery has the double capacity of creation or destruction, our Scientists and Technicians applied themselves to finding combative uses for the First Ones' technology until we were ready to do battle with the Insects—their vast numbers versus our weapons and military experience.

The period of preparation, once the Warriors were awakened, was both rushed and crowded. Like most of the Warriors, I had realized the urgency of our training and had focused most of my concentration on the specific tools of our caste, such as the flyers and the new weapons, covering the balance of the vast storehouses of knowledge suddenly at our disposal with a minimal skim and a glance.

In our current predicament, however, I found increasing need for the information I had so lightly passed over, and was immensely grateful for the presence of Zur and his library of information discs. I occasionally encountered difficulty keeping him from digressing into more detail than I deemed necessary; but even restricting the scope of our studies, I was astounded at the length of time required to cover the necessary material. As the days and weeks marched on, my respect for Zur grew. While I had always regarded him highly as a Warrior, this increased awareness of these seldom-glimpsed depths of his talents surpassed even my stringent requirements of effectiveness.

I commented on this to him once as we paused in our studies to eat and rest, reclining on the ground. Even in his after-feeding lethargy, his thoughts were quick and concise as he replied.

"There is a balance at work here, Commander, which at times I think you overlook. Knowledge is a powerful weapon, but only if it is used. Had the Coalition of Insects utilized the knowledge of the First Ones as we have, it is doubtful we would be here today. The Tzen are effective not because we have knowledge, but because we use it. The Scientists seek and organize the knowledge, the Technicians render it usable, and the Warriors apply it. On a smaller scale, my information would be of little value if you as the Commander were unwilling to benefit from it. As I pointed out when we first met, I feel there are many officers who would be reluctant to take advantage of my assistance."

"I must disagree with you, Zur. I do not feel I am that unusual as an officer. In all phases of our training we rely heavily on the Scientists and Technicians. Why should it be any different in the field?"

"Why indeed? Perhaps some notion that once in the field, none know combat as well as a Warrior and information is something best left for the classrooms. I do not say that no other Commander would listen, but how many would listen as readily or for that matter seek out my advice?"

"I would like to believe the majority of officers would," I insisted. "If not, we are being less than efficient in our ways of waging war."

"Perhaps you are right. Commander," he conceded. "I will readily admit that like your appreciation of the Scientists' caste, my own appreciation of the Warrior caste, particularly their officers, has grown significantly on this mission. There have been many small things I was previously unaware of, Kor's development as an example."

"What about Kor's development?"

"I assume you are aware that she now has definite opinions about each of her teammates. I assume this knowledge on your part because even if she has not reported her opinions to you, you were instrumental in her forming them."

I raised my head to look at him severely.

"It is a characteristic that any veteran Warrior has definite opinions about his or her teammates. Many consider it vital to their own survival," I said carefully.

"I am aware of that, Commander. That is why I specifically refer to it as development on Kor's part. I merely suggest that she may have had outside assistance in this phase of her development which enabled her to progress much more rapidly than might normally be expected."

"If you are observant enough to have noted that, then you have also noted that it is Ahk that she spends most of her off-duty time with," I pointed out. "Realizing that he has more combat experience than anyone on the team including myself, I should think it obvious that if anyone is advising her in her development, it is he."

"Agreed, Commander. However, I have also noted that you were the one who encouraged him to take an interest in Kor's development."

"Surely you are aware, Zur, that no Tzen Commander can order a Warrior to share his knowledge and experience with another."

"Indeed I am, Commander. What I had not been aware of prior to this mission was the possibility of informally convincing a veteran Warrior that it is in his own best survival interest to advise another less-experienced Tzen in the finer points of field survival."

I was silent for a few moments, then reclined again, lowering my head to the ground.

"I would be inefficient as a Commander if I did not strive to obtain maximum effectiveness from each Warrior in my command regardless of methods."

"That is what I am learning, Rahm. This is also why I do not regret having aligned myself with your command."

Chapter Nine

I have never felt as helpless as a Warrior, much less as a Commander, as when I was forced to idly watch while Ahk died.

It was early spring, and the activity level of the Leapers was unknown. That lack of knowledge was what prompted me to wake Ssah and Ahk from Deep Sleep. We needed to send out scouts to determine if the Leapers were active in sufficient quantities to justify waking the rest of the team.

The two of them had gone out with the usual strict orders to avoid contact with the Enemy, while I remained behind as entrance guard. They headed out shortly before dawn to minimize the possibility of chance encounter, as the Leapers seldom moved about until several hours into daylight.

While remaining motionless as entrance guard for long hours, there is little to do except think. Ironically, my thoughts that day were on how well our team had survived under adverse conditions. We had survived the shutout and ensuing crash landing, and although only six in number, had held out for almost a year in Enemy-infested terrain. Not only had held out, but had gathered valuable information for the Empire, and had done it without losing a team member.

It occurred to me to ask Zur to set aside one of his blank

information discs for me to record my notes as Commander. In addition to information on the Enemy, there were valuable lessons to be learned here about survival tactics. To that end, I set about mentally organizing my thoughts on how I had led the team in the period since our landing, the methods of utilizing the strengths of each individual on the team, the points I would change, the items I would leave intact . . .

My thoughts were interrupted by the death cry of a Leaper. I snapped my senses back into focus and listened intently, but heard nothing more.

I was surprised to note it was nearly sundown. While I had been watching the terrain unblinkingly the entire day, my thoughts had been so intense I had failed to notice the passage of time. It was time for the scouts to return.

Another shriek sounded. I was fully alert now. The source of the sound was out of my line of vision, somewhere beyond the hills that hid our cavern, somewhere in the vicinity of the forest line where Ssah and Ahk were. The Leaper activities corresponding with the time of the scouts' return could not be coincidental. We had trouble.

"Zur . . . Zur . . . Zur . . . Zur . . ." I beamed desperately into the cavern behind me.

It took a distressingly long time to arouse him.

"Zur here!" came the weak response finally.

"Trouble on the forest line . . . Possibly our scouts . . . Going to check it . . . Rouse the others and stand by."

As I beamed the last part of my orders, I was on my feet and running. As I plunged down the slope of the first hill, another scream split the air. I redoubled my speed, laboring uphill, then plunging into the next valley.

Suddenly my training returned to me. This wouldn't do. Dashing around blindly and recklessly in a crisis situation is the action of a panicky, soon-to-be-extinct, non-intelligent species, not a Tzen Warrior. I forced myself to a halt, clenching my fists as another shriek sounded. I needed information—information to relay back to the rest of the team and to govern my own actions.

I turned and hurled myself back up the slope I had so recently descended. A rock formation jutted up into the sky on this ridge, one we had occasionally used as a lookout post. It would serve me now.

I clawed my way up onto one of the ledges and flattened, scanning the distant forest line. I caught a faint movement and forced focus, accepting the inevitable headache for the advantage of temporary telescopic vision.

It was Ahk. I glimpsed him briefly as he crouched breathless at the foot of a tree, spring-javelin in one hand, flexi-steel whip in the other. Then he disappeared, darting around the tree trunk as a Leaper in midleap struck the spot he had so recently vacated. The insect backed up, momentarily stunned by the impact. Before it could recover, Ahk was back in sight. His whip flashed twice in the setting sun, and the Insect heeled over, two of its legs missing. Ahk was running again, along the tree line. Knowing the Leapers would outdistance him in open terrain, he was using his maneuverability to best advantage. There were several twitching carcasses in view giving mute testimony to the effectiveness of his tactic. It must have been their death throes that had alerted me to the situation.

I wondered why he did not simply duck into the forest to elude his pursuers. There were eight of them that I could see, a small pack, maneuvering to cut him off. Suddenly he dove flat as another Leaper bounded over his prostrate body from the shadows of the forest. That's why he was working the tree line! The Leapers were entering the forest now!

He rose to one knee and hurled his spring-javelin at the Leaper that had just threatened him, pinning it to the ground.

Suddenly he was down, another Leaper landing on him from behind as he threw.

I tensed, sending a sudden stab of pain through my straining eyes. Then the Insect was flipped backward, and Ahk was on his feet again. For a moment I was at a loss; then I realized what he had done. He had triggered another spring-javelin while under the creature, using the force of the ends telescoping out to push the Leaper up and off him.

He was running again, stumbling now, as two more Leapers crawled into view from the forest's depths. How many were there? Where was Ssah?

I started to look for her, but had my attention wrenched back to the action. A Leaper caught Ahk as he turned to change directions, closing its mighty jaws around his waist and lifting him into the air. He dropped the javelin and his hand went to the small of his back, and the Insect fell away, rolling in agony. The acid belt!

He was moving again, but now was in visible pain. There were terrible wounds in his sides from the Leaper's attack, and they slowed his movement. The other Leapers also saw it, and redoubled their efforts to catch him.

Casting about desperately, Ahk tried one last desperate move. The whip darted out again, but this time not at the Insects. His target was a low-hanging tree limb jutting above him. The whip wrapped around the limb and held. In a flash he was up, pulling his weight upwards with the strength of his arms.

Too late! One of the Leapers caught his legs, tugging mightily to pull him back to the ground. He tried to raise the additional weight, then let go with one hand, groping for another weapon. Another Leaper clambered up its comrade's body and fastened its jaws around the Warrior's neck. Ahk jerked once, then his head toppled off, severed completely from the body. The body clung to the whip for a moment, then fell heavily into the gathered pack below.

I did not watch the pack devouring its victim. I was looking beyond them. As I followed Ahk's upward progress, I had seen something else.

I saw Ssah crouched in a tree some ten meters beyond the action. More importantly, I saw the unfired hand-burner in her hand.

Chapter Ten

There were three of us moving through the predawn gloom. Kor, Zur, and myself were undertaking this assignment, leaving Ssah and Mahz behind on entrance guard.

This allotment of duty stations was not random. Combat was a certainty on this mission, and that would require cooperation and confidence in the unit to engage with the enemy. Both Zur and Kor had separately requested that I not assign them to a mission with Ssah, and I will admit to a certain reluctance on my part to rely on her. In fact, of the entire team, only Mahz maintained any contact with her beyond what was required for assigned duties. Unfortunately, this resulted in Mahz being avoided as much as Ssah was.

The team members' opinions of Ssah, while never high, had degenerated to an all-time low after Ahk's death. In fact, things had reached a point where I had to overstep my authority as Commander and outlaw dueling for the duration of our stay on the planet. This order understandably caused a great uproar of protest among the team members, including Ssah and Mahz, but I stood firm on my decision. A duel now, regardless of who was involved or what the outcome was, would weaken the team, and we couldn't afford to lose another member. Instead, I reminded them that although they had a

Warrior's right to protest my order, it was still a direct order in a Combat Zone. As such, while they could press charges with my Superior once the mission was over and we had rejoined the Empire, for the time being they were to follow my orders to the letter. If any member chose to defy a direct order under these conditions, I could level whatever punishment I felt necessary, up to and including death, without benefit of a trial, and call on any other team member to assist me in enforcing that sentence. There is no known case of this regulation's being enforced in the entire history of the Warrior caste, but the rule was still on record should I need it.

It was perhaps a misapplication of regulations, which, if challenged, would give rise to a debate on interpretation of authority and order priority versus personal judgment. However, I felt that this in itself was just. A personal interpretation of regulations had gotten me into this situation; so, by the Black Swamps, a personal interpretation of regulations would get me out of it.

My interrogation of Ssah following Ahk's death had been one of the most frustrating and unsatisfying conversations of my career. I had not returned to the cavern after witnessing the incident, but instead waited in the foothills for her to appear. The first loss of a Tzen under my command and the physical strain of prolonged close-focus had combined to erode my mental state so that by the time she arrived, my mood was not good.

"Explain!" I demanded as levelly as I was able.

"Explain, Commander?"

"We have just lost a team member, Ssah. As Commander, I wish to know why, so that we might avoid similar occurrences in the future. You were on assignment with Ahk at the time of his death and are therefore the logical source for information regarding the 'incident.' Now explain!"

She still seemed puzzled, but launched into her story. "Ahk and I moved out this morning specifically assigned to scout Leaper activity. We roamed several sectors, but by the close of the day had detected no activity, either individual or group. We were returning to the cavern when we heard the sounds of a pack of Leapers approaching rapidly from behind. As we were under strict orders to avoid contact with the Enemy, we attempted to escape notice by seeking refuge in some overhanging branches. Whether his foot slipped in the soft soil as he leaped or he simply misjudged the distance, I don't know; but Ahk missed his first jump. Before he could jump again, the first of the Leapers burst into view and spotted him. Rather than betray my position, he chose to attempt to elude his pursuers in a running fight. His efforts failed, and after the Leapers left the area, I climbed down and proceeded back to the cavern. Before I could reach the cavern, you approached and engaged me in this rather unconventional debriefing."

I stared at her in silence until she began to cock her head quizzically.

"Is your hand-burner functional?"

"Yes."

"Then why didn't you provide cover fire for Ahk when he was caught by the Leapers?"

"It would have been against direct orders."

"What orders?"

She cocked her head in question again. "Your orders, Commander. Before we left you gave us specific orders to avoid contact with the Enemy and to enter into combat only in self-defense. I was not threatened in that situation, so to open fire would have been in direct disobedience of your orders."

I considered this for several moments before continuing with my questioning.

"Are you then claiming that had I not issued orders against contact with the Enemy that you would have given Ahk supporting fire?"

She paused for thought before answering. "No. I still would have withheld fire."

"Explain."

"It has become quite apparent since our landing that the hand-burners could be a decisive factor in any battle with the Leapers. Realizing this, I could not justify depleting the power of my burner to benefit any single individual. Rather, I would feel obligated to preserve its power in lieu of a situation critical to the entire team. Secondly, priority had to be given to getting the report of our scouting mission back to the team. Entering into needless combat could have jeopardized the delivery of that report."

"But your report was of no activity, a fact which was proven invalid by the Leaper's attack."

"On the contrary, Commander. The attack gave us something to report. By my inaction, I have survived to report definite Leaper activity in the area."

The debriefing was getting circular, but I pressed on.

"To clarify something you said earlier, you claim you withheld fire to conserve the power charge. Isn't it true, however, that the Leaper pack was small enough in number that you could have eliminated them with minimal drain to your burner?"

"True, Commander, but they were so scattered during the battle that it was impossible to estimate their number until they closed in to feed on Ahk's body. At that time, with Ahk already dead and my presence undetected, it would have been foolish to waste power by entering into combat."

I sank into silence once again, but she continued.

"If I might add some unsolicited comments to the debriefing, Commander, your attitude on this matter puzzles me. You have constantly criticized me for taking reckless and independent action. Your only advice to me has been to try to become more team-oriented and less indulgent of my own desires and motivations. In this situation, however, when I have acted strictly by your orders and in the best interests of the team, you act more as if you were interrogating a criminal than like a Commander debriefing a Warrior. I cannot help but question whether you are asking pertinent questions seeking information, or if you are groping about for someone else on whom to blame your own incompetence as a Commander."

It was at this point that I decided we could not afford a duel, though the frequency with which I review my decision leads me to believe I am not particularly pleased with the conclusions.

However, now it was time to turn my thoughts to the mission at hand. Even though I acknowledged its necessity, I did not relish the thought of what it entailed. We had accumulated an impressive bulk of data on the Leapers. We were now familiar with their anatomy, breeding habits, life-cycle, and diet. There was still one bit of information missing that would be invaluable to the Empire, and that was what we were seeking today. This mission was to appraise the Leapers' military ability.

To date, we had witnessed only one tactic employed by the Insects in hunting or fighting. So far, all they had done was rush their victim, relying on their mobility, power, and strength of numbers to overwhelm any opposition. What we wanted to test was whether they could devise and execute an alternate plan given proper conditions.

Even though the sun still had not risen, I decided there was ample light for our final briefing. I signaled a halt, and the other two gathered about me. I squatted, cleared a space on the ground in front of me, and started scratching diagrams with my claw as I spoke.

"I want to take this opportunity to review our plan once more to be sure there is no confusion. The plan as stated involves danger enough without running the added risk of uncoordinated execution."

They studied the diagram intently.

"Some distance ahead is the river. The key point is, of course, the shallows."

I tapped the indicated position.

"Zur and I will wait there while Kor proceeds upstream a minimum of one thousand meters. At that point she will attempt to attract the attention of a pack of Leapers. Once she is spotted, she will evade them by retreating into the river and moving downstream."

I again indicated the point on my ground sketch.

"We know that the river between there and the shallows is both too deep to afford the Leapers footing and too wide for them to attempt attacking from the bank. The critical question is, Will the Leapers simply follow along the bank, or will they actually divide their forces and send a portion of their numbers ahead to the shallows? If they—"

"Commander!"

I was interrupted by a telepathed thought from Kor. I looked at her questioningly.

"Continue gesturing at the ground sketch," she continued to beam, "but unobtrusively scan the terrain around us."

I did, and saw the cause of her concern. In an unusual display of predawn activity, there were Leapers quietly creeping into view out of the shadows around us. Both from their stealth and from the focus of their motion, it was apparent that not only had we been spotted, but we were the object of their ambush.

Chapter Eleven

With the suddenness of a serpent's strike the situation had changed. We were the hunted, not the hunters.

Later I would look back on the reactions of my teammates with admiration and appreciation. They did not panic either physically or mentally. Not so much as an angry lash of a tail marred their performance as they waited. They didn't rail or beleaguer me with questions, but instead gave me several much-needed moments of silence in which to formulate our plans. Later I would remember, but now my mind was preoccupied, appraising our situation.

What at first glance seemed like more than a hundred Leapers on closer scrutiny proved to be fewer than fifty, still more than enough to make the situation desperate, but perhaps one not quite as hopeless as the first appraisal had indicated.

In many ways it was fortunate that the Leapers had chosen this expedition to ambush. As I noted earlier, we were expecting combat on this mission. As such, we were prepared both in armor, and more importantly, in frame of mind, for a fight. Therefore, the only real change necessary would be to adapt our tactics to the terrain chosen by the Enemy for the battle. It had been stressed frequently in our training as Warriors that the day that Tzen couldn't adapt to the

245

Enemy's terrain would be the day the Empire crumbled. It seemed we were to have the opportunity to test that axiom. I studied the terrain carefully.

We were on the downslope of the last foothill of our range, crouched in an area of open grassland dotted by large clumps of brush. About one hundred meters to our left the brush gave out, yielding to an open grassland. Two hundred meters ahead was the tree line that lined the river below the shallows, which was our original destination. To our right, the brush-dotted grassland continued, marred by only one notable geographic feature: The crest of the hill we were descending rose sharply to our right, almost trebling in height; and instead of a gentle slope, slide activity had exposed a steep sand-and-gravel cliff face.

The trees by the river would be our best chance for safety, so of course there is where the Enemy had allotted their greatest strength, fully half their force. The balance of the force was divided roughly equally, with half forming a line in the grasslands to our right, and the other half silently creeping down the slope behind us.

Any questions we had about their military aptitude were answered by that formation. We could read their plan in the patterns. They definitely did not want us to reach the river, and assuming we survived the initial clash, had aligned their troops to drive us to our right, out onto the open grassland. Once there, their superior mobility on open terrain would bring the affair to a rapid close. It was slightly ironic that we had walked into this ambush while on a mission to test if they had the intelligence to head off an escaping fugitive.

I reached my decision.

"Follow my lead," I beamed to my teammates. "Move as if we hadn't seen them, but ready your weapons."

With that, I rose and began walking to the right, paralleling the tree line. Zur and Kor followed, ambling along with such exaggerated laxness that I feared it would betray our plan. Although Tzen favor a surprise attack, we are not a deceitful race. As such, I was afraid our clumsy theatrical efforts would be immediately transparent.

It seemed my fears were groundless. The Leapers did not immediately charge or in any other way indicate they suspected their prey had been alerted. Perhaps they are even less deceitful than we are.

However, our feint was not having the desired effect. I had hoped that as we moved deeper into their trap they would shift some of their force from blocking the river to seal the trap, encircling us completely. If enough moved, it might weaken the wing at the tree line sufficiently for us to suddenly punch through their line to the river. Unfortunately the force by the river didn't budge.

My teammates were as ready as they would ever be. Zur had unlimbered the alter-mace and was idly snapping the heads off flowers as we passed. Kor was rolling one of her steel balls up and down on the blade of a wedge-sword as she walked and making it look easy.

It would be foolhardy to try for the trees with the Leapers in their current arrangement. The blocking force would simply move forward and engage us in the open, allowing the other two wings to close on us in an area with no cover. We would have to do this the hard way.

I leisurely removed the coiled flexi-whip from my shoulder. Actually, I shouldn't call it a flexi-whip, since it had been modified. I had affixed one of Kor's steel balls to its tip, the weight of which, combined with the whip's lashing action, could pulverize rock. It wasn't a flexi-whip anymore, it was a Bug-killer.

"Subtlety does not seem to be working," I beamed at the team. "Break for the cliff on my count . . . ready . . . three . . . two . . ."

As a unit we wheeled and began jogging for the cliff. As we ran, we spread the formation slightly until there was space of about two and a half meters between us to ensure weapons room, and we held at that distance. It is neither a fast-moving nor an impressive formation, but once set in motion it doesn't stop for anything. Though it is not a particularly terrifying sight, few have stood in the path of a jogging formation of armed Tzen and survived.

For a few precious moments there was no activity in the Enemy ranks. Apparently they were having difficulty comprehending that we had seen them and were charging them head-on. Then a series of chirps and squeals went up behind us, and the Leapers moved into action.

There were roughly a dozen of the Enemy between us and the cliff. Normally we could have dealt with them with ease, but by turning our heads slightly as we ran we could see the bulk of the pack closing rapidly on us from behind. The Leapers in our path would have to be dealt with swiftly if we were to survive.

I drew my hand-burner. The charge remaining had been too weak to assist Ahk, but at short range it might save us today. A Leaper bounded over a bush at Zur, who smashed its head with the alter-mace. It died with a shriek and battle was joined.

Three Leapers appeared in my path. I burned the second, caught the leader with the Bug-killer, and burned the third in midair. A spring-javelin flashed past me and out of sight behind a bush. As I passed it, I saw a Leaper that had been waiting in hiding pinned and writhing.

One appeared a scant two meters in front of me, seeming to pop out of the ground. I burned it and leaped over the body. My leap carried me into an unseen dip, and into the midst of three more. I burned one and clubbed another out of the air in front of me with the butt of the whip, but the third sank its jaws into my blaster arm and clung there. I tried to keep running and pull my arm free, but was slowly being dragged to a halt when Kor appeared, smashing the Leaper's head from behind with her armored fist while severing its jaws with her wedge-sword. It was painful, but I managed to twist the burner around and catch another that was crawling over the edge of the dip.

Then we were free and running again. The cliff face was only a few more meters ahead, but we could see a group of two Leapers waiting there for us. The pack was almost upon us now.

"Kor! Clear the cliff, Zur, with me . . . turn!"

My second-in-command and I whirled and faced the charging pack as Kor continued on. We backed slowly toward the cliff as we fought, confident that Kor would have disposed of the last two by the time we got there.

"Clear, Commander!"

We dashed the last two meters and turned. With Zur on my left, Kor on my right, and a cliff at my back, I lowered my head and hissed in the face of the Enemy.

For a moment they hesitated, then surged forward in a wave. We weren't running now, and the bodies began to stack around us.

I draped the Bug-killer over my shoulder as I burned a Leaper, opened a spring-javelin and pinned a second, then caught a third as I snatched the Bug-killer from my shoulder again. I saw one go down to one of Zur's acid darts and another to one of Kor's thrown steel balls as I took two more with the Bug-killer.

"Caught!" came Zur's calm voice from my left.

I turned and saw him struggling in a tug of war with a Leaper for his alter-mace as he tried to keep two others at bay with his dart-thrower.

"Covered!" I called as I burned the Leaper that was clinging to his mace.

Suddenly I felt jaws clamp on my calf. A Leaper I thought dead had inched forward and attached itself to my leg. I started to burn it, but had to avert my shot to pick another target out of midair. Before I could recover, the Leaper that had my leg rolled, causing me to fall and lose my balance.

"Caught!" I said.

"Covered!" came a voice, and Kor was there. She chopped at the Leaper with her wedge-sword. Straightening quickly, she backhanded another out of the air as I shot between her legs to burn a third, which was creeping into her vacated position.

I forced myself to my feet as the battle continued.

The hand-burner finally gave out, leaving me barely enough time to snatch and open a spring-javelin and bat a leaping Enemy to one side. A throw to pin it, and I was ready again, Bug-killer in one hand and wedge-sword in the other.

There was a lull in the action as the Enemy fell back. I was both tired and puzzled. Either I had completely lost my feel for combat, or there were more Leapers than I had originally counted. I scanned the terrain.

There was another small pack of Leapers emerging from the tree line and still another pack visible in the distant grassland. All were heading in our direction. Apparently either Leaper communication or the sound of our battle was drawing reinforcements into the area.

"Weapons status check," I beamed.

"Eight . . . no . . . seven acid darts left," Zur corrected himself as he picked off another Leaper that was starting to creep close.

I noticed he was bleeding steadily from an ugly gash on his upper arm, and suddenly realized all three of us were suffering wounds. My calf wound began to throb, but I ignored it, opening a spring-javelin to meet a Leaper who was crouching to attack.

Before I could throw, the beam of a hand-burner darted from the crest of the cliff behind us, finishing the Leaper and in rapid succession several others. The ranks of Enemy surrounding us gave ground as the beam lanced out again and again.

I didn't have to look. It was Ssah.

Chapter Twelve

The reappearance of the Empire fleets did not come as a surprise. We had spotted their scout flyers with increasing regularity and realized invasion was imminent. Accordingly, we began to make our preparations.

Our flyers were light enough to be carried easily by two, but that was on level ground. Unfortunately, they were not designed for a takeoff, but rather required a drop or launch to become airborne. As such, it was necessary to carry or hoist them to a higher level of the cavern. By the time our task was complete and five flyers were balanced precariously on the lip of a ledge near the ceiling of the cavern, I had had more than one occasion to question the wisdom of my decision to use the flyers again.

It was our speculation that all or part of the force would be surface troops, roaming the grasslands on foot, hunting the Leaper packs. It would be an easy matter to join up with these forces without freeing our flyers. Still, I reasoned that we could be of greater service acting as air cover for the troops. The Wasps had long since died out, and I wanted to take advantage of the air supremacy that we had fought so hard for. Then again, there was always the chance our speculations would turn out to be wrong. I had no desire to be stranded here again because we had been too lazy to arrange our own transport.

Another major portion of our time was occupied in releasing the warm-bloods we had kept penned for food. This turned out to be a greater task than we had originally planned. We had known it would be necessary to take them some distance from the cavern before releasing them to avoid luring Leapers into the area with a sudden abundance of game. What we had not counted on was the warm-bloods' reluctance to depart. Apparently they preferred to be penned and fed to having to wander and forage, and resented our attempts to return them to their natural situation. They persisted in attempting to follow us back to the cavern, even when pelted with rocks. In fact, some of them were so stubborn that they would hide themselves and attempt to follow at a distance unnoticed. They were quite crafty at this tactic, and it was not uncommon for a Tzen on a release assignment to arrive back at the cavern with more warm-bloods than he had left with.

They became such a nuisance that we seriously discussed the possibility of killing them, a rare solution for a race such as ourselves, which only kills for food or defense and occasionally for honor. We considered the possibility and discarded it. We were Tzen. We did not kill simply because something annoyed us. Another solution would have to be found.

Before the elusive solution was discovered, the fleet arrived.

I was guarding the entrance at the time of their arrival. I had never viewed one of our attacks from the defender's viewpoint before and was impressed by its suddenness. One moment the view was clear and serene, and the next the air was filled with flyers. There was no warning, no opportunity to watch the formations approach; they were suddenly there, crowding the sky with their numbers.

There were swarms of the single flyers such as we used, but my attention was held by the huge flyers of a design unfamiliar to me. As I viewed them, I noticed streams of what looked like clear balls being dropped as they swooped low over the grasslands. Curiosity made me force-focus my eyes on these balls as they fell. The increased magnification of force-focus revealed a Tzen Warrior encased in each ball as it plunged downward. Apparently the ball was composed of a substance not unlike the gel-cushion of our fliers, and this was a new method of dropping surface teams.

I scanned the immediate vicinity one last time and retreated into the cavern again.

"Load your flyers," I announced to the team.

They needed no further explanation. As I said, we had been expecting the fleet's arrival. I joined them as they quietly gathered their personal gear and began their climb to the flyers.

Before entering my flyer, I paused to scan the cavern a final time. The last of the warm-bloods had long since been released and the pens dismantled. There was no trace remaining of our garrison.

I suddenly realized the others were already sealed in their flyers and waiting for me.

"Open fire!" I beamed to them and entered my flyer.

Four hot-beams darted out simultaneously, and before their assault the wall of the cavern began to melt away. By the time I had sealed my flyer an opening had appeared, and sunlight began to stream into the cavern again. I added my weapon to the group effort. I deliberately allowed the filing to continue overlong, burning an exceptionally large opening. It had been a long time since any of us had flown, and it was doubtful we were up to precision maneuvers.

"Cease fire!"

We sat motionless for several long moments waiting for the rock to cool and until we were sure that any rockslides caused by our burning had run their course.

"One at a time . . . Wait until the flyer ahead of you has cleared the entrance before following!"

With that, I set the foot disc and trod down on it to start the engine. As I felt it begin to convert its power, I rocked my body forward in the flyer. It slid off the edge of the ledge and plunged toward the floor of the cavern. Immediately I began working the controls, and the wings spread, catching the air and changing my fall into a swooping climb. A few adjustments, and I was out in the sunlight.

I quickly took the flyer into a slow spiral climb and hovered over the entrance, waiting for the rest of the team to emerge. As they appeared one by one and climbed to join me, I felt a certain sense of accomplishment. Over a year on Enemy-held terrain and we survived with all equipment intact and only one member lost. Then I thought about Ahk and the feeling faded.

I was about to signal for a formation movement, then noticed there was another formation of flyers working in the near vicinity. I activated my flyer's intrusion beacon to advise them of our presence.

"Identify!" came the beamed thought from the other formation's Commander.

"Commander Rahm and survivors of the last attack on this planet. We request permission to join your command for the duration of this mission."

There was pause.

"Survivors from the last attack?"

"Confirmed."

"Then you have not been informed . . ."

There was another long pause.

"Clarify," I prompted.

"The Black Swamps have been destroyed!"

My mind reeled under the impact of the news. Shocked disbelief swept over me, followed closely by a dark rage. The Black Swamps!

We had all known that this might happen. It was for that reason we had relocated the Empire into the colony ships before entering into the War. Still, the reality was a crushing blow. The Black Swamps! The Swamps were the point of origin of our race as well as our traditional burial grounds. We came from the Black Swamps and would return to the Black Swamps. It was part of our heritage, part of the Empire. Particularly with the new technology, it was one of the few stable elements of our culture. The Black Swamps! Destroyed!

A cold resolve settled over me. Before, we fought the Insects because we had to. Now it was a Blood Feud. We would do whatever we had to do, to destroy them. Completely.

I suddenly realized how long we had been hovering there inactive. The other Commander had maintained a respectful silence while we absorbed the shock of the news.

"Commander!" I beamed quietly.

"Yes?"

"We have gathered much data on the Enemy vital to the Empire and to this attack. Request permission for my second-in-command to rendezvous with the flagship as soon as possible to pass this information on for the Planetary Commander's consideration."

"Rahm," Zur's voice came to me. "I—"

"You'll follow the orders given you!" I snapped back, interrupting his protest. "Well, Commander?"

"Permission granted. I will relay the request and obtain data on an accelerated rendezvous point."

"I would further request permission to lead the balance of my force in attacking the Leapers."

"Also granted. Proceed at your own discretion."

"On my lead . . . Ready . . . three . . . two . . ."

We wheeled our flyers and dove on the grasslands.

I took them in low, dangerously low. We had to swerve around bushes as we ranged back and forth, pursuing and burning Leapers as we found them.

The Black Swamps destroyed! I signaled the team for another run. There was a frenzy to our attack above and beyond that displayed by the other teams. Unlike them, we knew we were working against a time limit. We wanted to kill as many of the hated Bugs as we could before Zur reached the flagship. We knew once our information reached the Planetary Commander, the mission would be aborted. By our analysis of the data we had gathered during our stay on the Planet, there was no chance that this type of attack would succeed against the Leapers.

Chapter Thirteen

". . . having a highly developed telescoping oviposition situated at the indicated point on the diagram."

The Planetary Commander paused as lights flashed on the Leaper anatomy diagram on the wall-sized viewscreen behind him.

We were in the main briefing room of the fleet's flagship. I and my teammates were arrayed along the walls at the front of the room on either side of the viewscreen, heroes on display. The Planetary Commander was completing an unenviable task, that of explaining to the Commanders of the fleet why the mission had been aborted so soon after its onset.

"In the absence of any evidence of egg beds or central nests, we had assumed that either the Leapers bore their offspring live, or that the eggs were carried internally until mature, so that they hatched soon after being laid. If this had been true, our plan of a surface attack to wipe out all existing Leapers would have been a viable tactic."

He paused to look at my team.

"The firsthand experience of Commander Rahm and his team has proved this assumption is incorrect. The Leapers lay their eggs singly and buried deep in the earth. The exact time required for an egg to mature and hatch is currently unknown, but it is far in excess of a year. There is even a possibility that they lay dormant until triggered by a specific telepathed command from an adult."

He looked directly at the assembled Commanders.

"This means that if we succeeded in eliminating every living Enemy, that the eggs would remain, hatching at unknown intervals over an indefinite period. The only current possibility for combatting this would be to establish a large standing garrison to constantly hunt the new hatchlings before they could lay more eggs. Even if this tactic could succeed, we are not equipped on this mission to establish such a garrison. As such, it is my decision as Planetary Commander to suspend action until such time as an effective plan can be formulated. This decision has been supported by the High Command, and orders to that effect are currently being relayed to the other fleets engaged in similar attacks.

"Finally, we are fortunate that our casualty estimates were for very light losses on this mission. Consequently, relatively few Tzen will have to be stranded on this planet. We will be able to leave them ample supplies and weapons to ensure their survival until our return. We have been assured by the High Command that space for them on the next return flight will be planned for, giving them a very high probability for rejoining the Empire."

He scanned the room slowly.

"Any questions?"

There were none. He turned to me.

"Are there any comments you would wish to add, Commander?"

I moved to take his place in front of the assembly.

"I would call the assembled Commanders' attention to the great assistance my second-in-command, Zur, rendered in the gathering of the data you have been given, as well as in the overall survival of the team. This was to a large part due to his earlier training in the Scientists' caste. I would suggest to the Commanders that they recall this in the future if their Warrior's pride prompts them to refuse the service of a Warrior who was not raised in the Warriors' caste. I will further be submitting a recommendation to High Command that the Warrior caste's training program be expanded to include rudimentary Scientist training, and that information discs containing data about the Enemy and the target planet be made a mandatory part of each Warrior's equipment when undertaking a mission."

I turned and looked at Ssah before continuing.

"Further, I would publicly commend the action of Ssah. Her rapid analysis and reaction to a specific situation saved the lives of half the team and ensured our survival to deliver our report to the Empire."

With that I turned to the Planetary Commander.

"I feel that with our participation in this meeting, our part of this mission is completed. At this point I wish to formally and publicly decry one of my team, specifically Ssah. Her lack of action, her failure to save a teammate in a fatal situation, her constant endangering of the team with her self-centered drive for power—all contribute to my thoughts when I state that I find her conduct intolerable and unworthy of a Tzen, much less a Warrior. I call upon the assembled Commanders to witness my formal accusation of ineffectiveness of my teammate Ssah."

The Planetary Commander looked at Ssah.

"Ssah, do you wish to reply at this time?"

"I deny the charges leveled at me by Commander Rahm. Further, I would lodge countercharge that the Commander himself created the situations he described by his failure to provide firm leadership and his inability to issue clear and definitive orders."

The Planetary Commander turned to me once more.

"Rahm, do you wish this matter settled in a Court of Warriors or by personal combat?"

"Personal combat."

"Choice of weapons?"

"Dueling sticks."

"Will you represent yourself or appoint a champion?"

I had given long thought to this question, knowing it would be asked. While I was sure either Zur or Kor would be willing to serve as my champion and would doubtless have a better chance of victory, this duel I wanted to fight myself.

"I will represent myself."

He turned to Ssah.

"Ssah?"

"The conditions set forth by Rahm are satisfactory."

"Very well. You will meet in precisely one hour. A proper site will be arranged, and the information will be passed to you. I will officiate at the duel myself."

Thus it was that an hour later I was standing in one of the flight team bays waiting to face Ssah. I stood with dueling stick in hand, facing the wall with my head down and my back to the room as is prescribed by Tzen dueling etiquette.

A Tzen dueling-stick was a deceptively simple weapon. Assembled, it was merely a metal rod one and a half inches in diameter and roughly four feet long, with a tapered point on one end. It was composed of several sections that fitted into each other, allowing it to be dismantled and carried in a pouch. It was in this ability to dismantle the weapon that its subtlety began to be hinted at.

Although it was primarily a thrusting weapon, there were many ways it could be used. It could be held one-handed like a sword, held two-handed like a short staff, or thrown like a javelin. By removing several sections and holding them in the other hand, it could actually be handled as two weapons. Although the possible combinations were finite, the arguments between Tzen as to what was the most effective manner of using it were not.

We waited with backs to each other and heads lowered to reduce the temptation of sneaking a look at our opponent's preparations. You were not to know what tactic you faced until you actually faced it.

"Ready!" As challenger, I replied first.

"Ready!" came Ssah's voice from the far end of the room.

"Turn and face your opponent!"

We did, and the Planetary Commander left, shutting the door behind him. His job was done. He had ensured that neither of us had brought extra weapons or assistants to the duel or had taken advantage of our opponent's exposed back during the waiting period. From here on it was up to us.

Ssah had retained the pointed section of her stick and assembled the other sections into one long rod, thus giving herself a staff and dagger combination.

I had correctly anticipated both her double-weapon move and her implied intent for a close battle. I had divided my own stick into two equal lengths, giving myself two short sticks, one with a point.

I began to move toward her warily. Instead of advancing to meet me, she moved sideways to a wall. I hesitated, puzzling over her tactic, and in that moment of hesitation she sprang up onto one of the wall walkways and stood looking at me expectantly.

I considered her position. Obviously she wished to fight in an area where the footing would be restricted, as well as the space in which to swing a weapon. She stood facing along the wallway, her dagger between her and the wall, her staff free to swing.

I accepted the challenge and moved to the other end of the walkway. As I approached her, I switched hands with my weapons so that the pointed stick would be between me and the wall and the blunt stick would be on the outside.

We eyed each other, neither willing to make the first move. I was counting on her youth and recklessness to goad her into action, and I was right.

She sprang forward, aiming an overhead blow at my head with her staff. I blocked it with my blunt stick, bringing my arm across my body for a backhand block, at the same time thrusting for her chest with my pointed stick. A split second behind the thrust, I snapped a backhand blow at her head with my blunt stick. She parried the lunge with her staff while ducking under the blow at her head, then jabbed at my knee with her staff.

The move caught me off guard. I had not expected her to thrust with the blunt staff. The attack landed, and even though there was no point, there was sufficient power behind the jab to cause my knee to explode in pain.

I backpedaled, clumsily, striking at her extended arm with my blunt stick. She avoided it easily, but it achieved the results I desired. It kept her from immediately following up on her advantage.

I was in trouble. My injured knee would seriously impair my footwork in a terrain where footwork was already restricted.

I braced myself for her next attack, then realized she was waiting patiently at a distance for me to make my next move. She was going to make me carry the battle to her, forcing me into additional movement on my already injured knee.

I considered retreating back to the floor of the bay, but realized that if I attempted it she would worry me with small attacks every step of the way, wearing me down and perhaps finishing the fight before I reached solid footing.

I debated jumping for the floor, but decided against it. The heavy impact of landing might injure my leg further. I would simply have to fight this her way.

I moved forward slowly and was surprised to see she stood her ground. I had been expecting her to retreat before my advance, forcing me into additional movement. I decided on a desperate tactic to settle the fight before it occurred to her to turn it into a foot race. I deliberately advanced within range of her staff, hoping to bait her into trying a long attack where I could attempt to wrest the staff from her grip.

She didn't take the bait. Instead, she gave a small hop and jumped off the walkway. The move surprised me so that I didn't see her twirling until it was too late. She twisted her body around in a neat circle and used the centrifugal force to make a whip-strike at my leg with her staff as she fell.

Because it came from a very low angle, I had no opportunity to block it. The staff smashed into my injured knee, and I felt my leg buckle. I fought for balance, lost it, and started to fall. At the last instant I glimpsed Ssah waiting below with her dagger upraised, and used my good leg to propel myself out off the walkway, turning my fall into a headlong dive.

I didn't have time to roll, and crashed into the floor with stunning force, taking the full impact on my head and arms. I was in pain, but didn't have time to recover. I knew Ssah was rushing on my fallen body, dagger ready to finish me before I could regain my feet.

I didn't try to regain my feet. Instead I rolled and thrust blindly up and backward with my pointed stick, aiming at a point between where I had landed and where I had last seen Ssah.

She was there, in midair, dagger poised. My weapon took her in the throat, and I felt the shock of the impact all the way to my shoulder. I released my hold on the weapon and rolled away as she crashed to the floor.

She tried to rise, my stick protruding from both sides of her throat. She turned hate-filled eyes in my direction, but I remained passively at a distance. Finally, the eyes glazed and she sank forward.

I waited for several minutes before moving. Then, satisfied that she was indeed dead, I limped painfully to the door and let myself out into the corridor.

The Planetary Commander was waiting there.

"It is finished," I told him.

He nodded and began sealing the door. When he was finished, he pressed a button on the wall, and we both listened as the bay floor opened, dropping Shah's body to the planet below.

In this, at least, she and I had agreed before the duel began. Whichever of us emerged triumphant would dispose of the other's body in this manner. Normally, when possible, Tzen preferred to be buried in the slime of the Black Swamps, where their decomposing bodies would remingle with the mud and water from which our species first evolved.

The Insects had ended that. Their ships had dropped swarms of the Aquatics on the swamps. The Aquatics were the only omnivorous members of the Coalition, and they bred abnormally fast, even for insects.

The Black Swamps were gone now, denuded and lifeless after the devastating assault. As such, we simply disposed of Ssah's body in the most convenient manner. With the Black Swamps gone, it really didn't matter where our corpses went.

Book Two

Book Two

Chapter One

I waited.

Perhaps for the first time I began to appreciate the difficulties of command. Unlike a soldier of the ranks or a flight commander, the problem is not how to perform the tasks ordered by your superiors. Rather, it is how to occupy periods of inactivity while waiting for your subordinate to carry out your orders. As a Tzen, this is particularly difficult for me. Prior to accepting this assignment, I had never experienced the phenomenon of leisure time. I was either fighting, training, or sleeping. I was not accustomed to doing nothing. It was not a manner of passing time I found favorable. It was not efficient.

Logically, however, I had no choice. I had been awake for several days finalizing plans with Krah, the ship's commander. Now that that planning was complete, I had given orders to awaken the section leaders of the expeditionary force for their final briefing. This had been done, but I found I had underestimated the time necessary for them to become coherent after prolonged Deep Sleep. This was clearly an oversight on my part. I should have recalled my own recovery period and planned accordingly. I hadn't, but I would not waste energy berating myself for the error. I would simply note it to ensure against its reoccurrence.

I waited.

I could have spent the time with Krah, but had decided against it. She was, of course, a Technician. I have found that Technicians as a caste are far more talkative than the Warriors. Since my awakening, she had been trying to draw me into conversation about the mission, and my failure to respond had only caused her to redouble her efforts.

As an effort to avoid potential friction with her, therefore, I elected to wait alone. In my opinion, Krah had as much information on the mission as was necessary to perform her duties. Explanation or discussion beyond that would be inefficient.

Horc entered the conference room and seated himself without a word or salutation. Perhaps I was judging the Technicians harshly in using Krah as an example. As head of the Technicians' portion of the expeditionary force, Horc would probably be a more accurate model to draw conclusions from. The smallest of the force, he was a foot shorter than Krah's six feet, and displayed none of Krah's tendency toward long-windedness. Then again, he himself might be considered atypical. He had left a position coordinating and directing the work of fifty Technicians to accept this assignment as head of a three-Tzen field team. I would have to inquire into this inconsistency in logic when opportunity presented itself.

We both looked up as Tzu, head of the Scientists' team, entered. It suddenly occurred to me that recovery time might be directly proportional to size of the individual involved. Horc, who had recovered first, was only five feet high, whereas Tzu, who was seven feet high, had recovered ahead of the Warrior leaders. I made a mental note to broach the theorem to the Scientists. If it proved true, then staggering the arousal times could eliminate the unpleasant periods of inactivity waiting for individual recovery periods.

As head of the three-Tzen Scientist team, Tzu's job was perhaps the most difficult on the force, next to my own; yet she seemed to bear the burden surprisingly well. This would be the first attempt of her or any of her team—actually, for any of the Scientist caste—to perform their duties in a combat area. I wondered whether her composure indicated control, or simply a lack of comprehension of what they were undertaking.

Zur entered the room last, closely flanked by Mahz. The team he was heading consisted of a full count of six Warriors, allowing him to bring his second-in-command to the briefing. Had I been asked, I would have questioned Zur's choice of Mahz over Kor as his second-in-command. Zur had not asked my opinion, however, and as always, a team leader is allowed autonomy in matters concerning his team. As might have been expected, his choice, whatever logic had prompted it, proved a wise one. Mahz was performing far better in his new role than I would have expected.

I paused for a final check of the attending staff's condition. All eyes were clear, none seemed sluggish of action or otherwise indicated any lingering effects of recovery. We were ready to begin.

"Let me open by putting your minds at ease. There have been no changes to the plans I have previously discussed with you individually, nor is the situation any different than anticipated. This meeting is to serve as a final review of plans with all staff members present, that each will be aware of the others' duties and restrictions."

I paused for reactions. There were none. Again, I felt the uncomfortable weight of leadership. Apparently none had considered the possibility that anything would occur in any way other than the one I had planned.

"We are currently in orbit over what is believed to be the home Planet of the Coalition of Insects. Our mission is to investigate the existence of a natural enemy of the Leapers, and to seek a means by which said enemy can be transported to Leaper-occupied planets in sufficient quantity to curb or eradicate the Leaper population."

I considered yielding the floor to Tzu for the next portion of the briefing, but decided against it. I was in command of the mission, and would have to accustom myself to exerting authority over others, even those of other castes. I continued.

"The records of the First Ones in our possession regarding this planet are incomplete. The Coalition launched their attack before the reports were complete, and the very fact that the First Ones were overrun by that attack would cause us to question the validity of the observations that were made.

"What we do know is what we have observed on our own and

other planets; that there exists a natural balance of population among living organisms. Every living thing has a natural enemy in its own environment. The High Command is therefore confident that somewhere on the planet below there exists a natural enemy to the Leapers which held their population in check prior to the First Ones' giving the Insects a means for spreading to other worlds. We must find it, devise a means to transport it, and above all, ensure that it is not more harmful to the Empire than the Leapers we seek to destroy."

I realized I was becoming long-winded. Apparently my exposure to Krah had affected me more than I had realized. I forced myself to continue with the agenda.

"To accomplish this mission, we have assembled a force consisting of members from all three castes in order to bring the full resources of the Empire to bear on the problem. We will work from a fortified base on the planet surface. While the ship will remain in orbit during the mission, the majority of the ship's crew will go into Deep Sleep shortly after our departure, leaving only a skeleton crew on watch. This means that while pickup is assured, we should not count on support from the ship once the mission is in progress."

The next part of the briefing I did not look forward to. If I encountered any difficulties with the team, it would be here.

"The team of Scientists under Tzu will carry the bulk of the mission, investigating, analyzing, and submitting recommendations on the target organism. Horc, you and your team of Technicians are to maintain the base, as well as design and build any devices as may prove necessary for the success of the mission. The Warrior team under Zur, with Mahz as his subordinate, will be responsible for security throughout the mission, as well as providing firepower to implement whatever plan is ultimately settled on."

"Question, Commander?"

"Yes, Tzu?" It had been too much to hope the delineation of authorities would go unchallenged.

"Under the current plan, the Warriors have responsibility for security, particularly in clearing the landing site. I would request that a Scientist be included in that landing party."

"Explain?"

"The Warriors are well trained for dealing with immediate and obvious dangers. I feel, however, it would be in the best interests of the mission to have a Tzen trained in scientific observation to detect potential dangers in the landing site."

"Zur will be leading the landing party and has been trained in scientific observation."

"I would prefer a Tzen who had been successfully trained as a Scientist."

I glanced at Zur, who remained impassive.

"Your point is well taken. We will include such a member."

"Commander?"

"Yes, Horc." The Technicians were not going to go unheard either.

"I would request permission to awaken the Technician team prior to the arousal of either the Scientists or the Warriors. This will enable them to complete our final check of the fortification unit prior to the dropping of the advance landing party, ensuring uninterrupted flow of the mission once it is set in motion."

I deliberately lowered my head a fraction as I replied. I wanted to stop this bickering in its early stages before it got out of hand.

"You have already submitted to me your time requirements for final equipment check. Simple comparison of those requirements with the time estimates of the Warriors for clearing the landing site shows you will have ample time to perform your duties after the landing party's descent."

"But what if our check discovers an equipment flaw?"

"Then I suggest you fix it. I trust your team's ability to effect repairs will remain consistent whether the other teams are awake or not."

"What I meant, Commander, is that if our check discloses equipment flaws requiring lengthy repairs, it could strand the landing party on the planet surface without support for a longer period of time than anticipated in the plan."

"I have been led to believe in my earlier discussions with the Technicians' team that the probability of such an equipment flaw is so small as to be almost nonexistent. Has your estimation of that probability changed, Horc?"

"No, Commander."

"Then might I further remind you that half of the Warriors in the advance party were able to survive for over a year on an enemy-held planet without support—in fact, without power sources. I therefore maintain that if the unanticipated equipment failure occurs, they should be able to hold position for a few extra days."

"Very well."

"However, that does raise a question of my own. Tzu, does your request to send a Scientist with the advance landing party change your time requirements for final checks on your laboratory equipment?"

"No, Commander, that factor was included in our original calculation. However, while I have the floor," she continued, "might I reemphasize the standing order that no team members other than the Scientists should enter the laboratory area unless accompanied by a member of the Scientists' team. The equipment and chemicals there could prove dangerous to any unfamiliar with them."

"The same order, of course, holds true for the Technicians' workshop," interjected Horc.

"Your comments are noted."

"Question, Commander," Zur interrupted.

"Yes, Zur?"

"You have said that the Warriors are to have supreme authority in matters regarding security. Does that authority extend to team members not of the Warriors' caste?"

What Zur was asking was if he had the right to kill a Scientist or Technician. I considered my reply for several moments before speaking.

"As in any mission, the first duty of each Tzen is to the Empire. Every Tzen, Warrior or not, has the right to move against another Tzen if in his or her opinion the actions of the other are jeopardizing the success of the mission. However, it should always be remembered that if such action is taken, the instigator should stand ready to justify that action before a Board of Inquiry."

I moved my head slightly to include all the staff members in my gaze.

"If reckless, careless, or independent action on the part of any member jeopardizes the mission, the offending Tzen should expect to suffer the consequences. I would not, however, want to see such action taken merely because a Tzen is from a different caste and therefore annoying. The possession of an extra sense is also not to be considered a capital offense.

"This is an experimental mission on several levels. First, it is the first joint field mission involving all three castes. Second, we have several team members from the new hatching who possess what is referred to as color-sight, an ability to see things the rest of us cannot. Finally, it is the first prolonged mission on the enemy's home planet.

"I will not attempt to minimize the difficulties inherent in the first two points. We are all painfully aware of the tensions involved in working with teammates whose logic priorities differ from our own. I freely admit I cannot comprehend the new color-sight and am therefore unaware of its potential advantages or difficulties. However, as a Warrior, I know we cannot fight a two-front war. We cannot fight the Insects and each other simultaneously. If we allow our personal differences to grow out of proportion, then the mission is doomed."

I looked around the assemblage once more. "Are there any further questions?"

"I have one, Commander."

"Yes, Mahz?"

"If the Scientists are to carry the main brunt of the mission, why do we have a Warrior as Mission Commander?"

I was both annoyed and glad that the question had been asked.

"For lack of a better explanation, I would say that it's because that's how the orders were issued by the High Command."

"Commander," interrupted Tzu, "with your permission I might have a more solid explanation."

"Permission granted."

"The Commander is being generous in his analysis of the structure. The keyword of the Warrior caste is *efficiency*. When you appraise a problem or set priorities, you ask, 'Is it efficient?' In the Scientists, our key word is *interesting*. Frequently our priorities are determined by what is the most interesting subject at hand to study. While this attitude is beneficial in the laboratory, it is not conducive to a specific field problem. It would be my contention that a Warrior was placed in command of this mission to ensure our efforts would be directed to the subject at hand. If not, we would be in danger of being distracted by a new rock formation or plant, whether or not it was pertinent to the immediate problem."

"While we are on the subject of avoiding distractions," interrupted Horc, "the Technicians also have a key word. That key word is *workable*. It occurs to me that whatever fine points remain can be settled in the field. For the time being, we have a workable team and a workable plan. Shall we set it in motion?"

As none disagreed, we adjourned the meeting and began the mission.

Chapter Two

We waited in the fortification.

Waiting seemed to be a major portion of my new position. If I had been aware of this beforehand, I might not have accepted the promotion, not that I had really been given a choice. I was the only Commander who had successfully led a force for an extended period of time on an Insect-held planet, so I was the logical choice to head this mission. Still, I did not appreciate inactivity.

The fact that both the Scientists' and Technicians' teams were also sharing my inactivity did nothing to ease my discomfort. It was taking longer than anticipated to secure the landing area, but not enough time had elapsed to justify calling for a report. Final equipment checks were completed, and like myself, the other teams were impatient for action. However, impatient or not, Warriors or not, they were still Tzen, and they didn't complain.

We all lay on gel-cushions waiting for the "clear" signal from the landing party. I was using the cushion originally intended for the third Scientist, the one who had dropped with the landing party. I must admit I found this a marked improvement over the original plan.

By that plan, I had a choice of using the turret gunner's scantily padded seat or one of the vats of gel set aside for keeping specimens.

Of the choices, I preferred the third. Any one of the three, however, was better than dropping with the advance team. The acrophobia I felt when being dropped in a flyer paled to insignificance when compared to what I experienced when forced to take part in a bubble drop. Even though it was proven bubble drops were currently the most efficient means to dispatch troops from orbit, my reactions to them were so strong that I would actually be incapacitated for several precious minutes upon landing. As such, our plans included my riding down with the fortification.

"Landing area secure, Commander," Zur's voice was beamed into my mind.

Involuntarily, I touched the booster headband as I replied.

"You exceeded your time estimates, Zur. Explain."

"We had to clear a nest of Wasps from the area."

"Wasps?"

"A different species than the Coalition Wasps we exterminated, but the Scientist, Zome, felt they constituted a potential threat."

"Understood. Anything else to report?"

"No, Commander. The homing beacon is in place and activated. We're ready to cover your descent."

"Very well. Stand by."

I shifted my focus to the Technicians. "Horc!" I beamed.

"Yes, Commander," Horc's voice answered in my mind.

"The Advance Party has cleared the landing area and set the beacon. Take command of the launch-land proceedings. Krah should be standing by for your orders."

"Acknowledged, Commander."

As the final step, I raised my voice to the Scientists in the immediate area.

"Stand by to descend. The advance party has confirmed a clear landing area."

"How long before departure, Commander?" asked Tzu.

"I would estimate—"

The fortification detached itself from the bottom of the transport and began its plunge to the planet's surface.

"I withdraw the question, Commander."

It was just as well. I was unsure of my ability to complete my answer. When I stated my preferences for mode of descent, it was not meant to imply that I enjoyed the prospect of being dropped in the fortification. Rather, I found it at best a meager improvement over being dropped in a bubble. Freefall in any vehicle is not a pleasant sensation to 'me. I made a mental note to inquire into the possibility of having ships land to dispatch troops instead of dropping them from orbit.

I have been told the fortification was a masterpiece of design, and that if its performance on this mission was satisfactory, it would be used as a prototype for similar installations in the future. The main body of the installation is a half-globe, ten meters in diameter, surmounted by a turret gun bay. The half-globe was hollow, and bisected by a wall, dividing the Scientists' lab from the Technicians' workshop. This entire structure was in turn mounted on a disc twenty meters in diameter and three meters thick. This disc contained the Warriors' quarters and armory as well as providing cover for the immediate perimeter of the installation. I was also told it was aerodynamically unstable and had the glide pattern of a rock.

Our descent was described to me by Horc as "not quite a glide . . . more like a controlled fall." This afforded me little reassurance as we waited for impact. The only comforting fact I had to cling to was that the Technicians were also on board, which meant they at least had confidence in its design.

I felt the gel-cushion surge up against me, a pause, then another surge. I deduced from this that Horc was using exterior engines, probably similar to those that powered our flyers, to slow our descent. Its surges became more frequent and longer in duration until it became one uninterrupted pressure, almost as if we were in a one and a half gravity field.

I began to relax. I should have realized that the Scientists and Technicians were less accustomed to physical hardship than the Warriors. As such, the landing would be understandably softer than those I had experienced before. This illusion was shattered as we impacted with a bone-jarring, eye-flattening crash.

There was a moment of silence as we collected our shattered minds and bodies.

Tzu broke the silence.

"Commander," she began hesitantly.

"We've crashed!" interrupted Rahk. The second of the two Scientists on board, he was of the new Hatching, color-sighted, and outspoken. "Trust the Technicians to—"

"That will be enough, Rahk," Tzu said, to stop her subordinate's tirade. "Your comments, Commander?"

Before I had time to answer, the hatch to the adjoining compartment opened and Ihr lurched into view. She was the junior member of the Technicians' team, also of the new Hatching, also outspoken.

"You might be interested to know," she informed us, "that according to the instruments, that was the softest landing this vehicle has achieved. If we had been allowed a bit more practice with the controls and time for a few polish modifications in design, we might have been able to set it down gently enough to conform to the delicate standards the other castes seem to require."

"Actually," I said before Rahk had a chance to respond, "the landing was well within our tolerance levels. Do not worry yourself about the Warriors' ability to withstand hardship, or the Scientists' either."

"Worrying about the comfort of the other castes is not one of my duties, Commander."

"Ihr!"

Even from the next compartment there was no mistaking the rebuff in Horc's voice.

"Horc asks," Ihr continued hastily, "that you remain stationary while we settle the fortification."

She disappeared before I could respond. Ihr was going to be a problem. Horc had warned me that his junior member did not like the other castes, and Warriors in particular, but I had not expected her feelings to be so obvious.

I stole a glance at the two Scientists to try to interpret their reactions. They were silent, but from the focus of their eyes I suspected they were communicating telepathically. Observing their respective postures, I surmised that Tzu was reprimanding Rahk for his earlier outburst. I hastily averted my eyes so as not to betray my awareness of the situation. Tzu was a Tzen. She could and would handle her own team.

We could hear the cold-beams mounted in the base of the fortification working as we began to settle. I directed my attention to the scene outside the dome, eager for my first glimpse of this new planet.

Even though I had not been enthusiastic over landing in this or any other free-fall vehicle, now that I was down, I could admit a certain admiration of its design. The dome afforded one-way visibility of the surrounding terrain. That is, we could see out, but nothing could see in. This could be a definite advantage in a hostile environment.

The fortification was sinking steadily. I could now see some of the area around us as well as view the activities of the advance party. Neither the Scientist Zome nor Zur were to be seen, but the bulk of the Warriors' team was in full sight, stationed at scattered intervals around the fortification. Weapons at the ready, they barely glanced at us. Instead, they scanned the sky and brush for any danger while we were in this vulnerable phase of our mission. Even though their deployment appeared random and haphazard, I saw Zur's handiwork in their arrangement. Zur did not approve of stationing guards at static, regular intervals. Rather, he positioned them as necessary to cover each other's blind spots, to leave no brush tangle or erosion gully uncovered. When Zur planned a defense, I knew I could relax . . . that is, as much as a Warrior ever relaxes.

I was mildly surprised to see Eehm, the third Technician, at work outside the fortification. She must have left the fortification as soon as it had touched clown. Apparently Horc shared Zur's near-fanatical obsession with effective deployment of troops. Eehm was busy unrolling the wires that were to be our outer perimeter alarm system. She was intent in her work, ignoring everything but the job at hand. This could be both good and bad. It was good because she was not allowing herself to be distracted, she wasn't worrying about doing the Warriors' job for them. It was bad because in Enemy terrain, no one can afford to completely ignore one's surroundings.

The sound of the cold-beams ceased. The upper surface of the disc was now level with the ground.

The fortification was secure.

"We're not level!" Rank was looking at a small instrument balanced on the floor next to his gel-cushion.

I didn't bother wondering what it was or where it came from. Scientists carry instruments the way Warriors carry weapons.

"I trust it will not seriously impair the performance of your duties?" I asked.

"We are used to working around the shortcomings of the Technicians," Tzu assured me.

"Commander!" Horc's head appeared in the hatch. "Could I see you a moment?"

He swept the Scientists with his eyes. If he noticed the instrument on the floor, he gave no indication.

"If you'll retain your places, we should be done in another few minutes."

He disappeared before they could respond. Technicians seem particularly skillful at timely retreats. I rose and followed him.

"Down here, Commander!" His voice came up to me from the armory.

I descended the ramp and found him bent over, unbolting a hatch in the floor.

"I see the Scientists didn't waste any time discovering we were out of level," he said, not looking up from his work.

"You heard?"

"It wasn't necessary to hear them. I saw the Q-Box on the floor."

"The what?"

"The Q-Box. The instrument they were using to check level. The Technicians built it for them, so of course they use it to criticize our work."

"Do you find the Scientists difficult to work with?"

"No worse than the Warriors." He paused in his labors to look at me directly. "You see, Commander, as a Warrior, you've been relatively isolated from the other castes. The Technicians, on the other hand, have to deal with both Scientists and Warriors as part of their normal work. Had I been asked, I would have said a Technician should head this mission if for no other reason than his ability to deal with the other castes."

He abruptly returned to his work. I was beginning to find the Technicians' habit of ending conversations before rebuttal vaguely annoying.

He lifted the hatch and set it aside. He stuck his head into the inky hole as his hand went to a mechanical box attached to his belt at the small of his back. The hiss and blinding light of a cold-beam filled the armory, startling me with its suddenness.

Horc grunted and pulled his head out of the hatch as the beam died.

"I was afraid of that. The number six beam is malfunctioning."

As he spoke, he detached the box from his belt and began adjusting dials and setting slides.

"Here, Commander," he said, handing me the box. "When I give you the word, trip the far left switch."

"Me? What about Ihr?"

"She's busy dismantling the control panel. That's why we're using the remote unit. It's not difficult, Commander. Just trip the switch when I signal you."

With that he slid through the hatch and disappeared.

I felt immensely uncomfortable waiting there with the strange device in my hands. The myriad dials and levers on its surface were completely foreign to me. Taking care not to change my grip or touch any of the controls, I turned the unit over to examine it more closely. My action was answered by a flash and hiss from below as the cold-beams activated.

For the first time in my career, I froze. Horc was still under the beams! My curiosity had triggered the box! I had killed one of my teammates!

As abruptly as they had started, the beams stopped. A heartbeat later, Horc slid out of the hole and began replacing the hatch lid.

"We are now level, Commander, and any Tzen that wishes to dispute it should—"

He broke off, looking at me for the first time.

"Is something wrong, Commander?"

I forced my voice to remain level. "You didn't signal."

"Oh, that! No insubordination intended. The problem was not as difficult as I anticipated, so I flattened into a dead zone and triggered the beams manually. I was under the impression you were reluctant to handle the controls, so I did it myself."

"In the future, Horc," I intoned, "if you or any of your team set a plan of action, you would be well advised to follow it. We are in a Combat Zone, and failure to communicate could be disastrous."

"I'll remember that, Commander." He bent to finish his task.

I decided to let the matter drop. If I pursued it further, Horc might realize my anger was more from relief than from concern for proper procedure.

"If my usefulness here is over, I'll give the 'all clear' to the Scientists. They are probably most eager to begin their work."

"Of course, Commander."

I started for the ramp, only to be met halfway by Ihr.

"Commander, the advance party is trying to get your attention."

I hurried past her up the ramp. Now that I was not concentrating on Horc's work, I could detect Zur's signal.

"Rahm here, Zur," I beamed.

"Commander, we have a problem here which requires your attention."

I was about to tell him to wait while I passed the movement permission on to the Scientists, then observed they were already moving about readying their lab for operation.

"Explain the nature of the problem."

I had visual contact with Zur even if he couldn't see me through the dome. He was standing in a small conference group that included him, Mahz, and the Scientist Zome.

"We have lost one of the Technicians."

Chapter Three

"How did the Technician die, Commander?"

"That is not necessary information for you to perform your duties, Commander." My head hurt from the prolonged use of the booster band. "Simply drop a replacement as soon as it is possible."

"I will have to deny your request, Commander," came Krah's voice in reply. "I do not have the personnel to spare."

"Perhaps you are right, Krah. Perhaps you should be more closely apprised of the situation." I realized I was starting to flatten my head in annoyance, which was a pointless gesture, as Krah was still in orbit above us and therefore unable to observe the gesture.

"The situation is this. I am in command of this mission, including the ship's personnel. In that capacity, I am not requesting, I am ordering you to drop a replacement for the dead Technician. Further, I happen to know you're overstaffed by two members. This was specifically planned by myself and The High Command. Do you know why?"

Krah did not answer, but I knew she was still listening, so I continued.

"It was planned this way so that if this very situation should arise, that I would be free to kill you in a duel and there would still be an extra Technician available. Realizing this, I would suggest you arrange to have the extra Technician dropped immediately. Yielding to the logic of the situation will allow you to operate with one extra member in your crew. Failing to do so will not only mean the ship has to function at normal staffing, it will have to function without you. Do you agree? Or do you honestly feel you can beat a veteran Warrior Commander in a duel?"

There was a long silence before the reply came.

"I will select and drop a replacement immediately, Commander."

"Very well. And Krah . . ."

"Yes, Commander."

"I would suggest you choose the replacement carefully. If we are given a Technician who is either incompetent or overly difficult to work with, I would be forced to consider it an attempt on your part to sabotage the mission."

"Understood, Commander. Krah out."

"I removed the booster band and surveyed the immediate terrain coldly. For all my officious arrogance in speaking with Krah, I was not pleased with the mission's progress. In my last assignment, I had lost only one Tzen in a year's time, even though we had crashed on a hostile planet. Now, despite our planning and equipment, we had lost a Tzen before we had even finished establishing the base camp.

I reviewed the incident for a trace of overconfidence.

The Technician, Eehm, had been laying the wires for the defense network. She had been so engrossed with her work, she had backed through a calf-high, meter-diameter patch of vegetation flagged by the Scientists as "unknown."

Well, we know about it now . . . or at least some things about it. The Scientists insisted it not be destroyed until they had an opportunity to examine and test it fully. What we did know about it was that when heavy contact was made with the stems, they shot out thorns that served as a fast-acting nerve poison, not unlike the wrist needle guns used by some of the Warriors.

Eehm had died with alarming speed, but not painlessly. She had not made a sound, however. Technician or not, careless or not, she was still a Tzen, and we were in Enemy-held territory.

I reviewed the situation once more. No, there was not overconfidence there, just carelessness. I considered telling Horc to warn the Technicians to be more careful, but decided against it. He had already been told, in far more convincing terms that I could ever achieve.

"Horc!" I beamed toward the fortification.

"Yes, Commander?"

"A replacement Technician will be dropped shortly. I want you to report to me immediately if he proves incapable."

"Very well, Commander. The defense wires are in place now, would you care to join me in inspecting them?"

I considered delegating the task to Zur. It would be a boring chore; and technically, as part of the defenses, it fell under his jurisdiction.

"Certainly. Do you have visual contact on my position?"

"I do. I'll join you shortly, Commander."

I had decided against delegation. Horc had specifically requested my participation in the inspection. It occurred to me this could be for one of two reasons. Horc was a Technician, and as such he might be sensitive to intercaste rivalries. If there were to be any criticisms of the Technician's work, he would prefer it come from me. This was a tacit acknowledgment of the impartiality of my position as Commander. He felt I would not find fault simply to make his team look bad, or at least that I would be less inclined to do so than the head of the Warriors' team. Then again, perhaps he simply wanted a conference.

He appeared, seeming to spring out of the ground by the now camouflaged fortification. Even though I knew its precise location, I was only barely able to detect it visually. I made a mental note to comment on it to Horc before our tour of the defenses was over.

"This way, Commander," he beamed.

I moved to his side and squatted. By looking closely, I could just make out the ultrafine wire running along the ground.

Without comment, he rose and began walking along the near-invisible line. I followed, not even pretending to watch the wire. Erect, I couldn't see it, so I contented myself with checking the pattern of its layout as we looped and twisted across the terrain.

The defense wires were still a marvel to me. They could be set to detect an object as small as a sand flea crossing their scan-field. Not only would they report the breach, they could feed back to the fortification the size, mass, and body temperature of the object, as well as the speed and direction of movement. Normally, this information would appear on a viewscreen for a guard to analyze. If we came under attack, however, the flip of a lever would feed the data directly into the turret gun mounted atop the fortification. It, in turn, could automatically direct fire against the intruder, escalating as necessary until the danger was eliminated. In short, with the system in full operation, anything that moved within three hundred meters of the fortification would be eliminated.

This was a vast improvement over our last stay on an occupied planet.

"Commander!"

"Yes, Horc?" I beamed back.

"Would you have been offended if I had asked Zur to conduct this inspection?"

"No. I would have delegated it to him except for the fact that you made your request to me."

"I would have approached him directly, but I felt you might interpret it as bypassing your authority."

So much for my theories.

"Might I suggest that we return to the fortification and let you and Zur conduct the inspection, as we both agree it is more logical?"

"Agreed, Commander."

"One question, Horc. Is the system operational?"

"It is."

"In that case," I spoke aloud for the first time, "I feel the area is secure enough for open communication."

He cocked his head at me quizzically.

"Do you not require approval from the Warriors before accepting the system?"

"Horc, you are as much a Tzen as any Warrior. Your life depends on the reliability of this system as much as ours does, perhaps more. If you feel the system is adequate, it is all the assurance I need. The inspection by the Warriors is more a token courtesy between castes than a required clearance."

He was silent for a few moments.

"I am finally beginning to realize, Commander," he said at last, "why you were chosen to lead this expedition."

I did not know what reply to make to this statement, so I changed the subject.

"I have been meaning to comment on the camouflaged design of the fortification, Horc. Could you explain to me, in terms a Warrior can understand, how you achieved the effect?"

"It is simply another application of flexi-steel, the same material we use on the wings of your flyer. All surfaces of the fortification which are exposed when it is entrenched are actually double-layered. The outer layer is flexi-steel, which we allow to contract, forming the buckles, ridges, and uneven surfaces which blend with the surrounding terrain; add a mock-up of a tree stump with exposed roots to hide the turret gun, and you have your camouflage."

"And we can still see out from inside?"

"Yes."

"How do you keep the uneven outer surface from distorting the view?"

He thought for a few moments.

"I could try to explain, but I'm afraid I would have to use some rather specialized technical terms."

"In that case, I withdraw the question. As long as it works, you'll have no complaints from me. Overall, it is the most undetectable job of camouflaging I have ever seen, or *not* seen, to be accurate."

"Perhaps."

Something in his voice caught my attention.

"You sound dissatisfied. Is there some flaw I am unaware of?"

"I'm not sure," he replied. "I wanted more information before I brought it to your attention, but perhaps it is better you were apprised of the situation immediately. It has to do with a comment made by one of our color-sighted team members.

"Would that be Hif, or Sirk?" I interrupted.

"Hif; but I checked her observations with Sirk, who concurred. It seems he had also noticed the problem, but was reluctant to infringe on the Technicians' domain."

"What was their observation?"

"According to them, the fortification does not match the surrounding terrain."

I studied the fortification before replying.

"Normally, I would say they were incorrect based on my own observations. I must admit, however, I do not fully comprehend this 'color-sight' the new Hatching has."

"Neither does anyone else, as far as I can discover. It's a genetic experiment the Scientists are trying, based on some of the notes found from the First Ones. We're supposed to find out in the field if it has any practical value to the Empire."

"But what is it?"

"It lets them see things we can't . . . Well, to be accurate, it lets them see the same things we see, but in a different way."

"That's what I have difficulty understanding."

"Perhaps I can clarify it a bit by describing a demonstration I once witnessed," suggested Horc. "Three blocks were placed on a table; one dark, the other two noticeably lighter. We were asked if we could distinguish between the three blocks. To a Tzen, all the witnesses replied that while one block was dark, the other two were identical. Then a color-sighted Tzen was brought into the room and asked the same question. He replied that each block was a different color, the dark one was what he called 'dirt', and the other two were 'sky' and 'leaf', respectively."

"I fail to see what that proves," I interrupted.

"There's more," he continued. "The demonstrator then picked up the light block which had been designated 'sky' and marked its bottom with an 'X'. The color-sighted Tzen was then told to shut his eyes, and the blocks rearranged. Time and time again, he was able to identify the marked block, even though the 'Y' side was down."

"Did he truly shut his eyes?"

"Sometimes he was asked to leave the room while the witnesses rearranged the blocks. Still he was able to find the 'sky' block unerringly. He could see something about that block that we could not."

I thought about this. "What good is such an ability to the Empire?"

"That is one of the things we are supposed to be testing on this mission, and we may have found our first example. The two color-sighted members claim our fortification is a different color than the terrain, that the fortification is 'steel' while the rocks around it are 'sand.' According to them, it will be immediately obvious to any color-sighted creature that comes across it."

Again I lapsed into thoughtful silence.

"Does anyone know," I asked finally, "if the Insects are color-sighted?"

"Not that I know of. You might ask the Scientists, but I don't think they even know what to look for."

"In that case, I feel the matter should take top priority. Pass the word to Hif and Sirk to report to me immediately. Also ask Tzu to join us. Finally, inform Zur to place his Warriors on full alert until I've had an opportunity to consult with him."

"Yes, Commander, but . . ."

"What?"

"Do you feel it wise to act with so little information?"

"Horc, there are thirteen of us outnumbered by a factor of several million to one by the Enemy. We lack information and we must act immediately, not in spite of that, but because of that. We need some answers and we need them fast. If we don't get them, we may well have to abandon the fortification."

Chapter Four

The resolution of the matter of whether or not the Leapers were color-sighted was so quick and simple it was almost anticlimactic. We could take no credit for the discovery. As sometimes happens in a combat area, the solution presented itself, and we merely capitalized on it.

We had not yet convened our meeting, when the defense web reported a small pack of twenty Leapers entering the area. Orders were immediately beamed to the team members outside the fortification, apprising them of the situation and instructing them to take cover. The rest of us gathered in the Technicians' side of the dome and watched, with Zur personally handling the turret guns.

The pack passed within ten meters, moving slowly, trying to flush game. There was a bad moment when we realized two of our teammates were directly in their path, but beamed warnings enabled them to shift position long before they were detected.

We tracked the pack as long as we could visually, then by the Defense Net when they had passed out of our field of vision. At no time did they give any indication of having noticed our fortification.

There was some debate as to whether their passing through the area was happenstance, or if our drop had been observed and they were actually searching for us. One point we were all in agreement on, however—the Leapers, at least, were not color-sighted. Hif and Sirk assured us that our position would be glaringly apparent to any color-sighted beast, yet we had gone undetected.

The subject of color would still have to be looked into, but for the time being it was removed from top priority status.

This, however, triggered another debate as to what was to take top priority instead. The Scientists, having now had their first view of Leapers in their native habitat, were eager to begin work.

"We should have a team trailing that pack," insisted Tzu. "The more firsthand information we can accumulate, the faster we can complete the mission."

"Not until we have completed our surveys of the immediate area. It was explained to you in our briefings, Tzu, that we will not engage in scientific expeditions until our mapping scouts have completed their work."

"Come now, Commander, this is not the Empire's first contact with this planet. We have undertaken three major campaigns: against the Wasps, against the Aquatics, and the aborted campaign against the Leapers. Surely we have sufficient geographic notations in our data files to proceed."

"It is true we have information in our files, Tzu," I stated. "Outdated information. As Commander I will not risk the mission or the lives of the individuals on the team needlessly, and that includes relying on outdated information when current data is readily attainable."

"But my team is impatient to get to work. We do not feel inactivity is a means of serving the Empire."

"Nor does anyone else, yet it seems inactivity is something we must all learn to deal with on this mission. As a possible relief, I would suggest you put your team to work checking the unidentified flora within the established defense net. We have already lost one team member to a plant your team did not have time to check."

It was admittedly unfair criticism, but Tzu seemed insensitive to it.

"Very well, Commander. But I will again stress the importance of field expeditions at the earliest possible time. Firsthand observation will enable us to direct our research to the most promising candidates, rather than attempting to study everything and hope to find our target by random chance."

I left her then, as there was nothing else to say on the subject. I sought out Horc, at work in the Technicians' lab. I could have beamed contact with him; but for this discussion, I wanted personal interface.

"Is the viewscreen ready yet, Horc?" I queried.

"Shortly, Commander," he replied, not looking up from his labors. "The arm-units are complete, if you wish to distribute them."

"I'll see that it's taken care of. Is the new Technician acceptable?"

"Krah? Quite acceptable, Commander. She'll be performing at less-than-peak efficiency, but that would be expected of any team member introduced at this late point in the mission."

He continued working without pause. I hesitated, casting about for a tactful manner in which to broach the next subject. Failing to find one, I simply took the approach that was most efficient.

"If I could have your undivided attention for a moment, Horc, there is a matter I would like to discuss with you."

"Certainly, Commander."

He set aside his instruments and met my gaze directly. Faced by this intent focus, I was suddenly ill-at-ease.

"Horc, you lost a team member today. Situations were such at the time I was unable to have private words with you on the matter. Though perhaps excusable, this was still negligence on my part as a Commander. To correct that situation, I have now set aside time to discuss the matter. Has the incident upset you or your team in any way? Should we make allowances for recovery time?"

"No, Commander. Aside from the extra time to brief the new team member which I have already noted to you, we require no special consideration."

"I am speaking here of your feelings in total, Horc. I wish to be informed if you harbor any resentment towards the Warriors' team for failing to provide sufficient protection, or—"

"Allow me to explain a little about the Technicians, Commander," interrupted Horc. "And perhaps it will clarify our position. Death is no more a stranger to the Technicians than it is to the Warriors, or, I suspect, the Scientists. Workshop accidents are a common occurrence, and they are frequently fatal. It is our job currently to find practical and safe applications for alien concepts and machinery, and in the process many are injured or killed. As an example, were you aware we lost over two hundred Technicians perfecting the design of the flyers?"

"No, I wasn't," I admitted.

"Few outside our caste are. Mind you, I'm not complaining. It's our duty, just as fighting the Enemy is yours. I am merely illustrating that this is not the first time we've lost a teammate. The main difference between your situation and ours is that we've never developed a combat zone comradery."

"A what?"

"A combat zone comradery. Unlike the Warriors, we are seldom in a position of working with teammates who have saved our lives. I would imagine that because of that, the Warriors feel a certain obligation to each other."

"The last Warrior who saved my life in battle was named Ssah. I killed her in a duel immediately after the mission was completed."

"I see," he said, apparently taken aback. "Perhaps I have overestimated my personal theories, and in doing so underestimated the Warriors."

"In the Warriors, we react negatively to needless death, particularly if it was caused by carelessness or incompetence."

"In that, you are not unlike the Technicians. To reply to your original question, if there was any carelessness involved in Eehm's death, it was her own. As such, we neither mourn her passing, nor harbor any grudges against the Warriors."

"Very well. Then we will consider the subject closed. I apologize for distracting you from your work, but I wanted to deal with the matter as soon as possible."

"No damage done, Commander. We are well ahead of schedule on the viewscreen. If you wish to pass the word to ready the flyers, the screen should be ready by the time they can take off."

"Excellent. The Scientists have been anxious to proceed with the mission."

"If I might comment, Commander?"

"Proceed."

"We Technicians have had more contact with the Scientists than the Warriors. They are a pushy lot given opportunity, and frequently short-sighted for all their wisdom. Though I expressed my feelings that I felt a Technician should lead this mission, I would add to that the observation that in lieu of a Technician, I feel much more confident of the success of the mission with a Warrior in command than I would with a Scientist in charge. In my opinion, you should trust your judgment over theirs."

"I had planned to Horc, but I will keep your comments in mind."

I strapped one of the arm-units on, and, picking up two more, went looking for Zur. Discussion was fine, but it was time we got this mission underway.

Zur and I stood watching as the two flyers departed. Arm-units had now been issued to all team members, and as promised the viewscreen was functional.

Mahz and Vahr were piloting the craft. I would have sent Kor instead of Vahr, but Vahr was a competent Warrior and a veteran of the Wasp campaign, and Kor was a valuable asset to fortification defenses.

"Shall we watch their progress at the viewscreen, Commander?" suggested Zur.

Even though our arm-units could monitor all data fed to the viewscreen, the larger screen would afford better monitoring. I signaled my agreement by starting for the fortification.

The flyers we had used in the Wasp campaign seemed crude when compared to the craft Mahz and Vahr were piloting. The new flyers had been modified to allow vertical takeoff and landing, a feature that would have negated the crash landing and jury-rig drop takeoff of our last mission. More important for the immediate assignment, the new flyers were each outfitted with three view-input units. These would scan the terrain the fliers passed over and feed the images directly back into the viewscreen data banks for storage and/or immediate viewing. With proper cuing, the viewscreen arm-units could then either display the entire area or give a close-up of a specific portion. This gave each member instant access to a three-dimensional pictorial map of our terrain once the data was input.

Horc and Tzu were already at the viewscreen when Zur and I arrived. That was one of the effortless parts of being a Tzen Commander. If something really important was happening, you seldom had to call a meeting. The staff would gravitate to the key point on their own.

The four of us watched silently as the map formed on the viewscreen. So far it was identical with our existing data, but it was good to have it confirmed.

"Horc!" I said, breaking the silence.

"Yes, Commander?"

"This ravine." I tapped the appropriate portion of the screen. "We're going to need some way of getting across it.

"An arc bridge?"

"A cable would be better. That and a jump ramp for skimmers. What we want is something we can cross, but the Leapers can't."

"Understood, Commander. We'll start on it as soon as we can get a Technician there for a firsthand look."

"Would additional close-ups help?"

"It would be advantageous."

I slipped on my booster band.

"Mahz!" I beamed.

"Yes, Commander?"

"The ravine you're approaching . . . after you've completed your preliminary sweep we would like some close-ups of the rim."

"Confirmed, Commander!"

As I started to remove the band, I noticed Tzu was checking something on her arm-unit.

"Something wrong, Tzu?"

"I'm not sure, Commander, but it is definitely interesting. Do you see those rock formations there . . . and there?"

"The large rocks with the small ones clustered about?"

"That's right. Do you notice anything strange about them?"

I studied them for a few moments.

"They seem to have a similar configuration. Each one is a large rock surrounded by brush and small rocks. Why? Are they some kind of marker?"

"I'm not sure, but look at this."

She extended her arm to share her arm-unit.

"This is the same area, but displaying data from the last campaign. The formations are there, but a different number of them, and in different locations."

I compared the display on her arm-unit with the display on the viewscreen. She was right. The configuration of the formations had definitely changed.

"Do you have similar, data from the other two campaigns?" I asked.

She cued an index list and studied it.

"No data from the campaign against the Aquatics . . . They were concentrating on the bodies of water then . . . but . . . yes, here it is."

She fed a cue into the arm-unit and extended again.

"This is the same area during the campaign against the Wasps."

Together we studied it. The rock formations on this display were arrayed differently from either of the others we had studied.

"Zur!"

"Yes, Commander."

"Take a look at this."

By the time he reached us, I had cued my arm-unit for the Leaper campaign display so we had all three examples in view.

"Look at these rock formations. They seem to be—"

"Commander!"

Mahz's voice beamed into my head, interrupting my discussion.

"Rahm here, Mahz."

"Coming onto your screen now! Request immediate instructions!"

"Commander!" Horc called.

"Coming! Tzu, Zur!"

We crowded around the viewscreen. There, coming into view was a large anthill.

The Ants! The last members of the Coalition after the Leapers! We knew they would be present on this planet, but none of our data had indicated their activity in this area. The hill was a new installation, constructed since our last campaign. It was less than eight kilometers from our fortification!

Chapter Five

The discovery of the anthill understandably threw our team into a bit of a turmoil.

Word was passed to all team members as Alert status immediately went into effect. Mahz and Vahr, however, were ordered to finish their survey sweep as originally planned. Whatever our future plan would be, we would require information on the terrain around us.

Zur placed Kor in temporary command of the defense forces and joined the rest of the staff in our emergency planning session.

Tzu, speaking for the Scientists, had very strong opinions, not only on the subject at hand, but also on how it was to be discussed. I was beginning to expect this.

"But, Commander, the course of action we have to recommend is the only logical approach to this situation."

"Recommendations for courses of action and discussion of those recommendations will take place after we have had the necessary informational reports from the staff."

"If I might point out, Commander, time is of the utmost importance in this situation," she argued, her tail lashing impatiently.

"I agree. Far too important to waste arguing over meeting procedures."

"But—"

"And I will further point out that had we followed your initial time-sensitive recommendations and pursued the Leapers, without a mapping sweep, we would have either missed the anthill completely or blundered into it unawares. Now I will again suggest you give your portion of the information report and save your valuable recommendations for later."

"Very well, Commander. How detailed a report do you wish?"

"Summary only. As you have pointed out, time is of the essence. Address specifically those behavioral points pertinent to the immediate situation."

She was silent for a few moments, organizing her thoughts; then she began.

"The Ants are the fourth species of the Coalition of Insects. According to the notes of the First Ones, confirmed by our own studies, they are the most intelligent members of the Coalition and hence the most dangerous. They were rated as being the most responsive to training in the operation of simple mechanical devices, and possess a definite-ordered society. In all probability, they were the masterminds behind the initial formation of the Coalition."

"Question."

"Yes, Horc."

"Are they still operating machines, and if so, of what level complexity?"

"Unknown. They are credited with being able to pilot primitive starships after the First Ones modified the controls for them, and the continued spread of the Insects through the Universe indicates some machinery is still being utilized. However, whether these are the original ships or if improvements have been made is unknown. This is why the Scientists recommend that we—"

She broke off as I caught her eye and flattened my head. For a moment she held my gaze, then continued.

"Although they will forage for food on the surface of the land, they are primarily burrowing creatures. The bulk of their civilization is maintained in subterranean caves and caverns interconnected by a series of tunnels. These colony nests may extend over a radius of up to twenty kilometers with installations to a depth of two kilometers.

"Physically, they are a bit larger than the Leapers, often reaching five meters in length. Even though it might be suspected they have poor eyesight from then-underground existence, they seem to forage on the surface both day and night. Their primary natural weapon is a set of powerful mandibles, and they are reputed to be strong, vicious, and tenacious fighters."

"You mentioned a civilization," I inserted. "What is known about that?"

"What little is known is unconfirmed. It is not unlike our own, having both Hunter and Constructor castes. The main difference would seem to be that they also have a Reproducer caste. However, this is all information from the First Ones."

"What are their vulnerabilities, physically?"

"Unknown, Zur; from their appearance we would postulate a similar physiology to the Wasps. But that is, at best, a guess."

"How fast do they dig their tunnels?" asked Horc.

"Unknown."

"How many Ants in a nest?" asked Zur.

"Unknown. It is believed to be in the thousands."

"Is the anthill we viewed a new nest, or a new outlet for an old colony?"

"Unknown, Commander."

There was a long moment of silence.

"If there are no further questions . . ." I began.

"There is one more bit of information which could be important to our planning, Commander."

"Proceed, Tzu."

"They possess some method of passing information among themselves. Whether this is done by direct contact, by telepathy, or even genetically is unknown. This characteristic of the Ants defied even the First Ones' attempts to explain."

The silence was longer this time as we digested the information.

"Horc," I said finally, "what does the presence of the Ants mean to the effectiveness of our Defense Network?"

"The Network was designed to detect and destroy surface

creatures such as the Leapers. While it will still be effective against surface hunters, it will be totally ineffective against burrowing," he replied.

"Will your team be able to devise an effective defense?"

"There are two possibilities we can explore. One would be a device to detect sounds of burrowing. The other would be a machine to locate subterranean hollow points. It is doubtful, however, that they would be effective to a depth of two kilometers. With the equipment we have on hand, we couldn't guarantee coverage much deeper than a quarter-kilometer, half a kilometer maximum."

"How long until the devices could be in place?"

"We would have to design them before I could give you an accurate appraisal of construction and installation time. I could have those estimates ready by this time tomorrow, however."

"Very well, Zur, what is your appraisal of our Warriors' defensive ability?"

Zur did not hesitate, but plunged into his analysis. "The campaign against the Wasps has given us undisputed air supremacy. The campaign against the Aquatics has guaranteed we will not have to fight for water. That leaves the Surface Packs, the Leapers, the Subterraneans and the Ants to present threats. As we are only required to fight a defensive holding campaign as opposed to a counterstroke, I am confident the Warriors will be able to hold the fortification against any surface or frontal attack up to and including a massed frontal assault. As to the possibility of a subterranean burrowing attack, we must rely on such devices as the Technicians are able to improvise for our defense. The Warriors will be unable to guarantee the safety of the fortification or the force in event of such an attack."

"I don't understand, Zur," commented Horc. "I was under the impression that part of the Warriors' duty was to be able to fight anything, anytime, anywhere. In spite of this you are telling us that in the event of a subterranean attack, the Warriors will be helpless and completely reliant upon the Technicians' devices?"

"You are correct in your observation of a Warrior's duty, Horc," answered Zur. "However, it is the duty of a Warrior Commander to give an accurate appraisal of his teams' abilities. We are not equipped physically or mechanically to enter into such combat, nor have any of the Tzen under my command received any training in subterranean battle. Though I can assure you that if such an attack occurs, the Warriors will fight in a manner befitting their caste, I would be lax in my duties as a Commander if I guaranteed their effectiveness. Unfounded assurance would only mislead the Commander and the other members of the staff, and could potentially prove disastrous should those assurances be relied upon."

"Question, Zur."

"Yes, Tzu?"

"You claim to be submitting a conservative appraisal of your team's abilities. Still, you arrogantly guarantee a capacity to withstand an unknown force with unknown armaments. Is this not in itself a form of unfounded assurance?"

Zur looked at me, but I remained silent, thereby giving him unspoken authority to speak for the Warriors.

"The factors you refer to, Tzu, are, as you have said, unknown," he began. "Unlike the Scientists, the Warriors do not deal in unknowns; we deal in realities. Were we to qualify our reports with provisions for the unknown, we would never enter into battle, for none can guarantee success against the unknown. The realities of the situation as set forth in your report are that we are faced with a force physically not unlike the Insects we have successfully battled in the past, capable of surface and subterranean movement, with no known weapons or machines modified for warfare. I must base my report on those facts, and by those facts my force will be able to provide security as long as the attack is made from the surface. Should the known facts be altered, I will have to reassess my evaluation. Until that time, my report stands unamended. In the past you have refused to accept my testimony as a Scientist. If you are expressing equal reluctance to accept my testimony as a Warrior—"

"Zur!" I interrupted. His head was sinking dangerously low. "Complete your report."

"Very well, Commander. There does seem to be a point of misunderstanding I would like to clarify. When I refer to the Warriors' ability to enter into subterranean battle, I am speaking of their ability to intercept and engage the Enemy in their tunnels. As the Tzen are themselves surface dwellers, the Enemy would be forced to surface to affect their actual attack. Once that happens, we are again referring to a surface attack, and our reservations concerning subterranean combat would no longer apply."

I surveyed the assemblage for several moments. They waited in silence. There were no additional questions.

"Very well. Having now heard the reports from the individual teams, I would be interested in hearing any recommendations from the staff regarding a course of action. Tzu, I believe you had some opinions in the matter?"

"I would apologize for my earlier impatience, Commander. You were quite right. Having heard the team reports, my recommendations are obvious and do not require formal verbalization."

"State them anyway, Tzu."

"Very well, Commander. All our plans are handicapped by a lack of confirmed information on the Ants. It is obvious from this that top priority must be given to a study of the Ants. This study would serve a double purpose: First, it would provide vital information for the Empire for its upcoming campaign against the Ants, and second, it would give us the necessary data upon which to base our decision as to whether or not to continue our current mission."

"Thank you for your recommendations, Tzu. Now here are my orders."

I shifted my gaze to include all three staff members.

"Our first concern is to secure the defense of the fortification. Horc, I want two of your team working on the design and installation of both types of subterranean detection devices you described. The third is to begin designing the requested method for crossing the ravine.

"Zur, I want your entire team on full alert until such time as the new defenses are in place. The only exception to this will be to establish an irregular observation flight over the area evidencing the unexplained rock movements. You are to avoid all contact with the Ants and particularly the anthill until our defenses are ready.

"Tzu, while the defenses are being prepared, I want your team to complete their study of the unidentified plants within the Defense Network. Also, I will expect a report from the Scientists as to their appraisal of the moving rock formations." I paused, then looked straight at Tzu as I continued. "Once the defenses are in place, we will proceed with our original mission as planned."

Tzu started to speak, then changed her mind and remained silent.

"In deference to the recommendations of the Scientists, the Technicians will construct two extra view-input units to be placed near the anthill, which will be fed into the memory banks for later review by the Scientists or the Empire. I will repeat, however, the current mission is to have top priority in our attention. "I will remind the team that the next campaign is the next campaign. Our primary assignment is the current campaign . . . against the Leapers. The High Command was aware of the presence of the Ants on this planet when we were given our assignment; yet we were not assigned to gather data on them. We are assigned to find a natural Enemy to the Leapers, preferably with minimal loss of life; but safety of the team is not and has never been our primary concern. We are going to find that natural Enemy, and the Ants are merely another threat to that assignment.

"Those are my orders . . . those are the High Command's orders . . . and I trust I do not have to elaborate on the fate of any Tzen who knowingly disobeys them?"

Chapter Six

If the scientists took exception to my orders, they didn't show it. Instead, they plunged into their assignments with enviable efficiency.

One by one the plants within the Defense Network were studied and deemed harmless, with the obvious exception of the plant that had killed our Technician shortly after our arrival. For a while I allowed myself to hope that by a stroke of good fortune we might find our natural enemy for the Leapers in that plant. This hope was ended when the Scientists submitted their report. The plant was deadly to Tzen, but not to the Leapers. As this was decidedly not what we were seeking, we continued our search.

The moving boulders continued to defy explanation, a fact I found increasingly irritating. This in itself surprised me, as I am not a particularly curious Tzen. Upon examining my reaction, I reached the conclusion that my increased curiosity was a result of my prolonged contact with the Scientists. Even though my discussions with them were largely attempts to quell their impatience, at the same time, I was being made aware of the vast number of yet unanswered questions.

Having identified and analyzed the source of my unwelcome emotions, I dismissed them. I am a Warrior, not a Scientist. I concern myself with solving the problems at hand, not speculating on the unknown. The moving boulders would have to wait until additional data could be gathered, which in turn would have to wait until the defenses were secure.

Waiting! I was getting enough waiting with this assignment to last a lifetime. While it was true my exposure to the Scientists was increasing my curiosity, another major factor was time, inactive time. Inactive time results in boredom, and boredom results in excessive thinking. I began wondering how widespread this problem was. With Deep Sleep being used only for space travel, the Tzen would be faced more and more with inactive time. Assuming others reacted as I did, filling the time with thinking, what affect would this have on the Empire?

I forced this line of thinking to a halt. I was doing it again. I am a Warrior, not a Scientist. Let the Scientists explore the implications and impacts of new patterns and discoveries. I would concern myself with immediate problems. Right now, the most pressing problem was . . . how to deal with inactive time!

I suddenly realized that though the Scientists and Technicians were busy working on their respective assignments, the Warriors were currently in a state of forced inactivity. Realizing my own dubious reactions to that situation, this could present a significant problem.

I sought our Zur, who confirmed my suspicions.

"You are quite right, Commander. In fact, Mahz and I were discussing this point earlier, but were undecided as to whether or not to bring it to your attention."

"How is it showing itself?"

"In questions not pertinent to the subject at hand.

That and overlong, wordy discussions. As a former—as a Warrior, Commander, I feel a concern for the effective performance of my team."

I cocked my head at him. It was quite unlike Zur to change thoughts in midsentence. Usually he was both concise and complete when he spoke.

"I am also concerned for the effective performance of my team, Zur. You started to say something about being a former Scientist. Why did you change your mind?"

He hesitated before answering, also quite unlike him.

"As you know, Commander, I have always been self-conscious about my non-Warrior background. Changing castes was not my desire or my decision, and I have always secretly regretted the move . . . until this assignment. Viewing the Scientists after a prolonged, forced separation, I find not only am I glad I was not accepted in their ranks, I wish that my name not be associated with them, even as a reference to the past."

I considered his statement with mixed emotions. On the one hand, I was pleased Zur now felt completely a part of the Warriors and not torn by divided loyalties. However, it boded ill for the mission for the head of the Warriors' team to harbor such strong and considered ill feelings toward the Scientists. Being at a loss for comment, I returned to the original subject.

"Have you considered a solution for the problem with the Warriors?"

He lapsed into thoughtful silence, but at least now his thoughts were diverted toward a constructive end.

"My analysis of the cause of the problem," he commenced finally, "is the marked difference between guard duty and active patrol. While both are necessary, guard duty is a prolonged, low-activity assignment. If guard duty is unbroken by an active pursuit, the mind tends to create its own activity, usually in an uncontrolled and therefore ineffective manner."

He was sounding like a Scientist again, but I felt it unwise to bring it to his attention.

"So you would propose . . . ?"

"Activity. Constructive activity. Perhaps some form of drill or practice."

"That could be potentially counterproductive, Zur. If the noise of target practice did not draw unwanted attention to us, the damage to the landscape would surely betray our position. Without the proper training equipment here, practice with the hand weapons could be potentially injurious to the Warriors, at a time we can ill afford casualties."

We pondered the problem in silence.

"What about the skimmers?" asked Zur finally.

I considered it. "Possibly. Let me speak to Horc about it."

Horc was understandably annoyed at the request. His team was already overloaded with assignments with the defense and ravine-span designs. Still, he was a Tzen and followed orders without complaint. In an impressively short time span, the Technicians had checked out the skimmers and cleared them for use by the Warriors.

The skimmers were a modification of the water darts used in the campaign against the Aquatics. As four of us—myself, Zur, Mahz, and Kor—had missed that campaign, the extra practice in their handling was more than justified.

They were a two-seater craft with the seats mounted in tandem to conform to the vehicles' extreme streamlining. Even though there were dual controls, allowing the craft to be operated from either position, only one set of controls could be operated at a time. This was a necessary safety precaution, as the craft normally traveled at such high speeds that attempting to coordinate the efforts of two operators would inevitably result in a crash.

The reason for the skimmer's being a two-Tzen craft was the modified weapons system arming it. Our flyers had fixed weapon mounts that fired in one direction only, specifically, the direction in which you were flying. The skimmers, on the other hand, had swivel-mount weapons that fired independent of the craft's movement. That is, you could move in one direction and fire in a different direction. This might sound like a remarkable and wonderful modification. It wasn't.

To understand this, one must first realize the reason the modification was necessary in the first place. The skimmers were originally designed for use on and under the water. The streamlining that made them so stable in that element, however, proved inadequate in open-air use. As such, they tended to rock or dip if you shifted your weight in them. This, of course, eliminated any hope of accuracy when firing a fixed-mount weapon. For a solution, instead of redesigning the ship, swivel-mount weapons were added. In theory, you could then keep your weapons trained on the target no matter what your craft was doing. In theory, I was actually looking forward to giving the Technicians firsthand experience of what it was like taking one of their brilliantly designed craft into an actual combat situation.

The reality of the situation was that instead of visually tracking a target and simply depressing a firing lug, you had to consciously aim the weapons. Of course, while you are doing this, you are supposed to be foot-piloting a high-speed craft. While it could be done, to accomplish it kept you busier than a lone nursery guard in the middle of a premature Hatching. Because of this, we used two Tzen per craft, one to handle the weapons and one to steer the craft. The only time we were called upon to do both would be in the unlikely event of one crew member's being killed or disabled. This situation was highly improbable. If one member is killed, usually both are destroyed, along with the craft.

There were other problems inherent in the swivel guns. With fixed-mount guns, as long as you held formation, you were safe. Not so with the swivel guns. If you tracked a target too far, you would find yourself cutting the stabilizer off the skimmer next to you.

I have noted that more and more Warriors are abandoning the use of the swivel guns, preferring instead to close with the target and use a hand weapon from the open cockpit. Because the skimmers operate at such high speeds even using a dueling stick like a club will result in a fatal wound.

The Warrior hierarchy did not discourage this practice. The Warriors were merely making the best of a bad situation. We had lodged formal protest over the design of the skimmers, and had been ordered to continue using them until a better craft could be designed. As such, we used the craft, though not always as the Technicians had intended. We practiced with them as often as situations would allow. We also, as a caste, waited for the opportunity to send a Technician into battle in one.

As Zur had predicted, the skimmer practice provided much-needed activity for the Warriors. We practiced maneuvering the craft at both high and low speeds, we practiced patrol formations, we practiced maneuvering two formations in a confined area. Zur suggested we devise a drill on the use of hand weapons from a skimmer, but I refused. While we did not discourage the practice, I did not want to encourage it by ordering them to practice the maneuver. Instead, we gave them a specific time period each day for "unstructured drill" during which time they could practice handling the skimmers in any manner they wished. I suspect they used the time to drill with the hand weapons, but I have suspicions only, as Zur, Mahz, and I took great pains to be occupied elsewhere when such practice was taking place.

Finally, when we had exhausted our imagination finding new drills, we jury-rigged nets on our own without the assistance of the Technicians and set the Warriors to work running down warm-bloods with their skimmers to supplement the food stores. The Technicians' team was openly scornful of our net design, but it worked.

However, despite all our efforts, the Warriors had an unaccustomed surplus of inactive time at their disposal. Much of this was spent in idle conversation, a pastime hitherto unheard of in the Warriors. The Warriors from the New Hatching seemed particularly susceptible to this. I chanced to overhear such a conversation one day.

"The more I think about it," Hif was saying, "the more it occurs to me that all our training as Warriors, the skimmers, the hand weapons, everything, is futile if not needless. What do you think, Kor?"

Kor was still held in awe by many of the New Hatching, and justifiably so. Not only was she a noted veteran, she still possessed one of the most spectacular sets of combat reflexes in the Empire, despite several generations of selective breeding and genetic experimentation.

"I am a Warrior," she replied abruptly. "I wasn't trained to think; I was trained to fight."

"But Kor," Sirk persisted, "we're talking about fighting; or not fighting, to be specific. Surely there are better ways to handle the Insects than direct combat. Chemical or bacteriological warfare would be so much more effective. The Warriors' decision to—"

"If you want decisions, talk to one of the Commanders. I'm not trained to make decisions; I'm trained to fight."

"But—"

"I have no time for such talk. I'm going to check my weapons. I'd advise you to do the same."

"Again? We just wanted to . . ."

But she was gone.

"There goes a Warrior's Warrior," came Vahr's voice. "She's right, you know. There's reason for everything in the Empire. Asking about it is only a waste of time. If there wasn't a reason, the situation wouldn't exist. The fact that the High Command issues an order is all the proof you need that a reason exists."

"But don't you ever ask questions?"

There was a moment of silence before Vahr replied. "I did once, just after the campaign against the Wasps. The casualty rates on the planet we hit exceeded even the Empire's calculations. When I saw so many Tzen die, I asked questions not unlike the ones you asked Kor. Wasn't there a better way? Why risk lives unnecessarily. In fact, I got permission to take time out from training to try to find the answers."

"What happened?"

"Two things. First, I found the answer to my questions. In short, we don't use chemicals or bacteria for the same reason you don't cut off your arm to get rid of scale mites. We don't want to destroy what we're trying to save. We're in this war because the First Ones upset the ecological balance of the Universe. They allowed the Insects to spread off-planet, away from natural enemies or control. Unchecked, they'll spread through the Universe, denuding every habitable planet they find. That is the imbalance we're trying to correct . . . for our own sakes. We won't do it by unbalancing things further. Chemicals kill indiscriminately. Bacteria, once started, may be impossible to stop. If we want to preserve the Universe, not destroy it ourselves, the war must be fought on the simplest level possible."

"But, by that logic, aren't we the same as the Insects? I mean, aren't we spreading beyond our planet and therefore disrupting the balance?"

"Possibly. But unlike the Insects, we respect the balance and try to upset it as little as possible. If we destroyed planets to dispose of the

Insects, we'd be as bad as they are. We don't. So the gamble is the possibility of our disrupting the Universe against the certainty of the Insects' doing it if left unchecked."

"You mentioned two things happened as a result of your research. What was the other?"

There was a long pause before he replied. "I lost two teammates in the campaign against the Aquatics," he said softly. "Ridiculous situations. With a little more practice, I might have saved them. But I hadn't been practicing. I had been looking for answers to questions I had no business asking."

"Warriors die in combat."

"I know that, Hatchling. Better than you ever will!"

"But there's no guarantee you could have—"

"No guarantee, but a possibility. That possibility is worth my full concentration. Kor knows that, and so should I. I'm going to check my weapons."

"But we wanted to . . ."

I missed the rest of the conversation. I had just been beamed by Horc. The defenses were in place. We could begin the mission.

Chapter Seven

"We're in position, Commander."

"Does Hif observe anything unusual about the boulders?"

"No. She claims they are identical in color to the rocks which abound throughout the area."

I studied the boulders in the viewscreen. The Technicians had established a bank of viewscreens in the fortification, allowing us to monitor the images relayed by the view-input units mounted on either the flyers or the skimmers. By this method we were able to indirectly observe whatever transpired on a patrol or assignment.

The boulder stood alone in a small field of knee-high grass. It was three meters high and roughly spherical in shape. There was nothing particularly noteworthy about it except for two things. First, it was identical to several other boulders we had observed in this area. Second, it hadn't been here two days before. However innocent it looked, this was one of our mysterious "moving boulders."

"Any reaction from the Scientist?" I beamed.

"Zome? No, he seems quite content to follow our orders."

"I meant does he have any comments on the boulder?"

"No. He is as much at a loss to explain the phenomena now as the entire Scientists' team was from studying the viewscreens."

Beside me in the fortification, Tzu shifted her weight impatiently. Unable to hear the telepathic communication between Zur and me, she was doubtless wondering what the delay was. However, this time, for a change, she remained silent.

"Bracket the boulder with your skimmers and use far-focus for closer examination."

The scene in the viewscreens changed as the two Skimmers moved to take positions on opposite sides of the boulder.

Now it was my turn to wait as they studied the target and telepathically discussed their observations. During the interim, I considered the scout team. I had been in conference with Horc when they departed, and this was my first opportunity to check Zur's choice and deployment of the troops.

The team included three Warriors and, reluctantly, a Scientist. We were trying to keep the Scientists inside the fortification as much as possible, minimizing the chances of losing them to an attack. Of the three teams, they were the hardest to replace and therefore the most valuable. This tactic, however, was easier to order than to enforce. The natural curiosity of the Scientists led them outside whenever opportunity presented itself or was manufactured. In this specific situation, however, I had to admit their logic was justified. Firsthand observations of a Scientist in this puzzle could be invaluable, even though so far he had not made a significant contribution.

I studied the pairings, now visible in the screens as the skimmers faced each other.

The Scientist, Zome, and Kor shared one skimmer. Because the Scientist was inexperienced, Kor would probably be controlling both the steering and the weapons. Well, if any Tzen could do it, Kor could.

Zur and Hif were teamed in the second skimmer. I supposed Hif's color-sighted ability made her a logical choice over the more experienced Vahr. Also, if they weren't included on assignments, how would the new Warriors gain experience?

"The team reports nothing unusual in the appearance of the boulder, Commander," came Zur's message. "It seems to be a rock; nothing more."

It occurred to me that if indeed our target turned out to be a rock and nothing more, we might be indulging in one of the most massive overkills in the records of the Warriors. If it wasn't, however . . .

"Proceed with the investigation, Zur."

"Acknowledged, Commander."

The skimmers were moving now. The craft with Zome and Kor moved to a position forty meters from the boulder and settled facing it. Good! They would act as a fixed position covering the other craft. Not having to control its movements, Kor could devote her full attention to handling the weapons. When Kor concentrated on weapons, I was confident she could handle two boulders, unknown or not.

Zur's craft, probably with Hif piloting, moved off to a distance of some hundred meters. It waited until Kor was in position, then darted forward. Taking care not to pass between the boulder and Kor's guns, it swept past the target at top speed, almost brushing it as it passed. Carrying by, they turned the skimmer and swept by the target again.

There was no apparent change in the boulder . . . Or was there? My eyes darted from screen to screen. Had it quivered? Or was the movement I detected due to the shifting of the view-input units?

Zur's skimmer was approaching again, slower this time. I could see them in the viewscreens relaying Kor's input units. Zur had his flex-mace out. Apparently he had joined the ranks of Warriors who shunned the swivel-mount guns.

Suddenly it happened, with such speed that only later review enabled us to sort the action out. The boulder exploded into life, pouncing on Zur's craft with a leap that defied description. A spider.

A monstrously huge Spider.

The screens showing Zur's display flashed a sight of the ground, then blanked out. My eyes jumped to Kor's screen, just in time to see the spider turn and start in that direction. It was incredibly fast, swelling swiftly in the screens to blot out all view of anything else. Quick as it was, though, Kor was quicker. We could see the cold-beams lance out, striking the spider repeatedly as it moved, but with no apparent effect. The view started to shift, and at first I thought Kor was attempting to maneuver the craft. Then it jarred to a halt, displaying a bush and an expanse of grass, and I realized what had happened. Two skimmers down, visual contact lost.

"By the Black Swamps!" Horc exploded, echoing my thoughts. "Whoever designed those skimmers should be killed, if I have to challenge them myself."

"What's wrong with those cold-beams, Technician?" Tzu interrupted. "Can't your team even maintain existing equipment?"

"Nothing's wrong with them," Horc retorted. "The beast's natural defenses stopped them."

"Ridiculous. Those beams will cut through—"

"See for yourself. We'll recall the sequence from the memory—"

"Use another screen," I said.

"But Commander, another screen would—"

"Anyone who interferes with the current monitor display answers to me. I want to see this as it happens, not out of a memory recall."

"Forgive my asking, Commander," Horc inserted with quiet politeness, "but see what?"

I realized he was right. Staring at a picture of a bush was not going to give me any additional information. I also realized that despite our height differential, I was staring up at him.

Slowly I forced my head up to its normal level.

"Leave it," I said, but more calmly.

"Zur here, Commander."

I held up a hand to the other two as I replied to Zur's beamed message.

"Report, Zur."

"Situation is in hand, Commander. Our assailant has been eliminated."

"What is the condition of your team?"

"Hif's arm is broken. No casualties beyond that."

As I received the message, the view of the bush changed as the downed skimmer was pivoted to point back at the scene of the recent action. Zur was apparently beaming as he turned the skimmer; we could see the other three team members in the screen. Kor was working to right the other skimmer. Hif was assisting despite her broken arm. Zome was apparently examining the body of the dead spider.

"Both skimmers seem to be operational," Zur's report continued, "though my own flyer seems to have sustained some surface damage in the nose area."

"Confirmed, Zur," I replied. "The view-input units on your skimmer are unoperational."

I noticed Tzu was trying to get my attention.

"What is it, Tzu?"

"With your permission, Commander, I'd like to communicate some instructions to Zome."

"Certainly."

I had no hesitation in yielding on this point. Zur had given me his assurances the situation was in hand. Details could wait until their return. For the time being, it was more important to let the Scientists proceed with their work.

"Zur," I beamed, "pass your booster band to Zome."

"Acknowledged, Commander."

"Horc," I said as I passed my booster band to Tzu, "a word with you?"

"Certainly, Commander."

We retired to the far side of the dome to avoid distracting Tzu at her work.

"You made a comment just now I would like to have clarified."

"About the cold-beams?"

"No, about the skimmers."

"Oh, that. My apologies, Commander. It was an unforgivable outburst. I would ask that you recall we Technicians are unused to viewing combat firsthand."

"Actually I was interested in your implied criticism of the design of the skimmers. I was under the impression the Technicians considered it a masterpiece."

"You are confusing the Technicians as a caste with the individuals who compose it."

I waited, but he did not continue. I fought a brief battle with myself over conduct befitting a Warrior, but this time curiosity won.

"Explain, Horc."

"Commander?"

"The differences you referenced. I would like them clarified . . . for my information as Commander of this mission," I added hastily.

"I am unsure as to the necessity of an explanation. Surely there are differences of opinion within the Warriors' caste? Why should you expect the Technicians to be any different? Regardless of caste, we're all still Tzen."

I considered his answer. It was logical, so logical in fact I was surprised it had never occurred to me before. "I had never considered it in that light before, Horc. The Technicians always seemed a very united, stubborn caste to me, both in attitude and opinion."

"That is not unusual, Commander. Do you recall my question about the duty of the Warriors' caste at the conference on the Ants?"

"Yes."

"Well, until then I had considered the Warriors to have a caste identity: effective, but swaggering and arrogant. Zur's admission of the limitations of his team forced me to view the Warriors differently than I had previously. Perhaps our difficulty is that prior to this mission, we only dealt with the lower echelon of each other's caste. I have observed that the lower individuals stand in their caste, the more fiercely they will defend it."

I suddenly realized I was being drawn into a much more thoughtful discussion than I cared to partake.

"Returning to my original question, Horc, what is your opinion of the design of the skimmers?"

He hesitated before answering. "Normally I would not criticize a project I was not working on, just as you would not criticize a campaign in which you had not fought. However, as in my moment of weakness I let my feelings be known, I might as well clarify my position.

"The skimmers were modified from the water darts. That in itself indicates the High Command was concentrating on other priorities. When you modify a design instead of devising a new one, inadequacies and shortcomings are inevitable. Then you modify the modifications. The result is the kind of sloppy performance you just witnessed. In short, you invest a lot of time and effort to produce a device of dubious value. I personally would rather see the work put in on something specifically designed for the situation it will be used in.'

"Then you agree the skimmers are poorly designed?" I asked.

"To a point, I was surprised the Warriors accepted them."

"We didn't. Our formal protest was turned down by the High Command."

"Really?" He sounded surprised. "My respect for the Warriors is strengthened knowing that."

I decided to seize the opportunity while it presented itself.

"Realizing we are in agreement on this point, is there a chance your team could design further modifications to the skimmers?"

He thought for several moments.

"Possibly," he said at last. "Though after watching the actual performance of the craft, I would be more inclined to discontinue it completely. We could disassemble them and perhaps use the parts in another design completely."

"How long would it take for such a project?"

"I obviously can't commit to a specific time span, but with the team I have here—"

"Commander."

Tzu was beckoning from the viewscreens.

"Zur wants to confer with you."

Something was wrong. Zur wouldn't need my counsel unless there was a major change in the situation. Breaking off the conversation, I strode hurriedly to the screens, accepting the booster band as I went.

"Rahm here."

"Commander, I'd like your advice on this."

I hurriedly scanned the operational screens. They displayed a view of ridge and brush, but nothing noticeably unusual.

"Explain, Zur."

"The clump of brush by the dead tree. Examine it closely."

I did. At first I saw nothing, but as I used far-focus I saw it. An Ant.

"Kor just noticed it, Commander. It seems to be observing us."

"How long has it been there?"

"Unknown. It may have been there through our entire skirmish with the spider."

I studied the Ant, but my mind was elsewhere. Mentally, I was reviewing the briefing we had received from Tzu: intelligent . . . capable of understanding machinery . . . able to communicate with the nest.

Chapter Eight

Surprisingly enough, the Scientists did not seize upon the incident to renew their arguments for a closer study of the Ants. If anything, their efforts in that direction slackened. They even abandoned their covert monitoring of the view-input units by the anthill, leaving the viewscreens unwatched for unprecedented periods of time. Instead, they pursued the mission with renewed, almost frantic energy. Not that there wasn't enough to occupy their time: there were countless specimens to collect and observe. Also, there was the spider.

After they had realized they were being observed by the Ants, the team had cut short their field studies. Instead, they had transported the spider's carcass back to the fortification, intact. This was accomplished with no small difficulty by draping this spider across one of the skimmers and piloting it back. This involved actually crawling under the body and peering from between its legs to steer. I was quite proud of the nerves of the Warriors who performed this task. It is not pleasant to spend a prolonged period of time in such close proximity with the body of an Enemy, particularly one that has come close to killing you. Still, they carried out the assignment without falter or complaint. It did cause quite a stir when they hit the defense network, though.

Zur had beamed ahead that they were coming in. He neglected to mention the spider. The Warriors on guard had not taken cover and were caught in the open when the team burst into view. When you are expecting to see a teammate, the sight of a huge spider coming out of the brush at you can be unsettling, particularly if it is skimming the ground at unnatural speed.

Only the fact that the second skimmer, unadorned, was clearly accompanying the spider averted disaster. If a Warrior is startled, he tends to react with his weapons.

I was disappointed when I learned the Scientists had almost immediately dismissed the spiders as being unsuitable as a natural enemy for the Leapers.

"Rahk, Zome, and myself all concur, Commander," stated Tzu, as if it were both a unique and final statement.

"While it will be interesting to study the exoskeleton, which was impervious to our cold-beams, and its poison will give us a definite advantage, the spiders cannot be considered a serious candidate for the desired natural enemy."

"Explain."

"First is their hunting pattern. They appear to be primarily ambush hunters, remaining in one place until a victim wanders in range before striking. This method is far too random and slow for a species we want to exterminate the Leapers.

"The size of their digestive tract also indicates a light hunter. It gives every indication of a creature which feeds only occasionally, taking long rest periods to allow the food intake to digest. Again this is unsuitable for our needs. What we are looking for is a creature or plant with a high metabolic rate, one which is driven to feed constantly and gluttonously.

"With the displayed hunting and feeding pattern, it would require capturing and transporting them in vast numbers if the tactic were to be at all successful."

"What about egg masses?" I interrupted.

"Also out of the question."

She stooped and picked up a fist-sized rock at random from the ground.

"Is this a spider egg mass?" she asked.

"No," I responded immediately.

"We Scientists are not so sure. The clusters of rocks we first observed around the spiders are actually egg masses, camouflaged like the spider itself. They are produced in a variety of sizes, apparently depending upon the feeding habits of the adult, and adhere to the sides of the female before dropping off. As I have said, they are extremely well camouflaged, to the point where we are unable to differentiate egg mass from rock until we attempt to break it."

To demonstrate her point, she picked up a second rock and smashed it against the first. The rock split open at the impact, and she examined it out of habit.

"It seems you were right, Commander," she said letting the pieces fall. "It was just a rock. However, had it been an egg mass, we would have destroyed it performing that test."

"Couldn't you devise some other test?"

"Possibly, but there is no point in designing one."

"Why?"

"Because whether transported as adult specimens or as egg masses, the number of spiders necessary for the campaign would exceed safety limits."

"Safety limits?"

"As you recall, Commander, we encountered some difficulty in securing the specimens we have. While it is unlikely we would fall within the Spider's natural diet, it is obvious they will attack Tzen if provoked. We would therefore not only be spreading an Enemy for the Leapers, but one for ourselves as well. What is more, to effectively deal with the Leapers, they would also constitute a threat to the empire. The last thing we want to do is replace one Enemy with another, and particularly not an Enemy who is immune to our cold-beams."

"Speaking of that immunity, Tzu, what is the possibility that the Ants may have a similar exoskeleton?"

She considered for a few moments before answering.

"Unknown, Commander. The Scientist team is currently praying to the Black Swamps we never have occasion to find out."

This surprised me, as it seemed contradictory to the curious nature of the Scientists.

"Explain, Tzu."

"The time to investigate the Ants would have been before they knew about our presence. Now that they know we are here, it is only a matter of time before they act on that knowledge. As such, the Scientists feel it is in the best interest of safety to complete our mission in the shortest time possible and depart. Our position here is tenuous at best, and it becomes more so with the passage of time."

With that, she turned and strode away.

While she had given me much to think on, I postponed such activity until later. There were other, more pressing matters demanding my time currently. To that end, I sought out Zur.

"How is Hif's arm?" I inquired.

"Fine, Commander. The Scientists injected her with a compound to speed the bone mending. She should be ready for light duty in time for the next guard shift, and for full duty by tomorrow."

"Good. Has Horc spoken to you about the skimmer design?"

"Yes, Commander."

"What is your opinion?"

"While it was enlightening to learn a Technician shares the Warriors' opinion of the skimmers, I declined his offer."

This answer was unexpected. "Explain, Zur."

"Although obviously unstable, the skimmers are still the fastest means of ground transport available to us. As the mission progresses, we will be forced to canvass farther and farther afield seeking specimens for the Scientists. To accomplish this efficiently, we will have to cover great stretches of ground as fast as possible. While the flyers can serve to a certain degree as spotters, actual observations and capture can only be effected at ground level."

"It has been observed on numerous occasions, Zur, that the instability of their design all but negates the use of weapons. Do you not agree that the skimmers are apt to place you in potentially dangerous situations, while at the same time stripping your team of their ability to deal with those situations?"

"It is our plan, Commander, to utilize them as transports only, dismounting and proceeding on foot when the desired area is reached. As you well know, a Tzen Warrior is a formidable opponent, even when afoot."

"I still do not understand your position, Zur. While what you say is logical, it is a solution to a problem which could just as easily be circumvented. What is your objection to allowing the Technicians to redesign the vehicle to fit our needs?"

"Time, Commander. While I will not dispute the efficiency of the Technicians, such work would take time, time we can ill afford. In the time it would take them to redesign the skimmer, we might be able to find the object of our mission and depart."

"Am I to take it, then, that you share the Scientists' position that—"

Suddenly he held up a hand to silence me. He stood motionless, head cocked to one side, and I realized he was receiving a telepathic communication. I waited, but as time stretched on, I grew impatient, and curious. He was obviously either receiving a report or engaged in a lengthy exchange. I knew of no current activity of the Warriors' requiring such a communication. Finally he turned to me once again.

"Commander, a situation has developed you should be apprised of."

"What is it?"

"One of our Warriors, Sirk to be specific, has disappeared."

"Explain."

"He was on guard, fully armed and wearing a booster band for communication. He failed to report in, and has been unresponsive to attempts to contact him."

"Was he within the Defense Network?"

"Unknown, Commander. As you know, the detectors have been set to ignore the movements of a Tzen. As such, we have no knowledge as to whether he was lured outside the Network or if our defenses have been breached."

"Very well. Institute a search at once."

"It has been done, Commander. Mahz led the search party. That was him reporting in just now. There was no trace of Sirk, nor any signs of a struggle."

"A search has already been conducted? Why wasn't I informed?"

Zur hesitated before answering.

"The Warrior team has been dissatisfied with our conduct in the battle against the spider, particularly as it was witnessed by the other castes. As such, we were reluctant to sound the alarm until we were certain a crisis existed. We had no wish to look foolish in addition to being ineffective."

"You haven't answered my question, Zur. I am of the Warrior caste and would have held the information in confidence. Why wasn't I informed?"

The pause was longer this time. "Whether you are aware of it or not, Rahm, you have been becoming increasingly distant from the average Warrior. My team has not been insensitive to this, and tends to view you as something apart from the team. They were as reluctant to appear foolish in front of you as they were to avoid embarrassment before the Technicians or Scientists."

I also took time before answering, but in my case it was a struggle for control rather than thought. "Zur," I said finally, "in the future I would ask that you remember two things, and that you pass them on to your team. First, I am the Commander of this mission and as such, am entitled to be apprised of each new development regardless of who it embarrasses.

"Secondly," I dropped my voice to a low hiss, "I am a Warrior, and the next team member who deliberately withholds information from me, regardless of caste, will answer to me on the dueling ground, either here or upon completion of the mission."

Chapter Nine

We never found Sirk's body. Even though a disappearance such as this is not an unusual occurrence of the Warrior's caste, it was annoying. Without the body, we had no additional information. We did not know what killed him or how, or even if our defenses had been breached. It was an ineffective way to die.

Still, the mission progressed at a satisfactory speed. An astounding number of specimens were observed, analyzed, and discarded by the Scientists. After several uncomfortable attempts to serve as moderator, I approved a plan allowing the Scientists to make their requests for additional equipment directly to the Technicians. This plan proved workable, and the Technicians were kept busy in their labs designing and building the desired items.

The Warriors were not idle either. When not standing guard or collecting specimens, they were escorting observation expeditions into the field.

My own time was occupied trying to absorb and coordinate the reports and plans fed me by my staff. My insistence to be included on any new developments had been relayed through the entire team, and now every incident was being passed on to me, no matter how small or insignificant. I might have regretted the order, were I not so grateful for something to do to keep me from being inactive.

As you may gather from this, the problem of inactive time continued to plague our mission. Despite the frequency and intensity of assignments, individual members still found themselves with long periods of inactive time at their disposal. Idle conversation was now considered commonplace, almost unworthy of notice. The latest development was idle conversations between members of different castes. While this should have been predictable, it still took me a while to get used to.

I recall one conversation in particular that surprised me, as it transcended not only caste lines, but chain of command as well.

"A word with you, Commander, if you have a moment?"

"Certainly, Rahk."

Rahk was the junior of the three Scientists, and I had had little contact with him since his outburst when the fortification first landed.

"I have a theory I would like you to consider, Commander. One which I think has not been previously brought to your attention."

"Have you discussed it with Tzu?"

"Yes, but she has been reluctant to forward it to you."

"Did she explain why?"

"Yes, she gave two reasons. First, she pointed out we are adequately equipped to test the theory. It is her wish that we present proven theories only to you."

"Do you disagree with the policy?"

"In most cases, no, but in this instance I must take exception. Even though my theory is unproven, if correct it could have direct bearing on the success of the mission."

"Very well, I can understand your position. However, you mentioned Tzu had two reasons for withholding the information. What was the other?"

"Actually, her second reason was merely an extension of the first."

"Clarify."

"The Scientists have frequently voiced suggestions or opinions in the past which you have countermanded. Not that we are critical of this. You were within your rights as Commander, and the progress of the mission has proven your judgment to be sound. However, it has caused Tzu to feel, perhaps unjustifiably so, that you will have a tendency to reject out-of-hand recommendations of the Scientists on future plans. In an effort to reestablish the credibility of our caste in your eyes, she is screening our reports to be sure that only firm, proven facts and recommendations are passed to you.

I considered this. "I acknowledge the logic of her beliefs, Rahk, though I do not agree that they are accurate. For this reason, I will listen to your theory.

"I will ask, however," I continued before he could speak, "that you pause first and reconsider its importance. Bypassing the chain of command, particularly in the field, can have long-lasting and undesirable aftereffects and should not be taken lightly. Are you sure your theory's impact justifies such a risk?"

Rahk thought for several moments before responding. I waited patiently.

"I am, Commander," he said at last.

"Proceed."

"It has to do with our sleep patterns."

"Sleep?"

"Yes, that and our eating habits."

"Continue."

"Historically, Tzen of all castes have gone into Deep Sleep between periods of activity. This was necessary to ensure minimal consumption of food and other resources. This has changed with the advent of the new technology. Food and space are plentiful on the colony ships, and space travel has placed an ever-increasing number of planets at our disposal. As a result, the necessity of Deep Sleep has become obsolete. In fact, with the exception of the sick or injured, the only time a Tzen is required to undergo Deep Sleep is when traveling in a transport ship to attack a new planet."

"I am aware of all this, Rahk," I interrupted. "Proceed with your theory."

"It is my contention that Deep Sleep performed a function beyond simple conservation of resources. There is a replenishment of body cells which takes place during sleep which is necessary for a Tzen to function efficiently."

"A replenishment of what?" I asked.

"Allow me to rephrase that, Commander. The body and mind of a Tzen experience fatigue in prolonged use, similar to a weapon which is fired at full force for an extended period."

"I assume you are referring to the blasters as opposed to our traditional hand weapons."

"Yes, I am. Now just as a blaster must be allowed to rest to function normally, a Tzen must sleep to rejuvenate mind and body."

"I am not sure I understand your analogy, Rahk," I communicated. "Every blaster has two specific rates of use: the maximum rate, and the maximum sustained rate. The maximum rate is that rate a weapon is capable of firing at any given moment at full force. Firing a weapon at that rate will give a great amount of energy for a short time, but after that time the weapon will malfunction. There is also, however, the maximum sustained rate. This rate is lower than the maximum rate, but if used at that rate, the weapon can function indefinitely, at least theoretically. If your analogy is correct, then it should be possible for a Tzen to function at a maximum sustained rate forever without sleep."

"That is correct, Commander. However, there is some question as to what that maximum sustained rate is. It is my contention that we normally function at a level well above our maximum sustained rate. As such, unless a schedule of regular periods of sleep is established and enforced, I fear we will find that we are functioning at less than peak efficiency." I pondered this.

"How does our feeding pattern enter into this?"

"The cells require certain—" he lapsed into thoughtful silence for a moment. "I'm sorry, Commander. I am unable to think of a simple way to explain it. I am unaccustomed to speaking to Tzen not of the Scientist caste. I will have to ask that you simply believe me when I say that, like sleep, a certain regular intake of food is necessary."

"And you say you are unable to prove this theory?"

"Not to Tzu's satisfaction. It would require extensive testing of Tzen from all castes both before and after sleep to determine their relative effectiveness. For at least cursory proof, however, I would like to point to the performance of our current team."

"What about the performance of our team?"

"Few if any of the team have slept since our arrival on this planet.

I feel this is beginning to show in our performance, specifically in the Warriors' difficulty in dealing with the Spider. I feel a continued decline in our effectiveness could be disastrous, particularly as the insects will undoubtedly become more efficient as our stay here grows longer."

"You are convinced the Insects will give increased resistance?" I asked. I was not eager to comment on the performance of the Warrior caste.

"I have been examining the reports of your first expedition, Commander. As a result, I am of the opinion the Empire is underestimating the intelligence of the Insects."

"Explain . . ."

"When you first were forced to crash land, the Leapers would not venture under the trees, yet your account of Ahk's death specifically references the Leapers' attacking while under cover of the forest. This in itself indicates an alarming adaptive ability. Later, however, you describe in great detail how the Leapers laid an ambush for you and your two companions. This cannot be ignored. In an amazingly short time, the Leapers had not only recognized the Tzen as an enemy, they were actively mounting countermeasures. They were not merely pursuing you on chance encounters, they were actively hunting you. Also, remember we are speaking of the Leapers, a species rated as being less intelligent than the Ants."

He stopped, suddenly aware he was being carried away by his emotions. Composing himself, he continued. "Based on these observations, I feel it is not a possibility, but a certainty, that as the mission progresses, we can expect increased difficulties with the Insects. For this reason, I recommend that the team be encouraged, if not required, to get as much sleep as possible . . . now, while they are able. We will need every Tzen operating at peak efficiency soon."

Despite my skepticism, I was impressed by his arguments.

"I will take your recommendations under consideration, Rahk," I said.

I was sincere in my promise, and planned to implement his plan as soon as I had consulted with my staff. Before I could, however, something occurred that forced me to change my priorities.

I was in conference with Horc concerning the priority of the Technicians' assignments when I noticed something.

"Horc," I said, interrupting his speech, "all the skimmers are here."

"Yes, Commander."

"But isn't there a patrol out?"

"Yes, Commander. They declined the use of a skimmer."

"Why?"

"I was not consulted in the decision."

Breaking off the conference, I sought out Zur.

"It was the team's decision, Commander," he informed me. "As the destination for their patrol was less than two kilometers beyond the Defense Network, they decided to walk the distance rather than utilize the faster but less stable means of transport afforded by the skimmers."

"Who is on the patrol?"

"Kor and Vahr, escorting Tzu."

I approved of the use of veteran Warriors on such a mission, but still felt uneasy.

"Without a skimmer, we do not have visual contact."

"That is correct, Commander. I pointed this out to them, but they stood by their decision. They have, however, been keeping regular contact by booster band."

"Contact them and confirm their status."

"But they aren't due to contact us for—"

"Contact them. If they complain, tell them it was on my orders."

"Very well, Commander."

He slipped on his booster band. I waited impatiently. I wondered if I was misusing my authority as Commander to quiet my own fears, but discarded the thought. I had learned as a Warrior not to ignore my instincts, and seldom had I experienced misgivings as strong as I experienced when I learned the patrol was out without a skimmer.

"They are not responding, Commander."

"Contact Horc and have him get two flyers ready. You and I are going to—"

"Commander!"

It was Zome's voice beaming into my head.

"Rahm here," I responded.

"Set your arm-unit for the input unit by the anthill, immediately!"

Zome did not have the authority to give me orders, but something in his voice made me respond. Reflexively, I extended my arm to allow Zur to share the view as the scene swam into focus.

There was a frenzy of activity at the anthill. A party of Ants was returning, bearing aloft a prize. They were triumphantly carrying our three missing teammates. Judging from their lack of movement, they were either dead or unconscious as they were dragged out of sight down the hole.

Chapter Ten

The loss of three teammates had a definite impact on the remaining members. Of particular note was Tzu, sorely missed as a Scientist, and irreplaceable as the head of the Scientists' team. Of no less loss, though some might dispute it, were Kor and Vahr. The loss of two veteran Warriors, particularly one of Kor's abilities, could only lessen our chances of success or even survival. Although still nine strong, the team was disproportionately weakened.

The situation was serious enough to require my calling a staff meeting. I was loath to do this, as I felt our meetings were becoming needlessly frequent, but we could ill afford uncoordinated action or thought at this time. Lack of information, and therefore lack of unity, has doomed many a campaign in a crisis that could have been salvaged.

"An appraisal of the Warrior situation, Zur?" I asked, to begin the meeting.

"The Warriors should be able to perform with the existing force, Commander. It cannot be discounted, however, that with the loss of four teammates, three of them Warriors, we may be pitted against a force we are incapable of dealing with. Of particular concern is the potential ineffectiveness of our cold-beams. Both Warriors lost on the last assignment were armed with cold-beam hand blasters, and Kor's reflexes were known to all. Still, they were unable to secure sufficient time to beam a distress call or even a warning to the fortification. From this we must assume increased probability that such weapons are as ineffective against the Ants as they were against the Spiders. I would therefore recommend we give serious consideration to widespread use of hot-beams for the duration of the mission."

I considered this. Zome, now representing the Scientists remained silent, a fact for which I was grateful. It was obviously the Scientists' role to raise protest at the danger to the local ecology that use of the hot-beams would involve. The danger was obvious enough to go without saying, and he didn't say a thing. Lost in concentration though I was, I appreciated it.

"Horc," I said finally, "would it be possible for the Technicians to devise some method for containing any incidental fires started by the use of the hot-beams within the Defense Network?"

"We could do it either by establishing a firebreak around the network, or by a similar circular array of heat-triggered fire extinguishers. Of course, neither of these solutions are acceptable."

"Why not?"

"Either method would be difficult if not impossible to camouflage, and would therefore effectively pinpoint our position to the enemy."

"If I might point out, Horc, we have already lost three, possibly four, teammates to the Enemy. This indicates that they are fully aware of our presence, and if our exact location is not currently known, it very probably soon will be. I will therefore instruct you to install the necessary devices for fire containment. It is better that we begin to plan our defenses for such a confrontation than merely hope it will not occur."

"Very well, Commander."

"Zome, I realize the difficulty of your position, and would normally allow you a certain grace period to reacclimate yourself to the duties of command. Unfortunately, circumstances do not permit this. Do you have even an estimate for us as to how much additional time will be required to find an acceptable natural enemy to the Leapers?"

"I do, Commander. It is my belief we have already found it."

"Explain."

"For some time now the Scientists have been investigating a species of warm-bloods indigenous to this planet. They are small, only about a half-meter in length, and are completely harmless to the Tzen. Their specific food is the eggs of the Leapers, which they sniff out and burrow after, each one consuming ten to fifty a day. It is our belief that seeding the Leaper-held planets with large quantities of these warm-bloods, coupled with a concentrated ground and air strike against the adult Leapers, could effectively eliminate that species of the Insect Coalition." His voice was uncharacteristically enthusiastic.

"Warm-bloods are notoriously short-lived," interrupted Horc. "How will they survive the flight back to the colony ship?"

"This particular species is highly prolific," answered Zome. "They should be able to produce new generations while on board the transport ship to replace those that die."

"If they are so potentially effective," interjected Zur, "why have they been unable to eliminate the Leapers on this planet?"

"The natural enemy for this species, a carnivorous plant, also abounds on this planet. It claims such a high percentage of the species' population that only its high reproductive rate has allowed the species to survive at all. For this particular planet, we would raise a high population in the colony ships to offset the normal mortality rate. Then, including the carnivorous plants on the target list along with the adult Leapers, we would dump them back here to deal with the eggs. By the time the plants reestablished themselves from seeds, the warm-bloods' work should be done."

"What do they eat besides Leaper eggs?" asked Horc. "What would we feed them in transit, or on the colony ships for that matter?"

"We have induced them to accept a chemical substitute in the lab, one which we can easily produce, even on board ship. I should note that we were careful to test one thing. They will not eat Tzen eggs."

"How hard are they to catch?" Zur inquired. "What will be involved in obtaining a breeding stock to take back with us?"

"There is a particular chirp they emit when ready to breed, a chirp they use to attract a mate. It is possible to reproduce this sound mechanically, and properly amplified by the Technicians, it should be easy to draw them to our fortification for capture and transport.

"This trait is particularly advantageous, since if they begin to overpopulate the target planets, we will be able to attract them to a central point for disposal or dispersal."

"I have a question, Zome."

"Yes, Commander?"

"The species you describe seems to be the perfect solution to our problem. In fact, it is so perfect, I must inquire as to why it was not brought to our attention before?"

For the first time in his presentation, Zome hesitated before replying.

"Tzu does . . . did not like warm-bloods. She was at best reluctant to recommend spreading this species or any warmblood through the universe. As such, she delayed reporting our findings while she searched for another alternative. She was investigating another predatory species of Insect, one outside the Coalition, when she had her encounter with the Ants."

"What was her objection to warm-bloods?" asked Zur.

"She expressed what I believe to be a personal theory. It maintains that considering the brain-size-to-body-mass ratio, that the warm-bloods are potentially intelligent, even more intelligent than the Insects or even the Tzen. If properly directed, that intelligence could be a potential threat to the Empire."

"Warm-bloods?" interrupted Horc. "A threat to the Empire?"

"Having insufficient data to calculate the relative intelligence of warmblood species, much less the probability of such an occurrence, she was prone to treat all warm-bloods with equal suspicion."

"I'm no Scientist, Zome," Horc commented, "but I find that theory hard to accept. To challenge the Empire would require not only intelligence, but technology. To the best of my knowledge, warm-bloods are not physically able to operate machines, much less develop them."

"As you have said, Horc, you are not a Scientist. Species of warm-bloods have been discovered with grasping forepaws not unlike our own hands, and therefore capable of operating machinery. What is more, until we discovered the notes of the First Ones, we would have insisted it was physically impossible for an Insect to operate a machine. Intelligent beings will develop devices which can be operated by their own physical configuration."

"Zome—" Zur began, but the Scientist raised a restraining hand.

"Before we pursue the subject further, I would like to clarify my own position. I personally disagree with Tzu's theory. If nothing else, I feel the narrow temperature range warm-bloods can tolerate negates their effective danger to the Empire. However, as a Scientist, I must acknowledge the possibility just as Tzu did. I merely discount the probability."

"Tzu's apprehensions are noted, Zome," I said. "However, I believe we are in agreement. Any species we find will have potential dangers inherent, and searching for a probably nonexistent perfect species is both time-consuming and dangerous. The one benefit I can see to the species under examination is that if we have made a mistake, it can be recalled by the chirp machines. If there are no objections, then, I will accept the designated warmblood species as our target, and we will proceed with collection."

Once our target was agreed upon, the mission proceeded smoothly. The chirp machine devised by the Technicians drew the warm-bloods in at such a high rate that for a while we were hard-pressed to construct cages fast enough to hold them.

A booster beam call to the transport ship brought the crew back to full active status, and the cage problem was soon solved. The Technicians on board began constructing large holding pens, and daily runs from the shuttle craft began filling them, leaving us with empty cages to fill.

The ground team was not lulled just because the end of the mission was in sight, however. Horc and Rahk had taken assignment on board the ship looking after the warm-bloods as they were ferried up, leaving us with only seven team members on the ground. To counterbalance our weakness, Zome and Ihr armed themselves from the arsenal and accepted temporary assignment with the Warriors as guards, leaving only Krah to collect the warm-bloods and load the cages.

It was interesting that these two, Zome from the Scientists and Ihr from the Technicians, would volunteer for this duty. I had detected in Zome's eagerness to accept field assignments a hunger for action and admiration for the Warriors. In his case, it was a chance to try another role without changing castes.

Ihr was a different story entirely. From the onset of the mission, she had been openly disdainful of the Warriors, to a point where Horc had found it necessary to reprimand her several times. Her willingness to stand guard could only be interpreted in one way—she was out to prove that she could do a Warrior's job as well as or better than any Warrior.

Two non-Warriors, one friendly, one hostile—I did not care what their motives were. They were Tzen, and I was glad to have them armed and watching the perimeter.

Despite the smoothness of the mission, I was uneasy. My Warrior's instinct told me no plan, including our current one, would transpire as predicted.

I was right.

I was in conference with Zome when it happened. We were discussing the necessary quantities of warm-bloods to transport and had reached agreement. The load currently waiting to be picked up and one more should provide breeding stock of sufficient quantity for the proposed project. It was then the call came.

"Attack Alert! Weapons ready!"

I reacted instantly to the message beamed into my head, as did every other team member in sight. We waited for clarification, but none came. The message had been in a strained tone, negating identification.

"Who sounded the Alert?" I beamed at last.

There was no answer.

"Mahz!" I beamed. He was currently covering the gun turret.

"Yes, Commander!"

"Anything on the Network?"

"No, Commander."

I pondered the problem, weapon in hand.

"Commander!"

It was Hif's voice beamed into my head.

"Report, Hif!"

"I have visual contact. Something moving toward the fortification from the southeast . . . fifty meters out."

"Identify!"

"Unknown. I can see brush moving, but that's all."

"All members pull back to the fortification!" I beamed. "Mahz!"

"Here, Commander."

"Anything on the network to the southeast?"

"No, Commander."

The team was assembling now, Zur hastily assigning them positions with gestures and telepathy.

"I can see it now, Commander," came Mahz's voice.

"It's Kor!"

"Kor?" I echoed.

It was Kor. We watched her final painful approach, Zur moving to help her. She was badly mangled and missing one arm.

"Hold your position," I beamed to the rest of the team.

Chapter Eleven

Zur assisted Kor to a position behind our defensive line and eased her to the ground near the base of the fortification.

"Permission to leave formation, Commander?" called Zome softly.

"Reason?"

"To bring medical supplies and administer—"

"No!" Kor's voice interrupted, firm, and surprisingly calm.

"Kor!" Zur admonished.

"I must report first . . . important."

"Commander, she'll die if I don't—"

"They are going to attack . . . the Ants. . . . They'll try to stop the information from reaching the Empire . . ."

"Commander!" Zome was insistent.

I made my decision.

"We'll hear her report. Zur, I want you to rearrange the defenses. I want you, Zome, and the ranking Technician . . . Ihr, stationed near enough to hear this report, but I want you all facing outward to watch for attack."

"Yes, Commander," and he was moving, acting instantly to carry out the order.

"Thank you, Commander," whispered Kor weakly.

I ignored her.

"Mahz!" I beamed.

"Yes, Commander!"

"Put on a booster band and contact the transport immediately. Tell them we need the shuttlecraft down here as soon as they can manage it."

"Yes, Commander."

"Ready, Commander." Zur was back.

"Very well, Kor, proceed with your report."

"They have machines . . . They . . . they're studying us . . . using data to plan tactics—"

"What kind of machines?" interrupted Ihr.

"How are they studying us?" asked Zome.

"Ihr, Zome, I will say this once. We will not tolerate interruptions to this report. Kor, you are of the Warrior caste. You therefore know how to report in a concise orderly fashion. Cease this undisciplined babbling and report properly!"

The rebuff seemed to calm her.

"Yes, Commander. We were captured . . . all three of us . . ." She paused as if trying to organize her thoughts. I waited patiently, wondering about the fate of the other two captives.

"Some sort of stun ray . . . carry it slung under their bodies . . . Maximum range unknown . . . trigger mechanism unknown. We were hit at about fifty meters . . . They struck Vahr and me first, possibly because of our weapons, then took Tzu . . . Only saw two weapons. So they can be fired at least twice without recharge or reloading . . . Efect is immediate . . . full loss of motor nerve control and partial loss of mental faculties . . ."

She was weakening. I noticed the wound from her missing arm was still bleeding. Using my hand, I tried to pinch off the arteries. I was not wholly successful, but at least now she was losing blood at a slower rate.

"The Ants were both swift and organized in their movements . . . We were stripped completely, weapons, harness, even booster bands before we could think clearly enough to try to send a message. We were then carried back to the anthill and inside . . . We could see and think, but couldn't move . . . dim lighting . . . dumped on floor . . ."

She stopped and stretched her head back. I realized she was suffering from the pain of her wounds. I waited.

"Dumped on floor in room with dim lighting . . . We were examined . . . probed by their antennae . . . checked for sex . . . Knew what they were looking for . . . then piled together . . . Examining Ants withdrew . . . replaced by six guards . . . larger, heavier mandibles . . .

"Finally gained control of motor nerves . . . Effects of stun beam wear off eventually . . . Examined chamber . . . Tzu said it was specifically a chamber for captives . . . one entrance, water supply . . . Particularly noted lighting . . . came from luminous rocks . . . not a natural formation . . . brought in . . . changed occasionally by guards . . . Light not necessary for Ants; must be for prisoners . . .

"Examining Ants returned once we were conscious . . . Crowded first Tzu, then me toward Vahr . . . Tzu deduced they wanted us to breed . . . Vahr and I complied, Tzu would not . . . Warm-bloods brought and given to Vahr and me . . . Tzu prevented from eating . . .

"Pattern continued . . . Laid eggs, but would not let Ants near them . . . They did not insist . . . Suggested Tzu also comply . . . refused . . . Would not help Enemy learn about Tzen . . .

"Began planning escape . . . Could approach entrance, but guards would not let us leave chamber . . . From entrance we could see another chamber across the tunnel . . . machines . . ."

"Commander!" came Mahz's voice into my mind.

"Rahm here."

"I have a report on the shuttlecraft."

"Delay report."

I focused my attention on Kor as she continued.

"Could not see entire chamber . . . There was a kind of viewscreen . . . not full image like ours . . . stick figures on glowing screen . . . Display showed our fortification and the anthill . . . stick figures of Tzen around fortification . . . Number of Tzen changed from time to time . . . assumed showing defenses and patrols . . . Could not see controls or operators.

"Planned escape . . . Had noted speed of Ants while being carried on surface . . . used estimated speed and memorized turns taken carried in dark . . . Thought we could find our way out . . . Decided not to carry glow rocks . . . would pinpoint position . . . Vahr and I would provide fighting cover for Tzu's escape . . . get Scientist out . . ."

"Commander," came Mahz's voice again.

"Rahm here."

"Intruders in the Network, southeast."

"Identify."

"Leapers. Twenty of them."

"Movement?"

"Holding position at seventy-five meters."

"Attack Alert," I called to the team. "Leapers massing. Seventy-five meters, southeast."

I turned back to Kor. "Continue your report."

"We made our escape attempt . . . Vahr began to act erratically . . . running back and forth . . . falling on floor . . . Finally ran to eggs and began smashing them with his feet.

"Three guards moved to subdue him . . . He fought . . . They seemed unwilling to hurt him . . . Killed one . . . Tzu and I made no move to escape . . . two of the remaining guards moved to assist . . . only one guard left on entrance . . .

"There were several rocks in chamber . . . same size as my steel balls . . . Used one to kill entrance guard . . . We ran . . . Vahr broke loose and took position at entrance to slow pursuit . . .

"Running blind in dark . . . Hit walls . . . Tunnels not patrolled . . . Ran into an Ant from behind . . . killed it . . . Ran into one head-on . . . caught me by arm . . . Tzu continued alone . . . Killed the Ant but lost the arm . . . kept running.

"Message beamed from Tzu . . . Encountered large number of Ants . . . blocking tunnel to surface . . . She ran down another tunnel . . . led them off . . .

"I got to the surface without encountering another Ant . . . headed for fortification . . . Several Ants emerged and started after me, then turned back . . ."

"Commander!" came Mahz's voice, "More Leapers north, accompanied by several Ants!"

"Confirmed," I beamed.

"That concludes my report." Kor's voice was suddenly coherent again. "Special commendation recommended for Tzu. She died like a—" Her body spasmed, and was still.

"Mahz," I beamed, "status report."

"No visual contact, but instruments still show the two groups. No activity since the last report. They seem to be waiting for something."

"Estimated arrival of shuttlecraft?"

"The transport is in a bad orbital position. If they send it out it won't have enough power to lift off again. Earliest possible arrival is just after sunset."

"Update status as conditions change, but report directly to Zur."

"Confirmed, Commander."

"Zome!" I called softly.

"Here, Commander."

"Examine Kor and stand by to report."

"Confirmed."

He moved to Kor's body.

"Ihr! Analysis of Kor's report."

There was no response.

"Ihr!"

"Yes, Commander. I . . . in a moment."

I started to press her, then realized she was taking Kor's death badly.

"Ignore it," I beamed to her. "Make your report. You are acting head of the Technicians.

"But Commander," she beamed back, "the last thing I said to Kor . . . before she was captured . . . I said I thought the Warriors—"

"Warrior or Technician, she was a Tzen. So are you. Now report."

"But—"

"She's dead . . . and the rest of us could be the same unless we learn from her report. Now give your analysis!"

"The Ant's technology is apparently inferior to our own. The viewscreen described indicates two things. First, they have not yet mastered direct input methods. Stick figures as opposed to full visuals indicate a display of manually input statistics. It is possible that there are several input stations, and also the possibility of several viewing screens displaying common data. It seems unlikely, however, that they would content themselves with representative figures if full visuals were possible.

"Secondly, they are apparently unable to modify equipment." Her voice was strengthening as she continued. "The fact that our teammates could observe the screen from a distance would imply it was a light display. This feature is probably unnecessary to the dark-dwelling Ants. The fact they have not modified this to their own use, despite the fact they have had access to the First Ones' technology longer than we have, indicates a low technical ability."

"Could it be," I interrupted, "that they did not anticipate another species penetrating that far into their nests? That would make a modification for an unlighted display an unnecessary expenditure of time."

"Being familiar with the design of viewscreens, I can definitely state that visual light displays are more difficult to build and operate. To a being with technical knowledge, an unlit display would be a simple modification, and one which would ease both construction and operation. As they have not made that modification, I feel it indicates they do not fully understand the principle of the machinery they are operating, and are simply imitating what has been done before."

"Understood. Proceed."

"The stun rays are another example of faulty technology. There are far more effective methods for an Insect to employ a weapon than slinging it under its body. Used in the current manner, it would be extremely difficult to aim on uneven terrain. What is more, to use it when firing from cover would mean the Ant would have to expose itself completely to the Enemy before its weapon could be brought into play."

"How would you explain the fact that they have a weapon not currently in our arsenal?"

"You would have to ask the Scientists, Commander. To the best of my knowledge, however, the Technicians have never been asked to construct one."

"Zome! Your comments and analyses?"

"Kor is dead, Commander."

"Yes, I assumed as much. Now your analysis."

"None of her injuries seem to be caused by any mechanical weapon. From this we can assume that unless specifically prepared for combat, the Ants rely upon their natural weapons.

"As to the stun ray, while the Scientists are not currently aware of such a weapon, it is logically a device such as would have been employed by the First Ones. It could have been passed over in their notes as being unsuitable to our purposes. Tzen will usually either kill an organism or leave it alone."

"It would be useful on missions such as this, when we are assigned to capture live specimens," I commented.

"That is true, Commander, but investigative expeditions such as this are a relatively new venture. Stun rays could have been discarded and forgotten before the need for these missions was known."

"Possibly. Proceed with your report."

"The examination described by Kor indicates prior knowledge of Tzen anatomy. This means the Ants have either obtained data from our earlier campaigns here, or that we have finally discovered what happened to Sirk. In either case, it shows the Ants are also capable of investigative study. They are both aware of the Tzen, and eager for additional data. This last is demonstrated by the fact they were willing to risk attempting to capture live and armed Tzen to obtain subjects for study. We will have to assume if they are intelligent enough to do that, they are intelligent enough to use what they learn."

I waited for a moment to be sure he had completed his report.

"Mahz!" I beamed.

"Here, Commander."

"Resume reporting updates directly to me."

"Confirmed, Commander."

"Zur, report and analyze."

"There are currently three groups of Insects in the immediate vicinity. From their position and actions, they are all aware of our presence, and preparing for attack. There are two groups of Leapers, apparently under the command of Ants, located southeast and north of the fortification. There is another group, composed entirely of Ants, directly west of us. All groups are currently stationary, apparently waiting for some signal or occurrence before they begin their attack.

"The shuttlecraft will not arrive until after sundown. It would be optimistic to assume they will not attack until then, so we must plan our defense.

"We will assume all three groups will attack simultaneously, though possibly the group of Ants to the west will delay their attack, hoping the other two groups will cause us to shift our positions. If there are weapons used in this attack, they will probably be with that group.

"There are several points in our favor in the upcoming battle. First, the Enemy is apparently still unaware of our Defense Net, which is currently pinpointing their positions and movements. Second, as we killed the spider with hand weapons only, they are not aware of our hot-beams or their effect.

"It is doubtful the stun beams described by Kor are effective beyond fifty meters. If nothing else, it would be next to impossible to use them accurately at a greater range. The range of our hand blasters and particularly the turret gun greatly exceed that.

"Unfortunately, the turret gun can only fire in one direction at a time.

"Our strategy will be to deal with the Enemy at maximum distance. The turret gun will concentrate its fire on the group of Ants to the west, as that is the most potentially dangerous. The rest of us must deal with the groups to the North and southeast."

"Zur!" I interrupted. "Is it not true that the swivel guns on the skimmers have a greater range than our hand blasters?"

"That is correct, Commander."

"Then if we array the skimmers—"

"Commander!" Mahz's voice came to me.

"Rahm here."

"Instruments indicate digging. There is a tunnel in progress to the southwest."

Chapter Twelve

"Request, Commander."

"Yes, Zur?" I beamed back.

"If opportunity presents itself, I would like your permission to dispose of Kor's body personally."

"What method would you propose?"

"I would use my hand-blaster to obliterate her body."

"Explain."

"She was an exceptional Warrior. She deserves a better end than serving as Ant food."

"Permission granted . . . providing opportunity presents itself. We do not want to prematurely display the power of our weapons."

"Of course, Commander."

Trust Zur to think of details like that under the most adverse situations. Then again, Kor's body was on his side of the fortification. He and Krah would have little to do but stare at it as we waited for the attack.

Our position was tenuous at best. The tunneling from the southwest had stopped about thirty meters out. The other three groups of Insects had not moved, though another pack of Leapers had joined the group to the southeast.

ஃ ஃ ஃ

We had opened the top of the base disc of the fortification, giving us a circular trench from which to operate. Our force was split into three two-Tzen teams: Zur and Krah covering the group to the southeast, Hif and Zome covering the north, and Ihr and I covering the all-Ant group to the west. Mahz at turret gun was assigned to watch for the tunnel opening when it appeared, and cover anything that emerged with his superior firepower.

I scanned the terrain to the west of our position, but could see nothing, even using far-focus. A thick stand of trees fifty meters distant obscured my view. If it were not for our Defense Network, I would be unaware of the Enemy lurking there.

I wondered what the Insects were waiting for. It was almost sunset. Perhaps they were planning a night attack. I discarded the idea. That would be too much to hope for. Besides, the Leapers were not that effective as night fighters.

"Commander." It was Mahz's voice.

"Rahm here," I beamed back.

"More Ants arriving to the west. They're moving slowly, apparently dragging something."

"Identify."

"Unknown, Commander. Large and bulky, possibly mechanical."

I didn't like the implications of that. I shot a glance at the cages of warm-bloods, still stacked in place beside the fortification. They alone seemed unmoved by the situation.

"Shuttlecraft status report?" I beamed.

"Still has not departed . . . Attack Alert, groups from north and southeast closing."

"Attack Alert!" I relayed, but it was unnecessary.

The sounds of the hot-beams were deadly soft as the other two teams opened fire on the advancing Enemy. The sound was soon lost in the shriek of dying Leapers.

"Zur," I beamed, "the hot-beams are effective against the Ants?"

"Most satisfactory, Commander," came the reply.

"West group is closing, Commander," Mahz beamed. "Moving slowly."

"Confirmed," I replied.

"Enemy incoming," I said to Ihr softly.

"Ready, Commander." Ihr's voice was tight.

I reminded myself that she was a Technician and as such unused to combat.

"West status report?" I beamed to Mahz.

"I can't see anything," Ihr complained, glaring through the gathering twilight shadows.

I ignored her.

"Still closing, Commander," came Mahz's report.

"They're out there," I informed Ihr.

"Then let's see them."

Before I realized what she was doing, she rose and fired blindly to the west. Her hot-beam immediately touched off a small brushfire. In its light, I could see a small group of Ants gathered behind a large piece of machinery.

"Ihr . . ." I began, but too late.

A ray lanced out from the Ant's machine, cutting her in half at the torso. So much for the self-styled Warrior-Technician. The beam shot out again, opening a gash in the fortification dome behind me.

"Cold-beam!" I broadcast to the other teams, kicking Ihr's body to one side.

"Shall I try for it, Commander?" came Mahz's hail.

"No! Continue watching for the tunnel."

I did not want to disclose the turret gun's presence until absolutely necessary, particularly not with cold-beams around.

I moved along the trench to my left, then cautiously raised my head for a look.

"It seems to be a large, bulky mechanism," I beamed to the force at the fortification. "Any indication of similar devices in the area?"

"Nothing on the Network," reported Mahz.

"No visual contact to the southeast," Zur beamed.

"Nothing to the North," came Hif's voice.

The Ants were close now. I raised my hand-blaster, aimed carefully, and fired. I was rewarded by seeing the machine collapse and smoke as the attending Ants abandoned it. Then the advancing Ants were on me.

I burned two to my right, then spun and got another as it tumbled into the trench behind me. I back-pedaled, burning another, not realizing until later that it had some mechanism attached to its underside, presumably a stun ray.

Such weapons might be effective to ambush patrols, but not in open combat against a Tzen of the Warrior caste. I was constantly moving, presenting an ever-shifting target to the Enemy. Twice I abandoned the trench, clearing a space in the swarm with my blaster before rolling back to relative safety.

My wedge-sword was out now, and I used it freely on living and dead foes alike as the trench became more congested with bodies. I crawled sometimes over, sometimes under the smoldering corpses of Ants in my frantic evade-and-attack pattern.

Suddenly, the flow ebbed. I realized it was dark; the scene was lit by scattered fires touched off by our hot-beams. A beam hissed out from above me, scoring heavily in the ranks of the Ants. It was Mahz, giving me cover fire from the turret gun.

"Mahz! I ordered you to cover the tunnel!"

"I stopped that thrust, Commander. They broke off the attack after I burned the first ten as they emerged."

I burned another Ant.

"Cover it anyway."

The Ants had spent a lot of time building that tunnel. I couldn't believe they would abandon it so easily. Too many battles had been lost by assuming a retreat.

"Incoming from your right, Commander," came Hif's voice, and a moment later she appeared.

"The north group?" I queried, blasting at a group of Ants by the burning tree stand.

"Eliminated. Apparently it was only a feint."

"Zome?"

"Helping Zur and Krah," she replied.

"Change places with Krah," I ordered.

"But, Commander . . ."

"I need a Technician over here." I gestured at the tree stand. "Their extinguishers are putting out the fires we need for light."

"Understood, Commander."

She moved off. I glared at the fires as they flickered out. We'd just have to rely on the firebreak to prevent widespread ecological damage. Right now we needed that light.

"Status report on the shuttlecraft?" I beamed to Mahz.

"On the way, Commander."

"Incoming from your right, Commander!" and Krah appeared. She was wobbly, but apparently taking to combat better than Ihr had.

"Do you know the exact location of the extinguishers you planted to the west?" I asked, sweep-burning three Ants that were attempting to flank us.

"Yes, Commander."

"Start burning them out with your blaster. We need those fires."

"Commander!" came Mahz's voice.

"Rahm here."

"Strange readings on the tunnel. The hollow indicator shows it's lengthening, heading for the fortification, but there are no digging sounds."

"Cold-beam! Cold-beam in the tunnel!" I broadcast.

"I'll handle it, Commander," came Hif's voice.

"Shuttlecraft is down, Commander. Twenty meters due south."

"Evacuate at once!"

The shuttlecraft was unarmed, and I did not want it overrun.

As one, Krah and I left the trench and began sprinting for the shuttlecraft, burning Ants as we ran.

I saw Hif by the tunnel opening. She dropped a mini-grenade down the opening, stepped back to avoid the explosion, then jumped in herself, blaster at ready. She knew as well as we did there would be no returning from the tunnel, but now our withdrawal was covered from that direction.

Zur and Zome were waiting by the shuttlecraft, pouring fire into a group of Ants pressing them hard from the southeast. Apparently the Ants had taken up the bulk of the battle after the Leapers had been eliminated.

"Where's Mahz?" I asked, turning to train my weapons on the Ants pursuing us from the west.

"Still in the gun turret, providing cover fire as ordered," replied Zur.

That had not been my intention.

"Mahz!" I beamed.

"Here, Commander."

"Set the destruct mechanism on the fortification, then put the turret gun on auto-target and withdraw."

"Confirmed, Commander."

"Shuttle pilot!" I beamed.

"Here, Commander." I was surprised to hear Horc's voice.

"Stand by for immediate takeoff when our last member reaches us."

There was a hesitation before he replied.

"Confirmed, Commander."

I realized he had been expecting to pick up a larger force than was currently in evidence.

"Concentrate cover fire for Mahz's withdrawal," I called to the rest of the team.

We could tell when the turret gun went on auto-target. It began swiveling randomly back and forth, choosing its targets by Network-triggered priority.

Mahz appeared a moment later. He had to blast his way through several Ants who apparently realized a lone Tzen was an easier target than our group by the shuttlecraft.

We concentrated our fire on the other Ants moving to block his retreat, but as so often happens with uncoordinated group fire, we missed one.

The Network was set to ignore Tzen, and it did. The turret gun swiveled and fired on the remaining Ant, coldly unheeding of the fact that Mahz was in its line of fire as it triggered the beam.

Book Three

Chapter One

I paced restlessly around the confines of my private quarters. Though theoretically solitude was supposed to aid the thought process, I found it disquieting.

I was not accustomed to solitude. In my entire career, from early training into my combat experiences, I had been surrounded by other Tzen. Even in Deep Sleep, I had shared a rack or a bay with other Warriors. Any moment alone had been both fleeting and coincidental.

Now I and all the other Candidates on the colony ship had been assigned private quarters until we had completed our analysis. Although it was a direct order from the High Command and doubtless for the best, it made me feel uncomfortable.

My tail thumped against the wall, and I realized it was beginning to lash uncontrollably. This would not do. Mental agitation was acceptable only if it did not adversely affect my performance. It was time to curb my wandering thoughts.

I considered eating, but rejected the thought. I was not really hungry, and an intake of food at this time would only make me sluggish.

Sleep was another possibility. We were now required to devote a certain percentage of our time to sleep, whether in regular small allotments or in periodic long slumbers. I also rejected this thought. I had not progressed sufficiently with the analysis for my satisfaction. The sooner I completed my task, the sooner I could leave the isolation of private quarters. I would sleep while my analysis was being reviewed.

Clearly, the best plan of action was to return to my work. I turned once more to my work station, viewing it with mild distaste. There were several racks of data tapes as well as multi-screen viewer, which crowded the small confines of the room.-

The tapes were sorted into five groups. The first group was the accumulated data on the Ants, both confirmed and speculative, though carefully labeled to distinguish between the two. The second group contained the Technicians' report on the equipment that would be available for this campaign. The last three groups dealt with specific data on three different Ant-held planets.

The task confronting me and the other Candidates was to devise battle plans for assaulting each of the planets. The High Command's review of these plans would determine which of us would be assigned as Planetary Commanders in the upcoming campaign. There are no guaranteed assignments in the Warriors. Many of my fellow Candidates in this exercise had been Planetary Commanders in the last campaign. They would have to reprove their analytic abilities if they were to retain their rank for this campaign. Also, it was common knowledge that there were many Warriors who had previously been Planetary Commanders who were not included in the current list of Candidates.

There was a rasp of claws on the door. I positioned myself in the doorway and triggered its opening. Zur was standing outside in the corridor holding a small box in his hand. I stood aside to show my willingness to accept his company, and he entered.

"I saw your name on the list of Candidates, Rahm," he stated without ceremony.

"That is correct," I confirmed, "though by the Black Swamps I don't know why. My progress with the assignment thus far verifies my original impressions that I am not qualified for this type of work."

He cocked his head at me in question.

"I should have thought that a Warrior of your experience would be quite adept at this analysis," he commented.

"Perhaps in theory," I replied. "In actuality I find little in my prior experience to assist me in this."

"Explain?" he requested.

"Even though I have held certain lower-level authoritative positions, they have always been of an execution nature. I have been a tactician, not a strategist. I have always been presented with a plan, and my task was to modify it according to existing conditions and put it into action."

I gestured to the racks of data tapes.

"Now, instead of adapting an existing plan, I am required to devise a plan and state its requirements. Instead of being given a plan, an objective, ten Warriors, and three skimmers, and told to deploy them, I am given an objective, and asked how many Warriors and what equipment would be required to achieve that objective. It involves an entirely different logic process, one that I am not sure I possess."

Zur thought about this for several moments.

"I see your difficulty," he said at last, "but I may have a possible solution for you, if I might suggest it."

"Accepted," I said.

"You are being overwhelmed with possibilities. There are so many variables you are unable to focus on any one course of action. My suggestion is this: choose an arbitrary force, a specific number of Warriors, and a random selection of equipment. Then go ahead and devise a battle plan as if that was all you had to work with. Organize your assault and estimate your casualties. Then halve the force and devise a new plan. Then double the original force and plan it again. If I am correct, you will rapidly discover that in one situation you are handicapped by a shortage of Warriors, in another there are excess Warriors. Perhaps in one situation you will find yourself realizing that two or more pieces of equipment would take the place of ten Warriors. In any case, by establishing some of your variables as constants, you should be able to better analyze the problem."

I considered this. It seemed a logical approach.

"I will attempt to implement this method, Zur," I said. "It seems an efficient approach to problem solving."

"It is one of the primary systems employed by the Scientists' caste," Zur commented. "I see no reason why it should not work equally well for a Warrior."

Somehow, this made me uncomfortable, but I withheld comment.

"This is actually the reason for my intrusion," Zur said, placing the box he was carrying in the corner. "It may aid you in your efforts."

I examined the device from a distance. My exposure to the Technicians on my last assignment had reinforced my normal instincts to not touch any machinery with which I was not familiar.

"Explain?" I requested.

"The Scientists have found that many of the older Tzen are unused to the silence inherent in privacy. To assist those individuals in their adaptation to the new systems, they instructed the Technicians to construct sound boxes such as this."

He paused, and flipped a switch on the side of the box. Immediately, faint sounds began to issue from the device. There were sounds of feet moving back and forth, tails rasping along the floor, the low murmur of voices. Intermittently, I could make out the clank and rasp of weapons being tended to.

"It is designed to emulate the sound of other Tzen," Zur continued. "I have specifically set the sound mix to resemble a group of Warriors. Hopefully it will create a more familiar atmosphere for you to work in."

I listened for a few moments. It did indeed sound like I was in the middle of a bay of Warriors pursuing their normal activities. I realized that as I was listening, much of the uneasiness I had been experiencing of late was slipping away. My muscles were relaxing from unrealized tensions, and my mind was focusing better. As my thoughts became more settled and orderly, a question occurred to me.

"Why are you doing this, Zur?"

"Although I am no longer a Scientist, I have maintained my habit of scanning the listings of theories and discoveries of the Scientists' caste as they are made public. This particular innovation was given such a low-priority rating I was almost certain that with the pressures of your new assignment, it had escaped your notice. I therefore took it upon myself to bring it to your attention, as it could potentially ease your task."

"That is specifically what I am inquiring after, Zur. Why are you concerning yourself with my well-being? What bearing does my success or failure have on you?"

"My plan is for the good of the Empire, Rahm," he stated, "though I will acknowledge it is selfish in that it favors my interpretation of what is best for the Empire."

"Might I inquire as to the nature of your plan, as I seem to be an integral part of it?"

"Certainly. First, I should inform you that I refused assignment as a Candidate."

This was a double surprise to me. I had not noticed that Zur's name was not on the list of Candidates. Had I given it any thought, I would have assumed if my name was there, his would be also. But more than this, I was surprised he had refused assignment.

"I have spent much time studying the structure of the Warriors' caste since I transferred," he continued. "As a result of those studies, I am of the opinion I could best serve the Empire in a specific position, but that position is not as a Planetary Commander. My logic is that I will stand a better chance of being appointed to my chosen position if a Commander I have worked with, specifically you, attains the rank of Planetary Commander and requests me for his force. To that end, I am being individually supportive of your efforts."

"What is the position you desire, Zur?"

"Second-in-command and Commander of the reserve force," he answered promptly.

I considered this. "Might I inquire," I asked, "why you prefer that position over assignment as a Planetary Commander?"

"My reasons are two, Rahm. First, my experience in the Warriors caste thus far has been of a supportive nature as opposed to a direct leadership role. I am confident of my abilities in that capacity, and would prefer to continue in the role I feel most efficient."

"You were in command of the Warrior contingent in our last assignment," I pointed out.

"Reporting directly to you. That is entirely different from being the final authority in the field."

"Acknowledged," I said.

"Secondly, though I still lack the eagerness for combat that marks one raised in the Warrior caste, I find that once I enter into battle I am as effective as any Warrior, and often more so. I feel my original training as a Scientist enables me to more rapidly observe, summarize, and appraise the factors weighing on any specific situation. This ability would be best utilized in directing the efforts of a reserve force, where the situation they would be facing would be significantly different from that in the original battle plan."

His answers were, as always, well thought out and logical.

"I will take your thoughts under consideration, Zur, if I receive assignment as Planetary Commander. It occurs to me, however, there may be a reluctance on the part of the High Command to assign two Warriors with our firsthand experience at dealing with the Ants to the same strike force."

"That is a factor beyond our control, Rahm. For the moment, I am content in the knowledge you would find my proposal worthy of serious consideration."

"My opinions will have little importance if I do not receive a Command assignment," I reminded him.

"Of that I have every confidence," Zur answered. "Perhaps I did not make myself clear, Rahm. I offer assistance only to make your analysis easier, not because I feel you would not be assigned if I did not contribute. I am sure that in your case this exercise is merely a formality. The High Command would have to be foolish to pass you over for a Command assignment, and although I have not always agreed with their decisions, I have never known them to be foolish."

He turned and left without further comment.

I pondered his last statement. Zur was seldom, if ever, wrong in his analysis. He had correctly anticipated my first appointment as flight leader even before he joined the Warriors' caste. His thoughts were not to be taken lightly.

Grudgingly, I turned my attentions once more to my analysis.

Even if Zur was correct, even if this analysis was merely a formality, it still had to be done.

The familiar noises issuing from the sound box aided my concentration as I readdressed myself to my proposed battle plans.

Chapter Two

I studied my four strike team Commanders as they familiarized themselves with the data packs they had just been issued.

I assumed that Zur was engaged in the same study, though neither of us spoke. It was a natural enough reaction, as this was the first time we had met these Warriors.

This was not to imply, however, that they were unknown to us or that we had never discussed them. On the contrary, they had been carefully selected by Zur and myself after several long wake-spans of reviewing individual records of available Warriors.

This selection process had proved to be far more difficult than I would ever have imagined. There were numerous qualified Warriors with little among their records to distinguish them. They were so similar, in fact, that it was a momentary temptation to simply state "no preference" and allow the High Command to assign the necessary Warriors to us. In the end, however, we took the time to examine the records and select our strike team leaders. If there was a slight edge to be gained by selecting certain qualifications over others, it was well worth the time spent.

There were no specific qualifications, such as seniority, breeding, or test records, that decided our choices. Rather, we looked for specific individuals whom we felt would be best able to fill our needs.

Heem's last assignment had been as a Warrior advisor to the Scientists' caste. He had served in this capacity, sometimes observing, sometimes taking weapons in hand to demonstrate a point, during the period when the Scientists were performing the tests and experiments that constituted the main database on the Ants currently used for reference. I had been advised by Zur that not all the test results known to the Scientists were published. Mostly this was to insure concision of reporting, but occasionally data was omitted because no satisfactory explanation had been found. Scientists were loath to state speculation or opinion as fact. As a Warrior, I was more concerned with reliable observation than with explanation. If an organism I'm fighting breathes fire, I want to know about it even if no one has figured out exactly how it is accomplished. It was hoped that Heem would be able to provide such firsthand data.

Tur-Kam was selected for different reasons. Her prior experience had been as a trainer. Her extensive knowledge of current training techniques and the comparative merits of available facilities and trainers would provide valuable counsel as to how to get maximum effectiveness out of the available preparation time. Her own combat and leadership potential ratings were impressively high, and the frequency with which she had been bred bore mute testimony to the High Command's respect for her abilities.

Zah-Rah I anticipated would be one of our strongest strike team leaders. She would have to be, for the target anthill for her force was exceptionally complex and difficult. She was one of the candidates who had not been assigned to a Planetary Commander position. I had requested and received copies of her attack proposals, and upon reviewing them found her methods and philosophies meritorious and compatible with my own. I felt we were extremely fortunate to have acquired her for our strike force.

Kah-Tu had the least experience of any of the strike-team leaders. However, his combat and leadership potential ratings were phenomenal. It was noted in his records that only his lack of combat experience had kept him from being assigned as a Candidate, and therefore a potential Planetary Commander. Selecting him as a strike-team leader might have been considered risky by some, but not by me. Others would not attach any significance to another entry in his record—the one stating he was the result of a breeding between Kor, who had served with me in two earlier assignments, and Zur, my current second-in-command.

The group's attention was drawn to the door as one final Warrior entered the squad bay we were using for a headquarters. She walked with the slight unsteadiness that marked one who had only recently boarded a colony ship and was still adjusting to the centrifugal force gravity.

This was Raht, the last of our five strike-team leaders. Her tardiness was acceptable, as there was valid reason for its occurrence. She had just returned from assignment, leading a flight of scout flyers on a mission over one of the Ant-held Planets. She had accepted her current position in our force while en route back to the colony ship.

"Are you capable of participating in our briefing, Raht?" I asked.

"In a moment, Commander," she replied unhesitatingly. "As soon as I refresh myself with a drink of water."

We waited as she stepped to the water dispenser and drank deeply. It was not uncommon for a Tzen to experience a dehydration from space travel.

Raht was another valuable member of our team. Her work as a scout meant she was familiar with all the latest equipment available and had firsthand knowledge of the inevitable difficulties and idiosyncrasies inherent therein. What was more, she doubtless had additional knowledge of the Ants that was even now being studied by the Scientists and High Command prior to general release.

"Ready, Commander," Raht stated, taking her data pack from Zur. I was impressed by her perseverance. Most Warriors would have requested reorientation time between combat assignments. I wondered if her attitude could be at all traced to her longevity. For the last three Hatchings, the policy of assigning two-syllable names had been in effect. Thus her name, like those of Zur, Heem, and myself marked her as a survivor of an earlier era of the Empire.

"Before we begin," I said, "there is one point of clarification which should be communicated to you. It has now been confirmed that due to transportation timing, any Warrior accepting assignment on this

Force will be exempt from the final mission against the Leapers. By the time that strike force has completed its mission and returned to the colony ship, our own force will have finished its preparations for the upcoming campaign and be well on its way to its Target Planet. If any of you wish to withdraw your acceptance of position in this strike force so that you might be included in the final Leaper assault, you should do so at this time. Even though your participation in that assault would negate your rejoining our specific strike force, there would be positions available in the Planetary strike forces which would be forming and training after our departure."

I paused to give them opportunity to speak. The five team leaders waited impassively for me to continue. Zur was right again. I had been sure we would lose at least one to the final Leaper assault.

"Very well," I said at last. "I, Rahm, as Planetary Commander duly confirmed and authorized by the High Command, formally confirm the acceptance of appointment to the position of strike-team Commander of Heem, Tur-Kam, Zah-Rah, Kah-Tu, and Raht."

As I spoke, the team leaders looked at each other in mild appraisal. This was the first time they had heard the names of their fellow staff members.

"Zur has accepted appointment as my second-in-command and Commander of the reserve force," I continued. "In event of my absence or incapacitation, he will assume full command of the force until the High Command appoints a successor."

The formalities over, I nodded to Zur, who turned on the row of view tables, Immediately, tri-D projections of the five anthills appeared, one over each table.

"These are our targets," I said. "As you can see, we have been assigned one of the more formidable planets, one having five rather than the average two or three anthills. The mission of this campaign is to destroy the queens and the egg beds of the Ants."

I turned from the tables to address them directly.

"Each of you will command a team assaulting one of those anthills. The specific data and plans pertaining to your anthill are contained in the data pack you have been issued. You are to review that data immediately and inform Zur or myself of any proposed changes in the battle plan or support requirements. You will also prepare and present for the entire staff a summary of the battle plan for your specific anthill."

I paused and reviewed my words thus far for omissions before turning to the next subject.

"As we are one of the first wave of Planetary strike forces, you will have a wide choice of Warriors to build your specific teams from. I would caution you, however, not to take an excessive amount of time in submitting requests for specific team members. The longer it takes to form your team, the less time they will have to train. If I feel you are taking too long to name your preferences, I will give you a one-time warning. If after that you are still unable to make a decision, your force will simply be assigned to you.

"The quartering assignments for your teams and the tentative training schedules are included in your data packs. If you would propose any changes to that schedule, discuss them with either Zur or me immediately. I would anticipate one question, and point out that if the training period seems both long and intense, remember the nature of our mission will require that much of the combat be done in the tunnels of the anthills. As the Warriors are unaccustomed to fighting in complete darkness, maximum time must be allowed for familiarization with the new equipment if they are to perform at peak efficiency."

I faced them squarely for my closing comments.

"You will all be quartered here with Zur and me. Once your teams are formed, you will be on call to me at all times. If I call a staff meeting, I will expect to see you, not your second-in-commands. Serious illness or injury will be the only excuse for nonattendance, and if your impairment is serious, we will not expect you to recover and will seek a replacement. I mention this so you will not overextend yourselves between sleep periods. Do not allow yourself to become fatigued to the brink of exhaustion, for your planned sleep may be interrupted."

"As we are one of the first strikes forces to be sent out, we will have to adapt to any new developments or equipment in minimum time, or not at all. Are there questions?"

The team leaders were silent for several moments as they digested the briefing. I waited.

"Question, Commander!"

"Yes, Tur-Kam?"

"Would you clarify the necessity for destroying the egg beds as well as the queens?"

I turned to Zur and nodded for him to reply.

"It has been discovered," he began, "that in event of a queen's death, the Ants are able to inject additives to certain eggs to produce a new queen. Therefore, if we are to succeed in exterminating the Ants as a continuing species, we must destroy the eggs as well as the queens."

"Commander?"

"Yes, Raht?"

"In our selection of specific Warriors, particularly our second-in-commands, are there any Warriors you would deem unacceptable?'

"While you will be expected to review your choices with Zur or myself prior to acting on them, we currently have no prejudices against any individual, Hatching, or ability group which would result in an immediate veto."

"Question, Commander."

"Yes, Kah-Tu?"

"What are your anticipated casualties on this mission?"

"If the assault proceeds according to plan without unanticipated resistance, we expect to survive the mission with no more than seventy percent casualties."

No one said anything else.

Chapter Three

Zur accompanied me as I rode the shuttle flyer to the Technicians' portion of the colony ship. Actually, I realized, the term "colony ship" was a misnomer. The reality of the situation was that the colony was actually a collection of smaller ships traveling in close alignment without any physical connection between them. Although they theoretically could be joined together to form one massive unit, and each new module was designed with that purpose in mind, the fact of the matter was that they had not been so arranged since shortly after the Empire relocated its population into them. Each massive module was a self-contained, stand-alone unit. When it was necessary to form a new colony ship, orders were simply issued for certain modules to set a new course, and there would be two colony ships where before there had been only one. How many such colony ships there were currently in the Empire I neither knew nor cared.

The modules that composed the Technicians' portion of the ship were easily distinguished from the others on the screen. They were the ones that were solid discs as opposed to the rings that were the Scientists' and Warriors' modules. I had never known the reason for this until the first time an occasion arose necessitating a visit to the Technicians' section. Once there, it became obvious. Unlike the

Scientists and Warriors, who worked and trained in the centrifugal-force-simulated gravity of rim-module, the Technicians did much of their work in the near-zero gravity that existed at the center of the module. In fact, certain subcastes of Technicians, such as the pilot of our shuttle craft, the transport pilots, and the heavy construction workers, were specifically bred for zero-gravity work and spent the majority if not all of their lives in that condition.

The docking process interrupted my thoughts. We departed the shuttlecraft without exchanging words with the pilot. As I have noted before, exchanges between members of different castes are rare except at certain rank-levels.

A Technician was waiting to receive us as we disembarked.

"I am Or-Sah," he introduced himself. "I have been assigned to answer your questions."

"This is Rahm," Zur responded, "a Planetary Commander of the Warriors, here to inspect the progress on various pieces of equipment being prepared for the Ant campaign."

I did not question why Zur did not introduce himself. Part of the reason I had him accompany me on these trips was that he was far more familiar with intercaste protocol than I.

"First," I stated, "I would wish to inspect the new Borer units."

"Certainly, Commander," replied Or-Sah without hesitation. "This way."

The Borer units were an improvement on the fortification we had used in our last mission. Instead of simply burning their way into a ground-level position, the new units were fitted with telescoping walls that extended downward as a tunnel was burned to accommodate them. Although all the units were of the same general design, they had to be individually modified. As each anthill was unique, the Borers designated to each anthill had to be built to penetrate to different depths. In cases where the chosen path for the Borer intersected existing Ant tunnels, ledges and firing slots had to be added to enable the Warriors to defend the tunnel from assault.

"Here is the prototype of the Borer unit, Commander," Or-Sah said, leading us into a large chamber.

High above us, work crews were laboring, furiously constructing additional units. We ignored them and studied the unit at our level.

One feature that was immediately apparent to the eye was the additional armament. The weapons at the top of the dome were heavier and more numerous, and there were additional weapons mounted along the perimeter of the unit.

"Have the lock-out mechanisms of the auto-weapons been modified?" I asked.

"They have," Or-Sah confirmed. "They will now recognize and bypass a Tzen in their field of fire, though I personally have never understood the need for such a requirement."

I kept my silence, but involuntarily my head lowered.

"On our last mission," Zur commented conversationally, "the Commander lost a team member because one of the auto-mounts opened fire while he was in line with the target."

"But the specifics of this campaign state that no Warriors will be on the ground outside the Borer units," the Technician argued. "Why should the Technicians have to waste valuable time designing—"

"Are the walls of this tube in their finished state?" I interrupted.

"Yes they are, Commander."

"Why haven't they been treated for cold-beam immunity?"

"Because it isn't necessary, Commander," Or-Sah replied. "The Energy-Drain units should render the Ants weapons ineffectual."

I found the patronizing tone of his voice irritating.

"And if they do not, every Warrior in the tube will be vulnerable to having his escape route cut off," I commented.

"The Technicians have every confidence in the Energy-Drain units."

"Have they been live-tested?" I asked.

"The Warriors' caste vetoed any live testing," Or-Sah retorted. "The reasoning given was that if the units were successful, it would give the Ants forewarning and provide them with time to develop a countermeasure."

I noticed that now it was Or-Sah who was lowering his head. I considered his position, and found his anger justified. It would be irritating to be forbidden to test a piece of equipment, then have to answer complaints that it was untested . . . particularly when both the veto and the challenge came from members of the same caste.

"Perhaps," I suggested, "you could provide me additional information as to the nature of the Energy-Drain units. My lack of understanding of the official releases on them is doubtless contributing to my reluctance in accepting their effectiveness."

He seemed surprised at the request, but responded nonetheless.

"Certainly, Commander," he began. "The xylomorphic interface utilized by the Ants—"

Excuse me, Or-Sah," I interrupted, "but are you familiar with a Technician named Horc?"

"Yes I am, Commander," he replied. "I served under him on my last assignment."

"Would you happen to know if he is available for consultation at this time?"

Or-Sah hesitated before answering. "Horc is dead," he said finally. "Killed in a duel with a Warrior."

That surprised me. "That does not seem logical," I commented. "Warriors are currently forbidden to challenge outside their caste.

"Horc was the challenger," Or-Sah explained.

"Then are there any other Technicians available who are used to dealing with members of other castes?" I asked. "Although your explanations may be clear to another Technician, as a Warrior I find them beyond my comprehension and vocabulary."

He maintained a thoughtful silence for a few moments. "Perhaps I can try again, Commander," he suggested finally. "I feel there is a growing need for communication between the castes, and I will not develop that ability in myself if I delegate the job to others."

"Proceed," I acknowledged.

"Both the Ants and the Empire utilize the same power-source, specifically that developed by the First Ones. Even though we have succeeded in applying it to a higher level of technology, it is still the same energy-source. It is as if the Ants and the Empire each maintained a cave with a circular opening to let the sunlight in; even though the caves are different, the openings and the sunlight are the same. Because of this, the Ants can run their machines from our power sources and we can run our machines from theirs."

He paused. When I did not interrupt, he continued. "In preparation for the Ant campaign, we have made two major developments. First, we modified our power-source and changed the configuration of our machines to accept it. In the analogy, we have effectively created a new sun, one which will shine through the hole in our cave, but not through the hole in the Ants' cave."

"How is that done?" I asked.

"I would be unable to explain it without becoming extremely technical, Commander," Oh-Sah replied. "Simply accept that we have done it."

"Very well," I said. "Continue."

"Now. The situation exists where we can run our machines from our power-source or theirs. The Ants, on the other hand, can only utilize their own power. When that is used up, their machines become nonfunctional. Our second major development is a machine, one which runs on the Ants' power-source. It consumes their power at an unbelievable rate, and converts it to power which replenishes our own new power-source. These are the Energy-Drainers. In simple terms, they make us stronger by diverting the Ants' energy away from them and to us."

I considered his explanation. "Is this power drain instantaneous?" I asked.

"No," he admitted, "but the battle plans call for the units to be dropped in advance of the actual assault. The Ants' power should be drained prior to the strike-teams' landing."

"What if the Ants have power sources they do not activate until the assault begins?"

"Then they would have power for a short time before the Energy-Drain units could fully deplete them."

"In that case," I concluded, "I will formally submit a request to the High Command that all Borer units be treated for cold-beam immunity."

"That is your prerogative, Commander," the Technician replied.

"I would examine the progress in arming the shuttlecraft next," I stated.

"Certainly, Commander. This way."

Zur broke off his inspection of the Borer prototype and fell in step as we left.

"Might I ask a personal question, Commander?" Or-Sah said as we went.

"Proceed."

"Do you or your aide find the current designs for individual blasters ineffective?"

That question surprised me, though I could see where, as a Technician, he would be eager to know the answer. I glanced at Zur, who indicated no desire to respond.

"No," I said for the two of us, "we don't."

"I had simply noted that both of you wear only the old hand weapons," Or-Sah explained.

He lapsed into silence, apparently unable to bring himself to ask why. He had given me food for thought, however. In hindsight, I realized that all five strike-team leaders . . . in fact all the Warriors I had recently encountered, wore blasters either in addition to or to the exclusion of the old hand weapons. I made a mental note to add a blaster to my personal armament again. It would not do to have it appear a Planetary Commander was not staying abreast of new developments.

Chapter Four

I was performing one of my scheduled reviews of the force in training. Although these were normally one of my less distasteful duties as Commander, I was finding more and more that I had to schedule these reviews or they would be overlooked in my numerous other tasks in preparing for the upcoming campaign.

As prescribed by the High Command, the Warriors were all training in the new echo helmets. Unfortunately, this made it impossible to distinguish among individuals. During training, the echo helmets had extra face plates to obscure the vision, simulating total darkness and forcing the Warrior to rely solely on the data provided by the helmets' sensors. The difficulty was that the face plate also obscured the individual's features, making casual identification difficult if not impossible, save in cases where radical physical differences such as height or an amputated tail marked the Warrior.

Zur and the five strike team leaders accompanied me as I made my review. Aside from that, training progressed normally . . . at least theoretically. I say theoretically because there were numerous subtle points of difference between what I was observing and what I knew from experience to be a typical day's training.

For one thing, it was rare that a trainer would actively take part in the training. They, like myself, were usually overburdened with administrative details of scheduling and training design and therefore had to delegate the actual training process to their staff. It was not uncommon for a Warrior to cycle through an entire training phase without once directly encountering the trainer responsible. Today, however, the trainers were very much in evidence. Whether directly supervising the training or simply overseeing, their presence was extremely noticeable.

Then there was the appearance of the training bays themselves. Though orderliness is necessary when working with or around live weapons, there is usually a certain amount of clutter and disorder associated with training. When the primary focus is on training, Warriors tend to let things fall where they fall. They would police the area afterward, but for the time being their main concern was experimenting with new possibilities and combinations to perfect their skill as the fighting arm of the Empire. The training bays I was seeing were so orderly I had the definite impression that I was viewing an exhibition rather than a fighting force at practice.

I was not so sure of my observations as to raise comment at this time, however. Rather, I determined that my next review would be unscheduled and unannounced, even to my staff. I would compare my observations of that review with my current impressions before deciding if there was cause for alarm.

Something caught my eye as I scanned the training Warriors. I halted my progress, causing my staff to press closer to me and stand in a waiting semicircle around me.

We were on one of the elevated walkways overlooking a maze. The Warriors below were maneuvering the corridors utilizing the echo helmets, and pausing sporadically to fire at pseudo-Ant targets that appeared singly or in groups to block their path. The transparent walls of the maze gave clear view of the exercise, but what caught my attention was elsewhere.

"Zur!" I beamed to my second-in-command.

Because of the sensitivity of the echo helmets, we did not speak aloud in the training bays.

"Yes, Commander!"

"Summon that Warrior to me . . . the one who is waiting in line . . . third from the front."

"Certainly, Commander."

I waited as my request was relayed.

One of the specific things I was studying in this review was the weapons rigs of the individual Warriors. As I have mentioned, audible sound can have a confusing effect on the echo helmets, and individual weapons carried in the traditional battle rigs had a tendency to make noise . . . slight, but noise nonetheless. As many developments in the Warriors' caste have come from solutions individuals have devised in the field in response to specific problems, I was eager to see what modifications were developing.

That is what I had been looking for. It was not what caught my eye.

The indicated Warrior was approaching our group now. I was pleased to note he had not removed his echo helmet. The force was rapidly approaching the point where they would be as natural maneuvering from the echo helmet data as with their normal vision.

"I am Rahm," I beamed to him, stepping forward. "May I examine your wedge-sword?"

"Yes, Commander," responded the Warrior, smoothly snatching the weapon from his harness and extending it to me handle first.

I took the sword and examined it closely. It was identical to my own weapon in size, heft, and balance, except for the pommel weight at the butt of the weapon. It was this that had caught my eye. Rather than being smoothly tooled like my own, it was fashioned as an irregular lump.

"I am puzzled by the design of your pommel, Warrior," I beamed. "What improvement does this deviation from the normal pattern signify?"

There was a moment's hesitation before the Warrior replied.

"None, Commander."

"Then why use this design over the standard?"

"It's fashioned to resemble the head of an Ant, Commander."

I examined the pommel again. He was right. Now that I was looking for that specific feature, the pommel did roughly approximate the head of an Ant.

"But why would you want a pommel that looks like the head of an Ant?"

"It . . . it gives me pleasure to look at it, Commander."

I was beginning to think there was something significant indicated here. Perhaps a recurrence of the inactive time problem I had experienced on my last mission.

"Where did you obtain this weapon, Warrior?"

"From the Technicians, Commander, like any other weapon. I'm sure if the Commander is interested, one would be available for him, too. I notice several of his staff already have them."

Startled by this statement, I shot a glance at my waiting staff. The Warrior was right! Zah-Rah and Raht were wearing weapons similar to the one I was holding. I had simply not noticed before.

"Very well, Warrior," I beamed, returning his sword. "That will be all. You may resume your training again."

The Warrior turned and strode away.

I resumed my tour of review.

"One moment, Commander!"

It was Tur-Kam's voice beamed into my head. I halted and turned to face her. The ex-trainer was intently watching the retreating figure of the Warrior.

"What is it, Tur-Kam?" I beamed.

"With your permission, Commander, I would like to investigate something."

"Proceed."

The Warrior I had conversed with suddenly halted, turned, and retraced his steps back to our group. I realized he must be responding to Tur-Kam's hail.

She stepped forward to meet him, and there was a silent exchange for a few moments. Then the Warrior removed his echo helmet and handed it to Tur-Kam. She examined it closely.

"Commander! This warrants your attention."

I joined them, and she passed me the helmet.

"I thought this Warrior's movements were too sure for one just learning the intricacies of an echo helmet," she beamed. "If you examine this unit, you will see it has been modified to allow his normal vision to bypass the face plate."

She was right. Though undetectable while the helmet was on, the modification was readily apparent when viewed from this vantage.

"Zur!" I beamed.

"Yes, Commander."

"Spread this order. All training in this bay is to cease. All Warriors are to remove their echo helmets. Immediately."

I passed the helmet to my staff and waited for the Warriors below to comply with my orders. Within moments, they were all standing with faces upturned toward our position. I stepped to the edge of the walkway.

"The trainer of this Warrior will present himself to me immediately," I announced.

"Commander," Tur-Kam said, quietly stepping to my side. "If there is to be a duel, I would request permission to represent the Empire. This incident is a reflection on all trainers and therefore on me. I would therefore ask preference of challenge."

"I disagree, Commander," said Zah-Rah stepping to my other side. "This Warrior is in my strike team. If preference of challenge is to be awarded, it should be mine."

"Your opinions are noted," I replied. "Return to your places."

The trainer was approaching as they complied with my order. I took the echo helmet from Raht and passed it to her.

"Examine this helmet," I ordered.

She took the helmet and examined it closely. "With your permission, Commander?" she asked.

She stepped to the edge of the walkway and beckoned to one of the Warriors below, presumably her second-in-command.

We waited as the Warrior hastened to join us. The entire episode was potentially quite serious. The trainers are a privileged subgroup of the Warriors, but there is a price for their status. They are responsible for everything that takes place during training.

The new Warrior joined us, and the trainer passed the helmet to him without a word. The brevity of his inspection was not lost on me or the trainer.

"Your comments?" I asked.

"None, Commander," The trainer replied.

Her assistant started to step forward, but she held up a hand to restrain him.

"I am responsible for this portion of the training," she continued, "and therefore stand ready to answer for any transgression which may have transpired."

"Face the Warriors," I said.

She hesitated, then turned and stepped to the edge of the walkway.

I raised my voice to address the entire bay. "It has been brought to my attention that the progress in training I have viewed today has been falsified. If this had not been discovered, had I been allowed to think you were more prepared than you are, I might have committed you to battle before you were actually ready. If that situation would have occurred, you would have been soundly defeated. The Empire's campaign against the Ants would have failed, and we would have been too depleted in numbers to mount another attack."

I pointed to the trainer. "This Warrior was responsible for your current phase of training. Her neglect of duty does not constitute a difference of opinion or an affront to any individual, group, or caste. It is a direct threat to the Empire."

I signaled to Zur. His alter-mace came off his harness and struck in one smooth blur of motion. The trainer's body hurtled off the walkway and crashed limply on the floor below.

"She dies not as a Tzen and a Warrior in a duel or in service to the Empire, but as an Enemy and a threat to our existence."

I turned and continued my review, my staff accompanying me.

As we entered the next training bay, we could hear behind us the cautious sounds of the Warriors resuming their training.

Chapter Five

". . . The earlier possibilities of the Ant's utilizing either poison gas or an acid spray have been discarded. While these devices are within the grasp of their technology, there have been no indications to date of their use or development."

Of all my duties, I found these briefings with representatives of the Scientists' caste the most distasteful. The briefing was particularly uncomfortable as I was without Zur's counsel. He was justifiably preoccupied working with his reserve force. Unfortunately, this left me to deal with the Scientists alone.

"We are still working on a means of disrupting the Ants' communications, but at this time it seems unlikely an adequate counter will be perfected prior to your departure. Effective countermeasures have been developed, however, to deal with the stun rays."

She indicated a small flat mechanism on the table at the side of the room.

"They are worn strapped to the chest, and field tests have proved they will nullify the effect of a stun ray. The Technicians are currently producing them for issue in the near future."

"Has the exact range of a stun ray been defined yet?" I interrupted.

"No," the Scientist answered. "It seems to vary according to the amount of energy fed into the projector."

I made a mental note to require all transport crew members to wear these units. Having the Planetside Warriors immune to the stun rays would be of limited merit if the Ants could succeed in using them against the orbiting transports.

"We have continued monitoring the indirect surveillance of the spacecraft housed in the anthills," the Scientist continued. "There have been no sounds or other indications of work or modifications being performed. Therefore, it is assumed the Ants are still utilizing the primitive craft originally given them by the First Ones. The armed shuttlecraft should be sufficient to insure no Ants will escape once the final assault begins."

"Do the Ants' spacecraft utilize the same power source as their weapons?" I asked.

"That is correct."

"Then won't the Energy-Drain units perfected by the Technicians negate the use of the spacecraft?"

"The Energy-Drain units were developed independently by the Technicians," the Scientist pointed out. "Until the principle has been tested and confirmed by the Scientists' caste, I would be hesitant to comment as to its reliability."

"Will those confirmation tests be performed prior to my force's departure?"

"I am not familiar with that project's priority rating, Commander. I will investigate and inform you immediately."

"Very well. What is the next item for review?"

"That completes the agenda for this briefing, Commander. Do you have any questions?"

I thought carefully for several minutes before replying. "Would it be permissible to ask a question not related to this mission? One of a nonmilitary nature?"

"Certainly, Commander. I have been assigned to supply you with information. There have been no instructions limiting the scope of that information."

I considered my question carefully before verbalizing it. "Could you comment as to whether or not the non-active time now available to the individual is having an adverse effect on the Empire?"

The Scientist cocked her head, her tail twitched minutely. "Could you clarify your question, Commander?"

I began to pace restlessly. I was unaccustomed to expressing my thoughts to Scientists.

"Since returning from my last mission, I have become increasingly aware of certain changes in the Empire. For the most part, I ignored them, as they had no direct bearing on me or the performance of my duties. Recently, however, an incident occurred which I could not ignore for its potential implications."

"What incident was that?" she asked.

"The details are unimportant. It involved a deliberate deception."

"A deception? That doesn't seem logical."

"My staff discovered it in my presence," I reiterated. "A premeditated falsification of training progress. My question is, is this a widespread problem throughout the Empire or was it an isolated case?"

I waited as the Scientist pondered my question.

"No other such incidents have been reported to the Scientists, Commander," she said at last, "though I cannot say whether this is because no similar incidents have occurred or if they were simply deemed unimportant."

"Unimportant?" Despite my self-pledged control, I felt my head begin to lower. "Such a falsification can only be interpreted as a direct threat to the Empire."

"I find your logic unclear, Commander."

"If I had believed the deception, I might have committed my force prematurely."

"But would you have?"

My tail began to lash slightly.

"Clarify your question?" I requested.

"Your exact words were that you might have committed your force," the Scientist replied. "I was inquiring as to whether or not you actually would have. If the deception had gone undetected, if you had believed everything you saw, would you have immediately reported to the High Command that your force was ready for combat?"

"Certainly not," I responded. "The force's training is far from complete. There is considerable time remaining before our scheduled departure, and it is my duty and that of my staff to be sure that time is utilized to best advantage."

"Then by your own admission, the incident was of no importance."

"You have missed the point entirely," I said.

"Perhaps, Commander. Could you clarify your position?"

I paused to organize my thoughts. "As a Commander of the Warriors' caste, I must be sensitive to the implications of an event beyond the immediate. I must concern myself with potentials, not just confirmed realities."

"Commander, are you attempting to explain the necessity of considering potentials to a member of the Scientists' caste?"

I lapsed into silence realizing both the truth of her observation and the futility of my efforts. The break in the conversation lengthened as I cast about for a new way to phrase my question.

"Commander," the Scientist said at last, "might I ask a question?"

"Certainly," I replied.

"How many Hatchings have you survived?"

I cocked my head. "Clarify?" I requested.

"How many Hatchlings have there been since your own?"

"I have no accurate knowledge of that," I admitted. "My career began when the Empire was still in the Black Swamps. During those times the number and frequency of the Hatchings were kept secret, particularly from line Warriors such as I."

"Do you know why that was necessary?"

"Yes. There was a period, three campaigns before the current war, when the Enemy we were fighting, the Day Swimmers, were not only intelligent, they were also able to decipher our speech. Information on the Hatchings was withheld so that a captured Warrior could not be forced into yielding it to the Enemy. It has been an axiom among our caste that the only way to be sure a Warrior will not talk when tortured is to give him nothing to talk about."

"But," the Scientist persisted, "since that time, Hatching information has been available for the asking. How many Hatchings do you recall?"

"I have never concerned myself with such matters," I said. "I learned originally to function in the absence of such information, and have never encountered evidence since to convince me of its necessity."

"Commander, my own career began here on the colony ship, after the campaign against the Wasps. Though I have never kept close note, I personally know of over thirty Hatchings since my own. Perhaps you could estimate from that—"

"I fail to see the point of this line of questioning," I interrupted. "What is it you are attempting to discover?"

Now it was the Scientist who paused before answering.

"Commander," she began at last, "among my fellow caste members, I am considered old and knowledgeable. Yet I have only vague knowledge of life in the Black Swamps, and would have to go to the data tapes to obtain information of the War against the Day Swimmers you reference so easily."

"There is no doubt my veteran's status played a major role in my candidacy, if that is your point," I prompted impatiently.

"More than that, Commander. It means your attitudes were shaped and set in a period completely alien to today's Warrior's."

"Scientist," I said, "are you questioning my qualifications as a Commander of the Warriors' caste?"

"Not at all," she said hastily. "Hear me out, Commander. If my information is correct, the current battle plans allow for sixty-three- to ninety-two-percent casualties. In the early campaigns of the Empire, victory itself was uncertain. This could account for your difficulty in understanding the logic processes of the newer Hatchings."

"Clarify?" I requested.

I was growing increasingly aware of the time being consumed in this interview. What I had hoped would be answered with a brief statement was developing into a lengthy conversation.

"The newer Hatchings enjoy a security you never had, Commander. Whereas you were taught that the Empire hung in the balance in every battle, the younger Warriors have a strong conviction the Empire will survive. As such, they are more concerned with their standing in the Empire than you ever were. This is not to say they are not aware of the importance of the upcoming campaign against the Ants. They are still Tzen and Warriors and would never knowingly participate in any activity they believed would weaken the force. However, they also have an interest in their roles after the battle, and as such are not above trying to create the best possible impression on their superiors, in this case you."

I decided it was time to bring this discussion to a close.

"Your comments and observations have been most beneficial," I said formally. "I shall be on my guard to insure this new feeling of security does not endanger the force's preparations for battle."

"But, Commander—" the Scientist began.

"My duties require my presence elsewhere," I interrupted. "As always, the Scientists have proved their undeniable value in support of the Warriors' caste and the Empire."

I turned and strode away before she would resume her oration. As I went, I chided myself briefly for having attempted to pose a nonspecific question to a Scientist. As expected, the answer had been cryptic and had not directly addressed the question posed.

I resolved not to enter into another briefing session without Zur's accompanying me. Perhaps I would even delegate that portion of the preparations completely to him. My duty was to prepare my force for battle, not play word games with a Scientist.

Chapter Six

The tri-D projection maps of the anthills were a minor marvel. They were possible through a modification of the jury-rigged device the Technicians had developed on our last mission. The original device simply indicated the presence of a subterranean hollow such as a cave or a tunnel. This had proved to be an invaluable aid in setting our defenses, giving us forewarning of the Ants' attempts to tunnel toward our fortification.

The new modification, however, made the device a powerful addition to our offensive effort as well. Instead of simply indicating the existence of a tunnel, the new devices could also determine its size and depth from the surface. A scout flyer armed with one of these devices crisscrossing the air over an anthill could now bring back a map of the tunnels and caverns composing that network.

My staff was currently assembled in front of one of those maps, the map of the second anthill, Rant's assignment.

"The difficulties in assaulting this particular anthill are obvious," I stated in opening. "As you can see, one of the major egg chambers lies here, under this lake."

I indicated the specific location on the map.

"I have called this meeting to seek your counsel on a problem which has arisen, or more specifically has failed to be corrected. The latest progress report from the Technicians indicates they have been unable to perfect a watertight Borer unit. What is more, their current projections for a completion time on that task fall well beyond our anticipated departure date. That means our original plan to bore directly to that chamber is no longer valid. We will have to formulate and implement a new plan if the assault is to be successful."

I waited as they pondered the problem. Raht bent over to examine the map more closely, a gesture I realized was merely a formality to help her think, as she had long since committed the map to memory.

"Commander," began Zah-Rah," am I correct in assuming a force will have to traverse the tunnels from one of the other bore points? If so, it seems logical that they would have to come from this point, as it is the nearest to their objective."

"With your permission, Commander?" Raht requested.

"Certainly, Raht."

"That is not a viable possibility, Zah-Rah," she began. "They would have to travel one of these two tunnels. Our current plans call for both those tunnels to be collapsed by Surface Thumpers. Failure to do that would allow the Ants to bring support units into position to protect the queen's chamber, here."

"Have you considered the possibility of creating our own tunnels?" suggested Heem.

"Clarify?' I requested.

"It is a known fact that Ants utilize cold-beams in the construction of their tunnels. As we also have cold-beams, it occurs to me we could employ them in a similar fashion. If we sank a Bore shaft, say here, we could then use the cold-beams to tunnel horizontally to reach the egg chamber."

I considered the proposal. It seemed to be an effective and ingenious solution to the problem. I was about to comment to that effect, when I noticed Zur was consulting the data tapes.

"Do you have something to add to the discussion, Zur?" I asked.

"One moment, Commander. I seem to recall . . . yes, here it is."

He studied the data tape before continuing. "I regret to say horizontal tunneling will not be possible in this situation."

"Explain?" requested Heem.

"Although it is true the Ants employ cold-beams to bore their tunnels, it is merely to supplement their own abilities. Constructing a tunnel requires more than boring a horizontal hole. It also involves some type of bracing to prevent its collapse. The Ants accomplish this with a form of cement they make with their own saliva. We have no such ability, and to attempt to construct a tunnel without support could only be disastrous."

"What if the tunnel is through solid rock? Wouldn't that negate the necessity for additional bracing?" Heem asked.

"That is what I was checking on the data tapes," Zur replied. "The region of the second anthill is characterized by loose, sandy soil, not solid rock."

"Perhaps the Technicians could devise a spray cement for us to use," Heem persisted.

"I will, inquire as to that possibility," I intervened. "However, realizing we are in this predicament due to the Technicians' inability to comply with a simple request, and considering the lack of time before our departure, I do not feel it would be wise to rely completely on a new discovery as a solution to our problem. Another answer will have to be devised."

"Commander?"

"Yes, Zur."

"Perhaps we are treating the lake as an obstacle instead of utilizing it."

"Explain?" I requested.

"We know the eggs are vulnerable to water. Couldn't we simply drop one of the water darts we used against the Aquatics into the lake with instructions to direct its cold-beams against the lake floor at this point? Such an attack would flood the chamber, effectively destroying the eggs with minimal loss of personnel."

"What would prevent the Ants from evacuating the eggs through one of the tunnels?" asked Kah-Tu.

"We could collapse the connecting tunnels with Surface Thumpers," replied Zur.

"How could the water dart determine the precise spot to apply its rays?" commented Tur-Kam.

"The chamber is of sufficient size, the precise spot would not be important," Zur countered.

"I have to disagree," Heem injected. "In the campaign against the Aquatics, we discovered the cold-beam's effectiveness is severely restricted by water. In fact, it is doubtful that even with a precise target the beam would be able to break the chamber."

"Commander?"

"Yes, Raht?"

"I think I have the answer. Instead of collapsing both of these tunnels with Surface Thumpers, we could only collapse this one. That would leave this route to the egg chambers available for our use from the near Bore hole."

"As you pointed out earlier, Raht, that would jeopardize the attack on the Queen's chamber."

"I am aware of that, Commander. What I would suggest is that when we reach this point in the tunnel, we use our cold-beams and mini-grenades to collapse the portion behind us, thus barring its use to the Ants."

I did not bother to point out that this action would effectively seal the force's route of retreat as well. Raht was doubtless aware of that factor when she suggested the plan.

"Do you feel you could traverse the tunnel with a sufficient number of your force intact to destroy the egg chamber?" I asked.

"That is my plan, Commander. If I find our casualties have depleted our force too severely to be effective, I will order the weapons be brought to bear on the ceiling of the chamber. As Zur pointed out, flooding the chamber will complete our mission, and it should be easier to accomplish from inside the chamber than from the lake."

If there was any doubt that what Raht was proposing was a suicide mission, this last amendment dispelled it.

"Very well," I said. "You are aware that this could very well be the key to deciding whether our assault of this Planet is a success or a failure. I expect, therefore, that you will give careful thought as to which Warriors you assign to this mission, particularly the leader."

"I plan to lead that team myself, Commander," she replied.

"As you wish," I replied. "Feel free to draw personnel from the other strike teams as you deem necessary. Any disputes as to the availability of individuals for this mission I will deal with personally."

I swept the assemblage with my gaze. There were no lowered heads or other indications of any exception being taken to my order. That was good. Raht was an exceptional Warrior, and her loss would be noted. I did not want her sacrifice to be in vain. If that particular attack failed, it would not because another strike team leader was unwilling to release the necessary key Warriors for reassignment.

"That concludes our meeting," I said. "Return to your teams in training now, remembering time is short before our departure. Zur, I would have a word with you."

"Certainly, Commander."

We waited until the others had filed out of the room.

"Zur," I said finally, 'I require your clarification of something I noticed reviewing the equipment lists being prepared for loading onto the transports. Why is it that we require two different types of shuttlecraft?"

"One is the ground-to-space shuttle such as was used to pick us up from our last mission, Commander," Zur stated. "The other is of the type currently used between modules of the colony ship; only the ones we will be carrying will be armed as pursuit ships should the Ants attempt to escape via their spacecraft."

"Can't we use one kind of Shuttlecraft to fulfill both needs?" I asked.

"Not possible, Commander. The heavy armor of the ground shuttles is not compatible with the maneuverability necessary for a space shuttle pursuit ship. Besides, it has been ordered that the Technicians will pilot the ground shuttles, while the Warriors will pilot the pursuit ships."

"I remember now," I said. "The order seemed illogical to me at the time. The Technicians are far more accustomed to piloting the space shuttles than the Warriors are. It would seem natural that that assignment would fall to them, not us."

"In this instance, piloting the space shuttles involves direct combat with the Enemy," Zur pointed out. "As such, it is within the duties of the Warriors' caste."

"Very well, that completed my questions, Zur."

"While we have a moment, Commander, there is something I should report to you."

"What is it?"

"I was asked to oversee a duel in your absence."

"A duel? Who was involved?"

"Two of the trainers . . . actually they were only staff members, not full trainers. One of them you might recall, the second-in-command of the trainer you had executed."

"What was the duel over?" I asked.

"They didn't inform me, and I did not ask. The second-in-command I referenced emerged the victor and seemed satisfied that the incident was closed."

"Do you see any difficulties arising from this episode, Zur?" I queried.

"No, Commander. I merely felt you should be informed of what had transpired."

"I will make note of it," I said. "You may return to your duties now."

As he left, I tried to recall what else I had intended to ask him, but whatever it was eluded my memory.

Chapter Seven

I was reduced to waiting again. Perhaps the hectic pace of my duties on board the colony ship had reduced my tolerance for inactive time or increased my metabolic rate. Whatever the case, I found I liked waiting even less than I had on previous assignments. I was in one of three transports currently in orbit over the target planet. Zah-Rah's and Kah-Tu's teams shared one ship, Tur-Kam's and Heem's another. Raht's team and Zur's reserve force were quartered aboard my designated control ship.

The mission thus far had progressed smoothly. The reports and data from the advance scout ships showed no significant additions to the anthills. The team leaders had received their final briefing, which they were currently relaying to their respective forces. The power-sources and Energy-Drainers had been successfully dropped and were performing perfectly. I should have been pleased and contented. I wasn't. I was impatient.

Zur seemed unmoved by the delay as he waited with me in the control compartment. Rather than burden his force with the final briefings, we had decided they need only be given final data if the need for their involvement arose, and then only that data that applied to their specific assignment.

In the meantime, Zur stood as motionless as a statue in front of the bank of viewscreens, apparently oblivious to the passage of time. I wondered if he had discovered some modified form of sleep to drop into at times like this. I almost asked him, but decided against it at the last moment. If he had, it would be improper for me to interrupt his trance before it was absolutely necessary.

I decided to review the late dispatches from the High Command once again, more from wanting something to do than from necessity.

The Technicians had finally perfected a watertight Borer unit. Similarly the cement spray we had requested was now ready. Unfortunately neither of these had been available prior to our departure from the colony ship.

While it was a mystery to me why the High Command bothered to send dispatches such as these, it did set me to thinking. Before attaining my current level of command and therefore having access to such dispatches, I had not been aware of the time lapse involved in traversing space. It seemed mildly incredible to me that two, perhaps three, flights of Warriors had been trained and dispatched since our departure from the colony ship.

It made me realize that the complexities of coordination involved in my own position were dwarfed by the task of the High Command in bringing the resources of the entire Empire to bear in one massive assault against the Ants.

It also brought to mind an unresolved problem I had previously ignored pending inactive time to fully study the matter.

"Zur?"

"Yes, Commander."

"How many Hatchings have you survived?"

There was a pause before he answered.

"I am not sure I understand your question, Commander."

"How many Hatchings have there been since you began your career?" I clarified.

I had the vague feeling I had had this conversation before.

"I do not know," Zur replied. "Why is this information important?

"While on the colony ship, I asked a Scientist to comment on the changes in the Empire. She seemed to feel the answer to that question played a large part in her reply. I was unable to decipher what she said, and I was hoping you might be able to clarify her analysis."

Zur pondered the subject for several moments.

"Do you feel outdated, Commander?" he asked finally.

"Explain?" I requested.

"Are you finding it increasingly difficult to communicate with other Warriors, to comprehend their motivations?"

"The Scientist asked similar questions at the time," I countered. "Yet when I asked if she was questioning my qualifications as a Commander, her reply was negative."

"She probably wasn't," Zur explained. "She was pointing out that you were different—not incompetent, merely different."

"Clarify?" I requested.

"The Empire has changed since you and I began our careers. I am aware of it, and apparently so are you, although you cannot identify the specifics. Warriors today think differently, react differently than you or I do. You notice I do not say better, merely different."

Both our heads turned as one of the ready lights came on the control panel. That was for our ship. Raht was ready.

"I do not resent this change," Zur continued, "nor do I attempt to change myself. I am what I am, and I simply trust in the Empire to find an assignment where a Warrior of my attitudes and skills are necessary. While it is possible that a time will come when my usefulness will fade, I am confident that at some future date the need will arise again and I will be awakened from Deep Sleep."

"Could you elaborate on your views of the future?" I prompted.

"As you know, Tzen do not kill or destroy out of inconvenience," he said. "Even assuming the assault on the Ants is successful and the last of the Coalition is destroyed, the High Command will not abandon its Warriors. Whether from a yet undiscovered species which bars the path of our colonization or if Tzu's mythical race of intelligent warm-bloods develops, there will arise a threat to the Empire. Such is the Law of Nature. Just as the Coalition encountered a natural Enemy in us, we in turn will eventually encounter a natural Enemy whose power rivals our own. On that day, the Warriors will be awakened. As such, we need not worry about outliving our usefulness."

I thought about this for some time.

I must admit," I said at last, "I had never given serious consideration to outliving my usefulness."

"I would not concern myself with the problem," replied Zur, "were I you, Commander. In many ways, you have changed much more readily than I."

"Explain?" I requested.

"The change has been obvious, Commander," Zur asserted. "Whether your rise in rank has been because of your change, or you have changed to fit the rank is irrelevant. The change *is* there."

"I am not aware of a change," I stated.

"Only because you are not prone to self-analysis. There was a time when you knew each Warrior under your command intimately. You deemed it vital to the performance of your duties. Now, I doubt if you even know the names of your strike team leaders' second-in-commands. I would hasten to point out this is not intended as criticism. A certain amount of detachment is necessary in a Commander. But it is a definite deviation from your earlier patterns."

The second ready light came on. This time from Tur-Kam and Heem's ship. The period of waiting was nearly over.

Zur started to continue, but I held up my hand for silence. While his points were interesting to ponder in inactive time, I did not want any distractions when we finally entered into battle.

The third light remained unlit.

It occurred to me it would be ironic if the final assault against the Coalition failed because of a malfunctioning ready light.

The light still remained dark.

I considered summoning a Technician to check the device. I was about to ask Zur's opinion, when the third and final light came on, completing the pattern.

The entire force was ready.

With forced calm, I signaled the attack, and the final assault began.

Chapter Eight

There was a delay before the viewscreens were activated. The first move of our assault was dropping the flyers, both the old single-Warrior and the new, larger, three-Warrior variety.

The view-input units were mounted on the underside of the flyers, and did not begin sending images until the flyers leveled off to start their attack. I could have had a visual report via the viewscreens beginning the moment they were dropped from the transports, but decided the additional wait was preferable to having multiple displays of their free-fall to the planet.

The viewscreens were grouped by anthill to avoid confusion in interpreting their displays. Zur and I watched in silence as one at a time they winked to life.

"Heem, Commander," came a message. "Report view-input unit malfunction on flyer four."

"Acknowledged," I replied.

The report was audible because of a late development by the Scientists. To ease strain on Planetary Commanders, they had devised a unit that could convert booster-band-relayed telepathic messages into actual sound, and reversed the process to send messages. Even though messages to the Planetary Commander were sent by strike-team leaders only, in an assault such as this messages were numerous and complex enough to make this new device a major aid.

We ignored the single blank viewscreen and watched the others. The first assignment of the flyers was to seal the anthills, using explosives to collapse the tunnels at and around their surface accesses. Simultaneous with this action, they were to drop the Communication Disrupters. I personally placed little faith in these units, not because I disbelieved in their efficiency, but because we had no means of verifying if they were functioning properly or not. The blank viewscreen gave mute testimony that not all devices were foolproof, regardless of the reassurances supplied by the Technicians. We still used the Disrupter units, however, since in a combat situation communications are vital, and any possibility of sabotaging the Enemy's efforts to pool and coordinate information was to be pursued. I simply didn't rely on their success in my planning.

"Tur-Kam, Commander. Borer units landed and functioning."

"Acknowledged."

"Report," I ordered.

"Reason unknown, Commander. Flyer was dropping Surface Thumpers and failed to pull out of run. Assumed mechanical failure.

"Acknowledged."

I had hoped for more firm information. Mechanical failure in a flyer is rare.

"Kah-Tu, Commander. Borer units landed and functioning."

"Acknowledged."

Third anthill. The battle was now joined on all fronts. I checked the screens. The Ants were gathering in clumps and rushing the Borer units.

"Kah-Tu."

"Yes, Commander."

"Split your flyers. Half are to abandon their efforts to seal the tunnels and instead provide cover fire for the Borer units. The other half are to coordinate their efforts and using Surface Thumpers attempt to seal the surface access tunnels at a lower point in the Network."

"Acknowledged, Commander."

This would be a true test of the force's training and effectiveness under fire. It was one thing to drill and prepare to drop the Thumpers on a specific, preplanned target. It was another matter entirely to select a target from the tri-D maps, translate it to the actual field situation, set the Surface Thumpers, and successfully execute the maneuver, all while in the middle of a combat situation.

"Reserves standing by, Commander."

I had not observed Zur's entrance, but he was at my side again.

"Acknowledged."

"Another view-input malfunction?" he asked, noticing the second blank viewscreen.

"Flyer down," I said. "Unconfirmed mechanical failure."

As I spoke, another viewscreen went blank.

"Zah-Rah, Commander. Flyer down."

"Report!"

"Reason unknown, Commander. Situation similar to first incident."

Two flyers down at the same anthill!

"There is something wrong, Commander," Zur interrupted. "It is illogical that two flyers would suffer mechanical failure in the same area."

Something in his assertion prompted a question in my mind.

"Zah-Rah. Was the second flyer downed in the same area as the first?"

There was a pause before the response came. Zah-Rah was with one of the Borer units, so the question and reply had to be relayed to the remaining flyers.

"Affirmative, Commander. Second flyer went down after attempting a drop run over the same area as the first."

"Instruct flyers to avoid that area. Order a high-altitude sound scan of that area and report results to me immediately."

"Acknowledged, Commander."

I stared suspiciously at the viewscreens for the other anthills, but no similar crashes occurred.

"Raht, Commander. My section is in the tunnels and has collapsed the designated portion behind us. We are continuing toward the egg chamber. Forty-three percent casualties so far."

"Acknowledged."

"Kah-Tu, Commander. Surface access has been collapsed as ordered. Surface resistance weakening."

"Acknowledged."

That would be the fourth anthill. I checked the viewscreens to confirm the operation. The fourth anthill had only three accesses to seal, so it was logical they would be the first to begin the actual attack.

"Heem, Commander. Borer units landed and functioning."

"Acknowledged."

Fifth anthill. I hastened to obtain visual confirmation from the viewscreens. This was a relatively difficult task. As I have noted, the view-input units were mounted on the flyers, and the flyers were far from inactive at this point.

As the Borer units were landing, the flyers were drop-placing the Surface Thumpers, a job calling for precision handling of the machines. More often than not, the viewscreens afforded only a close-up view of the ground flashing by at high speed as the flyers raced to complete their mission.

There had been some debate as to whether the Surface Thumpers should be dropped prior to or simultaneous with the landing of the Borer units. If we had dropped them earlier, it would have given the flyers more time to perform the maneuver. Our utilizing the simultaneous drop gave the Ants less time to counter the move.

"Zah-Rah, Commander. Borer units landed and functioning."

"Acknowledged."

First anthill. Hopefully, by now the Ants would be in utter turmoil. Even if they had anticipated our attack, they should have had no forewarning as to its format. Without advance knowledge of the Borer units, they would have had to expect a direct assault on the tunnels. Our move of sealing the surface tunnels and collapsing others should have introduced an unexpected element into their defense plans.

"Raht, Commander. Borer units landed and functioning."

"Acknowledged."

Second anthill! Something was wrong. The third anthill should have reported in before the second.

"Kah-Tu!" I beamed.

"Yes, Commander."

"Report status immediately."

"Encountering unexpected surface resistance, Commander. The Ants are digging new holes to the surface as fast as we can seal them."

The kaleidoscope display on the viewscreens confirmed this. Despite the frenzied efforts of the flyers, Ants were boiling to the surface and dashing angrily about.

"There are loose soil conditions in that area, Commander," Zur informed me. "It is doubtful we will be able to successfully stop that countermove."

"Proceed with Borer unit drop," I ordered.

"Acknowledged, Commander."

We had fought the Wasps to gain air supremacy. Now was when it should prove its worth.

"Zur!"

"Yes, Commander."

"Alert your reserves to stand by and report back to me."

"At once, Commander."

If we were encountering difficulties this early in the assault, it could be taken as guaranteed we would need the reserves before it was over.

One of the viewscreens went blank.

First anthill! I waited.

"Zah-Rah, Commander," came the report. "Flyer down."

I started for the viewscreens to confirm the claim.

"Zah-Rah, Commander. Sound scan reports evidence of machinery in designated area. No visual confirmation."

"Acknowledged."

My worst fears were realized.

"Rahm to all strike teams," I beamed. "Suspected cold-beam activity from Enemy. Possible firing on flyers. All units report full current status on my command. Zah-Rah!"

"First anthill. Borer units extended or extending. One egg chamber breached. Fifty-seven percent casualties so far. Possible ground fire on flyers."

"Raht!"

There was no reply.

"Kah-Tu!"

"Third anthill. Borer units extended. Two egg chambers and queen's chamber breached. Cold-beam attacks reported on tubes, but they have ceased with no damage inflicted. Seventy-seven percent casualties so far."

"Tur-Kam!"

There was no reply.

"Heem!"

"Fifth anthill. Borer units extended or extending. Queen's chamber breached. Sixty-seven-percent casualties so far."

"Raht, second call."

"Second anthill. Borer units extended. Queen's chamber and one egg chamber breached. Fifty-four-percent casualties so far."

"Tur-Kam, second call!"

There was no reply.

"Rahm to fourth anthill flyer leader."

"Here, Commander."

"Status report on your strike force."

There was a pause before the reply came. "Unknown, Commander. We have not been contacted by our leader since the Borer units landed and are currently unable to establish communication."

"Acknowledged."

I turned to Zur. "Your target is the fourth anthill. Brief your team as they drop."

"In what force shall we attack, Commander?"

"Full force. Anticipated resistance is unknown."

"At once, Commander."

I returned to the viewscreens without watching him depart.

Chapter Nine

"Kah-Tu, Commander. Rain commencing at third anthill."

"Acknowledged."

We had known of the potential bad weather conditions when we commenced the assaults, but we were required to proceed to insure coordination with the other Planetary assaults. If anything, we were fortunate to only experience adverse weather at one of the five anthills. Rain would severely limit the effectiveness of the flyer support and could make the eventual withdrawal and pickup more hazardous.

"Mir-Zat, Commander. Assuming command at first anthill."

"Acknowledged."

First anthill! Zah-Rah was dead. The first . . . no possibly the second casualty among the strike team leaders.

"Zur!"

"Yes, Commander."

"Status report!"

"Fourth anthill, Commander. Ordered flyers to drop all Surface Thumpers in an effort to maximize disruption of defenses."

"Evidence of original strike force?"

"Negative, Commander. We will be in the Borer units shortly. Will report findings at that time."

"Acknowledged."

"Raht, Commander. Target egg chamber for our section defended by cold-beams. Suffering heavy casualties."

"Will you be able to carry the objective?"

"Affirmative, Commander."

"Acknowledged."

Cold-beams again! There was a pattern forming here, but I wasn't allowed time to analyze it.

"Heem, Commander. Have received reports of Ants moving eggs from one of the egg chambers as it was destroyed."

"Order immediate pursuit. Find the new egg catch and destroy it."

"Acknowledged, Commander."

The collapsed tunnels were supposed to keep the Ants from moving the eggs. Apparently it wasn't working at the fifth anthill. If the Ants succeeded in their gambit, if they saved some eggs from our attack, the species would survive and the campaign would have failed.

"Zur, Commander. We are in the Borer units and proceeding with the assignment against minimal resistance. Have discovered original strike force."

"Report."

"Strike force rendered helpless by stun rays. Borer units breached manually by Ants. No survivors of the original strike force. We have cleared the Borer units of Ants. The units are still functional, and we are proceeding with the mission."

"Were the members of the original strike force wearing the anti-stun plates?"

"Affirmative, Commander. Apparently the Ants have either modified their stun ray, or have in their possession a weapon we are yet unfamiliar with. Our reserve force, however, has encountered no difficulties such as those apparently encountered by the original strike force. Perhaps the Energy-Drain units have successfully stopped the weapon's functioning."

"Acknowledged," I replied.

That was it! I had the answer to the vague pattern I had been sensing. The Energy-Drainers had been effective, but each anthill had a reserve energy unit. Apparently the Communication Disrupters had prevented coordinated effort between the anthills, so each anthill had utilized the reserve unit in their own way before it too was drained of energy.

The first anthill had used their energy to attack the flyers, while the second anthill had used cold-beams in an effort to defend one egg chamber. Cold-beams had been used, too, at the third anthill, whereas the fourth anthill had successfully employed a modified stun ray to wipe out that strike force. That left . . .

"Heem, Commander! Urgent! Fifth anthill is launching spacecraft!"

"Acknowledged."

Now we knew what the fifth anthill was using their energy for.

"Rahm to space-shuttle pilots! Launch your craft immediately! Take position over fifth anthill."

I waited impatiently through their ripple of acknowledgments.

"Heem!"

"Yes, Commander!"

"Report."

"We investigated the tunnel through which the Ants had been evacuating eggs. This is a new tunnel, apparently constructed since we began our attack. The tunnel led to a chamber housing spacecraft. It was heavily defended, and we were unable to prevent launching."

"How many spacecraft were launched?"

"Only one, Commander."

"Proceed with your withdrawal."

"Acknowledged, Commander."

"Rahm to space-shuttle Leader. Your target is one, repeat one spacecraft. Stop it at all costs!"

"Acknowledged, Commander."

If that ship escaped with a cargo of eggs, we would have failed and the Empire would be in grave jeopardy.

"Ar-Tac, Commander. Assuming command of second anthill."

I forced my mind away from the escaping spacecraft. Raht was dead.

"Can you confirm completion of Raht's mission?"

"Affirmative, Commander. Flyers report water level in lake

dropping rapidly, indicating egg chamber successfully destroyed. Are commencing our withdrawal."

"Casualty report."

"Seventy-two percent so far, Commander."

"Acknowledged."

"Kah-Tu, Commander. All targets in third anthill have been destroyed. Eighty-seven-percent casualties so far. We are encountering strong resistance on our withdrawal attempts. Remaining force is insufficient to regain the surface. Request reinforcements."

I was afraid of this. The weather conditions were having their expected effect on the retreat.

"Reserve force has been totally committed. No reinforcements are available."

There was a pause before the reply came.

"I understand, Commander. Request permission to release our flyers to rendezvous with transport."

"Permission granted."

"Acknowledged, Commander."

Kah-Tu was dead. She acknowledged this and was attempting to salvage part of her strike force.

"Space-shuttle Leader, Commander. We have encountered the Ant spacecraft and destroyed it."

"Report."

"Spacecraft was apparently unprepared for combat. By going into low orbit, we were able to intercept it before it had an opportunity to change course from launch pattern. Cold-beams were effective in completely destroying the craft."

"Return to transports."

"Acknowledged, Commander."

It was reassuring to know some phase of this assault had been executed without difficulty.

"Mir-Zat, Commander. All targets in the first anthill have been destroyed. We are commencing our withdrawal. Sixty-eight-percent casualties so far."

"Acknowledged."

"Flyer Leader from third anthill to Commander. Request permission to land flyers and assist in strike team's withdrawal."

That gave me pause. Apparently the flyers from Kah-Tu's force were refusing her order to rendezvous with the transports, asking instead to try to rescue the stranded ground force.

"Permission granted. Land your flyers out of range of the auto-weapon scanners."

"Acknowledged. Our gratitude, Commander."

If there was a chance to save the stranded force, it should be pursued. While I would not have ordered Warriors into such a precarious position, I would not deny them their request for such action.

"Second transport pilot to Commander. Urgent! We are going down."

"Report!"

"Apparent maneuvering malfunction of space shuttle when attempting to dock with our transport. Damage severe and irreparable. We are losing orbital pattern and anticipate burn entry to planet's atmosphere."

"Acknowledged!"

One transport! Gone! This possibility had never entered into my plans.

"Rahm to space shuttle. Do not, repeat, do not attempt to dock with transports. Undetermined malfunction of your vehicles has caused destruction of Transport Two. Attempt to land in vicinity of anthills and regroup with strike teams for pickup."

I ignored their acknowledgments. The shuttle pilots knew as well as I that their vehicles were not designed to survive a planet landing. My order was only an acceptable alternative to waiting in space until their air supply ran out.

"Zur, Commander. All targets in the fourth anthill have been destroyed, commencing withdrawal. Fifty-nine-percent casualties so far."

"Acknowledged."

All anthills were accounted for now, except one.

"Rahm to Kah-Tu. What is your status?"

There was no reply.

"Rahm to third anthill flyer Leader. Report your status."

There was no reply.

"Rahm to any Warrior in the third anthill strike force. What is your status?"

There was no reply.

The attempt to rescue the stranded force in the third anthill had failed.

Chapter Ten

The loss of a transport severely changed our pickup calculations. Instead of thirty percent of our original force, we could now only transport twenty percent back to the colony ship. Even with the loss of two full strike teams, we would doubtless have to leave some Warriors behind.

I gave my last order of the attack.

"Rahm to all strike team Leaders and acting Leaders. Our attack has been successfully completed. Coordinate your pickup requirements directly with the transport pilots. Transports One and Three only are available."

As soon as I received their acknowledgments, I left the control compartments and headed for my sleeping quarters.

I understand now both why Planetary Commanders were required to eat prior to an assault, and why they were not required to report to High Command prior to their return to the colony ship.

Although I had not physically lifted a weapon against the Enemy in this last campaign, I felt more fatigued than I had after any previous assignment. I began to believe the claims of the Technicians and Scientists that they could be just as fatigued as the Warriors even though they never were involved in direct combat.

Still, I did not go to sleep immediately. Instead, I found myself idly pondering several questions.

Under what circumstances would I be awakened again? Would the High Command require a detailed report from me? Would I be involved in the colonization of new planets, assuming the War against the Coalition was truly over? Or would it be as Zur postulated, that I would only be awakened again if a major species challenged the Empire?

Zur! It suddenly occurred to me that his force was the last to complete their mission. Logically, this meant they would be the last survivors to be picked up, and therefore it was highly probable that all or some of them would be left behind. Would Zur be one of the survivors? Or would he be stranded, included among the casualties?

I realized suddenly that these questions bore no more importance to me than . . . than whether or not a species of intelligent warm-bloods evolved. I was a Tzen and a Warrior, and I had been efficient in the performance of my duty to the Empire.

I went to sleep.

Tambu

Interview I

As the airlock door hissed shut behind him, the reporter took advantage of the moment of privacy to rub his palms on his trouser legs; he wished that he had a bit more faith in his Newsman's Immunity.

He had never really expected to be granted this interview. The request had been made as the prelude to a joke: a small bit of humor to casually drop into conversation with other reporters. He had anticipated making lofty reference to having been refused an interview by the dread Tambu himself. Then, as the skeptics voiced their doubts, he could silence them by producing the letter of refusal. But his plans had come to a jarring halt.

His request had been granted.

His editor had been no less surprised than he; his cynical indifference was swept aside by a wave of excitement . . . excitement mixed with suspicion. An interview with Tambu would be a feather in the cap of any journalist; a much-sought-after feather which had thus far eluded the grasp of many older, more experienced reporters. It seemed strange that this prize would go to a junior reporter who in five years of working for the news service had covered only minor stories.

One thing was sure: this interview would not be filler material. It would be the turning point of his career, eagerly read and studied throughout the settled universe, focusing an incredible amount of attention on his work. If his treatment was equal to his subject, he would be flooded with job offers. But if his work was judged and found lacking . . .

Despite his daydreams and careful preparations, he found that now that it was imminent, he approached the meeting with increasing dread. There were a thousand ways this "golden opportunity" could sour, resulting in an abrupt end to his career . . . and perhaps his life with it.

He had half-expected, half-hoped, that when he arrived at the rendezvous, he would be greeted by empty space. But the ship had been there, dwarfing his own craft with its immense size. The reporter remembered being slightly disappointed at the outward appearance of the vessel. He had expected a sleek jet-black monster adorned with Tambu's well-known crest . . . the silver death's head surmounted on a nebula. Instead, the ship was little different from the hundreds of freighters which traversed the starlanes, shuttling their cargos from planet to planet. The only clues to this ship's potential savagery were the numerous gun turrets prominent on its outer hull. It seemed ready for combat, its sails taken in as if in preparation for flight or fight . . . though the idea of his tiny ship attacking this dreadnought was ludicrous.

Now, here he was aboard Tambu's own flagship, about to meet face to face with the most feared individual in the settled universe. He had only a moment to reflect upon these thoughts before a soft chime sounded and the inner door opened to receive him.

The first thing that struck him about the quarters was the psychological warmth of the room. He instinctively wanted to examine the quarters more closely, and just as instinctively suppressed the desire. Instead, he contented himself with a brief look at the cabin and its contents.

The walls were of a texture unfamiliar to him, of a dark gold in dramatic contrast to the customary white. The trappings of the room made quiet contribution to the atmosphere. There were paintings on the walls, and books lined the shelves—honest-to-God books, instead of the tape-scanner usually found in libraries and studies. Several easy chairs were scattered about the room, obviously at convenient points for reading or contemplation. Tucked away in one corner was a bed—double bed, the reporter noted with professional interest.

The only reminder that this was not simply a luxury cabin or a lounge was a huge communications console which dominated one full wall of the room. Even compared to the familiar network terminals at the newscenters, this console was impressive, with banks of keys and controls surrounding a modest viewscreen. After eyeing the console's array of flickering lights and gauges for a moment, he turned again to sweep the cabin with a wide gaze, seeking an overall impression.

The total effect of the room was quite different from what the reporter had expected. It had the lived-in, personal air of a home, rather than the cold efficiency of a command post. Anywhere else it would have been incredibly relaxing. Here it gave the room the feeling of a lair. The reporter glanced about him again. Where was Tambu?

"Please be seated, Mr. Erickson."

Startled by the voice, the reporter turned again to face the console. The viewscreen was still blank, but it was apparent that the unit was operational, and that Tambu was now watching him . . . watching and waiting.

Fighting off his apprehensions, the reporter seated himself at the console.

"I am addressing Tambu?" he asked with an ease he did not truly feel.

"That is correct, Mr. Erickson. I notice you've brought a Tri-D recorder with you. As I will not be meeting you face to face, it is unnecessary. The console at which you are seated is recording our conversation. You will be supplied with a copy. Visually, there will be nothing to record."

"I was promised a personal interview," Erickson half-explained, half-protested, then cursed himself mentally. If he didn't watch himself, he'd end up alienating Tambu before the interview even began.

"Personal in that you will be dealing with me directly rather than with one of my subordinates," Tambu clarified, apparently unoffended by the reporter's remark. "For security reasons, a face-to-face meeting is out of the question. I maintain several flagships identical to the one you are on now, and part of the problem confronting any Defense Alliance ship seeking to capture me is discovering which ship I'm on and when. My exact location is kept secret, even from my own fleet."

"Aren't these precautions a little extreme for meeting a lone reporter in a rented shuttlecraft?"

"Frankly, Mr. Erickson, reporters have been known to stray from their oaths of neutrality . . . particularly where my fleet and I are concerned. My defensive preparations for this meeting, therefore, go quite beyond what meets the eye. As an example, you might be wondering why you were granted this interview aboard one of my flagships when the smallest ship at my command has a viewscreen you could have listened at just as easily."

"It did cross my mind," the reporter admitted uneasily. "I assumed you were trying to impress me."

"There was that," Tambu laughed, "but there was also another, much more important reason: all my flagships, including the one you're on now, are rigged to self-destruct either from the captain's cabin, or by a remote signal from me. The explosives on board are sufficient to cause severe damage to any ships in firing range at the time of detonation. If your request for an interview had been a ploy to lure me or one of my ships to a predetermined point for an ambush, the appearance of a dreadnought-class flagship would have been a nasty surprise for the hunters. If the waiting ships were of sufficient size or numbers to trap and capture a dreadnought, the captain was under orders to trigger the self-destruct mechanism. It would have been a costly but necessary example for anyone who might entertain similar thoughts of entrapment."

"I thought the crew seemed awfully glad to see me," Erickson muttered, licking his lips nervously. "So I'm sitting here on a bomb that might go off at any time. That's certainly incentive for me to keep this interview short."

"Please, Mr. Erickson, there is nothing to worry about. I

mentioned the self-destruct mechanism as an example of our defensive arrangements, not as a threat to you. Take as much time as is necessary."

"If you say so," the reporter murmured doubtfully. The conversation was taking a dubious tack, and he was eager to change the subject.

"You're upset," Tambu observed. "If you'd care for a drink, there is a bottle of Scotch on the table by the bathroom sink, along with glasses and ice. 'Inverness' I believe it's called. Feel free to help yourself."

"Thank you, no. I don't drink while I'm working."

"Very well. However, I've taken the liberty of ordering the ship's crew to load a case of that particular liquor onto your ship. Please accept it as a personal gift from me."

"You seem to know quite a bit about me," the reporter observed. "Right down to the brand of liquor I would drink, if I could afford it."

"I probably know more about you than you do, and definitely more than you'd like me to know. I've reviewed your family history, health records, psychological records, as well as copies of everything you've ever written including that rather dubious series of articles you wrote in school under an assumed name. You were checked very closely before permission for this interview was granted. I don't talk with just anyone who drops me a note. In my line of work, my whole future and that of my forces hinges on my ability to gather and analyze data. If I didn't think you were safe, you wouldn't be here."

"Yet you refuse to meet me face-to-face and dispatched a ship rigged to blow in event of betrayal?" Erickson smiled. "Your actions aren't as confident as your words."

There was a moment of silence before the reply came.

"I've made mistakes before," Tambu said at last. "Often enough that I long since abandoned any ideas of infallibility. In lieu of that, I guard against all possibilities to the best of my abilities. Now may we start the interview? Even though I have tried to set aside time for this meeting, there are many demands on my time and I can't be sure how long we'll have before other priorities pull me away."

"Certainly," Erickson agreed readily, glad to resume the familiar role of an interviewer. "I guess the first question would be to ask why someone of your intelligence and abilities turned to the ways of war and world conquering as a way of life rather than seeking a place in the established order."

"Purely a matter of convenience. If you think for a moment, I'm sure you could think of several men both as intelligent and as ruthless as I in your so-called established order. As you pointed out, they have successfully risen to positions of power, wealth, and influence. I am not that much different than they; only I chose to move into a field where there was little or no competition. Why fight my way up a chain of command when by taking one step sideways I could form my own chain of command with myself at the top, running things the way I felt they should be run from the start instead of adapting someone else's system until I was high enough to make my presence felt."

"But to terrorism and violence as a way of life?" the reporter pressed. "It seems a rather harsh way to extract a living from the universe."

"Terrorism and violence," Tambu mused. "Yes, I suppose you could call it that. Tell me though, Mr. Erickson, do you apply the same phrasing to what the Defense Alliance does? Both my fleet and that of the Alliance earn their living the same way—selling protection to the planets. They include us as one of the threats they are protecting the planets against. Aside from that, we do not differ greatly, except in words; a 'police action' versus a 'reign of terror.' Perhaps I over simplify the situation, but I don't feel the differential is justified."

"Then you see nothing wrong in what you're doing?" the reporter asked.

"Please, Mr. Erickson, none of your journalistic tricks of putting words in my mouth. I did not say I don't see anything wrong in what I do; simply that I don't see that much difference between my own forces' tactics and those of the Defense Alliance."

"Are you then asserting that in the current conflict that it is you who are the hero and the Defense Alliance the villains?" Erickson prodded.

"Mr. Erickson I have asked you once, I will now warn you," Tambu's tone was soft, but deadly. "Do not attempt to twist my words into what I have not said. If I make a statement or express an opinion you take exception to, you are certainly welcome to comment to that effect, either in this meeting or in your article. However, do not attempt to condemn me for opinions which are not my own. I have shown my respect for you and your intelligence by granting this interview. Kindly return the compliment by remembering that in this interview you are not dealing with a dull-witted planetary sub-official and conduct yourself accordingly.

"Yes, sir. I'll remember that," the reporter promised, properly mollified. He would have to mask his questions more carefully.

"See that you do. Still, you did raise a curious point. The rather romantic concept of heroes and villains, good guys and bad guys. It would be amusing if I did not think that you actually believe that rot. That's the main reason I granted this interview. It stands out all over your writing, and I wanted to meet someone who really believes in heroes. In exchange, I offered you a chance to meet a villain."

"Well, actually—" Erickson began, but Tambu cut him off.

"There are no heroes, Mr. Erickson. There are no villains." Tambu's voice was suddenly cold. "There are only humans. Men and women who alternately succeed and fail. If they are on your side and succeed, they are heroes. If they're on the other side, they're villains. It's as simple as that. Concepts such as good and evil exist only as rationalizations, an artificial logic to mask the true reasons for our feelings. There is no evil. No one wakes up in the morning and says, 'I think I'll go out and do something terrible.' Their actions are logical and beneficial to them. It's only after the fact when things go awry that they are credited with being evil."

"Frankly, sir, I find that a little hard to accept," Erickson frowned. This time his challenge was planned, carefully timed to keep his subject talking.

"Of course. That's why you're here, so I could take this opportunity to show you a viewpoint other than that to which you are accustomed. As a journalist, you are no doubt aware that in the course of my career I have been compared with Genghis Khan, Caesar, Napoleon, and Hitler. I believe that if you could have interviewed any one of those men, he would have told you the same thing I am today, that there is no difference between the two sides of a battle except 'them and us'. There may be racial, religious, cultural, or military differences, but the only determination of who is the hero and who is the villain is which side he's on. That—and who wins."

"Then what you are claiming is that this moral equivalence of opponents also applies to today's situation?"

"Especially today," Tambu said. "Now that mankind has moved away from the bloodbath concept of war, it is easier than ever to observe. Despite the blood-curdling renditions of space warfare which adorn the newstapes and literature, actual combat is a rarity. It's far too costly in men and equipment, and there is no need for it. Each fleet has approximately four hundred ships of varying sizes, and there are over two thousand inhabited planets. Even at the rate of one ship per planet, there is always going to be over eighty percent of the planets unoccupied at any given time. For a ship of either force to move on a new planet means temporarily abandoning another. As such, there is little or no combat between the fleets. The objective is to either move into unoccupied systems and divert their tribute into our coffers, or move into an occupied system with sufficient force to where the opposing ships will abandon the system rather than enter into a lopsided battle. It's a massive game of move and countermove, with little if any difference between the gamesmen."

"A stalemate," Erickson suggested. "Yet there was a time when the Defense Alliance was substantially weaker than your fleet. I find it interesting that you were powerless to stop its growth.

"Just because we refrained from openly opposing the Alliance when it was forming doesn't necessarily mean we were powerless to do so. You might say that was my error. I seriously underestimated their potential at first and actually ordered my fleet to avoid contact with them. Remember, we were well established at the time, and did not consider them a serious threat."

"I remember," the reporter nodded. He didn't, but he had done his homework in the news service's backfiles. "Actually, I had hoped to get some information from you about those early days, before the Defense Alliance formed."

"That would take quite a bit of time, Mr. Erickson. I don't think you're aware of what you're asking. Most people never heard of me until we first started offering our services to the planets. In actuality, the fleet had been operating as a unit long before then. For me, the early days go back much farther than the point when we first appeared in the public eye."

"But that's specifically what I'm after. I want to be able to trace your career from its early days to the present, showing how you've developed over the years."

"Very well," Tambu sighed. "We'll cover as much as time allows. This will probably get quite involved, but I'm willing to talk if you're willing to listen."

"Then how would you say your career began?"

There was a moment's pause.

"There is a strong temptation to say I started out as a child."

". . . born into a poor, but honest family?" Erickson completed the old joke, smiling in spite of himself.

"Not really. Actually, my parents were fairly well off. Various people have speculated that I had a bitter childhood, ruthlessly fighting for existence in the streets of some backwater planet. The truth is my father was . . . successful, quite successful at what he did. I would even go so far as to say that I had more love and affection in my early childhood than did the average person."

"Then . . . what happened? I mean, why did you . . . choose the path you have?"

"Why did I turn renegade?" Tambu asked, echoing Erickson's thoughts. "First, allow me to clarify my home situation. While, as I said, I was not lacking for affection, there were certain expectations placed upon me. I was to exceed my father's achievements—a task which, I assure you, was not easy. It seemed that everything I set my hand to, my father had been there first and done it better."

"So your father's pressure eventually drove you out," Erickson prompted as Tambu paused.

"Not directly . . . nor intentionally," Tambu corrected. "Much of it was self-imposed pressures or expectations. When I flunked out of college—undergraduate studies, at that—I decided to strike out on my own rather than return home. This was done partly because I was ashamed to face my parents, and partly to make a name for myself as myself, not as my father's son."

"I must admit you've succeeded there," the reporter smiled, shaking his head ruefully. "So you ran away to space. Then what?"

"I worked tramp freighters for several years. I had a friend . . . a close friend. He was several years older than I, and gentle as a kitten for all his strength. We worked several ships together, and probably would still be doing just that except for the mutiny."

"The mutiny?" Erickson's attention focused on the story possibilities.

"Not in the sense you're imagining. There was no organized revolt, no dark conspiracy. It just happened. Unfortunately, I can't give you the details without seriously breaching security . . . both my own and the forces.'"

"Couldn't you omit specific details and change the names?" the reporter pleaded.

"Possibly . . . Actually, the important event was not the mutiny, but the decision we reached shortly thereafter."

Chapter One

The plump, red-faced man filled the small captain's cabin with his indignant anger, barely leaving room for his adversary seated behind the desk. This was not unusual. He was Dobbs of Dobbs Electronics, a man who fought his way to the top and who wasn't about to let anyone forget it—not his relatives, not his employees, and definitely not the captain of some second-rate tramp freighter.

His noisy indignation was his trademark, as was his presence for this transaction. Other business owners would sometimes relax and enjoy their success, delegating menial tasks to their subordinates, but Dobbs was cut from different cloth. He had been there for the unloading, riding the cargo shuttle from the ship to the spaceport planetside and back again. He had personally delivered the payment for the shipment. Therefore it was only natural that he would feel obligated to personally handle this last detail.

None of the proceedings had met with his approval, but this last oversight was a particular annoyance. He was in the wrong and he knew it, but that knowledge only increased his bitterness. More than anything, Dobbs hated to be wrong. Never one to hide his feelings, particularly his anger, Dobbs let his displeasure show. It showed in his stiff bearing and tight lips, in his ruddy complexion, and in the abrupt way he slammed the attaché case down on the desk.

"There it is." he announced flatly. "The balance of payment. I believe you said fifteen thousand was the difference between the original purchase price and the price you're asking now?"

"That's not entirely correct," the man seated behind the desk said. "It constitutes the difference in currency exchange between the time of purchase and the time of delivery."

"Semantics," the visitor countered. "It's still costing my company fifteen thousand more than we planned."

"As you will." The man at the desk sighed. "Would you care to have a seat while I count it?"

"I'd rather stand."

The seated man had been reaching for the attaché case, but at his visitor's rebuke he hesitated, then sat back in his chair frowning slightly.

"Mr. Dobbs . . . it is Dobbs isn't it? Of Dobbs Electronics?"

The visitor nodded stiffly, annoyed there had been any doubt as to his identity. He had been dealing with this man off and on for three days now.

"You seem both upset and determined to express your annoyance by being rude. I find both positions difficult to understand."

Dobbs started to protest, but the man at the desk continued.

"First of all, when you ordered your materials Cash On Delivery, you accepted the risk of currency-exchange fluctuations. That is standard in any contract of that kind, but it's still good business. If you paid in advance and our ship was attacked and taken by pirates, you'd be out the full cost of the shipment. As it is, you have to pay only for goods delivered, even though occasionally you have to pay a premium."

"Occasionally!" Dobbs snorted. "It seems like every time . . ."

"And even if I felt the system was unfair, which I don't," the man at the desk continued, "this ship is only the means of delivery. We don't make the rules. We only shuttle materials from point A to point B and collect the money, as instructed. In theory, we shouldn't have allowed your men to unload your cargo until we had collected our payment in full."

The man was leaning forward now, his eyes burning with a sudden intensity.

"In short, Mr. Dobbs, I feel we've treated you fairly decently through this entire affair. If you have a complaint, I suggest you write a letter. In the meantime, isn't it about time you came down off your high horse and started acting like a human being?"

Dobbs started to retort angrily, then caught himself, reconsidered, and relaxed, exhaling a long breath. Like most bullies, he would give ground when confronted by a will of equal or greater strength.

"I guess I have been making a bit of a jackass out of myself, haven't I?" he admitted ruefully.

"You have." The seated man opened the attaché case and began counting.

Dobbs responded by sinking into the offered chair and leaning forward, his elbows resting lightly in his knees. He had discovered in the past that people were more receptive when approached at eye level.

"I guess I forgot that the captain of a freighter is a businessman same as me." he confided. "You know, as much as we've seen each other these past couple days, I've never gotten around to asking your name. It's Blütman, isn't it? Ulnar Blütman?"

"No, it's Eisner, Dwight Eisner. I'm the First Officer. Captain Blütman doesn't like to handle the business end of things, so I take care of it for him."

"Isn't that a little strange?" Dobbs frowned. "Usually . . ."

"Mr. Dobbs," Eisner sighed, "if you had treated Ulnar Blütman the way you treated me, I guarantee he would have broken your nose and dumped your goods out the nearest airlock. He is, at best, an unpleasant man."

"I see," Dobbs commented, taken slightly aback. "Say, are you taking cargo on before you ship out? Maybe I can put together a shipment for you. You know, to make up for the way I've acted."

"That won't be necessary. We already have a sizable load to pick up at our next stop."

He set the case aside abruptly.

"The count tallies. Just a moment and I'll transfer it into our safe and you can have your case back."

"Keep it." Dobbs waved. "Consider it a present. How much have you taken in this run, anyway?"

"Nearly a quarter of a million. A little less than average, but it's not bad."

"Quarter of a million? In cash?" Dobbs was visibly impressed. "That's a lot of money!"

"I just wish it was mine." Eisner laughed. "Unfortunately, there are a lot of people waiting at the other end of the run to get their share. Our piece is ridiculously small considering the risks we take, but if we up our prices too much, the companies will buy their own ships and we'll be out of business."

"I suppose. Well, I've got to get going now. Watch out for pirates, and if you're ever back this way, look me up. I'll buy you a drink."

"I'll remember that." Eisner smiled, rising to shake the man's hand. "But don't even mention pirates. It's bad luck."

Dobbs laughed and departed, heading for the shuttlecraft standing by to take him back to the planet's surface.

Eisner sank back into his chair. For long moments he stared thoughtfully at the wall, then he turned his attention to the attaché case on the desk, running his hands softly over the leather finish.

His reverie was interrupted by a lanky youth who burst through the door like an exploding bomb.

"How did it go?" he demanded excitedly. "Is everything all right?"

Eisner smiled tolerantly. Nikki always seemed to be going in eight directions at once, even under normal circumstances.

"It went fine, Nikki," he said reassuringly. "The nice man gave me an attaché case."

"He what?" the boy blinked.

". . . and the extra fifteen thousand." Eisner concluded, opening the case dramatically.

"You did it!" Nikki exclaimed. "God, you've got guts, Dwight. I never would have had the nerve to go for the extra. I was afraid he'd get suspicious."

"The man was trying to pull a fast one. He would have been more suspicious if we hadn't called him on it."

"I know, but—"

"Look, Nikki, it's just like I told you. If we just conduct ourselves as if the captain were still alive, no one will suspect a thing. This way, we've got the ship and a quarter of a million."

"But didn't he say anything?"

"As a matter of fact, he did." Eisner smiled. "He warned us to watch out for pirates."

"He did?"

Simultaneously, the two burst into laughter, whatever tension they had pent up finding release in the absurdity of the situation.

"Did I miss something?"

The interruption came from the middle-aged black woman who had started to enter the cabin, only to stop short at the laughter within.

"No, not really, Roz." Eisner assured her. "Did Dobbs get off okay?"

"No trouble at all." Rosalyn sank into a chair. "He seemed a lot politer on the way out than on the way in."

"We had a talk. I explained a few facts of life to him, and he pulled in his horns a bit."

"That's nice," Roz grimaced. "Since you're in an explaining mood, maybe you wouldn't mind explaining a few things to me—like what do we do next?"

"We already know that," Nikki protested. "Now that we're pirates, we do whatever pirates do."

"Technically, we're mutineers," Eisner corrected. "We aren't pirates until we actually attack another ship. But Roz is right; we still have several options open to us at this point."

"We've been through those already," Nikki grumbled.

"If you don't mind, Nikki," Roz interrupted, "I'd like to go over them again. I'm not too wild about the choice we've made so far."

Eisner began hastily, before a fight could start. "First of all, we could continue business as normal. We could return to our home port, report that the captain died of natural causes in space, and run the freight business ourselves. Of course, that would mean we'd have to give the money we've collected to the proper people."

Nikki snorted derisively, but Roz silenced him with a glare.

"Second," Eisner continued, "we could sell the ship, divide the money among us, and either go our separate ways or set up another business. The main problem with that being that you need ownership papers to sell a ship, and as soon as we touch down planetside, someone's bound to get very curious about where we got our money."

He paused, but the other two remained silent.

"Finally, we can play the cards fate seems to have dealt us. We can turn pirate and become one more ship gone bad, preying on the helpless and defenseless."

"You don't have to be so graphic on that last point," Rosalyn mumbled, half to herself.

"Of course I have to, Roz." Eisner insisted. "That's what anyone else would say about us. That's what we'll say about ourselves sooner or later. We'd better learn to live with it now while we still have other options. Later it will be too late to change our minds."

"You missed an option, my friend."

They all turned to face the massive figure framed in the doorway.

"You could all turn me in to the nearest authorities and pocket a hefty reward. They still pay pretty good for murderers."

"Abuzar, that isn't even an option," Roz scolded. "We've told you a hundred times, Blütman was an animal. If you hadn't lost your temper and killed him, one of us would have. We aren't going to turn you in for that."

"But I was the one who killed him," the big man insisted. "And now, because of me, the rest of you are going to become pirates. You can't make me believe that's what you really want to do, Roz."

"Learn to live with it." Rosalyn winced, turning away. "It won't be the first time I've earned a living doing something I didn't like."

"Not so fast!" Eisner had been leaning back, his brows knitted. "There's another option here, one we haven't considered before." His voice was tense with excitement. "It hadn't even occurred to me until Abuzar mentioned rewards."

"What is it?" Roz asked.

"None of us are too wild about becoming pirates. Well, what if instead of becoming pirates, we hunt pirates? Besides what we get for salvage rights, there are bound to be businessmen who'll pay us if we can make a dent in the number of shipments and ships lost to pirates."

"Now you're talking!" Nikki exclaimed with the same enthusiasm with which he had accepted the idea of becoming a pirate.

"Pirates shoot back," Abuzar pointed out bluntly.

"But they're used to fighting freighters with little or no armament," Eisner countered. "If we're armed better than they are, with better sensors than normal so that we can see them before they know we're in the area, they're in trouble."

"Maybe." Abuzar conceded reluctantly. "But equipment like that could cost a small fortune."

"We've got a small fortune," Eisner shot back. "The first thing we'll have to do is find out what armaments and sensor equipment are available, and how much they cost."

"That's assuming we agree to take that option," Roz interrupted. "I seem to recall a few other choices."

There was an uncomfortable moment of silence. Then Dwight sighed.

"You're right, Roz. I guess the time has come when we have to make our final decision about the future. Anything after this is a commitment, and we shouldn't move unless everyone's in agreement. Speaking for myself, I'm willing to try being either a pirate or a pirate hunter, with preference toward the latter."

"I'm with you, Dwight." Nikki chimed in.

"I've got no choice." Abuzar shrugged. "Eventually someone will learn what I've done, and I'll be a hunted man. It's easier to run in space than on a planet."

"Well, Roz?" Eisner asked. "How about you? Are you with us, or do you want to shuttle down to planetside? We'll buy out your share of the ship if you want."

Roz chewed her lip thoughtfully for a few moments before she replied.

"Tell you what," she said at last. "You can count me in with two conditions."

"What conditions?" Eisner prompted.

"First, that we unanimously agree here and now that Dwight runs the show. That he becomes our captain officially."

"Why?" Abuzar asked suspiciously.

"Come on, Abuzar. You know as well as I do that there has to be one man at the top. Eventually we're going to be in situations where one person has to give the orders and make the decisions. I figure we should decide who that's going to be now, instead of arguing it out in the middle of a crisis. Dwight's been running things since Blütman died and doing a pretty good job of it. Nikki's too reckless, and even you don't trust your temper. I couldn't do it, and wouldn't want to if I could. To my thinking, that makes Dwight number one. If we can't agree on something as basic as that, we should call it quits right now."

"I don't think I'm all that reckless," Nikki grumbled. "But I've got no objections to Dwight running things."

"Abuzar?"

"If we need a captain, I guess Dwight's the logical choice."

"Okay, that's that." Roz nodded. "How about you, Dwight?"

"I guess I never thought about it. I'm like Abuzar. I didn't really think a chain of command was necessary for four people."

"But will you serve as captain?" Roz pressed.

"Before I agree, what was the other condition to your staying with us, Rosalyn?"

"Oh, that." Roz grimaced. "It's nothing really. Your agreeing to be captain was the big one. My second point was that I think we should all take new names."

"Oh, come on, Roz!" Abuzar exploded.

"Hold on a minute, Abuzar," Eisner said. "Why do you think that's necessary, Roz?"

"I don't know about you other space bums, but I've still got family out there. I'm not too wild about dragging their name into the crazy things I'm going to be doing, and I sure don't want some pirate tracking them down to get back at me. Besides, up until now we've all got pretty clean records. On the off chance that someday we want to quit what we're doing and go back to leading normal lives, it wouldn't hurt to have a 'clean' name to go back to. Whether the rest of you want to go along with this or not, I'm going to use a different name for my new career. From now on, I want the rest of you to get used to calling me 'Whitey.' "

"Whitey?" Eisner raised his eyebrows.

"That's right." She grinned. "All my life I've wanted someone to call me that. I guess this is as good a time as any to get it going."

"Whitey." Eisner repeated, shaking his head. "All right, what do you two think about the whole idea?"

"Puck." Nikki said thoughtfully.

"What was that again?" Eisner frowned.

"I said 'Puck,' " Nikki repeated. "That's what my dad always called me. It's the name of some cutsey-poo character in an old play. I always hated that name, but I like the idea of a feared pirate hunter called 'Puck.' "

"It fits you," Roz teased.

"It's no worse than 'Whitey,' " Nikki said.

"How about you, Abuzar?" Eisner asked.

"The only man who ever beat me in a fight was a retard they called 'Egor.' He couldn't count on his fingers, but I've never seen anyone fight like that. Yes, you can call me 'Egor.' I'd like that."

"How about you, Dwight?" Roz asked. "Are you going to get in on this?"

"Um . . . Dwight," Nikki said. "If you do, could you pick a name that sounds fearsome and ominous? I mean, you are going to be our captain, and it would help if you had a name that scared people when they heard it."

". . . and 'Dwight' just doesn't do it." Roz agreed. "What do you say, Dwight?"

"Actually, I'm not very good at names."

"How about 'The Skull'?" Nikki suggested hopefully.

"Be serious," Roz chided.

"I am serious," Nikki insisted. "His name should—"

"I think I've got one." Eisner smiled.

He had been doodling on one of the ship's receipt books, and held it up for the others to see. He had circled the logos: Ulnar Blütman's Moving and Transport.

"In honor of our departed captain who so generously left us his ship, I'll use the first letters of the old letterhead for my name."

"Ub-mat!" Nikki read. "I don't know, Dwight. It doesn't—"

"Reverse them. Reverse them, and what you have is 'Tambu'!"

"Tambu," Whitey echoed thoughtfully. "I like it. It's got a nice ring to it. Has it got any special meaning, or is it just a word?"

"There's no special symbolism." Eisner laughed. "It's just a name. Now that that's settled, I'm ready to give my first order as your new captain."

"Don't tell me, let me guess," Whitey quipped. "You want us to knock off the chatter and get to work. See how fast power corrupts?"

"Actually, I was thinking more in terms of breaking out a bottle of the good wine and toasting our new names and careers."

"And friendship!" Abuzar declared, clapping a massive hand on Eisner's shoulder. "You see, Roz? It'll take more than a new name or a new job to change this one. He'll always love his friends and his wine more than he loves work!"

They all laughed, though some laughed louder than others.

Interview II

"Ulnar Blütman's Moving and Transport?" Erickson asked, as Tambu lapsed into silence.

"Don't get your hopes up, Mr. Erickson." That was not a slip of the tongue betraying my original ship. It was a fabrication, as were the original names of the crewmembers, including my own. There is no—was no Ulnar Blütman. However, I assure you the actual origin of my name was equally inane."

"Well, what's in a name, anyway?" the reporter shrugged, hiding his disappointment.

"I assume you're being flippant, but there is an answer to that question. What's in a name is what one puts in a name. Tambu could have been a brand name for a new soap, but my actions and the legends which grew from them have made the name Tambu a household word of a completely different nature."

"You sound quite proud of yourself," Erickson commented dryly, unable to hide his distaste.

"That's another 'are you still beating your wife' sort of question," Tambu admonished. "But I'll try to answer it anyway. Yes, I am proud of myself. To get where I am today, I have overcome many obstacles and difficulties which would have stopped or crushed a lesser man.

That is not boasting, merely stating a fact. I should add, however, that just because I am proud of where I am does not necessarily mean I am proud of everything I did to get here."

"Then you're ashamed of the things you've done?"

"Not ashamed, Mr. Erickson. Just not proud. There are certain events and decisions I regret in hindsight. Perhaps it is a rationalization, but I've never felt this type of regret was a trait unique to me. Surely there are things in your own past you wish you could do over?"

"There are," Erickson admitted.

"Then allow me to give you a bit of advice. Or rather, share a philosophy which has helped me when I find myself preoccupied with past mistakes. When I review a decision which turned out bad, I remember it was just that . . . BAD. 'B' . . . 'A' . . . 'D'. Best Available Data. I made the best decision I could, based on the data available, within the time perimeters allowed for the decision. Even though the results may not have gone as I predicted, or as I would have liked, I console myself with the memory of that moment of decision. Given the same situation, the same information, and the same amount of time to reach a decision, I would probably choose the same course of action again."

"That makes sense." The reporter nodded thoughtfully. "Thank you."

"Actually, it's an old accounting expression. But I find it applies readily to other fields as well."

"Getting back to an earlier statement," Erickson pressed, suddenly aware of the interview. "You mentioned having to overcome many difficulties in your career. While it is obvious they would be there, I can only imagine what they must have been. What were some of the specific difficulties you encountered?"

"They are literally too many to count, Mr. Erickson." Tambu sighed wearily. "At times it seems all I've encountered were difficulties. Sometimes I wonder whether I would have started this project originally if I could have looked into the future and seen the difficulties involved . . . if I had known then what I know now."

"Once you made that decision, how soon did you begin encountering difficulties?"

"Almost immediately. Things one takes for granted suddenly become obstacles when confronted by them directly. For example, there was the basic task of outfitting our ship for combat . . ."

Chapter Two

"I don't like it, Dwight," Whitey cast a dark glance around the gloomy bar.

"It's Tambu. Remember?" He took a leisurely sip from the glass in front of him.

"I don't care if you call yourself the Queen of May," Whitey snapped. "I still don't like it."

The bar was a typical dive, indistinguishable from hundreds of its fellows which cluttered the streets around any spaceport. Its clientele was composed mainly of crewmen on leave and ground crews, with a few drab locals holding court at the grimy tables along the walls. A tired-looking whore was perched at the bar conversing with the bartender, her drooping breasts threatening to slip free of her low neckline when she laughed.

"I admit it's not what you'd call a class place," Tambu conceded. "But we're not here to deal with genteel folk."

"That's not what I meant," Whitey scowled. "I've been in worse places."

"Are you still worried about Puck? I don't like it either. Leaving a one-man watch on board ship is asking for trouble, but there wasn't any other way. All three of us had to be here for this deal: you for the

443

technical expertise, me for the negotiating, and Egor for protection. It's dangerous, but it's the only way we could handle it."

"That isn't it, either."

"What then?"

"It's this whole business. When I agreed to go along with this pirate-hunter bit, I didn't figure it would mean skulking around like a common criminal."

"It's only a temporary situation," Tambu assured her. "Just until we get the ship outfitted. Until then we don't have much choice."

"Sure we do. We could buy our weaponry through normal channels, like other ships do."

"No we can't, Whitey. The kind of weapons we want can't be picked up through normal channels."

"But other ships—" Whitey began.

"Other ships buy antiquated weapons which haven't helped them at all in stopping a pirate attack." Tambu broke in pointedly. "We aren't cruising around hoping the pirates won't spot us, we're going to actively hunt them. For that, we'll need weapons as good or better than the ones the pirates use."

"I suppose you're right."

"I know I'm right. We've tried a dozen weapons dealers and gotten the same answer everywhere. 'Weapons of that nature are not available.' Then they try to sell us some popgun or other with toothy reassurances that it will be enough to protect us in most situations. Twice we've been told about the black market in arms here on Trepec, so here we are. If we can't find what we're looking for here, we'll just have to look somewhere else. We can't risk going into battle with inferior weapons."

"We could opt against going into battle."

"Not a chance," Tambu insisted. "The first time we try to move in on a pirate, they're going to fight—particularly if they think we're overmatched in the weapons department. I wish it wasn't the case, but that's the hard facts of the matter."

"What I meant was that we could decide to give up the whole idea of pirate hunting."

Tambu leaned back in his chair and studied her carefully.

"What's bothering you, Whitey? We've gone over this a hundred times. The four of us. You were in favor of it then, and now suddenly you're against everything . . . the weapons, the fighting, pirate hunting . . . everything. What happened? Have you changed your mind?"

"I don't know," Whitey admitted. "I was never that wild about the idea, but the three of you kind of swept me along—especially you, Mr. Tambu. You can be awfully persuasive. Now that we're actually moving on the plan . . . I don't know. I guess I'm just scared."

"You can still deal yourself out if you want to," Tambu offered gently.

"I'm not that scared." Whitey broke into a smile. "Who knows what kind of trouble you three would get into if I wasn't there to watch over you. No, I may grumble a lot, but I'm still in."

"You're sure I'm not 'persuading' you again?"

"I'm sure, but don't laugh about your power to convince people. I was serious about that. You have a way about you . . . I don't know what it is, that wins folks over to your way of thinking. If you weren't so honest, you'd make an incredible con-man."

Tambu protested, "I hate to argue with you, Whitey, but you're wrong. Maybe you're susceptible to my logic, but not everyone is. I remember a couple of girls—twins, in fact—that Egor and I made a play for on Isle, who weren't persuaded at all. Neither were their parents—or the police, for that matter. We were lucky our captain interceded for us, and he stepped in only because he didn't want to lose two crewmen—not because I convinced him to."

"Speaking of Egor, where is he?" Whitey interrupted, peering at the door. "Shouldn't he be back by now?"

"Don't worry about Egor. He can take care of himself. He's just not particularly good at keeping timetables. Except for that, he's dependable to a flaw."

"If you say so. There! You did it again!"

"Did *what* again?"

"Convinced me not to worry with just a few words. That's what I'm talking about. You could calm a cat in the middle of a dog show."

"Not any more than anyone else could. Sometimes I can, sometimes I can't. It's no big thing."

"You don't believe that any more than I do." Whitey snorted. "If you didn't think you had an edge on most people, why did you come along specifically to handle the negotiations on this deal?"

"Because I'm a little better with numbers than most. Except for that . . ."

"And you talk a lot better than most. You know when to push and when to back off. That counts for a lot."

"I suppose you're right," Tambu admitted. "But why make such an issue out of it? You have a feel for the mechanics of a ship that makes me feel like a kid. Each of us has something we can do better than someone else. So what?"

"The difference is I work with machines and you work with people," Whitey said. "I know what I'm doing and what to expect in the way of results. I don't think you do."

"Probably not," Tambu admitted. "But I still don't see why you should get upset about it."

"Because it's dangerous! You think you're only doing what people want you to do, and never stop to think you're actually calling the shots. Just because we agree with you when you ask the final question doesn't mean we agreed with you when you started—"

Suddenly Tambu laid a hand on her arm, stopping her oration.

"Heads up! We're about to have company."

Three figures were approaching their table in a beeline course that left no doubt as to their intended destination. The girl was in her late-twenties, sporting close-cropped blond hair, a halter top, shorts and sandals. The dusky-complexioned boy was in his early teens, and wore a sleeveless shirt open to the waist. Loose-fitting trousers and soft ankle-high boots completed his outfit. While there was nothing uniform about their garb, there was something in their gaze which set them apart from the other denizens of the bar and bound them together into a unit.

The man in the lead was of an entirely different cut. In his middle fifties, his hair was close-cropped which, coupled with his expression, gave him the appearance of a Caucasian Buddha. Mechanic's coveralls gave his short, stocky figure the appearance of butterball fat, but there was a feline lightness to his walk.

All three wore guns on their hips.

"Mind if we join you?" the leader asked, smiling as he reached for one of the vacant chairs at the table.

"As a matter of fact, we do." Tambu smiled back, hooking the chair with his foot and drawing it out of reach. "We're waiting for someone."

For a moment, the man's eyes narrowed, but the smile never left his face.

"No matter," he shrugged. "What we have to say won't take long."

"Good," Whitey commented dryly.

This time it was the man's companions who reacted, shooting dark looks at Whitey as their muscles tensed. The leader, however, took the jibe in stride.

"A bit of a spitfire, isn't she?" he laughed, jerking his head at her.

"You said you had some business with us?" Tambu prompted, an edge in his voice.

The man nodded, showing even more teeth. "We've heard that you've been asking around after weapons of an exceptionally powerful nature."

"Where did you hear that?" Whitey asked sharply.

"Does it matter, as long as the information is accurate?"

"What makes you think it's accurate?" Tambu countered.

"The fact that she didn't deny it." The man smiled.

"Assuming for the moment you're correct, what business is it of yours?" Tambu asked. "Are you an arms dealer?"

The man threw back his head and laughed. "Me? Blackjack? An arms peddler? Not hardly." His laughter broke off and his eyes became wary. "And now that you've gotten that information out of me, maybe you wouldn't mind answering a direct question."

"Such as?" Tambu asked.

"Such as, are you a pirate?" Blackjack replied, his eyes darting weasel-like back and forth between the seated pair.

"No, we're not. If we were, we probably wouldn't admit it openly."

"Why not? I do. Blackjack's the name, piracy's the game. Been making a good living at it for over five years now. Now that I know you're not in the business yourself, I have a proposition for you."

"And what would that be?" Whitey asked, her curiosity getting the better of her.

"It's a straightforward deal. You tip us as to where you're going with your next shipment, we meet you, put a few picturesque but easily repaired holes in your hull, relieve you of your cargo, and we split the profits down the middle." "

"You lost me with your logic somewhere," Tambu said. "Would you mind backing up and starting over?"

Blackjack rolled his eyes in exasperation. "Look, if you're not in the business, then you're looking for big guns to protect your cargo. If you're willing to pay that much for weapons, it stands to reason what you're protecting has to be pretty valuable. Right?"

"Keep going," Tambu replied noncommittally.

"The odds of your bringing a valuable shipment through are low, at best. You can't keep something that big a secret, and every space wolf around will be waiting for you. If you put up a fight, like it looks like you're planning to do, you'll probably not only lose your cargo, but your ship as well and maybe your lives."

"And so you're going to be generous and offer us a better deal," Tambu said wryly.

"Why not? If you do it my way, neither of us lose any men, and we both come out of it richer. Everybody's happy—except the insurance company that has to cover the loss. But they've got plenty of money."

He beamed at them, obviously delighted with his own cleverness. Tambu matched him smile for smile.

"No deal," he said flatly.

Blackjack's face fell. "Why not?" he asked in a hurt tone.

"Just because we aren't pirates doesn't mean we're stupid. What if we give you our flight plan and run out the welcome mat when you show up. What's to keep you from shooting our ship and us full of holes and keeping the whole pie instead of just half?"

Blackjack was no longer smiling. "I'll assume you aren't willing to take my word for it . . ."

"Good thinking," Whitey said.

". . . and instead I'll point out that it's in my own best interest to keep this relationship going as a long-term business deal. Four or five halves add up to more than two halves, if you get my meaning."

"Don't you think the insurance company would get suspicious after a while? Not to mention our customers?" Tambu asked.

"We could stagger it a bit," Blackjack explained, eager again. "Let a few shipments through and only hit the really big ones. By the time anyone figured out anything funny was going on, you'd have made enough to retire."

"It's still no deal, Blackjack. I appreciate the offer, but I still think we're better off trusting in the guns we have pointed out than in the one pointed at us."

"You know what this means, don't you?" Blackjack rumbled, his expression darkening. "If we find you out there, it will be no quarter."

"On either side," Tambu nodded. "Be sure your crew knows that before you come barreling in on us."

"It's your funeral." Blackjack turned to leave.

"Just a second, Blackjack," Tambu called. "I have one last question before you and your playmates disappear."

"What's that?" Blackjack scowled.

"What would you have done if we said we were pirates?"

"Then I would have told you to stay away from my territory. I don't take kindly to folks trying to horn in on my range."

"And where is your range?" Tambu asked innocently.

"You'll find out when you cross it. Until then, just keep looking over your shoulder."

"No harm in asking," Tambu shrugged.

The blond girl was whispering something in Blackjack's ear. He listened intently, a smile spreading slowly across his face.

"That's a good question. Those weapons you're after cost a lot of money. Do you have it with you, or is it on your ship?"

A sudden tension filled the air as the two forces surveyed each other.

"I don't think I'll answer that," Tambu said.

"Why not? It'll save us the trouble of finding out the hard way."

"Because the person we were waiting for just showed up," Tambu smiled, meeting the pirate's eyes squarely.

"Really?" Blackjack jeered.

"Really!" Egor answered, looming behind the trio, gun in hand. "These three giving you trouble, Captain?"

"Trouble?" Tambu smiled at the frozen trio. "There's no trouble here. As a matter of fact, these three were about to put their weapons here, on the table, and go have themselves a drink. Isn't that right, Blackjack?"

The pirate nodded, tight-lipped, and eased his gun from its holster, placing it carefully on the table. One by one, the other two followed suit.

Tambu pointed. "I think that table there will do, where we can see you—and do keep your hands above the table, hmmm?"

"I'll remember this," Blackjack growled, leading the group away to the table.

"What was that all about?" Egor asked.

"That was some of the opposition," Whitey explained. "All of a sudden, I'm a lot more eager to see them through a set of gunsights."

"Speaking of that, did you find your contact?" Tambu interrupted.

"Sure did," Egor nodded. "He's waiting outside. I left him there when I saw the crowd at your table. He seems to be the nervous sort."

"Well, bring him in," Tambu ordered. "The quicker we get this done with, the better I'll like it."

"Do you think it'll be okay?" Egor asked, jerking his head toward the seated trio glaring at them from across the room.

"I think so," Tambu said judiciously as he hefted one of the guns from the table and glanced pointedly at Blackjack. "Go get him."

The man Egor escorted back to the table was a bespectacled, balding wisp of a man who clutched his attaché case to his chest like a drowning man clinging to a life jacket. His eyes kept darting nervously to the guns on the table as the introductions were made.

"There—there won't be any trouble, will there?"

"Relax, Mr. Hendricks," Tambu assured him. "Everything is under control."

"For an arms dealer, you seem awfully nervous around guns," Whitey observed.

"Just because I sell weapons doesn't mean I like to be around when they're used," Hendricks snapped defensively. "If I had my way, I'd deal only through the mail."

"Quite understandable," Tambu nodded. "Now then, Mr. Hendricks, if you could begin going over the weapons specs with Whitey here, I'd like to have a word with Egor."

The man nodded and began unsnapping his case as Tambu drew Egor aside.

"Egor, I have a couple of errands for you."

"I thought I would be here for the bargaining," the big man frowned.

"So did I, my friend, but this is more important. Get down to the spaceport and find out all you can about Blackjack's ship."

"Who?" Egor blinked.

"Mr. Personality at the table over there. Get a description of his ship if you can, and relay the information to Puck. Tell him to stand by the guns and open fire if that ship comes anywhere near ours."

"But our guns aren't good enough to fight off an armed ship!"

"I know, but until we close this deal, they're all we've got. If my guess is right, Blackjack's crew won't be too eager to get into a fight if he isn't there calling the signals."

"You'll keep him here? Then why do I have to—"

"He might be wired for sound," Tambu broke in. "If anyone on his ship picked up our conversation, they might be getting very curious about us."

"They might be going after Puck right now!" Egor exclaimed.

"Right! So hurry. There's no time to argue."

"Okay, but watch that table. I don't trust them."

"Me neither, my friend," Tambu admitted, but the big man was already on his way.

With a sigh, Tambu joined Whitey and Hendricks, pulling his chair around to where he could watch Blackjack's table without moving his head.

"Sorry to be so long," he apologized. "How are we doing here?"

"Hendricks has what we want." Whitey leaned back from the table. "Compatible with our ship's systems. If they were any bigger, we wouldn't have the power to fire them."

"That big?" Tambu said. "Where'd they come from?"

Whitey answered, "As near as I can figure, they were salvaged from some of the old Planet Tamer ships. Nobody else used guns that big."

"Professional ethics require that I never reveal my sources—or customers," Hendricks commented.

"How would these weapons stack up against their armaments?" Tambu asked, indicating the trio glowering at them.

"Blackjack?" Hendricks asked, peering over his glasses. "You'll have half-again the range of anything on his ship."

"Fine," Tambu nodded. "And now the big question. How much?"

Hendricks produced a small notepad and scribbled briefly on it.

"I dislike haggling," he announced, pushing the pad across the table. "This is a firm price, including installation."

Tambu glanced at the figure on the pad and smiled.

"Let's be realistic, Mr. Hendricks. "We want to buy the guns *without* a ship attached—used guns, at that."

"In mint condition," Hendricks countered. "Warehousing them has cost me dear."

"Which is all the more reason for you to be eager to sell them," Tambu pointed out. "And there can't be much demand for them if you've had to carry them in inventory this long."

Hendricks began to protest, but Tambu held up a restraining hand.

"Fortunately, I also dislike haggling. Here is my top offer, and we'll install them ourselves."

He crossed out Hendrick's figure and scribbled a number of his own on the pad.

"Ridiculous!" Hendricks scoffed, looking at the pad. "Just because I deal with pirates doesn't mean I'll stand still for being robbed myself. I'll let the guns rust away before . . ."

Tambu smiled to himself as he listened to the man's orations. Despite the volume and bitterness of his objections, Hendricks had not moved from his seat after examining their offer.

They would reach an agreement soon.

Interview III

"It sounds like you were getting it from all sides in the beginning," Erickson commented. Sympathy was always a good ploy to loosen a subject's defenses.

"Yes, we were quite alone then. Still, that is not particularly surprising. We were setting a new pattern, and change is always resisted. The people we dealt with were constantly assuming that we fit in the order they already knew. Our only consolation was that if they had realized then what we were about, they probably would have treated us much more harshly."

"How do you figure that?" the reporter urged.

"Well, I've always felt Blackjack could have given us more trouble, but he didn't. Pirates are not the devil-may-care adventurers people think they are. Even though they risk their lives in combat, they're usually very careful about the reward they are gambling their lives against. Before we armed our ship, we would have been easy prey for a ship such as Blackjack's, but there was no reason for him to fight us then."

"How about vengeance? You embarrassed him in front of his crew there in the bar. Wouldn't he want to get even for that?"

"Vengeance is an expensive habit, Mr. Erickson. It's a luxury few businessmen can afford, and for all his flaws, Blackjack was a businessman. No, he believed us to be cargo haulers and decided it would be better to wait until sometime when he caught us with a full cargo hold. If he realized our actual plan of becoming pirate hunters, he probably would have attacked us at the earliest opportunity."

"You make it sound as if a confrontation between your ships was inevitable. I should think it would be a long shot at best."

"Not really," Tambu corrected. "While space itself is vast, there are a limited number of settled planets, and even fewer which have substantial space traffic in and out. Most ship-to-ship encounters occur in orbit over a planet rather than in space. If both our ship and Blackjack's were prowling the heavily trafficked lanes, it would only be a matter of time before we collided—especially if we were looking for each other."

"I see," the reporter nodded thoughtfully. "Getting back for a moment to your early difficulties, what would you say was the greatest obstacle you had to overcome?"

"Ignorance."

"Ignorance?" Erickson echoed, caught off guard by the abruptness and brevity of the answer. "Could you elaborate on that a bit?"

"Certainly. Our biggest problem was our own ignorance . . . naïveté, if you will. We were out to beat the pirates at their own game, but we had no real idea of what that game was. Blackjack was the first pirate we had met face to face, and we wouldn't have known it if he hadn't told us."

"And this ignorance hampered your early efforts?"

"It did more than hamper them, it crippled them. I've already given you an idea of how long it took us simply to find our suppliers. If any of us had crewed on a pirate ship, we would have had the information and known exactly where to go."

"But once your ship was outfitted, things started to go easier, right?"

"Quite the contrary. It wasn't until our ship was fully outfitted and we went hunting for our first opponent that we began to realize how little we knew about pirates. In many ways, that's when our real problems first began . . ."

Chapter Three

"How much longer until they can see us?"

As Puck's voice came over the intercom, Tambu punched the "talk" button on his command console, not taking his eye from the two ships on the viewscreen.

"Stow the chatter, Puck," he ordered. "Just keep watching that upper turret."

As might well be expected, they were all nervous. The next few minutes could well be the culmination of nearly a year's preparations.

Refitting the ship had taken much longer than any of them had anticipated, not to mention costing considerably over the original estimates. The results were heartening, however. The ship, now named the *Scorpion*, had a sting to be reckoned with in the form of four long-range slicers. Hendricks had assured them that they were now armed better than any ship currently registered. The only discomforting thought was that not all pirate ships were registered.

Even more important than the weapons, and twice as costly, were the custom scanners which allowed them to appraise a situation from a position well outside the range of another ship's detection equipment.

That plus several months of practice made the *Scorpion* and her crew formidable opponents. When they were all in agreement that they were ready to do combat, a new problem arose. How do you find the pirates?

Their only solution had led them here, to the Weisner System, which reported the highest frequency of pirate attacks. Prepared for a waiting game, they had struck paydirt almost immediately. In orbit over Magnus, the largest inhabited planet in the system, their detectors found two ships lying side by side. One was disabled and showed signs of recent damage, while the other seemed to be unscratched, and had two turret guns prominently mounted on her exterior.

It could be a pirate in the process of looting a victim. Then again, it could simply be a commercial ship answering a distress call. The problem was one that captains had been wrestling with for over a decade; how do you tell a pirate from any other ship until he fires on you?

A hurried conference among the *Scorpion*'s crew yielded the current course of action. They would ease close enough to the two ships that their guns would be in firing range, but the smaller guns of the functional ship would be unable to reach them to return fire . . . hopefully. From that position, they would hail the ship, offering assistance, and try to determine the situation confronting them.

Of course, there were several precautions they took to insure their safety in the maneuver. First, they kept their solar sails furled, relying on their storage batteries for power. Although this meant less power for their weapons or for emergency flight, Tambu reasoned that the fighting, if there was any, would be over quickly one way or another.

They angled their approach so that they were not aligned with the guns of their potential opponent, thus guaranteeing themselves first-shot capability before any fire could be brought to bear on them. Finally, Egor and Puck were manning batteries of two guns each, keeping them closely trained on the turret guns of the ship they were approaching while Whitey handled the actual maneuvering of the *Scorpion*. Tambu stood by ready to handle the talking once they opened communications.

They had taken every precaution possible, short of simply

bypassing the entire situation. Both of the ships they were approaching had their sails out, obviously not combat ready in their vulnerability. Still the crew of the *Scorpion* were wet-palmed nervous—individually and as a group.

Another few minutes . . .

"Whitey?" Tambu asked abruptly.

"Yes, Captain?"

"Am I set with a hailing frequency?"

It was a needless question, one that he had asked before. Tambu was no more immune to the strain of nerves than any of the others in his crew.

"Sure are, Captain. They should be able to hear you now if you want to start."

They were within the range of the *Scorpion*'s armaments now. Tambu knew that if he waited much longer, they would be vulnerable to return fire from the other ship. Licking his dry lips, he reached for the hailing microphone.

"Captain!"

At least two voices called to him from the ship's intercom, their exact identity lost in the garble of their overlap.

"I see it!" he barked. "Open fire!"

One of the turret guns on the functional ship they were approaching had begun to move, swiveling toward them in smooth silence.

Even as Tambu gave the order, the guns of the *Scorpion* opened up, the orange beams of slicers darting out like striking snakes toward their would-be assailant.

Though the crew of the *Scorpion* had practiced often and long with their slicers in mock attacks on small asteroids and occasionally on the face of an uninhabited planet, they had never seen the actual effect of their weapons on another ship. Now they had a front-row seat.

There was no explosion, no shower of sparks or flame. The portion of the rival ship which came into contact with the orange beams simply melted away like thin plastic before a soldering iron. One of the beams hit a sail, severing the tip. The remaining portion of the sail crumpled slowly as the severed tip began to drift away into open space. Both turret guns simply vanished, erased completely by direct hits from the slicers.

"Cease fire!" Tambu shouted, finding his voice at last.

The beams halted at the sound of his command, and silence reigned as they surveyed their handiwork.

The stricken ship's hull was already healing itself. The outer hulls on all ships were triple thickness with auto guidance to slide new plates into place in event of damage severe enough to cause interior pressure loss. Soon the exterior of the ship would be repaired. They could only guess at the interior damage of their attack.

Tambu's eyes wandered to the third ship, floating silently next to their recent opponent. Having now seen how fast a ship could heal itself after an attack, he could appreciate anew the extent of the attack which had wrecked such havoc as to leave a ship gaping open like that.

"We got him!" Puck's awe-filled voice came over the intercom.

"Keep your guns on him!" Tambu snapped. "We don't know if he has any more surprises up his sleeve."

"Captain?" Whitey joined the conversation. "Aren't you going to try hailing them now?"

There was something in her voice that caught Tambu's attention. In contrast to Puck's enthusiasm, Whitey seemed almost pensive.

"Is something bothering you, Whitey?" he asked.

"Well . . . it occurs to me that except for some shooting, nothing has changed." she replied hesitantly. "We still don't know whether or not they're pirates."

There was a moment of stunned silence. Then the crew erupted in protest.

"Cm'n, Whitey!" Egor groaned. "He was getting ready to shoot at us."

"That's right," Puck added. "He wouldn't have done that if—"

"Sure he would," Whitey interrupted. "Any of us would. If an unidentified ship came easing up to us with its sails in and its guns out, what would we do? We'd crank our guns around and cover the bastard until he said who he was and what he wanted. That ship couldn't have known whether or not we were pirates just like we didn't know if he was a pirate—and we still don't."

"What were we supposed to do?" Egor snarled. "Wait until he opened fire and cut us in half?"

"Whitey's right," Tambu said softly.

"But—Captain—" Egor protested.

"She's right." There was a bitter firmness to Tambu's voice now. "We don't know. We've got to find out—if it's not too late. Whitey, are we still set for hailing?"

"Affirmative, Captain."

Tambu slowly picked up the hailing microphone, hesitated, then depressed the transmission button.

"This is Tambu, captain of the *Scorpion*. Identify yourselves and state your condition."

There was no response.

"This is the *Scorpion*," he repeated. "We want identification of either or both of the two ships in our vicinity. Do you require assistance?"

It seemed strange, offering assistance to a ship they had been firing at a few minutes before. Still there was no response, nor was there any sign of movement from either of the other two ships floating on the viewscreen.

Setting the hailing microphone aside, Tambu flipped several switches on his command console, then settled himself in the swivel chair, one hand resting on a small keyboard.

"Egor!" he called into the intercom.

"Yes, Captain?"

"I'm taking over your battery. Take a shuttle over and investigate that ship—the one we fired on. Check for survivors, and look for any records or logs to tell us what kind of ship she is. And Egor . . .?"

"Yes, Captain?"

"Go armed. Take along a hand communicator and stay in touch."

Then there was nothing to do but wait. Tambu keyed his mind to detect movement from either of the other two ships and blotted out everything else. Even when the shuttlecraft finally appeared on the screen heading out on its mission he did not comment or react. Instead, he thought.

Their procedure had been in error; yet there was no other course they could have followed. They had blundered forward, forcing a confrontation whether the opposing ship was a pirate or a legitimate commercial vessel. Even catching a pirate in the act, they were left unsure as to its identity or motives. Moving in blindly as they had done was wrong, yet they could not afford to let a pirate take the initiative. Just as in this encounter, if fighting was involved, whoever shot first and straightest survived. The other . . .

How could they identify a pirate? How did pirates operate? He'd have to think like a pirate. A pirate's main weapon would be his anonymity, not his guns. By approaching another ship under the guise of a distress call—perhaps a request for medical assistance or repairs—a pirate could strike the first and final blow before their victim was aware of its danger.

That only emphasized their problem. *Scorpion* couldn't wait to be fired on to identify her enemies. How to pierce the cloak of secrecy? How to anticipate . . .

Perhaps that was the answer. How did pirates know where to hunt? Surely pirates couldn't rely on circumstance to find ships to prey on. They needed some method to find target ships—specifically target ships with large, expensive cargos. If the *Scorpion* could find out how the pirates set their traps, if they could anticipate where the pirates would be and be there waiting for them, then they might have a chance.

But how were they to find out how the pirates operated?

"You're awfully quiet, Captain." Whitey's voice interrupted his thoughts.

"Just thinking, Whitey," he replied absently.

"You aren't blaming yourself for what happened, are you? Heck, we all had a part in it. If we made a mistake, we're all at fault."

"That's right." Puck's voice chimed in. "You didn't even do any shooting. Egor and I were the ones who jumped the gun."

"At my command," Tambu said pointedly. "Just as we moved in on the ships at my command."

"But like Whitey said," Puck insisted, "we all had a part in it—the planning and the execution!"

"Ships aren't run by committee," Tambu reminded him. "That's why you made me captain. Besides getting the lion's share of the glory and profits when we do well and having last say on policy, being captain means that I hold the bag if things go wrong. It goes with the job. Isn't that right, Whitey? You were the one smart enough to dodge the captain's post. Wasn't avoiding responsibility one of your main reasons? Then don't lecture me about how I shouldn't feel responsible."

"I've got an answer to that," Whitey answered. "It's called the Nuremburg trials. The weight of responsibility falls on everyone in the chain of command, not just the one who gives the orders. If we were wrong, if we just shot up a commercial ship instead of a pirate, then we're pirates—all of us. If they catch us, they'll hang all of us, not just you, Captain."

"Touché!" Tambu laughed. "But I wish you didn't have to be quite so morbid with your example."

"Not to change the subject, Captain, but can we afford to get a few more viewscreens installed?" Whitey asked. "Then we can keep one thing on the main screen and still have a couple of little ones for talking to each other. I don't know about you, but I like to see people when I'm talking to them. Otherwise I can't always tell if they're serious or joking."

"That will depend on what those two ships have on board," Tambu answered. "Whether we're pirate or pirate hunter, I figure we have salvage rights on both vessels."

"There should be a bundle after we sell the ships," Puck declared.

"We'll see," Tambu said.

"What do you mean, 'We'll see'?" Whitey asked, her voice suddenly sharp. "We are going to sell the ships, aren't we?"

"Egor to Tambu. Do you read me?" Egor's voice blared suddenly over the console speaker, cutting off their discussion.

"This is Tambu. Go ahead."

"We're in the clear, Captain. This is a pirate ship, all right."

Relief washed over Tambu like a cool wave, freeing his mind of its slowly building tensions.

"The ship's name is the *Mongoose*," Egor continued. "It inflicted the damage on the other ship. That one's called the *Infidel*."

"Wait a minute," Tambu interrupted. "What is the source of your information? How do you know the *Mongoose* is a pirate ship?"

"I've got a survivor here. Found him hiding in the corridor. He's more than a little hysterical. Keeps babbling that he doesn't want to be hanged. Claims he'll tell us anything or do anything if we don't turn him over to the authorities."

Tambu leaned forward with a new eagerness. The survivor might be able to supply them with the answers to some of the questions they had on how pirates operated.

"Is he the only survivor?" he asked.

"He's the only one on this ship. There were three others who bought it when we chewed 'em up with our slicers. But you ready for this? There are six more on board the *Infidel*."

"What?" Tambu was unable to contain his surprise.

"That's right. A bunch of the crew took a shuttle over to check the *Infidel*'s cargo just before we showed up. One of them is the *Mongoose*'s captain."

Tambu paused to think. On the one hand, the captured pirates could supply them with much-needed information. On the other hand, they outnumbered the *Scorpion*'s crew seven to four. That could be trouble—particularly if they still had their captain to lead them.

"Do you want me to take the shuttle over and check 'em out?" Egor asked, breaking the silence.

"No! Stay where you are for now. I need you there to make sure none of them try to sneak back on board."

Actually, Tambu was afraid the pirates would overpower Egor if he tried to board the *Infidel*, but he didn't want to say that. Egor was so proud of his brawling abilities that he might just take it as a challenge and try it on his own.

"Do you have any way of communicating with the boarding party?" Tambu asked.

"Just a second—I'll check."

There was a brief silence, then Egor spoke again. "They're using hand communicators, same as us. They're on a different frequency though. I can hold mine next to theirs if you want to talk to them direct."

"Just relay this message to their captain. Tell him to take their shuttle to our ship—alone. I want to talk to him. Let me know when you get confirmation."

Staring at the ships on the viewscreen, Tambu set aside the hailing microphone he had been using to communicate with Egor, then leaned forward to use the ship's intercom speaker.

"Okay, you've heard the plan," he said. "Now here's what I want you to do. Puck, you swing your guns round to cover the *Infidel*. Whitey, stay with the maneuvering controls, but be ready to take over Egor's battery if anything happens with the *Mongoose*. The guns should be set already, but check 'em out just to be sure. I want them set so that all you have to do is hit the firing button. I'll go down to the shuttle docking port to deal with the prisoner. Call me on the intercom if anything strange starts to happen. Any questions?"

"Just the one I asked before," Whitey drawled. "I'm still waiting for an answer."

"I'm sorry—I've forgotten the question." Tambu admitted.

"The question was if we were going to sell the two ships, and if not, why?" Whitey prompted.

"We'll discuss it after I've talked to the *Mongoose*'s captain."

"What's to discuss?" Whitey argued. "What would we do with three ships?"

"We could cover three times as much space, or have one very powerful strike force," Tambu snapped back.

"I should think you'd like that, Whitey. It would mean less fighting and fewer casualties on both sides."

"How do you figure that?"

"If you were running a ship and three heavily armed ships overhauled you and demanded you stand by to be boarded and inspected, would you do it? Or would you try to fight?"

"I see what you mean," Whitey admitted. "I sure wouldn't try to fight three ships. But where would we get crews for the other two ships?"

"That's what I want to talk to the captain of the *Mongoose* about," Tambu confided.

"You're thinking of hiring them?" Whitey was incredulous. "But they're pirates!"

"Egor to Tambu. Do you read me?"

"Go ahead Egor."

"I've got confirmation for you. The *Mongoose*'s captain is on her way over."

Tambu's eyes jumped to the viewscreen. The shuttlecraft was clearly in sight, steering a straight course for the *Scorpion*. Then something that Egor had said registered in his mind.

"Egor! Did you say 'her way'?"

"That's right, my friend. It seems your counterpart is female. Young, too, from the sound of her voice. Her name's Ramona. Have fun with your interview."

Tambu grimaced at the leer in Egor's voice, but nonetheless paused to check his appearance in a mirror before heading for the docking hangar.

The captain of the *Mongoose* was not beautiful, but neither was she repulsive—or even homely. She was small, barely five feet in height, and stocky without really being overweight. A shock of long auburn hair was pulled back into a pony-tail which descended past her waist, combining with her round face to give her an almost schoolgirl appearance.

". . . You could have bluffed your way out." Tambu finished the thought for her. "It's a little late for that now, don't you think?"

The girl stared wordlessly for a few moments, then threw back her head and laughed.

"Ramona, the crafty pirate," she declared, shaking her head. "Trapped by blind luck and her own big mouth. Forgive me, but if I don't laugh, I might start crying."

Tambu smiled at her. "Now that you're fully aware of the situation, perhaps you will realize why I'm willing to bargain the way I have. Our aim is to be pirate hunters—sort of a cross between bounty hunters and a police force. It's obvious to me now that we can't simply rely on luck to find our prey. We need to know how pirates think . . . how they operate. That's where you come in. For example, you've implied that you knew in advance where to intercept the *Infidel*. How did you get that information?"

Ramona blinked, then grimaced slightly. "You really listen close, don't you? Well, on this particular venture, our information came from inside sources."

"Inside sources?" Tambu frowned.

"That's right. I'll tell you my honest opinion. If you're planning to make a living at this, you've got your work cut out for you. The name of the game is information, and it can take years to build up an effective network. How you're going to get informants who will inform on other informants is beyond me."

"Back up a little," Tambu said thoughtfully. "Who are these informants that make up a network?"

"Almost anyone who has information about shipments and an eye for easy money. When I say 'inside sources,' I'm talking about people within the corporate structure of the outfit shipping the cargo out. It could be a shipping clerk, an accountant, or a secretary. Sometimes the information comes directly from upper management when they want to cash in on a little insurance money."

"So you get your information from the shippers themselves?" Tambu asked.

"Some of it," Ramona corrected. "Sometimes it comes from corporations out to sabotage a rival's shipments. People working at the spaceports themselves are good sources. We even get tips from receiving merchants and corporations who don't want to pay the full price of a shipment."

"I see," Tambu said, pursing his lips. "It sounds as if you have a lot more information than I imagined."

"And you aren't about to let us go until you've pumped it all out of me. Right?" Ramona scowled.

"Actually, I was thinking along different lines. How would you like to come to work for me?"

She held his gaze for a moment, then turned away.

"If you insist," she said flatly. "But you drive a hard bargain. It's extortion, but I don't really have much of a choice, do I?"

"Of course you have a choice!" Tambu thundered, slapping his hand down on the desk hard enough to make it jump with the impact.

Ramona started, taken aback at this sudden display of temper, but Tambu recovered his composure quickly. He rose and began to pace about the room.

"Forgive me," he muttered. "I suppose you have every right to think the way you are. It serves me right for trying to be so cagey instead of laying my cards on the table from the first."

He stopped pacing and perched on the edge of his desk facing her. "Look," he said carefully, "it's been my intent all along to offer you and your crew positions in my force. I need experienced people—particularly people with experience in space combat—to man my ships. What I don't need are a bunch of sullen animals who think they were blackmailed into serving and who will jump ship or turn on me at the first opportunity. That's why I was saying I'd let you go instead of turning you over to the authorities. If you or any of your crew want to sign on, fine. If not, we'll let them go. Now do we understand each other?"

Again their eyes met. This time Ramona's expression was thoughtful, rather than guarded.

"I'll talk to my crew," she said at last. "For my part, though, the main hesitation isn't money . . . it's position. I worked a long time to get where I am, captaining my own ship. In all honesty, I'm not sure how content I'd be working under someone else again. Still, if you let me go, I'll probably end up crewing again for a while. I just don't know. I'll have to think about it."

"What if I offered you a position as captain of your own ship?" Tambu asked.

Hope flashed across the girl's face for a moment. "I don't want to sound suspicious again," she said carefully, "but that sounds a little too good to be true. You capture a pirate ship and crew, then offer to turn them loose again intact? What's to keep us from going back to business as normal as soon as you turn your back?"

"For one thing, your crew would probably be divided up among the available ships under various commanders. For another, we'll probably be operating as a fleet for a while, which would tend to discourage independent action. There is also the minor detail that I plan to be on board your ship."

"That sounds to me like I'd be captain in title only."

"Not at all," Tambu assured her. "It's my plan that the captains under my command have complete autonomy on their ships, providing, of course, that they stay within the general guidelines I set forth for them. I envision my own position to be more of an overall coordinator for the entire force. I suspect that if all goes well, that will occupy my time to a point where I will have neither the time nor the inclination to bother with the operational details of a single ship—including the one I'm on."

He uncoiled from his perch and seated himself at his desk once more.

"My decision to travel on board your ship is to enable myself to more readily obtain specific information from you rather than to imply any distrust. That is actually the answer I should have given you in the first place. I'll have to trust you, as I'll have to trust all my captains. If I don't, the force hasn't a hope of success."

Now it was Ramona's turn to rise and pace as she thought.

"Just how large a fleet are you envisioning?"

"I have no exact figure in mind," Tambu admitted, "but I expect we will grow well beyond the three ships we have currently."

"My crew isn't big enough to man even these three ships," she pointed out.

"I know. We'll have to do some additional recruiting. I'll want your advice on that, too."

"Aren't you risking trouble using ex-pirates for crew? I don't mean with mutiny, I'm thinking more about your reputation."

"My crew might object a bit, at first, but they'll accept it. If not, they can be replaced."

"I was more concerned with reactions from the people you'll be dealing with outside the force. I'm not sure how the merchants will take to being protected by the very people who were stealing from them not too long ago."

"We already have a solution to that," Tambu smiled. "We'll change the names of the ships and crew. That way no one outside the force has to know anything about your past. In fact, there's no reason for anyone to know within the force, either. Your crew doesn't know anything about my crew's background or vice versa. There's no reason they should be told, just as there's no reason we should have to give any background information to the new recruits."

"It'll sure make recruiting a lot easier if the new people don't have to admit to any past indiscretions." Ramona admitted. "Even though God knows what we'll get as a result. It's a little like the old French Foreign Legion."

"It's not a bad parallel. I don't really care what the crew did before they joined, as long as they toe the line once they're under my command."

"Discipline could be a problem," Ramona observed thoughtfully. "You know what would really be effective?"

"What's that?"

"If we made you into a real mystery figure. An omnipresent power with no face." Her voice grew more excited as she warmed to the idea. "You know how superstitious crewmen are. You could become a kind of a boogey-man. It could work against the ships we'll be fighting as well as within our own force."

"And just how would we accomplish that?"

"Hell, we've got a good start already! My crew is already spooked by the way you popped up out of nowhere and blitzed our ship before they could even get a shot off. All we have to do is keep you out of sight, and they'll do the rest. Sound doesn't travel through space, but rumors do. The myth will grow on its own. All we have to do is give it room."

"It won't work." Tambu shook his head. "The one thing I do insist on is meeting each person who's going to serve under me. I have to know who and what I'm commanding if we're going to be effective."

"Do it over a viewscreen. If you keep your sending camera off, you can talk to them and observe them to your heart's content, and all they'll see is a blank screen. As a matter of fact, that would help to build the mystery. Everyone would form their own impression, which means they'll talk about you among themselves trying to get confirmation."

"I'll have to think about it."

"Now is the ideal time to start," Ramona pressured. "Right now, the only ones who know what you look like are your crew and myself. If you wait, then you'll have to try to get cooperation out of the combined crews as well as any new recruits. The sooner you start, the easier it will be."

"But if I'm planning to be on your ship—"

"You can board ahead of the crew. There's a room off my cabin you could take up residence in without anyone being any the wiser. When they talk to you on the viewscreen, they won't know if your signal is coming from somewhere on board or from another ship."

Tambu leaned back and stared at the ceiling as he turned the thought over in his mind.

"It's a good idea," he admitted finally. "Maybe we can give it a try and see how it works. I'll talk to my crew."

"It'll work," Ramona declared triumphantly. "You know, I think we'll work well together. Who knows? If we play our cards right, we might end up ruling the universe."

"Who wants it? Right now I'll settle for eeking out a humble, but substantial, living."

"I know, I know. But when you talk to the new recruits, you might make some veiled references to a secret master plan. It'll help us fill the rosters if they think they're getting in on the ground floor of something big."

"They are," Tambu announced solemnly. "The question is how big—and I figure we won't know the answer to that for a long time yet."

Interview IV

"Then your original crew was surprised by your plans of expansion?" Erickson asked. Tambu seemed tyrannical, even in his early career.

"I had not deliberately withheld the information from them. The plan had been half-formed in my mind for some time, and I had simply forgotten to tell them about my thinking on the subject. If I had reached a firm decision before encountering the *Mongoose* and its captive, I would have discussed it with them."

"How long had you been thinking about it before you actually implemented the plan?" the reporter pressed.

"I guess it had been in the back of my mind all along," Tambu admitted. "I was always aware of the limitations of a single ship, both in terms of firepower and of coverage."

"Coverage?"

"One ship can be in only one place at a time. If the pirates could figure out where our one ship was, they would know where we weren't, and therefore where it was safe for them to operate. Three ships complicated the problem for them."

"I see," Erickson nodded. "Once you had three ships, though, how did you deploy your original crew—the ones you could be sure of in terms of loyalty?"

"Egor and Whitey were each placed in charge of a ship. I assigned Puck under Whitey."

"Didn't that cause problems with Puck? Giving him a subordinate position while Ramona kept command of her own ship?" the reporter asked, eager for clues of dissention.

"Surprisingly enough, not. I expected him to be much more upset than he actually was. Egor gave me more problems than Puck did."

"What kind of problems did Egor cause?" Erickson pressed.

"It was strange. I had expected problems with Whitey and Puck, but it never occurred to me that Egor would object. Whitey and Puck took the change in stride, but Egor put up an unholy argument. He flatly felt he wasn't qualified for an independent command."

"But you changed his mind, right?" the reporter smiled. "Whitey had commented before on your powers of persuasion."

"Not really," Tambu sighed. "I still maintain Whitey was wrong in attributing superhuman persuasive powers to me, and this is just one example of my failures. I did get Egor to accept a command position, mostly by pointing out there was no one else available with the necessary qualifications whom I trusted."

"What about Puck?"

"Even Egor admitted that Puck was too young for command. Not so much in years, but he lacked maturity. On that basis, Egor accepted command, but he never really agreed with me as to his qualifications."

"So in essence, you forced your will on him?"

Tambu hesitated a moment before answering.

"I suppose you're correct," he said finally. "If that was an error, it's one I paid for a hundredfold afterward. I was constantly receiving complaints, both from Egor and from the other captains as to his shortcomings as a commander. He was probably the least effective captain who ever served under me."

"Why didn't you relieve him of command, then?"

"That is one of those hindsight questions we were speaking of earlier," Tambu admitted. "I've asked myself that a hundred times in the last few years and still haven't come up with a satisfactory answer—mostly because I'm unsure of my own motives during that period. Mostly, I think, it was because of friendship. Egor was my friend, and I gave him command of a ship because I believed in him and his abilities. To take this command away would have been a sign that I no longer believed in him. Balanced against that was my own stubborn pride. I didn't want to admit I had been wrong in my assessment of his abilities, and I sincerely felt that the problems he was encountering were manufactured by him in an effort to prove me wrong. I genuinely believed that once I made it clear that I wasn't going to remove him from command, he would resign himself to the task and solve his own problems. I saw it more as a test of wills than as a sign of incompetence on his part."

"That must have been pretty rough on your friendship."

"It was, particularly as the force continued to grow. As my time was divided across an increasing number of ships, my rapport with my original crew—with my friends—became dangerously thin."

"I can see that," Erickson commented thoughtfully. "Even adding to your fleet by conquest, the number of ships would grow geometrically."

"Even faster than that," Tambu countered. "Few people realize exactly how fast the fleet did grow. You see, not all the new ships came to us as fruits of battle."

Chapter Four

"You're sure she'll be all right?" Tambu asked again.

"Look, will you relax?" Whitey scolded, her exasperated expression received clearly on the command console viewscreen. "Women have been having babies since prehistoric times. The hospital is more than able to handle any complications that might arise."

"I still don't know why you didn't sign her into the hospital on Carbo when you were there last month," Tambu grumbled. "It's a better facility."

"We aren't talking about a limb transplant," Whitey argued. "It's a childbirth, a simple childbirth. Besides, I tried to talk her into staying on Carbo and she wouldn't do it. Derry can be very strong-willed when she sets her mind to it. What was I supposed to do? Force her to go on shore leave and strand her there?"

"It isn't your fault, Whitey," Tambu sighed. "I know that. It's just this is the first childbirth in the fleet, and I don't want anything to go wrong. I guess I've been taking it out on you. Sorry."

"That's all right," Whitey shrugged. "If you can't sound off at us, who can you sound off to? Most of the new recruits would faint dead away if you talked to them direct, much less shouted at them."

"It's not quite that bad."

"Well, anyway, Pepe's staying with her here on Bastei, so he'll be able to handle any problems that we've overlooked," Whitey continued. "We'll be back in a month to check on things and pick them up if they're ready."

"You're sure they're set on rejoining?" Tambu pressed. "Shipboard is no place to raise a kid."

"I already tried that argument, and it didn't work. Derry was raised on shipboard."

"But that probably wasn't a fighting ship. There's a difference."

"We haven't done any fighting for a long time," Whitey observed. "Anyway, they both want to keep working for us, and I'm not about to stop them. Do you want to overrule me?"

Tambu shook his head, then remembered she couldn't see him.

"No," he said hastily. "It's your ship, and if you're willing to put up with it, I won't interfere."

"Good," Whitey nodded. "Then it's settled."

"She is registered at the hospital under her real name, isn't she?" Tambu frowned.

"Yes, she is!" Whitey exclaimed, "And her medical records have been transferred from her home planet. That's what I meant in my original report when I said we were following recommended procedures. Your recommended procedures."

"I'm doing it again, aren't I?" Tambu said.

"Yes, you are." Whitey was still annoyed. "Do you get this wound up over everything that happens in the fleet?"

"Not everything," Tambu admitted, "but a fair number of things."

"You can't afford that—not with eight ships under you. If you can't keep some distance between yourself and the minor hassles of running a ship, it'll tear you apart in no time."

"But if I don't keep track of what's going on—" Tambu began, then broke off.

A small red light had begun to blink insistently on his command console accompanied by a soft chime.

"I'll have to sign off now, Whitey," he explained hurriedly, "I've got a 'blinker' emergency coming in."

"What's up?"

"I don't know. It's from the *Dreamer*."

"Puck's ship?" Whitey exclaimed. "He hasn't been in command for a month yet. What kind of trouble can he have gotten into that quick?"

"That's what I'm about to find out," Tambu announced grimly, reaching for the cutoff switch.

"Well, sometime when you get a few minutes, give me a call so we can talk about other things than business." Whitey called desperately. "We never just talk anymore."

"Right," Tambu agreed absently, "I'll do that. Tambu out."

He was hitting buttons as he spoke, switching the communications relays to accept the Dreamer's transmission. Whitey's face faded, to be replaced immediately by Puck's worried features.

"Tambu here," he announced, forcing a calm tone into his voice. "What's the problem, Puck?"

"I'm—I'm not sure it's a problem," Puck stammered in return.

"Well, then, why don't you just tell me why you put in a priority call?" Tambu suggested patiently.

"We've got a pirate ship here. It came up out of nowhere and caught us with our sails out."

"How big a ship?"

"About twice our size. And armed to the teeth. If it opened fire, we wouldn't have a chance."

"Then I'd say you have a problem," Tambu announced grimly. "I take it from your comments that so far it hasn't fired on you?"

"That's right. It's just sitting out there watching us. We've got its captain on the horn, and he says he wants to talk to you."

"To me? About what?"

"He won't say, but he says if you aren't on board our ship, we should relay his transmission to you."

"All right, patch him through."

"Will do," Puck acknowledged. "Should we try to get our sails in while you're talking?"

"Negative. If he wants to talk, let's hear what he has to say before you try anything. Monitor the conversation, though, and keep your weapons manned. If you hear me say my name—the one I was using when we first met—open fire and try to knock him out before he returns fire."

"Got it," Puck nodded vigorously. "Oh, Tambu, one more thing you should know. The captain says his name is Blackjack. I think he's the same one you met back on Trepec."

"I see. Very well, patch him through."

There was a few moments' pause. Then Puck's face faded and was replaced by the impatient countenance of Blackjack. Tambu watched in silence for several moments as the man fidgeted.

"You wanted to speak with me?" he said at last.

Blackjack started, then squinted at the screen as his hands went to the control dials.

"Excuse me," he apologized hastily. "There must be an equipment malfunction. I'm not receiving a picture. If I had known you were standing by—"

"It is not an equipment malfunction," Tambu interrupted. "For security reasons, my picture is never transmitted."

"Oh," Blackjack blinked. "Of course. A very sound policy."

Tambu smiled in wry amusement. As incredible as it seemed, Blackjack hadn't recognized his voice. The difference between the swaggering bully he had met on Trepec and the servile figure on the screen was ludicrous.

"You said you wanted to speak with me?" he asked levelly. "My time *is* limited."

Blackjack licked his lips nervously. "Well, sir, we've heard that you're forming a peacekeeping force and were accepting members who were . . . that is, regardless of their past records."

"That is correct. And in answer to your unasked question, some of our crews have been pirates in the past."

Blackjack smiled. "Good, because we'd like to join up. I mean, we'd like to become a part of your force, if that's possible."

Tambu raised his eyebrows in surprise. This was a turn of events he hadn't anticipated.

"I know this is irregular," Blackjack continued hastily,

misinterpreting the silence. "But if you could just supply us with a few details as to what you're expecting—"

"Why?" Tambu interrupted.

Anger flashed momentarily in Blackjack's eyes, and his posture stiffened. Then he regained his smile.

"I know it's an annoyance, but it's been hard getting a line on your operations. We figured maybe if we went right to the source—"

"I meant, why do you want to join. I was under the impression you had a lucrative business of your own going."

"You've heard of me?" Blackjack seemed both surprised and flattered.

"We have our sources," Tambu countered, smiling to himself. "It was my belief that you were a diehard loner. I fully expected that if our courses crossed, that you'd be taken dead or not at all. As such, I'm quite curious about your sudden change of heart."

"Well, the business has never been all that stable, and it's been getting rougher lately. You should know that. You're one of the reasons things have been going bad."

"We have had some modest success."

"It was shaky enough when things were one-on-one and every ship for itself. But now that we're up against ships working together in teams or packs—well, let's say the odds are getting pretty high against us."

"Have you thought of quitting?" Tambu suggested.

"We talked it over, the crew and me, but none of us were wild about finding work planetside, and cargo-hauling seems awfully dull after the life we've been living."

"Besides, it doesn't pay as well," Tambu observed dryly.

"Exactly. Well, anyway, we decided to go with the old saying . . . you know, 'if you can't lick 'em, join 'em.' So here we are. What do you say?"

"It still sounds like a rather abrupt change of face to me. I'm surprised your crew isn't more averse to changing sides this way."

Blackjack shrugged. "Cops or robbers, the game's the same on both sides of the fence. The big difference is that playing it your way, we can mix with polite company."

"Well, we haven't exactly been swamped with invitations to society balls," Tambu countered. "And I'd like to think there are a few differences between the cops and the robbers. The main one that comes to mind is discipline. If you join the fleet, you play by my rules. You'll be allowed to run your ship your way, but the final decisions are mine. No solo jaunts or independent action."

"I know that. That's the price we pay for joining a group. Between you and me, though, in a lot of ways, it's a plus, not a minus. I don't mind at all passing the buck on some of the rougher decisions."

"Exactly what are you expecting to get out of this?"

"You don't buy the 'noble cause' bit, eh?" Blackjack grimaced.

"Let's say I have limited faith in it. I think the best business relationships exist when both sides benefit from the arrangement. If you join, I get another ship complete with a trained crew. Now what are you seeing that you'll get out of this?"

"Support. Both military and financial. Not only do we have allies we can call on if we get our ass in a sling, by sharing profits and losses, we stabilize our cash flow."

"Now that's the kind of selfish answer I can relate to. For the first time, Blackjack, I'm starting to believe you."

Blackjack sighed. "Now that that's settled, where do we go from here? Do we have to actually fight with your ship here, or can we just surrender and save wear and tear on everybody?"

"I think we can dispense with that in this case. Instead, why don't you have your ship tag along with the *Dreamer* for a while. I'll instruct the captain to fill you in on our procedures and fleet policies. Then we can talk again."

"Fine by me." Blackjack smiled. "Anything else, boss?"

"Yes, start organizing the personnel records for your crew. I'll want to go over them with you next time we talk."

"Why?" Blackjack asked suspiciously. "I thought selection and assignment of the crew was my responsibility."

"It is," Tambu soothed. "I just like to be familiar with the individuals serving under me."

"Ah, right. It might take a while, though. I was never big on recordkeeping."

"I'm particularly curious about two of your crew," Tambu commented, unable to resist the jibe. "One of them is a short-haired blonde in her late twenties; the other is a boy in his mid-teens, Spanish-looking. I think you know who I mean."

Blackjack was visibly unsettled by the request.

"You weren't kidding when you said you had your sources, were you?" he said wonderingly.

"No, I wasn't. Tambu out."

He waited until Blackjack's face was gone, then leaned into his console once more.

"Are you still there, Puck?" he asked.

"Didn't miss a word," Puck replied, his features materializing on the screen.

"Good," Tambu nodded. "Try to get invited on board Blackjack's ship—and take a few extra people with you. I want a report from you on their armament and personnel to check against Blackjack's data. Can do?"

"Affirmative, boss."

"Keep me posted, then. Tambu out."

For a few minutes, Tambu leaned back in his chair smiling to himself. He considered calling Whitey, but rejected the thought. The board was clear, and his eyes hurt from staring at the screen for so many hours.

On an impulse, he rose and moved to the door of his cabin, activating the small intercom set into the wall. Hearing no conversation in the adjoining cabin, he depressed the button by the volume knob.

For long moments he waited, knowing that Ramona might not notice the small light glowing on her console even if she were in her cabin.

"Yes, boss?" Her voice came through the intercom at last.

"Can you come in here for a moment? Nothing important. I just want to talk to a live person for a while."

"Sure. Coming through."

He reached down and unlocked his side of the door, and a moment later heard the click as she unlocked her side.

"Care for some wine?" he offered as she entered the cabin. "I opened a half-bottle a couple hours back and haven't gotten around to drinking more than a glass."

"Only if you'll join me," she smiled. "It's silly, but my mother always told me a lady never drinks alone."

"Why not?" he smiled gesturing at the blank callboard. "The fleet seems to be handling its own problems for a change."

He draped himself over a chair and waited while Ramona poured two glasses of wine. Passing one to him, she pulled up another seat and sank into it, curling her legs up under her.

"You seem to be in an exceptionally good mood tonight," she observed, cocking her head to one side. "Good news on the board?"

"Not really," he frowned. "Just no bad news. There was one funny incident, though."

"Tell me about it."

"Well, I just got done talking with Blackjack. You remember I told you about him? The pirate we ran into on Trepec? The one who was going to get even with us?"

"I remember," Ramona nodded, sipping her wine. "What did he want?"

"He wanted to join the fleet, but that's not what tickled me. The funny part was that he didn't recognize me—my voice, that is. I wonder how he'd react if he knew the Tambu he was dealing with in such humble tones was the same man who took his gun away from him in a bar on Trepec?"

"That's it? That was your laugh of the day?"

"Well, I suppose it doesn't sound like much," Tambu admitted, crestfallen. "You would have had to have been there."

"I just don't think it's all that surprising that he didn't recognize you. You've changed a lot, you know."

"How so?"

"I didn't mean that as a criticism. It's just that since you've been coordinating things for several ships instead of one, you've taken on different mannerisms. Your voice has a no-nonsense ring of command to it that wasn't there when we first met."

"I haven't been aware of any changes," he protested.

"You're too close to see it," she pointed out. "But you're taking to command like a duck takes to water. You may have started out playing a role, but now you're it. You're the boss, the chief, the old man. There's a distance between you and everyone else, and it shows in how you talk."

"You mean that now, as we're talking here, I'm putting on airs?" he challenged.

"Not so much now when we're in the same room," Ramona conceded. "But when you're talking to me over the viewscreen, I can feel it. And it isn't putting on airs—it's just a clear knowledge of who orders and who follows."

"You make me sound awfully dictatorial."

"It isn't overt," Ramona insisted. "But there's no doubt in anyone's mind that there's an iron hand in that velvet glove. Nobody ever forgets you've done what no one else even thought of trying—building a united fleet from a bunch of individual ships."

"I'll have to think about that," Tambu sighed thoughtfully. "I thought I was just doing what had to be done to keep the fleet together."

"Did you let Blackjack join?" Ramona asked.

"Tentatively. It may be a mistake. I can't help but wonder how he'll act once he's operating on his own."

"It's my bet he'll be a model captain," Ramona stated. "In case you haven't noticed, the newer the ship, the closer they toe the line. The stronger the fleet gets, the less any individual ship wants to cross you."

"I'd rather have respect and loyalty than fear," Tambu stated flatly.

"You're going to get all three," Ramona insisted. "You're becoming a power, and that tends to polarize people's reactions. Some will love and respect you; others will migrate toward hate and fear."

"That's a bit too much for me in one evening." Tambu rose and stretched. "I'm going to get some sleep while I can. I still maintain I'm just doing my job."

"I'm not so sure it's always going to be that simple," Ramona retorted, uncoiling and starting for the door. "Remember, even now, the only one defining your job is you!"

Interview V

Erickson took advantage of the recess to inspect the room more closely. His confidence had grown until now he was more relaxed than at the beginning of the interview. Of particular interest to him was the collection of books which adorned the walls.

Much to his surprise, the titles were mostly of an economic or philosophical nature. For some reason, he had been expecting the main thrust of the literature to be military history. Like Tambu, the library was proving to be inconsistent with his preconceived notions.

He was about to take a volume down for closer inspection when Tambu's voice came over the console's speaker once more.

"I'm ready to continue now, Mr. Erickson. Please forgive the interruption."

"It's quite all right," the reporter waved, taking his seat once more. "I must confess, however, that it had somehow never occurred to me that the feared Tambu would occasionally have to go to the bathroom like anyone else."

"It's a common misconception surrounding public figures," Tambu said. "When the average person thinks of an actor, a politician, or an athlete, they always view them within the context of their specialty. The thought that they must occasionally perform some very ordinary tasks such as shining shoes or doing the laundry never enters into the picture."

"That's true," Erickson admitted. "I guess it's just a matter of ego-defense."

"Ego-defense? I don't believe I understand your point."

"Well, when an ordinary Joe looks at a celebrity, there's always one question in the back of his mind: 'What has he got that I don't?' If he lets himself view the celebrity as just another person, it means he must see himself as inferior. Since most people strive to see themselves as above average, they reject the thought that an ordinary person can achieve that much more success given the same materials to work with. As a result, rather than accept an inferior self-image, they are more comfortable projecting the celebrity into superhuman status. The view then is: 'I'm above average, but they're special! I don't have to compare myself with them because they're another species completely.' As I said, it's self-defense—or rather ego-defense."

"An interesting concept," Tambu commented after a moment's pause. "While I've observed the phenomenon, that is one interpretation I had never considered. Perhaps we can discuss it further later, if I have any extra time left at the end of our interview."

"I somehow doubt that." Erickson smiled. "Just what we've covered so far has raised so many questions in my mind that I'm sure the interview will last as long as time allows."

"In that case, we should probably proceed," Tambu said. "What questions do you have so far?"

"One question I've been asking in various ways since the beginning of the interview still sticks in my mind. You've answered it indirectly with your narrative, but I'd still like a simple 'yes or no' response. When you began organizing your force, did you think you were doing the right thing? Did you see your force as the good guys?"

"The simple answer is 'yes'!" Tambu replied. "The actual answer is far more complex. I was hoping you could see that by now."

"The complexity escapes me. It seems a very straightforward question."

"It becomes complex when I add that what we were doing was right in my own mind, not just at the beginning, but to this very day.

However, I am aware that I do not have an exclusive patent on truth. What's right in my mind is not necessarily right in the minds of others. From there it's a matter of who you believe or which philosophy you embrace."

"But facts are facts," the reporter argued impatiently.

"Very well," Tambu sighed. "The facts are that we were successful. We waged war against the pirates infesting the trade and made enough of a dent in their numbers that their activity all but ceased. That is a fact which can be confirmed through your own newspaper's files. By examining our record you can see we were a law-enforcing group."

"Enforcing whose law?" Erickson jibed. "Yours?"

"You're defeating your own arguments, Mr. Erickson. You're attempting to interpret the facts. The factual response to your question, however, is that yes, we were enforcing my laws. There were no interstellar laws until I formulated them with my fleet. To judge beyond that requires interpretation. Was I bringing law and order to the previously lawless starlanes? Or was I an opportunistic bandit taking advantage of that lawless state?"

"I'm beginning to see your point," the reporter admitted hesitantly. "But what happened next? What happened once you gained the upper hand over the pirates?"

"Then," Tambu reminisced, "we began to encounter the same problem which has confronted peacetime armies since the dawn of time."

Chapter Five

"There's no sign of them at the other two inhabited planets in this system either. We've checked with instruments and confirmed with firsthand investigation. They aren't here."

Tambu slouched in his chair studying the angry face of the *Candy Cane*'s captain on the viewscreen before him. He was as concerned over the mental state of the captain as he was about the unfortunate turn of events being reported.

"Have you checked planetside?"

"On all three planets," the captain confirmed. "There hasn't been a ship in this system in weeks. With your permission, I'd like to find the lying bastard who sold us this information and get our money back—with interest!"

Tambu grimaced at the suggestion, confident the captain could not see his expression. He had several unconfirmed reports on the captain of the *Candy Cane,* all regarding unnecessary brutality. The last thing he wanted to do was to give the man carte blanche to lean on one of their informants.

"Have you checked the uninhabited planets?" he asked, stalling for time.

The expression of anger on the captain's face gave way to one of uneasiness.

"We've run an instrument check, but not a firsthand confirmation," he admitted. "I figured if the Chameleon was putting in for R and R and supplies they'd be at one of the inhabited planets. I mean, there's no point in giving your crew shore leave on a hunk of barren rock. Shall I go ahead and check out the other planets?"

Tambu had reached his decision as the captain spoke.

"No, that won't be necessary. I want you to hold firm at that system for a while, though. Wait at least a week and see if our target pops up. He might just be running late."

The captain grimaced, then remembered that Tambu could still see him and rearranged his features into a forced smile.

"Hold position for a week," he repeated. "Affirmative."

"For the record." Tambu said casually, "What are you figuring as your modus operandi for that week?"

It was an unfair question. The captain had just gotten his orders, and it was obvious he couldn't have a set plan of action in mind yet. Still, Tambu expected his captains to be able to think on their feet. Besides, he hadn't liked the way the captain reacted when receiving his orders.

"Umm . . ." the captain began, licking his lips nervously, "we'll leave a crewman at each spaceport on the three inhabited planets, then take up position close enough to the furthest uninhabited planet that it will screen our position. If the target ship shows up, our watchers can contact us by closed communicator and we'll move in."

Tambu let the captain suffer in silence for a full minute before he answered.

"That plan seems adequate. How do you intend to select which crewmen are to serve as watchers?"

"On the merit system," the captain replied promptly, his confidence apparently bolstered by the acceptance of his plan. "An all-expense-paid week planetside is a pretty nice plum. I figure it should go to my best performers."

"That also means your best performers will be off-ship when you take on the target vessel," Tambu commented pointedly.

The captain's face fell at the admonishment, but Tambu continued. "It's good to hear that. I wish more of my captains had that kind of faith in their crews instead of letting a few key crewmembers handle all the dirty work."

"I—Thank you, sir," the captain gulped.

"One suggestion, though," Tambu drawled, smiling at the captain's discomfort. "You might choose one of the watchers by random draw, then rig it so one of your newer crewmembers wins. Send someone with a bit of experience along to be sure he stays out of trouble, but make it clear it's the new man's assignment. Also, I think you should put all the watchers on a budget just to make sure they don't get carried away with their spending. They're there to do a job, not to go on a binge."

"Yes, sir."

"And announce to the crew that if you nail the target, there will be a week's shore leave at a planet of your choice."

"Yes, sir. Thank you." The captain was smiling now.

"Tambu out."

Tambu didn't smile as he clicked off the viewscreen. He took no pleasure or pride in dealing with situations such as this. They were all too commonplace now, more the rule than the exception.

Swiveling his chair away from the communications console, he faced his desk once again. The jumble of papers and notepads stared back at him in unswerving accusation. He realized that he viewed the work before him with neither enthusiasm nor distaste. He was too tired to muster any reaction.

He briefly considered the possibility of a short nap, but rejected the thought. He would double-check these figures once more, then take a break. With an involuntary sigh, he reached for a pencil.

Behind him, the communications console chimed softly, signaling an incoming call.

Tambu turned from his desk and reached for the switch to activate the mechanism. His eye fell on the call board, and he hesitated. The incoming call was being relayed through several ships. This was the normal precaution taken to hide his exact location. The ship originating the call was the *Scorpion*. Egor!

Tambu scowled at the board, his hand poised over the activator switch. For a moment, he was tempted to ignore the call. Then the console chimed again, and he threw the switch. As long as Egor was one of his captains, he would be afforded the same prompt attention as any other captain, no matter how annoying it was.

"Yes, Egor?" Tambu asked, forcing his voice into a neutral tone.

"Saladin says you approved the transfer of Jocko from the *Scorpion* to the *Ramses*." Egor's snarl exploded over the speaker even before his face blinked into focus.

"That is correct," Tambu replied levelly.

"Did you know Jocko is the second-best navigator in my crew?" Egor's face was on the screen now, and his expression matched his voice.

"I knew it," Tambu admitted without apology.

"Why wasn't I consulted?" Egor demanded. "Doesn't my say matter for anything anymore?"

As Egor spoke, the door of Tambu's office opened a crack, and Ramona's head appeared. She cocked an eyebrow in silent question, and he waved her inside.

"In this case, Egor, your opinion was already known," Tambu explained patiently. "You had already turned down Jocko's transfer request. That's why he came to me directly."

"So you just countermanded my authority," Egor scowled. "Without even bothering to ask my reasons."

"As Jocko explained it to me, he was either going to transfer or leave the force." Tambu's voice had an edge to it now. "Either way, the *Scorpion* was going to lose him. At least this way he's still in the force. As you pointed out, he's a good navigator."

"I still don't think you should have let him blackmail you." Egor was sullen now.

"What are we supposed to do? Chain him to his bunk?" Tambu's annoyance was beginning to show. "We can't hold people against their will. Even if we could, I wouldn't. I want ships crewed by free men, not slaves."

"Well, I still think you should have talked to me," Egor grumbled.

"I was going to, Egor," Tambu apologized. "But things have been so hectic at this end I haven't had time."

"That's been happening a lot lately," Egor complained bitterly. "I always seem to be at the end of your priority list. You can find time for everybody but your old friends."

"Damn it, Egor," Tambu snapped. "I spend more time talking to you than with any three of my other captains."

"Which is less than a tenth of the time you used to have for me! Of course, now that you're a big shot, I can't expect you to waste your precious time on my problems."

Tambu drew a long breath before responding. "Look, Egor," he said gently. "Speaking for a moment as an old friend, you might ease up a little on your crew. If you did, a lot of the problems you're having would never arise."

"Don't tell me how to run my ship! I'm allowed to do things my way as long as it doesn't go against the rules. You just worry about the fleet and keep your bloody hands off my ship!"

"*Captain* Egor," Tambu replied coldly. "If you wish to retain full responsibility for the running of your ship, I suggest that you be man enough to begin taking full responsibility for solving your own problems instead of whining for me to clean up your messes. Tambu out!"

"But—"

Tambu smashed his fist down on the activator switch, cutting off Egor's response.

A touch at his shoulder made him jump. He had forgotten that Ramona was in the room.

"I'm sorry, Ramona," he sighed, sinking back in his chair. "I didn't think things were going to get that hot."

"How many times do I have to tell you," she said gently, standing behind him to massage his neck and shoulders, "it's Ratso now, not Ramona. You should follow your own rules."

"I don't like the name Ratso," he complained. "I'll use it in formal communications, but privately you'll always be Ramona to me."

"Other crewmen have picked names you don't like, but you use them," she teased.

"I don't sleep with the other members of the force! I just can't accept the idea of sharing a bed with someone called Ratso."

They had drifted into an affair after several months of working together. What began as a shared moment of passion had grown into a gentle and tender partnership which neither of them questioned.

"When are you going to do something about Egor?" she asked absently.

"Egor's one of our oldest captains. His seniority gives him certain considerations."

"He's a braggart and a bully. Everyone in the fleet knows that."

"He has an irritating manner," Tambu admitted, "but he's a good man. You've just got to know him before you can see through his bluster."

"If so, you must be the only one who can do it. The other captains are wondering why you don't boot him out, or at least pull his command."

"Look, just drop it, huh?" Tambu winced. "Egor is my problem, so it's up to me to come up with a solution. Okay?"

"Sure," she shrugged. "Didn't mean to get on your back. Did you get any sleep at all last night?"

"Not much," he sighed, relaxing under her skillful hands. "It seems everyone has decided that the easiest time to get through to me is the middle of the night. Then again, there's all this."

He gestured at the papers on his desk.

"What is all that, anyway?" Ramona asked. "You've been working on it nonstop for a couple of weeks now."

"I've been going over the books checking our cash flow," he explained. "I've got to check the numbers again, but if the preliminary figures hold true, we're going to be out of business by the end of the year."

"Are things that bad?"

"Actually, things are that good." Tambu laughed bitterly. "We're suffering from being too successful. There are only so many pirates for us to capture, and the ones that are left are giving us wide berth. We've been paying the crews out of the treasury for nearly a year now, and we aren't making enough in salvage and reward money to replenish it. In short, our expenses have remained constant while our income has gone down. We're in trouble."

"Actually, our expenses have gone up," Ramona commented thoughtfully. "Now that we're up to twenty-four ships . . ."

"Twenty-eight."

"Twenty-eight?" she echoed. "Where did the other four ships come from?"

"One captured, three joined." he recited mechanically.

"Joined?" Ramona frowned. "But you can't keep letting new ships into the fleet."

"I thought you were the one who argued for that in the first place," Tambu teased. "Most of the ships in the fleet are joiners."

"At first, yes. But we can't keep expanding if we're running out of money and targets."

"We need the extra ships and the contacts."

"But that just means more . . ." She broke off and looked at him suspiciously. "You've got a plan, don't you? You always have a plan."

"Not always, but most of the time."

"Well, come on," she prodded, poking him in the ribs. "What is it?"

"Nothing much," he said casually. "Just a complete reformatting of our force."

He paused, as if expecting her to respond enthusiastically. Instead, she gnawed her lip.

"How complete?" she asked warily.

"Well, so far we've been living on rewards and salvage. The books show the flaw in that system—no fighting, no loot. I figure we're ready to move onto the next logical stage."

"And that would be . . .?"

"That we hire ourselves out as a peacekeeping force. That way we get paid whether there's fighting or not. In fact the less fighting there is, the more we should be paid."

"How do you figure that?"

"Easy," he smiled, "in theory, we'll be paid to keep the trade routes free of pirates. If we botch the job and somebody loses a shipment, we might have to refund part of our fee; but as long as things go smoothly, we get full payment."

"Full payment from who? Refund our fee to who?" Ramona pressed. "Just who are you expecting to foot the bill for all this?"

"The ones who are benefiting from our services. The corporations and the merchants. I still have to figure out how to spread the cost around proportionately but I figure it should be a small percentage of the value of each shipment, to be paid equally by the shipper and the receiver."

"What if they won't pay?" Ramona asked pointedly. "So far they've been getting the service for free."

"If they won't pay, we take our ships away and guard the systems that will pay. When the word gets around that a system is unguarded, the pirates will move in again. Sooner or later, the systems will come around to seeing it our way and will ante up."

"I don't know. It sounds a little too good to be true. I'd like to hear what a couple of the other captains have to say about this."

"I can go you one better than that. You'll have a chance to hear what all the captains have to say about it."

"How so?"

"I'm planning to have a mass meeting of the entire fleet, specifically to get the captains all in one place so I can sell this idea to them all at once. It's a little too big for a unilateral decision."

"And if they don't agree with you?"

"Then I'll resign and let someone else take a shot at running the show." Tambu's tone was light, but his sagging shoulders betrayed the depth of his emotion. "I see it as our only hope for survival, but I can't lead if no one will follow."

"Then it's a unilateral decision," Ramona stated flatly. "No one's going to buck you if you feel that strongly about it."

"Don't be so sure. Sometimes I think some of the captains automatically take the opposite position I do just to be ornery."

"I am sure," Ramona insisted. "And if you don't realize what's going on, it's about time you took another look at things. Sure the captains argue with you, because they know you respect people who think for themselves and speak their minds. You tell each person who signs on this force that you won't tolerate 'yes men,' and they take it to heart. They'll argue because you tell 'em to, but don't kid yourself into thinking they'll go against you on anything big. You're Tambu, and you call the shots in this outfit. They wouldn't have it any other way."

Tambu stared at the blank viewscreen, avoiding her eyes as he thought.

"I don't know," he sighed finally. "I hope you're wrong, but a lot of what you're saying fits what's been going on. You know what they say about absolute power corrupting absolutely? Well, I'm no different from anybody else. It scares me to think what I'd be like if I let myself believe I've got total control over the force. I mean, even with the ships we have now, without any further expansion, we're strong enough to seize and hold a half dozen systems—not planets, *systems*. We could do it, and there's not a force in the universe that could stop us."

"You know, I hadn't thought about it, but you're right." Ramona admitted.

"But, you see, that's what bothers me," Tambu pressed earnestly. "I *do* think about those things. That's what scares me. Do you know the thing that makes me suppress the thoughts? I don't think the force would go along with it. The fact that it's immoral or wrong doesn't enter my mind, just that I don't think the force would back me. I think they'd finally be convinced I'd lost my mind and toss me out on my ear. Maybe I shouldn't say it, but I like being Tambu. With all the arguments and the lost sleep, I *like* running the force."

"I know," Ramona soothed, rubbing his shoulders again. "I'd hate to think you were putting up with all this if you didn't like it. As you say, you're no different than anybody else. There's a need inside everybody to make an impact on society or history . . . to make a difference. Where you're special is that you can do it. How many people could run this force, much less build it? You have something— call it charisma or whatever, but people trust you and believe in you. They believe that you'll make that difference in history, and if they follow you, they'll be a part of it. They believe that in serving under you, they'll go further than they ever would on their own, and they're right. Would Egor or Puck ever command a ship of their own if you hadn't given them the opportunity? You talk about the force. You are the force. The captains and their crews are loyal to you, not the force. They tolerate each other because you order it, but you're the glue that holds the whole thing together."

"That's the other reason I'm calling for a mass meeting," Tambu muttered darkly. "I want the captains to start interacting more, not just tolerating each other. I'm betting that once they're all together, talking and sharing drinks, they'll find out that their problems are not unique or individual, but shared by every other captain in the fleet. With any luck, friendships will spring up and they'll start calling each other for answers instead of coming to me all the time. I'll wait until the end of the meeting to see if anyone else suggests making the meeting an annual affair—and if no one does, I'll suggest it myself."

"I don't know if you're overestimating the force or underestimating them," Ramona commented, shaking her head. "But it's not going to work."

"Thanks. I always appreciate a little support for my plans."

"Oh, the meeting will go okay, but I don't think it will accomplish what you want it to—your hidden motive, I mean."

"Hidden motive?" Tambu frowned.

"You should listen to yourself as closely as you listen to the captains," Ramona laughed. "What you've been saying is that if the captains start talking to each other and find answers among themselves, then maybe it will ease your status as answer man, that it will give you a chance to ease down off your pedestal. What you're overlooking is that you're still instigating it, and the captains will see that. None of them thought of getting together to help each other until you ordered it, just like no one thought of assembling a space fleet until you did it. It may get you off the spot for specific questions and issues, but you'll still be Number One who can do things no one else even thinks of."

"I don't know. I'm too tired to think straight anymore. Maybe it will seem clearer tomorrow."

"How tired are you?" Ramona drawled, pressing herself against him.

"Well . . ." Tambu mused with mock solemnity, "I was thinking of going to bed."

They kissed and moved toward the bed with their arms around each other's waists.

The communications console chimed softly.

Ramona groaned dramatically, and Tambu swore under his breath.

"I'll try to keep this short," he promised.

A glance at the call board identified the call as coming from the *Raven*. Whitey!

"Yes, Whitey?" he asked flipping on the activator switch.

As Whitey's face swam into focus, he noted there were circles of fatigue under her eyes.

"Sorry to call you so late," she apologized, "but I just finished a brainstorming session with my crew and wanted to get a hunk of uninterrupted time with you."

"What's the problem?"

"Well, we just finished investigating a complaint by some of the planetside folk that a couple of our boys busted up a bar and put two people in the hospital."

"Which crewmen?"

"That's the whole point. When we checked, it turned out that it wasn't our crew at all. A couple of planetside toughs were throwing their weight around and saying they were Tambu's men so they could get away with it We've had the authorities go through our crew roster, and the witnesses confirmed it wasn't any of our crew; but in the meantime the pilot of our shuttle got jumped at the spaceport and was beaten pretty badly."

"That's unfortunate, but I don't see what I can do about it."

"There's nothing you can do about this specific incident," Whitey agreed, "but the crew came up with an idea that could affect the whole fleet. They say they're tired of taking the blame for things other people do posing as Tambu's men. They suggested we adopt an emblem or something that could be worn by each crew member when they went planetside so that folks would know who they are. We're going to try it for the *Raven*'s crew, but you might want to consider doing it with the whole fleet."

"What kind of emblem?" Tambu queried.

"We haven't decided yet," Whitey admitted. "But we're thinking in terms of a belt or an armband, something like that."

"How are you going to keep those same toughs from making their own copies?" Tambu frowned.

"I'll tell you one thing," Whitey grinned. "If they do, I wouldn't want to be in their shoes if any of my crew caught them."

"That's not good enough," Tambu insisted. "Tell you what; call the main spokesmen for your crew up to your cabin and let's kick this around a little more."

Insulated by the intricacies of this new problem, he never heard Ramona as she quietly let herself out of his cabin.

Interview VI

"I assume the captains approved your plan?" Erickson asked.

"Unanimously. In hindsight, it wasn't surprising. It was either that or disband."

"So you began offering the services of your fleet to the planets on a retainer basis?" the reporter prompted.

"That is correct. And the key word there is 'offered.' When you stop to think about it, it was a good deal for the planets. We had built, armed, and organized the fleet at our own expense. All we were asking them to do was contribute toward maintaining it."

"Yet you encountered resistance to your offer," Erickson recalled. "Didn't that surprise you?"

"Yes and no. We knew from the onset that not everyone would want to contribute. There's an old medical saying which states, 'An ounce of prevention is worth a pound of cure.' The anticipated problem was convincing a healthy patient that he needed an ounce of prevention, however reasonably priced it might be."

"Perhaps they thought they were being asked to pay for a pound of prevention where an ounce would suffice."

"I would believe that if they had haggled about the price," Tambu said pointedly. "However, what we encountered was flat refusal. In essence, the planets wanted to reap the benefits of our work without paying a cent."

"They did pay reward money when you destroyed the pirate ships," the reporter reminded him gently.

"The actual fighting was only a fraction of our work," Tambu argued. "If a pirate chose to run or even avoid a planet completely rather than tangle with our ships, we got nothing even though we had effectively performed a service."

"But in that situation your ship hadn't actually done anything," Erickson countered.

"Are your planetside police paid by the arrest? Part of the value of a uniformed patrolman is as a deterrent. Their job is as much to prevent crimes as it is to solve them."

"I take it the planets weren't swayed by your arguments?"

"Some were," Tambu said, calming slightly. "I tend to overgeneralize when I refer to the planetside resistance. Many planets did subscribe to our service, but there were few enough that in my eyes they had to pay an inflated rate. As such we were continually approaching and re-approaching the other planets to subscribe, in an effort to reduce the costs to the individual planet."

"That sounds awfully considerate," Erickson observed, not really believing it.

"Only partially," Tambu admitted. "The other side of the coin was that we were afraid if we didn't find a way to spread our fees more, that the subscribing planets would decide they were paying too much and withdraw from our roster."

"While you're speaking candidly," the reporter prodded, "I couldn't help but notice a note of bitterness in your voice when you spoke about the resisting planets. How deep did the emotions run in your fleet over that initial resistance?"

"There were two kinds of bitterness prevalent in the fleet at that time. The first was over the injustice of the refusals. We lost numerous ships in our campaigns against the pirates—ships with friends and comrades on board. It did not sit well with us to be told by the planets that we hadn't really done anything or risked anything. That was a bitterness we had anticipated, and as such kept under control."

"And the other kind?" Erickson urged.

"The other kind was over the method of the refusals. As I mentioned earlier, we hadn't expected all the planets to agree to our proposal. Though we felt our position was reasonable and justified, we held no grudge against an opinion to the contrary. What did surprise us was the venom with which our offer was refused. While most of our crews owed no allegiance or loyalty to the planets, neither did they harbor any ill-will—that is, until they encountered the warm greeting some of the planets had prepared for anyone off a Tambu ship."

Chapter Six

Tambu bent forward over his console and pressed his palms over his ears, unsuccessfully attempting to block out the babble of voices gushing from the viewscreen's speaker. Failing that, he drew a breath to speak angrily, then reconsidered. Almost of its own volition, his hand flipped a switch and the scene on the viewscreen changed, now displaying the space outside his ship.

Looking at the stars was becoming a habit with him, a ploy he relied on more and more to put his own problems in perspective. This time, however, the stars were partially obscured, upstaged by the vast armada of ships gathered here. Militarily, it was the strongest force in the universe, boasting more fighting ships than any planet—than any system could field. Many people outside the force feared its power. They were all too aware of the potential danger of this many ships united under a common cause.

United! Tambu smiled wryly. Those people would worry less if they had the vaguest idea of what actually went on within the fleet. The babble of voices rose in volume. Tambu sighed and readjusted the screen back to its original display.

It was a large room, one of the cargo holds of the *Raven*. Chairs had been packed in wall-to-wall to provide seating, but at the moment most of the room's occupants were on their feet shouting and arguing with each other.

Tambu watched for a moment, then shook his head and leaned toward the microphone.

"I will entertain a motion to gas the room," he announced firmly.

Heads snapped around and arguments died in mid-sentence at the sound of his voice. Silence spread through the crowd like a wave, leaving shocked and wary stares in its wake.

"Now that I have your undivided attention, allow me to remind you of our situation. Each of you is a captain of a ship under my command. You are here to represent your ship's interests in discussions of the fleet's policies and procedures, as well as to exchange ideas with your peers."

He paused for a moment, then continued, allowing his voice to harden noticeably.

"As such, you are expected to conduct yourselves as mature, responsible adults, not as bickering children. Our agenda will require at least four days to cover, but it will take four months if you cannot contain yourselves. Now, if you will resume your seats, I would like to continue with the subject at hand."

The group began to obediently sort themselves out and shuffle toward their seats. One captain, however, remained in place. She was short, middle-aged, and grossly overweight, but her ferocious expression gave her additional stature as she waved her hand in the air, demanding recognition.

"Yes, Momma?" Tambu asked, acknowledging the woman's hand.

"I think what you said points out our need to limit the size of the fleet," she declared without preamble. "We're getting too big to function effectively, even in a meeting like this."

"Am I to understand that you feel being too big has hampered your effectiveness?" Tambu quipped, deliberately misunderstanding in an effort to lighten the mood.

The group chuckled appreciatively, but Momma was not to be sidetracked.

"Not me, the fleet," she insisted.

"Plans for expansion are on the agenda for tomorrow," Tambu

pointed out. "I would appreciate it if you would hold your comments and opinions until that time."

"Well, I want to put a motion on the agenda then," Momma pressed stubbornly. "I think we should put a top limit of a hundred ships on the fleet."

Tambu noted the murmurs and nods of assent among the other captains. There were also several angry faces and hands being thrust violently into the air. The meeting was poised on the brink of another argumentative digression if he didn't exert control immediately.

"Momma," he asked, "are you volunteering to withdraw your membership from the fleet?"

"Me?" the woman blinked, taken aback. "No! I never said that."

"The fleet is already over a hundred strong," Tambu pointed out solemnly. "To adopt or even consider your proposal would imply a willingness to remove several existing member ships from the roster. I assume you would not suggest such a thing unless you were ready to accept the same exile as you were suggesting for others."

"No," Momma admitted, "I—I didn't know there were that many ships already."

Defeated, she sank into a chair, avoiding the eyes of the other captains. Tambu deliberately waited several moments before offering a lifeline.

"You have raised a good point, one I feel all the captains should ponder prior to our expansion discussion tomorrow. The subject currently under consideration, though, is the treatment of our crewmen during their visits planetside."

Several hands went up, seeking recognition. Tambu's attention, however, was drawn to one figure whose raised hand was accompanied by a thoughtful expression, a marked contrast to the eager or angry faces around him.

"Yes, Puck?" Tambu asked.

"I've been listening for the past hour, and it seems to me we're saying the same thing over and over. Now, we could all take turns telling horror stories and have a lot of fun one-upping each other and get everyone all worked up, but I don't see much point in it. We're all in agreement that our crews are being treated shabbily. Once that's been established, I think it's a waste of time to continue recounting the gory details. The real question we should be discussing is what are we going to do about it?"

There was scattered applause as Puck sat down. Tambu smiled to himself. Puck had come a long way from the cocky, hair-trigger kid he used to be. He was rapidly becoming one of the most valuable and popular captains in the fleet.

"I think Puck has put his finger on the problem," Tambu announced firmly. "If we can dispense with further itemizing of complaints, I'd like to hear some discussion from the floor as to proposed courses of action."

"We've got to hit them back," Blackjack called, leaping to his feet. "As long as the Groundhogs think they can gang up on our crewmembers and get away with it, they're going to keep doing it. I say we should teach them that if they lean on someone off a Tambu ship, they're going to get it shoved back down their throats."

Tambu frowned at the growls of assent that responded to Blackjack's suggestion.

"Whitey?" he said, recognizing the scowl on her face.

"We can't do that, Blackjack," she argued. "Last time I checked, we were still a law enforcement organization. Now, the one rule that's always held for law enforcement groups is that to gain and keep public support, you can't use undue force. That means if someone jostles you on the street, you can't break his arm. If we start going around exacting vengeance with interest for every insult or injury, we'll never get any public support."

"Public support?" Blackjack roared. "The last public support my ship got put three of my crew in the hospital!"

"How do you know your roughnecks didn't start it?" Whitey challenged.

"Three men don't start a fight with a whole bar," Blackjack shot back.

"They might," Whitey corrected. "Or they might try to hassle a hooker with a lot of friends."

"Are you saying my men—"

"That's enough! "Tambu barked. "It was decided that we weren't going to discuss specific incidents, nor am I going to allow this discussion to degenerate into childish name-calling."

Though they couldn't see him, the anger in his voice was sufficient to subdue the two combatants.

"Now then, Blackjack, you've proposed a program of retribution. Whitey has raised two questions. First, how much force are you suggesting we employ; and second, what level of investigation do you plan to carry out before launching your retribution? I am also curious as to your answers to those questions. Would you care to comment?"

"I haven't thought it through that far," Blackjack admitted. "I was just suggesting it as a possible solution for discussion."

"I see," Tambu commented. "Very well, does anyone else have anything they'd like to add to this proposal?"

Cowboy, the lanky captain of the *Whiplash,* rose slowly to his feet.

"Ah'd like to add a thing er two to what Whitey said. My paw, he used to be a policeman, and I learned a lot listenin' to him talk over dinner."

"Is that how you managed to dodge the law for so long?" someone quipped from the back of the room.

Cowboy shrugged and smiled, drawing a round of laughter from the assemblage.

"Anyway," he continued, "Paw used to say anytime there was a fight, both sides would insist the other side started it. Usually they weren't even tryin' to cover up or anythin'; they really believed it was the other folks doin'. More often 'n not, my paw never could sort out whose fault it really was."

He paused to look around the room.

"Now, Ah'm not say in' it's always our fault when there's a fight, but Ah don't think we kin always say it's the Groundhogs' fault neither. What's more, Ah don't think that even if we tried to investigate each problem that anyone'd believe we was bein' fair and impartial. Heck, Ah don't think we'd believe it ourselves."

"But we can't just ignore it!" Blackjack roared, surging to his feet again. "Just because I don't have a plan doesn't mean we should just sit back and do nothing. Our crews are being discriminated against. We owe it to them to take some kind of firm action."

Several voices rose in both support and protest, but Tambu cut the growing pandemonium short.

"Jelly," he said, "I believe you're next as soon as we have some quiet."

"Thank you, sir." The old man bowed as the voices died down around him. "I would contest Mr. Blackjack's last comment. I do not feel our crews are being singled out for special treatment."

There were several growls at this; but for the most part, the audience held its peace, waiting for the old captain to have his say.

"Mr. Cowboy's father was a policeman. Well, I was a policeman, too. Incidents such as those which have been recounted here, beatings, attempted rapes, minor extortion by spaceport personnel, are not unique to members of our fleet. Police blotters are filled to overflowing with such cases, and have been since long before our fleet was established. The areas we most often frequent planetside—the bars, the places of amusement which surround the spaceports—have always experienced a higher than average occurrence of such crimes. I feel we are reacting emotionally because our friends and families are directly involved. I am concerned, as all of you are, but I cannot believe we are victims of a vast conspiracy on the part of the planets, or that the authorities sanction such activities against us."

"What about the times when the police have been directly involved with the beatings?" someone called angrily.

"Unscrupulous men in law enforcement uniforms are neither new nor rare," Jelly argued. "It is sad, but a part of reality. I still feel it is the work of individuals rather than of some sanctioned group."

"That's real pretty, Jelly," Ramona challenged, "but I don't buy it. My crew and I have been cruising the starlanes for a long time and had our share of hassles with the Groundhogs, but nothing like we've been getting lately. You can't convince me that what's been happening is just random street violence."

Tambu raised his eyebrows. Until now he hadn't been aware of how deep Ramona's feelings ran on this subject.

Individual arguments were raging among the captains again as he cleared his throat to restore order. This time, however, someone beat him to it.

"Shut up! All of you!"

The naked rage in the voice cut through the clamor like a sword stroke, and the captains abruptly lapsed into silence and gave ground from its point of origin. Exposed by the crowd's parting was a pixyish woman, standing tall on a chair. Her skin was poisonously mottled, marking her as a victim of New Leprosy. Though hers was an arrested case, many still felt uneasy in her presence.

"The chair recognizes A.C.," Tambu smiled.

The irony of his voice was lost on the stormy woman as she launched into her tirade.

"Never in my entire life have I heard such crybaby moaning and weeping," she announced bluntly. "Screw what Cowboy and Jelly are saying. I'll give you what you want to hear: 'We're being picked on . . . discriminated against.' So what!"

The assembled captains sat in stunned silence as she continued.

"Most of you don't know what discrimination is," A.C. challenged. "Well, I do. For eleven years now I've been a New Leper. No matter what laws have been passed, that's still a stigma I have to live with. Jelly there's a black. He's been discriminated against so long he doesn't even notice it anymore. A lot of you are other things that some people don't like: Orientals, Jews, witches, women, young, old, smart, dumb. You don't get hassled working for Tambu and instead of being grateful, you get spoiled rotten. You forget how unfair reality is!"

She dropped her eyes and took a deep breath as if trying to calm herself.

"You're discriminated against because you're different," she said softly. "You all are—your crews are. You ride around on ships instead of working in a hardware store down the street. You're transients on any planet, outside the local order. That makes you different. That's all it takes to have people envy, fear, and hate you all at once. You can't change that by breaking heads, just like you can't change that by acting nice and polite. You don't change it at all. You learn to live with it."

A.C.'s head came up and her voice hardened.

"There are only two options to that. You can be stampeded into damn-fool useless action, letting any ignorant spaceport bum who mouths off or takes a swing at you control your actions, or you can tuck your tails between your legs and quit. I don't know about the rest of you, but it'll take a lot worse than what I've heard today before I holler for help or quit. If any of you or your crews can't take a few lumps in stride, I say good-bye and good riddance. Go ahead and fold, but don't try to justify your own weakness by asking the whole fleet to follow suit."

There was total silence when A.C. sat down. Tambu waited several moments, then cleared his throat.

"I think I've heard enough discussion to reach a decision," he announced. "Until further notice, my orders on the matter are this: any incidents or complaints concerning fleet members and planetside citizenry are to be reviewed as individual isolated affairs and will be resolved in cooperation with planetside officials. While fleet members are allowed and expected to defend themselves if attacked, no retaliation in excess of the affront will be tolerated. Should there be any doubt as to the proper course of action in such an incident, or if a question arises as to interpretation of these orders, a priority call will be made to me so that I can personally guide the decision."

Tambu paused for a moment as he always did before concluding a ruling.

"Any captain who feels he cannot obey this order or enforce it within his crew rosters should signify it at this time. If a majority of captains so object, I will either reconsider my order or step down as fleet commander. If those objecting are in the minority, they will be removed from the rosters of the fleet. Those who do not object are thereby accepting the order and will be subject to discipline if it is breached. Dissenters, show yourselves at this time by standing."

There was a shifting of chairs as the captains craned their necks to look around the room, but no one stood.

"Very well. As the hour is late, I adjourn the meeting for today. I believe the *Raven*'s crew has prepared refreshments for you, but remember, we reconvene tomorrow at 0800 hours, shiptime."

With that, he clicked off his console and sagged back in his chair. Though a decanter of wine was just a few steps away, he was too weary to fetch it. All energy seemed to drain out of him as soon as he adjourned the meeting.

He was suddenly aware that his shirt was drenched with sweat, and shook his head in dull recognition of the emotional output necessary to control these meetings. The fleet was a tiger—a multi-headed, multi-personalitied tiger. It would turn on the planets, on itself, or on him if he relaxed his control, however briefly. Like a wild-animal trainer, he only had his belief in his own goals and abilities to buoy him, and that only gave him limited control. If he tried to clamp down too hard, all hell would break loose.

Leaning back, he began to mentally review the arguments surrounding the fleet's planetside difficulties. He always did this after a major decision, probing for prejudices or hasty thought on his part, as well as any lingering resistance or resentment among the captains. Later, he would review the actual recordings of the meeting, but for the first pass he relied on his memory and impressions.

Cowboy's oration had been disappointing. His argument had supported Tambu's position of inaction, but in this case that support was annoying. From numerous arguments in the months prior to the meeting, Tambu knew that Cowboy personally favored retaliation, yet today he had spoken in favor of moderation.

A generous interpretation of the lanky captain's change of heart would be that his opinions had been over-ruled by his crew, and that he was speaking today as their representative. A more probable explanation supported criticism voiced by both Ramona and Whitey as to the value of the yearly meetings.

They steadfastly maintained that most of the captains—particularly the newer ones—were not voicing their true feelings in the discussions, but rather attempting to curry favor with Tambu by saying what they thought he wanted to hear. While Tambu argued firmly that this was not the case, he had to admit to himself that he had no way of knowing for sure—and hearing Cowboy contradict himself made him wonder anew if he was deluding himself as to the sincerity of the captains' statements.

An insistent chiming interrupted his thoughts, and he looked to his console. The priority call light flashed red, drawing a frown to his face.

There was supposed to be a ban on personal conferences for the duration of the meetings, sparing him the annoyance of captains "stumping" for support of their proposals. For a moment he considered ignoring the call, then he noticed it was coming from the *Raven*. Was there trouble among the captains? A duel?

With a sigh, he activated the viewscreen once more. To his surprise, however, it was Egor's face, not Whitey's that appeared on the display.

"What's wrong, Egor?" Tambu asked, instantly regretting having spoken. If he had kept quiet, Egor never would have known that his call was answered.

"Nothing's wrong," Egor answered hastily. "Whitey let me use her gear to call you is all."

"There are to be no personal conferences until the meetings are over," Tambu growled. "If there is no emergency, then—"

"It's not an emergency, but it's important," Egor interrupted. "I thought you'd want to talk it over with me first, but if you're too busy, we'll do it from the floor during the meeting."

There was a warning tone in the big man's voice that caught Tambu's attention. Swallowing his annoyance, he leaned into the mike again to apologize.

"Sorry to be so abrupt, my friend, but these meetings always set me on edge. That's part of why I avoid personal conferences until they're over—it keeps me from taking my frustrations out on people close to me. What was it you wished to discuss?"

The anger drained from Egor's face, and he dropped his eyes.

"I would like—I want you to relieve me of command," he said softly.

Tambu's annoyance flared anew, but he kept it out of his voice.

"Why?" he asked.

"These yearly meetings emphasize something we've both known for a long time now. I'm no leader. I don't belong in the same room with these others."

"You're a captain, the same as they are," Tambu retorted. "I fail to see the difference."

"The other captains know their crews," Egor protested. "When they talk at the meetings they speak as representatives of their ships."

"And you?" Tambu pressed.

"My crew doesn't like me. I don't know their minds or how they feel on the issues. I can run a ship, but I'm clumsy with people. Please. I'm asking as an old friend. Put someone else in my place. Let me go back to crewing like I did before."

"What makes you think the other captains know what their crews want?"

"It's obvious. You can see it in their stance and hear it in their voices when they talk."

"They don't know their crews any better than you do," Tambu declared harshly. "You're confusing good oratory with good leadership."

Egor frowned, trying to grasp the concept as Tambu continued.

"Look, Egor, a lot of those captains aren't as sensitive as you are. It never occurs to them that their crew might have opinions. They speak their own minds and assume their crews are in agreement with them. A lot more know their crews don't agree with them, but they don't care. They're the captains, and that's that."

"Are you sure?" Egor asked suspiciously.

"In my position, I can see it. If I were going to single out poor leaders for replacement, it would be those captains, not you. Most of them are Johnny-come-latelies who substitute words for action. Their records are so empty that they have to save their arms to call attention to each little victory. You've successfully commanded a ship for me for nearly five years now, Egor. Your record speaks for itself."

"But my crew doesn't like me," Egor insisted with characteristic doggedness.

"I'm running a business, not a popularity contest!" Tambu exploded. "Can't you get that through your head? Your crew is working because they're getting paid, not because they have any great love for you—or me, for that matter. As long as they're doing their jobs, then you're doing yours. Beyond that I don't want to hear about it."

The words hung heavy in the air as Egor stared out of the viewscreen at him with a frozen expression.

"You're right," the big man said at last, not changing his expression. "I shouldn't have bothered you."

"Egor," Tambu began, his anger gone, "my friend, I—"

"Don't worry," Egor interrupted levelly, "I'll command my ship for you. I'll command it for you until you remove me yourself. Egor out."

The viewscreen went blank.

Tambu sat motionless, staring at the screen and trying to remember when, if ever, a captain had broken with him instead of vice versa.

Interview VII

"It sounds as if those yearly meetings were quite something," Erickson commented.

"They still are," Tambu said. "The captains' meetings are still one of the high points on the fleet's yearly calendar. Though they are usually much calmer than the episode I just mentioned, occasionally they can become as spirited and emotional as those conducted during our formative years."

"Yet despite their emotional outbursts, they seem to be fairly levelheaded when it comes to advice or debate."

"Never underestimate the abilities of a ship captain," Tambu warned. "No matter how often I tell myself that, I still forget sometimes that just because someone dresses funny or doesn't speak well doesn't mean he is any less capable or intelligent. To survive as a ship captain, particularly a fighting ship captain, requires a wide range of skills and abilities. One must be a tactician, a diplomat, a father-confessor, a personnel manager, and an accountant all rolled into one. Then, on top of it all, be a leader: one who can command and get respect and cooperation from a wide range of individuals."

"I must admit that's a different array of characteristics than has been displayed when one of your captains has been interviewed by the press," Erickson observed, cautiously.

"Of course it is!" Tambu snapped. "When you interview someone, they'll tell you what they think you want to hear. Not that they'll lie to you, mind you—just change their priorities and emphasis a bit."

"Then the captains have been deliberately trying to create the impressions they have?" the reporter blinked.

"Certainly. First of all, a captain is an administrator. If a captain tried to tell you about drudgery and paperwork involved in his job, you'd lose interest. Instead, they tell you all about the dangers of space, the ship-to-ship duels, and the harrowing escapes they've had—much of which is simply rehashings of stories they've read in adventure novels."

"And of course reporters like me eat it up," Erickson smiled appreciatively. "Tell me, do you think this editing of information is unique to ship captains?"

"Not at all. I feel it's a normal human tendency. If I asked you to tell me what it was like being a reporter, would you tell me about having to write stories about things that didn't interest you, while older, less capable reporters got the prime assignments? Or would you regale me with tales about gathering news under dangerous conditions and bravely exposing the truth despite the pressures of a corrupt establishment?"

"Touché! It sounds like you know the news business."

"I know people," Tambu corrected. "I have to. In your line of work, if you make an error in judging people, you lose a story. If I make an error, people die. It's a great incentive for me to get to know people as well as is humanly possible."

"Yet you still make mistakes," Erickson noted quickly.

"Too often," Tambu admitted. "But then, at the stakes I'm playing at, one mistake every five years is too often."

"I can see why you established the yearly captain's meetings. That's a lot of weight for anybody to carry alone. At least the meetings let you spread the responsibility around a little."

"Yes and no. While the discussions are helpful, the final decisions are still mine. I've discovered that having additional viewpoints and opinions does not always ease the decision-making process. Then, too, I have to make independent decisions on things which arise between meetings."

"Could you estimate a percentage split as to the number of decisions that come out of the meetings versus those that are made unilaterally?"

"No, I couldn't. There have been so many decisions made over the course of my career that I literally couldn't count them, much less divide them into categories. What's more, the varying magnitude of the problems would make a numerical comparison meaningless."

"I see. Well, how about decisions of major importance or impact? Would you have a feel for that?"

"I'm afraid the answer is still no," Tambu replied, but more hesitantly. "I've never thought of decisions in numerical terms. If I correctly interpret the direction of your questioning, however, there was one specific major decision I recall having to make unilaterally. I also recall that it was one of the most difficult decisions I've ever had to make."

Chapter Seven

Tambu sat alone, slouched at his command console. The viewscreen display showed the starfields outside, but his eyes were directed at the cabin wall, unfocused and unfeeling.

Moving as if it were not a part of him, his hand picked up the decanter to fill the wineglass before him. Only after setting the vessel down and raising the glass to his lips did he realize that both glass and decanter were empty.

Annoyance and puzzlement filled his mind as he frowned at the glass, momentarily driving out all other thoughts.

How much had he drunk? He wanted another glass, but knew he had to keep his mind clear to sort out the current situation. Had he filled the decanter this morning? How long ago was morning?

He ran a weary hand over his chin and noted with some surprise the well-developed stubble which met his touch. It had obviously been more than twelve hours since he shaved, but he couldn't remember shaving.

With a growl of self-disgust, he pushed the glass and decanter away from him. If he couldn't even remember what time of day it was, he certainly was in no condition to drink.

"Are you with us again?"

Tambu turned his head slowly and found Ramona perched on the foot of his bed. He hadn't heard her come in and didn't have the faintest idea how long she had been there.

"I'm sorry, love," he apologized, smiling faintly as he stretched. "My mind must have drifted a bit. Did you say something?"

Ramona shook her head.

"You know, lover, for a grim, humorless type, at times you have an incredible talent for understatement."

"Meaning what?"

"Meaning this is the first time you've come up for air in over two days. When your mind drifts, you don't kid around!"

"Two days!" Tambu exclaimed, ignoring her jibe. "What happened? Was I drinking? What about the fleet?"

"Whoa!" Ramona interrupted, holding up her hand. "The fleet's fine—or as good as could be expected. You haven't been drinking, you've been working. Nonstop. What's more, you worked thirty hours straight before you stopped talking to me or acknowledging there was anything in the universe except you and that damned viewscreen."

"But the fleet's all right?" Tambu pressed. "Who's been handling their calls?"

"You have. But I'll bet you couldn't tell me who you talked with or what they said without looking at your notes."

"You're right," he admitted ruefully. "I can remember generalities, but not specifics. I guess I'd better review this mess before I go any farther."

"Not so fast! The other side of the coin is that you haven't eaten or slept in that whole time. Now that you're back in the land of the living, I'm not going to let you plunge into this again until you take care of yourself."

"But I've got to reach a decision on this—and soon! "I've already stalled too long. The fleet's counting on me."

"Sure, the fleet's counting on you," Ramona argued. "So what happens to the fleet if you end up in sick bay from exhaustion and malnutrition? I'll give you two choices: Either make your decision now, if you won't rest until it's done; or if you want more time to ponder the problem, rest, then make your decision. One of the two, but I want you in bed in the next fifteen minutes!"

Normally, Tambu would have been livid if any of his captains—even Ramona—had tried to give him orders. But now, he couldn't even muster the interest or energy to argue. This, more than anything else, indicated to him that she was probably right.

"All right," he sighed, shooting a covert glance at the console's call board. "But wake me up again in a couple of hours."

"I'll try once after six hours. But if you won't budge, I'll let you get another four."

"Under no circumstances more than eight," he insisted. "Even if you have to throw ice water on me. I've got to get this problem resolved."

"Agreed," Ramona nodded, rising to her feet. "I'll run down to the galley and swipe a couple of sandwiches for you. If you doze off, they'll be here on the side table when you wake up—and quit looking at the call board! I'm giving orders to put any incoming calls, on hold until you wake up."

"Not the blinkers!" Tambu ordered, his head coming up with a snap. "I'm not going to lose a ship because I need a little sleep!"

Ramona chewed her lip.

"Can I try to do a little screening?" she asked hesitantly. "We both know that some of the captains abuse the emergency priority to get your attention."

"Very well," Tambu agreed wearily. "But I want to take any genuine emergencies."

"I know." Ramona stooped to give him a quick kiss. "That's why you're top dog in this outfit."

He remained seated at the console for several minutes after her departure, pondering the true nature of his current status. Was he top dog? He didn't feel like it. There was no power or joy in his routine—only incredible fear.

It was as if he was at the controls of a ground skimmer with the throttle jammed wide open, trying desperately to avoid obstacles darting at him from the distance, fighting certain knowledge that eventually he would react too slowly or steer in the wrong direction. The longer he survived, the faster the skimmer was going, making the inevitable crash that much more terrible when it finally came.

With effort, he closed his mind against the image. Ramona was right. He needed sleep, if only to steel his nerves.

He was stretching his legs, preparing to rise from his seat, when a chime sounded and a light came on the console.

Tambu smiled as he looked at the signal. Ramona was slipping. The light was red, but not blinking. Either she hadn't issued her orders yet, or a call managed to slip past her blockade.

His eye fell on the indicator, and his smile faded abruptly. The call was from the *Raven*! From Whitey! Whitey had never used a priority signal of any kind.

Without thinking, his hand went to the transmission switch.

"Tambu here," he said even before the signal appeared on his screen. "What's the problem, Whitey?"

Whitey's face appeared on the screen, her features frozen in a mask of anger.

"Tambu?" she asked. "I want to know what's going on!"

"About what?" Tambu blinked, then it all came back to him. Of course! That's what Whitey would be calling about.

"All right," Whitey snapped. "If you want to play games, we'll take it from the top. I was just down on Elei making our sales pitch. They were receptive—very receptive for a planet that had never agreed with our position before. They were so receptive, in fact, they wouldn't even let me talk. They just signed up—said they'd pay whatever we asked."

"And you want to know why," Tambu finished for her.

"I asked them why," Whitey spat. "And you know what they said? They said they were paying so my ship wouldn't burn their capital."

Tambu ran his fingers wearily through his hair, but didn't interrupt.

"Of course I laughed at that," Whitey continued bitterly. "I told them I was one of Tambu's captains and that Tambu doesn't operate that way. You know what they said to that?"

"They told you about what happened on Zarn," Tambu answered tonelessly.

For several moments Whitey stared at him out of the screen, her anger melting into hurt puzzlement.

"Then it's true?" she finally asked in a soft voice. "I was hoping they were lying—or had been lied to."

"It's true," Tambu admitted.

"And you want to know why I'm calling?" Whitey demanded, her anger returning in a rush. "What's going on in the fleet? We never agreed to anything like this."

"I doubt they told you the whole story," Tambu began.

"How many ways can you read the facts?" Whitey interrupted. "One of our ships burns out a whole city—a city that has no way of fighting back. How can anybody justify that?"

"Nikki's dead," Tambu said softly.

"Nikki? Puck?" Whitey blinked. "What happened?"

"He went to pay a call on the Planetary Council, much as you did on Elei," Tambu explained. "It seems they not only refused our services, they were exceptionally unpleasant about it. Among other things, they stated that their planet was going to bar their spaceport to any of our ships."

"But spaceports are open to any ship, regardless of origin!" Whitey protested.

"That's right," Tambu confirmed. "But the Council seemed ready to overlook that detail, along with numerous other niceties humans usually extend to each other—niceties that usually transcend planetary or racial differences. Anyway, to keep a long story short, Puck lost his temper and told him what he thought of them and their decisions. He was complete enough in his oration that he finished it by spitting on the floor, whereupon the Council guards shot him down in cold blood."

"Good God!" Whitey gasped. "What did they do to the guards?"

"Nothing," Tambu replied grimly. "Not only were the guards not disciplined, the Council had his body delivered back to the ship's shuttlecraft with the message that he was to be taken offplanet for burial. I believe the specific quote was they 'didn't want him or scum like him on their planet, alive or dead.' Shortly thereafter, his ship opened fire on the capital."

"You're sure he didn't attack them physically?" Whitey pressed.

"He was alone and unarmed, Whitey," Tambu said softly. "When they carried his body through the streets to the spaceport, the crowds cheered the guards and spit on his body."

"How do you know all this if he was alone?" Whitey challenged.

"From reports submitted by our informants who were there at the time. I've even got copies of the official reports of the incident prepared by the Council guardsmen. Most of my time since the blow-up has been spent piecing the facts together and checking them."

"You mean you ordered the strike *before* you checked the story?" Whitey exploded.

"I didn't order it at all, Whitey. I didn't even approve it."

"You didn't?" Whitey's face showed a mixture of relief and concern. "Then who did?"

"Puck's second-in-command—with the full support of the crew." Tambu sighed. "Puck was a very popular captain."

Whitey rubbed her forehead absently as if trying to erase her frown wrinkles.

"I still don't think they were justified, hitting the whole city that way," she said at last.

"They didn't mean to hit the whole city," Tambu said quietly. "They were trying for the Council Building. It might have worked, except for two things. Nobody has any experience shooting at a planetside target from space. They missed—missed badly. They also underestimated the devastation caused by weapons designed for long-range work in space."

They both lapsed into silence again, each lost in their own thoughts.

"I wish you had told me sooner," Whitey commented finally. "It was bad, hearing it the way I did. I don't know which was worse; the news itself or hearing from someone outside the fleet."

"I'm sorry," Tambu said sincerely. "I've been trying to put together a new policy statement for general release, and it isn't easy. I've been trying to alert any captain due for planetfall, but the *Raven* wasn't due at Elei for another two days."

"Puck was a friend of mine," Whitey observed dryly. "You might have made an exception to your rules in this case."

"I said I was busy!" Tambu snarled. "What do you think I do with my time? Sit on my butt and play darts? I would have called you if I could, but I couldn't. There were more important things to do. I don't like saying that, but that's the way it is. The good of the fleet has to take precedence over my personal friendships."

"What's so all-fired important?" Whitey challenged. "How long does it take you to issue a statement saying you had nothing to do with Zarn—that the ship was acting against your orders and is going to be disciplined?"

"It—it isn't as simple as that," Tambu replied hesitant for the first time in the conversation. "There are a lot of factors to be considered."

"Like what?" Whitey pressed. "Don't you realize that the longer you let things sit without comment, the more people are going to assume you ordered the strike?"

"I realize it . . . more than you do, Whitey. As far as our personal friendship goes, I should tell you that except for the crew of Puck's ship and myself, you're the only one who knows I didn't order the strike."

"You mean you're going to take the blame for Zarn?" Whitey gaped. "Why, Tambu? You weren't responsible."

"They're a ship under my command," Tambu countered. "Technically, that makes me responsible. I've taken a lot of indirect credit in the past for things my captains did. I can't just wash my hands of what happened because things went sour."

"I don't agree. But even if I did . . . if I felt you were responsible, it doesn't change anything. You've got to do something. You've got to level some kind of punishment against the ship."

"For what?" Tambu demanded. "For being loyal to their captain? For going after a bunch of bastards who think they have the right to gun down anyone from one of my ships?"

"How about for leveling a city and everybody in it?" Whitey shot back. "Don't you think that was a little extreme?"

"Yes, I do," Tambu retorted. "But I'm in a bad position to judge. I haven't set foot off a ship in over six years. I don't know how bad things are for the crews when they go planetside. I've got no comprehension of what they've been putting up with. You tell me, Whitey. If things had worked out differently—if you had been gunned down on Elei instead of Puck getting killed on Zarn, how would your crew react?"

"I—I don't know," Whitey admitted. "I'd like to think they'd react with more restraint."

"But you can't be sure," Tambu pointed out viciously. "Okay, let's go a step further. If they reacted the same way Puck's crew did . . . if they did that and you were in my position, what would you do to them? What kind of punishment would you level? A wrist-slap? Would you have them all hunted down and executed? What?"

"I'd have to think about it. I can't just come up with an answer on something that big."

"Then why are you leaning on me for trying to take time to think?" Tambu accused. "Do you think I've been planning in advance for this? Am I supposed to have a master plan in mind for every disaster?"

"Okay! I was out of line! But you've had time now. You'd better come up with something fast. Lord knows how the planets will react when they hear—or the rest of the fleet, for that matter."

Fatigue made Tambu's laugh harsh.

"Do you want to know how they're reacting? Over two-thirds of the fleet has called in already. Less than three percent have objected to what happened—and the main protest there was that they weren't notified in advance of the policy change. That's how upset the fleet is!"

"But the planets—"

"Right along with those call-ins," Tambu interrupted, "came a tidal wave of sign-ons. Our crews don't even have to go planetside and ask anymore. Planets are calling them to subscribe. Some of them are relaying calls through other planets. Financially, this is the best thing that's ever happened to the fleet. We could cut our fees by a third tomorrow and still show a profit."

He suddenly noticed that Whitey was shrinking on the viewscreen. Not that the reception was bad, but rather that she seemed to be sagging . . . folding in on herself.

"Are you all right?" he asked, suddenly solicitous. "I didn't mean to shout at you. It's just that things have been pretty rough at this end."

Whitey shook her head, but this time she didn't raise her eyes.

"That's all right. It's what you're saying, not how you're saying it that's made up my mind."

"Made up your mind about what?" Tambu frowned.

"I'm quitting," Whitey sighed. "Getting out while the getting's good. I'll recommend Pepe, my second-in-command, as my replacement. He's as solid as they come, and the crew respects him."

"Wait a minute," Tambu protested. "I haven't reached a decision on this mess yet. Don't—"

"Yes, you have," Whitey corrected gently. "You may not know it yet, but you have. I know you, Tambu. Maybe better than you know yourself. If you were going to jump the way I think you should, you would have done it by now. Just the fact that you're still seesawing back and forth tells me something. It tells me I can't follow you anymore."

Tambu felt the truth in her words wash over him as she spoke, though he wouldn't admit it even to himself.

"Isn't this a bit sudden?" he asked quietly.

"Not really. I've thought about doing it a hundred times since we started. I want out, but it has to be sudden. I can't ease away from it."

Unlike his conversations with Egor, Tambu knew instinctively that he could not argue or wheedle Whitey into changing her mind once it was made up.

"Very well. It will take some time to make the arrangements. You're due a substantial pension—and we'll have to set up a cover for you."

"Put my pension in the general fund. I've saved enough on my own to live on. As for a cover, I figure I'll just have the shuttle run me down to Elei and settle there. It's as good a place as any."

"But on Elei they know you're one of my captains," Tambu objected. "It shouldn't be safe."

"They'll also know I've quit the fleet," Whitey pointed out. "And why. I don't think I'll have much trouble."

"It sounds like you've thought this through pretty carefully," Tambu observed bitterly.

"I've given it some thought, ever since they gave me the news on

Elei. Just for the record, Tambu, I think you're wrong. The fleet was never popular with the planets before, but now you're taking on the role of an extortionist. I don't think they'll put up with that for long. There's going to be trouble, and I for one don't want to be around when it hits."

"That's one person's opinion."

"Maybe," Whitey shrugged. "But then again, maybe it's the opinion of a whole lot of people. You should listen to the folks planetside as much as you do to the people in your fleet."

"At the moment, I'm more concerned with my fleet."

"I know," Whitey sighed. "That's where you're going wrong. Goodbye, Tambu. Whitey out."

Ramona reentered the cabin in time to see the viewscreen fading to darkness.

"What was all that about?" she asked. "I thought you weren't going to take any more calls until after you got some sleep."

"That was a call from the *Raven*," Tambu explained, staring at the dark screen. "We just lost another captain—the hard way."

"Whitey?" Ramona exclaimed, setting down the tray she was carrying and moving to his side, "Whitey's been killed?"

Tambu rose and started for the bed, ignoring the sandwiches on the tray.

"No, she wasn't killed. But we still lost her the hard way."

Interview VIII

Erickson was silent for several minutes after Tambu finished his narrative.

"So that's the way it actually happened," he said at last.

"Yes," Tambu sighed. "That's how it happened. You may use it in your article, if you wish. Enough incidents have occurred since then, it is now an item of historic curiosity more than anything else. I don't believe it will change anyone's mind one way or the other."

"It's certainly given me something to think about."

"But it hasn't changed your mind noticeably. You disapproved of the Zarn incident before, and you still do . . . regardless of the circumstances."

"You're right," Erickson admitted. "But I will say I'm glad the decision wasn't mine to make."

"In case you ponder the problem at leisure sometime in the future, let me give you one extra thought to complicate things. I believe that we are in agreement that if consulted in advance, neither of us would have ordered the strike on Zarn. Remember, though, that you're trying to put yourself in my place, and that means deciding a course of action after the fact. By the time I entered the picture, the strike was already over—and nothing I could do or say would change that."

"So the real question was whether to atone for the deed or capitalize on it."

"That's right," Tambu acknowledged. "I chose to capitalize on it. Even in hindsight, I don't know how we could have atoned for what happened. Perhaps it was weak of me, but it was easier to take advantage of the situation."

"But was it an advantage?" Erickson pressed. "I mean, it seems to me in the long run it would have been better business if you could have disassociated yourself and the fleet from the incident."

"I fear you're a better reporter than a businessman, Mr. Erickson. There were many factors I took into consideration in that decision, most of which were business-oriented. Group image: I don't feel it would have enhanced our position to let it be known to the planets that they could kill our crew members and throw us offplanet without repercussions. Internal morale: It would have had an adverse effect on our crewmen if they were to feel the hierarchy of the fleet not only did not act when one of ours was attacked, but punished them when they performed what in their eyes was a demonstration of loyalty and affection. Profit and loss: I've already pointed out that our list of subscribers increased substantially after the incident. As far as business goes, my decision was actually quite wise."

"But isn't part of business catering to one's public image? You could have avoided a lot of bad feeling if the criminal label had not been attached to you and your fleet."

"Could we?" Tambu asked sarcastically. "If you recall, even before the incident at Zarn, we were being treated like criminals or worse. If given a choice between being viewed with contempt or with fear, we'll take fear. Zarn gave us that choice."

"So, in your opinion, Zarn actually made things easier for the fleet," Erickson suggested, eager to move the interview away from the delicate subject.

"I did not mean to imply that. Richer does not equate with easier. In many ways, our newfound success increased our internal problems. In fact, there were so many decisions to be made that really important issues tended to be lost in the shuffle. Some decisions I made in haste— assuming them to be minor—came back later to haunt me mercilessly."

Chapter Eight

"Coffee, love?" Ramona asked, poking her head into Tambu's cabin.

"Thanks, I could use a break."

"We finally found our problem." Ramona gave him a steaming cup and curled up in a nearby chair. "It took three rounds of check-inspections, but we found it."

"Where was it?" Tambu asked curiously.

"There was a flaw in one of the circuit boards in the Emergency Life Support Override System. It took only three minutes to replace—once we found it. Could have been nasty if we hadn't caught it, though."

Tambu frowned.

"Isn't that a sealed system? When was it last inspected?"

"Two years ago," Ramona recited. "During its scheduled preventative maintenance cycle."

"Then the problem's been with us that long?" Tambu winced.

"No," Ramona insisted firmly. "It's a recent development."

"You seem awfully sure of that."

"I am, for two reasons. First, it was triple-checked during that inspection. I know the crewmembers whose initials were on the seal. They aren't the kind who would fake an inspection or miss a defect that obvious."

"And the other reason?"

"The other reason is the tapping started only recently."

"I thought so." Tambu smiled. "You know, sometimes I wonder if superstitions would survive if we didn't force feed them."

"Now, look," Ramona flared, "I'm not saying I believe in all the superstitions that we keep in space, but the tapping on the outer hull of a ship as a warning of impending disaster is fairly well documented."

"By searching until something wrong is found?" Tambu teased. "In any network of circuits and machinery as complex as a ship, at any given point in time, a close inspection would reveal something wrong. Are you trying to say you honestly believe that if we had inspected that system, say, a week ago, that we wouldn't have found the flaw?"

Ramona glared. "All I know is that on five separate occasions I've been on board a ship when the tapping was heard. Each time a pending malfunction was found. That's enough to convince me to stop everything and run a check-inspection if we hear it again. Wouldn't you?"

"Sure I would," Tambu acknowledged. "But even though I keep the superstitions right along with everybody else, there's part of my mind that reminds me that what I'm doing is silly. You'd think man would have outgrown such childishness, but instead we find technology and superstition advancing hand in hand down the starlanes. I just find it a bit ironic is all."

"Well, I don't think we'll ever get away from it," Ramona grumbled, still annoyed at his teasing. "Let's face it. Our crewmembers aren't the brightest representatives mankind can muster. A lot of them don't have much education other than what they've picked up on shipboard. That means they learn the superstitions right along with everything else."

"Right," Tambu nodded. "Oh well, I'm glad we're under way again. If that's the biggest hassle on this ship, it's the shining star of the fleet."

"Speaking of shipboard hassles," Ramona said, "has there been any more word about the crewman who died on board the *Scorpion*?"

"As a matter of fact, the investigation's closed. The final ruling is suicide."

"Suicide?" Ramona frowned. "Any report as to the reason?"

"Space-depression." Tambu shrugged. "Egor says the guy was a borderline basket case when he signed on. Probably joined out of a death wish and decided to do it himself when he found out how slow things really are working for the fleet."

"Egor?" Ramona echoed. "You let Egor investigate it himself?"

"I didn't *let* him do it," Tambu protested. "He did it on his own initiative. Wouldn't you if it happened on your ship?"

"Aren't you going to conduct your own investigation as a check?"

"What for?" Tambu countered. "I have no reason to doubt Egor's conclusions. I thought you were the one who was always after me to delegate more and quit trying to run everything personally."

"Maybe I shouldn't say this," Ramona hesitated, pursing her lips, "but there have been a lot of rumors of discontent on the *Scorpion*."

"You're right, you shouldn't say it," Tambu commented grimly. "There are problems on the *Scorpion*. Egor has reported them to me himself, and the last thing he needs right now are a lot of rumormongers fanning the flames."

"In that case, maybe I'd better take my rumors and leave."

"Hey, hey!" Tambu soothed, holding up a hand. "I'm sorry. I didn't mean to lean on you. Look, I know you're trying to help . . . and I appreciate it. It's just that I'm a bit on edge. I really hate wading through all this." He gestured toward the table behind him.

"The yearly financial statements?" Ramona raised her eyebrows, her anger mollified by her curiosity. "I thought you *enjoyed* playing with numbers, love."

"There's a limit! Nine boxes of paper and data tapes is a bit much, even for me."

"Why don't you just review the summaries?" she suggested.

"These are the summaries. The support data behind them would fill several cargo holds."

"Well, it should solve your leisure-time problem," Ramona joked. "Seriously, though, why do you bother? I mean, just the fact that everyone has to submit yearly reports to you should serve as a deterrent against embezzlement without your having to review them all."

"Don't bet on it." Tambu sighed. "Sooner or later, people would figure it out if I just filed their reports. Sometimes . . . wait. Here, let me read this to you."

He fished around on the table for a specific sheet of paper, found it, held it aloft, and read: "If you have gotten this far in our report, we will buy you a case of your favorite whiskey. Simply call so we know what brand to buy."

"Really?" Ramona laughed. "Are you going to collect?"

"I sure am," Tambu grinned. "And on the other eight notes like it I've found buried in other reports. I also get to send about a dozen terse reprimands to references to my parentage or sexual preferences."

"What are you going to do with all that liquor?" Ramona asked. "You don't drink anything but wine."

"Another year like this last one, and I'll be ready for the hard stuff. But, I can't actually accept the shipments. If nothing else, it would show which ship I was on. Instead, I'll have each donor send it off to a different ship, with a note that the ship's crew is to enjoy the gift with my compliments."

"Sounds like a good deal. Any chance my ship can get in on that?"

"I'll have to check my lists," he retorted with mock severity. "You know I won't play favorites. Just because you successfully seduced me doesn't mean you should expect special privileges."

"I stand duly chastised." She hung her head dramatically.

"Getting back to the original question, jokers like these would be able to tell in no time flat if I wasn't reading their reports."

"Which would be an open invitation to gimmick the books," Ramona acknowledged.

"Even if I trusted everyone implicitly, which I don't, but even if I did, I'd still take the time to review the reports. There's a lot of information here once you learn to read between the lines."

"Such as what?"

"Well," Tambu squinted, "I can tell how often they conduct target practice, what the condition of their ship is, the state of the crew's morale—"

"Wait a minute. You lost me. How can you tell all that from just looking at numbers?"

"By studying various expense items. For example, if a ship is spending less than half the amount on maintenance and parts as other ships the same size and age, I can make an educated guess that its condition is less than excellent."

"And crew morale?"

"If a captain is paying his crew low wages and is spending little or nothing on employee luxuries, they will be noticeably less happy than a well-paid crew on a ship with a new lounge and game room."

"I see," Ramona commented thoughtfully. "Maybe I should take another look at my own reports."

"I'm not sure how much good it would do you without other reports to compare it to. What you might do is call a couple of the other ships and ask for copies of their reports."

"I just might do that," Ramona nodded. "Now you've got me wondering."

Tambu's simply giving her copies of the reports submitted to him was not mentioned by either of them. Yearly reports were strictly confidential between Tambu and the individual captains.

Tambu continued, "Besides checking on individual ships, I use the reports to look for new ideas. There's one ship in the fleet, for example, that's shown significant savings on their food expenses by allowing planetside food services to open a franchise on board the ship. Food preparation and planning becomes the service's problem, and the crew buys their meals in a cafeteria."

"Interesting. Does it work?"

"I'm still checking into it," Tambu said. "Even though their food costs have been reduced, they've had to pay their crews more to cover the price of the meals. It could be a false savings."

"I can see where it gets a bit complicated," Ramona commented.

"Oh, that's not the complicated part," Tambu replied innocently. "Where it gets rough is trying to use the reports to find answers to nonspecific quantitative questions."

"You're showing off now!"

"You're right. But it's true nonetheless."

"I'll call your bluff," she challenged. "Give me an example of a nonqualitative . . . whatever it was you said."

"Gladly. Do you remember the item on the agenda about next year's captains' meeting that calls for a review of the funds allocation methods?"

"I glanced over it, but I didn't read it carefully. Why?"

"You should look at it. It's going to be one of the hottest items on the agenda. Most of the other captains are gearing up for a major brawl."

"Maybe it's the terminology that's putting me off. What's it all about? In nonaccounting terms."

"Simply put, the planets who subscribe to our services pay their money into a big common pool," Tambu explained. "From that pool, the money gets divided down among the individual ships which comprise the fleet. The question that's being raised is what is a fair basis for determining which ship gets how much."

"Aside from the fact that everybody gets emotional when there's money on the line, what's the problem?" Ramona yawned. "I mean, how many ways can you carve a pie?"

"Lots. The trouble is, each way has its drawbacks."

He rose and began to pace the room as he spoke, unconsciously falling into a lecturer's role.

"We can't just give a set amount to each ship. Some of our ships are twice as big as others and require larger crews and more maintenance. Similarly, we can't give a set amount to each crewman or captain. On a small ship, a crewman has to do more than one job. Should a navigator gunner be paid the same as a man who is only a gunner?"

"Or should the captain of a five-man cruiser be paid as much as the captain of a forty-man dreadnought?" Ramona supplied.

"Exactly." Tambu nodded. "And then there's seniority. Should a five-year crewman be paid the same as someone in the same job who just signed on?"

"It *could* get a little sticky."

"I haven't even gotten to the good part yet. There's also the matter of the patrol range of the individual ship. If two ships are the same size with the same size crew, and one of them is patrolling eight planets and the other patrols twenty, should they be paid the same? Of course, there you have to figure in the currency exchange rates and price of supplies on the various planets."

"Stop!" Ramona cried. "Okay! I get the picture. It's a morass. What has all this got to do with the financial reports?"

"Between now and the meeting, I have to formulate a plan. If I don't have something firmly in mind before the item comes up on the agenda, the discussion will degenerate into a dogfight."

He poked listlessly at the heap of paper and tapes on his table.

"Going through this stuff, I'm trying to find a pattern to our costs—by ship and by man. Then I get to sort through it again to define the modifying factors such as patrol sectors. Hopefully, then, I can rough out a proposal that will make everybody happy—or at least make everybody equally unhappy."

Ramona rose to her feet and stretched lazily.

"Well, this time I think I'm going to do what everybody else usually does."

"What's that?" Tambu asked.

"I'll let you figure it all out, argue for a while, then go along with what you propose. No sense in both of us losing sleep over this."

"But don't you want to conduct an investigation of your own to check against my findings?" Tambu gaped in mock horror.

She stuck her tongue out at him.

"Even if I had access to the data you've got, which I don't, I wouldn't know what to do with it—or have the time to do it if I did."

Tambu shook his head sharply as if trying to clear his ears. "Could you repeat that last part? It didn't make any sense at all."

"Simply put," Ramona sniffed in imitation of his earlier lecture style, "I've got my hands full running my ship. Running the fleet's your job, and you're welcome to it! Bye now!"

Tambu laughed and returned her wave as she left. But after she was gone, his smile faded.

Even though she had been joking, she was right. The whole mess was sitting in his lap. It wasn't that the captains didn't care or that they weren't intelligent, it was just that no one else in the fleet had the overview he had when it came to problem solving. Ramona knew much more about the intricacies of running the fleet than she had shown during their conversation. It was obvious to Tambu that she had been playing 'straight man' to his show-off performance so that he would have a chance to talk things out a bit. Still, even she couldn't aid him directly in this work. Like the other captains, she lacked the detailed comparative data which currently only he had access to. The captains' jealous hoarding of information was inadvertently giving him sole proprietorship of the job of fleet coordinator.

With a sigh, he started to turn towards the desk again when a light on his command console caught his eye. It was only an amber call—next to no importance or priority, but he was glad to answer it. Anything to stall his return to the reports.

The viewscreen showed an empty chair, causing Tambu to smile as he leaned toward the mike.

"Tambu here," he announced in carefully modulated tones.

Blackjack appeared on the screen, hurrying to his chair, shirtless and half-hopping as he tried to pull on a pair of pants.

"Sorry, boss," he apologized. "I didn't think you'd answer so fast."

"It's been a slow day," Tambu explained dryly. "What've you got?"

Blackjack hedged. "Well, it might be nothing. But when we dropped in on Trepec here, I picked up a bit of information I thought you should have."

"And that is—" Tambu urged impatiently.

"It seems there's been a run on guns—big ones like we use on our ships."

"Interesting." Tambu frowned. "Any word as to who's been buying?"

"As near as I can find out, they've sold a few each to a lot of planets."

"Strange." Tambu pursed his lips. "Which planets?"

"I've got a list here. Some of 'em are on our subscription list, but most aren't."

"Oh, well," Tambu sighed. "I guess it was bound to happen sometime."

"What's that?"

"The planets are arming themselves," Tambu explained, "though what good they expect ground-mounted guns to be against ships in orbit is beyond me."

"Arming themselves? Against what?"

"Maybe against pirates," Tambu smiled. "But more likely against us. We have hit a few planets in our time, you know."

"But that's ridiculous," Blackjack protested. "Ground-mounted guns wouldn't stop us if we decided to hit a planet."

"You know it, and I know it, but apparently the planets don't know it. Oh well, it's their money."

"Are you going to alert the fleet?"

"Why bother?" Tambu yawned. "Any ship of mine that can't hold its own against a ground-mounted attack deserves what they get."

"But if they set up a battery near a spaceport, they might ambush a shuttlecraft," Blackjack cautioned.

"I suppose you're right. All right, give me the list, and I'll pass the word."

He jotted down the names of the planets as Blackjack read them. The list was surprisingly long, between fifteen and twenty planets. Still, it was nothing to worry about.

"Very well, I'll make sure the fleet is warned. Take a couple of extra days while you're there and see if you can find out anything else."

"Right, boss. What are your orders for dealing with one of the planets on the list?"

"I don't know. Hail them from orbit and see what they have to say, I guess. If they make nasty noises, avoid 'em and head for another planet."

"You mean back down?" Blackjack asked.

Tambu smiled at the disappointment in the captain's voice.

"We have to fight often enough already. There's no point in looking for trouble."

"But you said yourself that taking a ground-mounted gun would be no problem," Blackjack argued.

"There are lots of planets, Blackjack. Why would we risk a ship in a needless brawl, however one-sided, when there are so many that won't put up a fight at all?"

"What if they shoot at us?" Blackjack pressed.

"If you're fired on, you can defend yourself, of course. But under no circumstance will one of my ships fire the first shot. Got it?"

"Affirmative," Blackjack scowled.

"Good enough. Tambu out."

He stared thoughtfully at the blank viewscreen for several moments after signing off. His orders to Blackjack had been rather vague and poorly defined. He'd have to take some time to phrase them better before he sent them out to the fleet. Of course, that would have to wait.

He set the list of planets to one side and turned back to his work table.

Right now he had to wade through these reports. He had stalled long enough—too long. He owed it to the fleet to be selective about his priorities.

Interview IX

"Though I didn't realize it at the time, that was the start of the Defense Alliance. It never occurred to me that they might be mounting the weapons on ships, much less that they were planning to band together against us."

"That must have been an ugly surprise," Erickson laughed.

There was a moment of silence before the reply came.

"I lost five ships the first day the Defense Alliance began functioning as a unit. The humor of that escapes me."

"I'm sorry," the reporter squirmed. "I didn't know. I didn't mean to make light of it."

"You aren't the only one who didn't know," Tambu sighed. "You see, Mr. Erickson, the Alliance's counteroffensive came before I had gotten around to passing the warning to the fleet."

"So when the Alliance attacked, they were totally unprepared," Erickson finished softly. "I can see where you would feel guilty about that."

"I never like losing a ship, but I don't feel particularly guilty. They were fighting ships and should have been ready for trouble. They fell to attack because the years of low resistance had taken the edge off their alertness."

"But if you had warned them, it might have made a difference," Erickson insisted.

"It might," Tambu admitted. "But I don't think so. Remember that the warning I would have issued would have been against ground installations, not armed ships. One of the things I neglected to mention was that Blackjack's ship was one of those lost on the first day—and he had been warned."

"What happened? Was he caught unaware?"

"Again, the answer is yes and no," Tambu replied. "He saw an armed ship in his vicinity, but he wasn't expecting to be attacked. As a matter of fact, he was on the viewscreen asking me for instructions when the Alliance ship opened fire on him."

"You seem surprisingly unmoved by the memory."

"Do I? That's a strange criticism coming from someone who was just appalled at the Zarn incident."

"Both examples show a callousness to loss of life," the reporter countered.

"True enough," Tambu acknowledged without rancor, "but you must try to see my side of things, Mr. Erickson. In the course of my career I have lost ships, men, and close friends. I feel their loss, but for self-defense I must keep my distance emotionally. If I didn't, I would go insane."

Erickson refrained from comment.

"So the Alliance's threat was felt from the first day on," he said instead.

"You flatter the Alliance with your word choice. The Defense Alliance has never constituted a serious threat to my fleet—then or now."

"But you just said they destroyed five of your ships!"

"Five out of nearly two hundred," Tambu remarked pointedly. "I'll also admit they've downed several of our ships since—just as we've destroyed several of theirs. I tend to attribute their victories to shortcomings in my own captains rather to any brilliance or competence on their part."

"Excuse my asking, but isn't that a little conceited of you?"

"What's so conceited about acknowledging the weakness of my

own fleet?" Tambu asked innocently. "If I wanted to brag, I'd claim that it requires an expert tactician or an ace crew to down one of my ships. The truth is that it's really quite easy to do—if you're faced with a hot-headed captain who won't follow orders."

"I thought your captains followed your orders to the letter," Erickson probed.

"I've never claimed that, Mr. Erickson," Tambu corrected. "In fact, I've given you several examples to the contrary. My captains are human, and they follow popular orders much more strictly than orders they disagree with."

"Then you've issued orders which were unpopular with the fleet?"

"Yes, I have. Orders that were very unpopular."

Chapter Nine

Tambu glared at his console viewscreen, fingers tapping his thigh in fierce impatience.

"I would ask that the captains *sit down!*" he ordered in a tone that left no room for rebuttal.

Slowly, the forest of figures on the screen sank back into their chairs—individually, as each captain lost the battle with rebellious indignation.

Tambu waited impatiently until all were seated.

"Put your hands down, too!" he growled dangerously.

Again, the captains complied with grudging hesitancy.

"Very well. I'm going to say this once and once only. This meeting is too large for any vague semblance of democracy. With nearly two hundred of you jammed into one room, I can't even see everyone, much less recognize them to speak."

He paused to wet his lips.

"What is more, even if I could, with this many people present, simple time parameters dictate that not everyone who wants to speak would be able to."

Mentally he crossed his fingers.

"It is therefore my decision," he announced, "that for the duration of this discussion, I will not recognize speakers from the floor. Instead, I will call upon specific captains whom I feel are most representative of the feelings I have heard expressed over the last several months and let them speak for the fleet."

A low growl of disapproval rose from the assemblage.

"If you are called upon and have nothing to say or feel someone else can say it better," he continued, ignoring the protests, "you may yield the floor to a speaker of your choice. However, independent outbursts or interruptions will not be tolerated. Do I make myself clear?"

A sea of angry eyes glared back at him from the viewscreen, but no one chose to challenge him openly.

"Good." He nodded. "Our first speaker will be Pepe, captain of the *Raven*. Pepe, if you were to be the only speaker for the fleet, how would you describe the current views of the Defense Alliance?"

The swarthy little captain rose slowly to his feet, eyes downcast and brow furrowed as he struggled to organize his thoughts. The crowed waited in patient silence until he was ready to begin.

"The Defense Alliance is not a good thing for us," Pepe managed finally. "We've got a whole bunch of ships there who do nothing—nothing but chase us away from planets we're supposed to be protecting. That's bad for business. How are we going to do our jobs if we've always got to be watching the screens for Alliance ships, eh?"

Tambu broke in. "Excuse me for interrupting, Pepe, but how many planets were you patrolling before the Defense Alliance began their operations?"

"Maybe twelve," Pepe answered.

"Your reports say ten. And how many now?"

"Fifteen," Pepe admitted.

"So at least, in your case, your business has increased—not decreased—with the appearance of the Alliance," Tambu observed.

Pepe flushed.

"You told me to speak for the fleet, not my ship," he argued.

"Quite right." Tambu smiled. "Continue."

"What is truly bad," Pepe explained, his voice rising, "is the unhappiness in our crews. For many years now we tell them, 'Practice with your guns . . . be ready to fight.' Now, for the first time we have someone to fight, and we tell them, 'Run away . . . don't fight.' Our crews . . . don't know what to think anymore. They are confused. Are they fighters or runners, eh? We can't keep telling them to be both."

Scattered applause and murmured approval swept the room as Pepe sat down. Tambu pursed his lips and frowned as he watched, then leaned towards the mike.

"Thank you, Pepe. Before we go much further with the discussion, however, we should define our terms. What is this Defense Alliance we're all so concerned about? While most of you know some of the facts, allow me to take a few moments to summarize the information which has come to me, so that we're all on even footing."

There were loud groans and the sound of people shifting in their chairs impatiently, but Tambu ignored them. Despite his awkward speaking form, Pepe had been a little too good at stating the fleet's complaints. Tambu wanted to slow the pace of the meeting before it got out of control.

He began in his best lecturer's monotone. "The Defense Alliance is a collection of some forty ships fielded by the planets with the intent of forming an interstellar peacekeeping force. In this, they are not unlike our own force."

There were mutters of disagreement.

"There are numerous differences, however, which separate the two fleets," he added hastily. "The most obvious is the chain of command on board an individual ship. As you know, many of our ships joined the fleet with crews intact from their previous engagements. The captain and crew are used to working together, and any replacements are selected by the captain."

The crowd was fidgeting, obviously bored by the oration.

"In contrast," Tambu continued, "the Defense Alliance is composed of ships and crews donated by the various planets, and their captains are appointed by the Alliance's High Command—a group which functions independently of any specific planet."

He paused to emphasize his next point.

"This means that the captain and crew of an Alliance ship do not share a common origin, nor do they necessarily agree on methodologies, custom, or tactics. I personally feel this is a major flaw in their organizational logic."

There were more interested faces listening now.

"To emphasize this for a moment, consider how the ships are run. Within our fleet, each ship and ship's captain has autonomy as long as their actions do not go against established policies and guidelines. The High Council of the Defense Alliance, on the other hand, has laid down a strict set of rules as well as a code of conduct which every ship, captain, and crewmember must obey to the letter. Having seen copies of their rules, I can only say that if I tried to get this assembly to abide by them, there would be an armed revolt. The only way the High Council can realistically expect adherence to their rules is if they've crewed their ships with saints and angels."

Laughter greeted this speech, and Tambu began to relax slightly.

"For the rest of it, they are not dissimilar to us. They finance their fleet with taxes from member planets, taxes which do not vary greatly from the monies paid us by our subscribers. Also, in their effort to form an impartial force, the ships each severed commitments with their planets of origin. As a result, like our fleet, the Defense Alliance answers only to itself—not to any planet or system."

Tambu reviewed his captains on the screen and found them to be calmer and more settled than when he had begun speaking.

"Now that we all understand what we're talking about, let's continue the discussion. Cowboy? Do you have anything to add to what Pepe has already said?"

Tambu had expected that Cowboy would be caught off-balance and would have to flounder while trying to remember Pepe's comments. Instead, the lank Captain surged immediately to his feet and launched into his comments.

"What the Boss sez sums up what we all know," he declared. "We can whip the tar out of them Alliance ships, so what are we running fer? While we're all together for the meeting, Ah think we should take a little extra time and do us some hunting. Ah don't know what the bag limit is on angels an' saints, but Ah bet we could fill it in no time at all!"

Tambu gritted his teeth and rubbed his forehead while the crowd cheered Cowboy. So much for slowing down the pace of the meeting.

"If I understand your logic, Cowboy," he commented dryly after the noise had died down, "you feel that since we can attack and destroy the Alliance fleet, it automatically follows that we should. Is that correct?"

"Well . . . yeah," Cowboy stammered. "Ah guess that's what Ah'm sayin.'"

"I see." Tambu smiled. "Then why stop with the Defense Alliance? The fleet's strong enough to totally destroy any planet or system in the universe. After we're done with the Alliance fleet, why not start attacking the planets one by one? We can do it, so why shouldn't we?"

"Yer pokin' fun at me," Cowboy declared, drawing himself proudly erect. "We're supposed to be protectin' the planets, not attackin' them. That's our job."

"Forgive me," Tambu apologized sarcastically. "My mind must be slipping. I wrote the contract we use with the planets, but obviously I've forgotten an important part of that agreement. Could you refresh my memory? Just what part of that agreement says that chasing and destroying the Defense Alliance is part of our job?"

Cowboy dropped his eyes uncomfortably.

"We're—we're supposed to fight against pirates," he murmured lamely.

"Are you saying the Alliance is actually a band of pirates?" Tambu pressed mercilessly. "No one's reported this to me before. That changes everything. Tell me, though, which merchant ships have they attacked? I'll need that information for my records."

Cowboy shook his head silently, not looking up.

"I see," Tambu said at last. "Thank you for your comments, Cowboy. Ratso? Do you have anything to add to the discussion?"

He was careful to use Ramona's fleet name, but her response caught him totally unaware.

"I yield the floor to Captain Egor," she announced without rising.

A murmur of surprise ran through the assemblage. Egor had never spoken before at a captains' meeting.

"Very well," Tambu managed, recovering himself. "Egor?"

The big man rose slowly to his feet and surveyed the room

carefully before he spoke. Tambu tried to read the expression on his old friend's face, but found he could not. The only thing he could say for certain was that Egor looked older.

"I'm not as good a talker as most of you," Egor began hesitantly, "but there's something I've got to tell you about. Something that affects all of us in this room."

He paused for a moment, frowning as if trying to choose his next words.

"Most of you know Whitey," he said at last. "She was captain of the *Raven* before Pepe. She's an old friend of mine, and I kept in touch with her after she left the fleet and settled on Elei. I've found out . . . well, she's dead."

There was a moment of stunned silence. Then everyone tried to talk at once. Pepe was on his feet, his face pale and drawn, trying to say something to Egor, but his words were lost in the clamor.

Despite his own shock at hearing the news, Tambu's mind was churning with suspicion. Why hadn't Egor informed him of this sooner? More important, why had he chosen now to make his announcement?

Egor was holding his hands up now, motioning for quiet. Slowly, the other conversations subsided as the captains turned to listen.

"What is particularly important," he continued, "is not the fact that Whitey's dead, but rather how she died. The Defense Alliance killed her. One of the Alliance ships visited Elei, and someone told its crew that Whitey used to be with our fleet. They went to her home, dragged her out in the street, and hung her. There was no formal arrest by the Elei authorities, no trial, nothing! Just a lynch mob—a Defense Alliance lynch mob!"

Tambu frowned at the ugly sounds coming from the assembled captains, but Egor wasn't finished yet.

"How do I know?" he called in answer to one of the many questions shouted from the group. "I'll tell you how I know. The *Scorpion* was there! We were there at Elei!"

His words stilled the rising babble like a bucket of water tossed on a fire. All eyes were on him as he turned to stare at the viewscreen.

"The *Scorpion* was orbiting Elei when the Alliance ship arrived," he announced coldly. "Under orders, we withdrew rather than put up a fight. When we returned later, we found out about Whitey."

Tambu bowed his head as the icy rage in Egor's words washed over him. It was obvious that Egor blamed Tambu personally for Whitey's death.

Egor continued, "Unfortunately, my crew heard about it first when they went planetside. I had to exert every bit of discipline and authority at my command to keep them from retaliating against Elei for what the Alliance had done. What's more, I've blocked them from meeting or communicating with the crews from any other ship. It wasn't a popular thing to do, but I felt it was necessary to keep the story from spreading through the fleet before we could discuss it here at the meeting."

Egor faced the other captains, inadvertently turning his back on the viewscreen.

"Well, we're at the meeting now," he growled, "and the question I want to put before the assembled captains is: what are we going to do about it? How long are we going to let the Defense Alliance push us around before we push back?"

A chorus of angry shouts answered his challenge. Tambu gritted his teeth. Egor was showing an unsuspected talent as a rabble rouser. The captains were teetering on the brink of an emotional commitment the fleet could ill afford. Tambu would have to move now if he was to maintain control of the meeting.

"Order!" he barked. "Order, or I'll adjourn the meeting right now! Order!"

Grudgingly, the captains complied. One by one, they returned to their seats, but their faces were tense and expectant as they stared at the viewscreen. Tambu knew they were barely holding their emotions in check. He considered his words carefully.

"Egor," he said after the noise had subsided, "I can only say that I share your grief—as I'm sure all the captains do. Whitey was liked and respected by all who knew her, as a captain and a friend." He paused and took a deep breath before continuing.

"However," he added in a harsher tone, "I must also say as the chairman of this meeting that what you say has no bearing at all on the subject under discussion."

Heads snapped up, but he pressed on.

"Whitey was no longer with our fleet, and therefore outside our sphere of protection. I personally offered to establish her in a location where her past would be unknown, but she refused. She chose instead to live among people who knew her as a fleet captain. She knew the risk, but make her decision anyway. The fact that she lost her personal gamble should have no bearing on the policies or decision of the fleet."

The room was staring at him out of the viewscreen, but no one seemed to be in violent disagreement.

"As such," Tambu concluded, "if you're finished—"

"I'm not finished!" Egor cried.

"Very well," Tambu sighed. "Continue."

"Since you only want to talk about the fleet," Egor glared, "we will forget about Whitey. Fine. Let's talk about the *Scorpion* and ships like her who are supposed to follow your orders. We were driven away from Elei by an Alliance ship without firing so much as one shot—following your orders. Speaking for myself, my crew, and the rest of the fleet, I want to know why. I can accept not chasing Alliance ships, but why do we have to run?"

Tambu asked, "When you left Elei, were there other planets unpatrolled by ships of either fleet?"

"Of course," Egor nodded. "With so many planets and so few ships, there are always unpatrolled planets."

"Then I'll ask you a question of my own. You ask, 'Why run?' I ask you, 'Why fight?' To protect the planet? The Alliance won't attack them. To protect yourself? They never fired a shot at you. To keep the revenues of the planet? Why bother when there are so many other planets that can replace it?"

Tambu leaned back and sighed.

"What it boils down to, Egor, is that you want to fight because of your pride. You don't want to back down to anyone, anywhere, anytime. That's pride. Now I ask you: do you think it's right to risk not just your life, but your ship and the lives of your crew in a fight that could have been avoided? How much is your pride worth to you?"

Egor flushed and sat down, still angry, but unable to reply.

"Thank you, Captain. Now, if we could hear from—"

"I smell a rat!"

There was no mistaking the diminutive figure standing on a chair in the middle of the assemblage.

"I never thought I'd see you climb on a chair to avoid a rat," Tambu observed attempting a joke. "Sit down, A.C."

"I have something to ask," she called back defiantly.

"I said I would not tolerate any outbursts or interruptions, and I meant it! Now sit down!"

A.C. hesitated, then dropped back into her seat.

"Thank you. Now then, Jelly? Would you like to say something at this time?"

The old man half-rose. "I'd rather yield the floor to Ms. A.C," he announced.

A titter ran through the group, and Tambu knew he was outmaneuvered.

"Very well," he said politely, trying to salvage his dignity. "A.C? I believe you had some comments?"

"I have an observation and a question. The observation is that we're being flimflammed! Flimflammed, bamboozled, and hustled! What's more, the one doing the hustling is none other than our own beloved chairman!"

She leveled an accusing finger at the viewscreen, and the assemblage turned to stare.

"No offense, boss," she called. "But I've sat through a lot of these meetings, and I know your style. If this is a free discussion, then I'm Mickey Mouse. You're playing divide-and-conquer games with the meeting, and it's about time you admitted it. By controlling who speaks and in what order, you're choosing what arguments you want to hear and when. Then, after forbidding anyone else to interrupt, you use your position as chair to interrupt as often as you want with questions or observations. You're taking our arguments one at a time and carving them up. That's not your normal style, but that's what you're doing."

She paused for breath.

"Go on," Tambu encouraged, amused despite himself at the accuracy of her statements.

"Well, I've been sitting here trying to figure out why you're doing this, and I can come up with only one answer: Your mind's already made up on the subject of the Defense Alliance. What's more, you don't think that your decision is going to be particularly popular with the captains, so instead of just coming out and speaking your mind, you've set up this cat-and-mouse game. It's my guess you're hoping you can talk us around to where we come up with your idea and think we did it ourselves."

She paused, licked her lips, and continued, her shoulders drooping slightly.

"I don't know. I may be entirely wrong about this, but it's the only thing that fits what's going on. If I'm wrong, I apologize."

Her head came up and her eyes bored out of the viewscreen at him. "But if I'm right, I think I can speak for all of us when I say could you knock off the bullshit and tell us what you're thinking? You can save everyone a lot of time and emotional stress by just being honest with us. We might not like it, but it beats being treated like children."

She dropped back into her seat, and Tambu winced as the room stared at the viewscreen, waiting for his answer.

"Thank you, A.C.," he said slowly. "And I really mean that. All I can say is that you're absolutely right."

The captains shifted uneasily and muttered to each other as he continued.

"There are two points of clarification before I share my thoughts with you. First, though I was manipulating the discussion, I was not being close-minded. If a point had been raised from the floor that had escaped my earlier studies on the situation, I would have given it my full consideration. Second, knowing my decision would be unpopular and therefore require considerable explanation, I was trying to bundle that explanation in a choreographed discussion rather than simply lecturing and dictating. Now, I can only apologize to the captains. Whatever my intentions, my methods in dealing with you were less than honest, and therefore in clear violation of my own principles and the spirit of these meetings. I'm sorry. It won't happen again."

He paused for a moment. There was dead silence in the room as the captains waited.

"As to my position on the Defense Alliance, I have given the matter considerable thought and attention. Like all questions, it involves both logic and emotion, and unfortunately my final solution is also logical and emotional.

"As to the logic, I have tried to strip the problem down to the bare essentials. We have always considered ourselves a peacekeeping force. While we will fight to defend our ships or our crews, a peaceful person outside our fleet has nothing to fear from us. The charges and criticisms of us we have attributed to misinterpretation, misinformation, or outright lies.

"The Defense Alliance is also a peacekeeping force. While we seem to be their primary targets, I am sure they would not hesitate to attack a pirate if they chanced upon one. In short, they are in the same business we are—except they aren't as good at it as we are. I'm not talking about fighting here, even though I believe we could beat them man-for-man and ship-for-ship. I'm talking about the day-to-day drudgery once the romanticism wears off. They're all bright-eyed and bushy-tailed, planning to beat us at a game we've been playing for ten years. I don't think they can do it."

He paused for emphasis, scanning the rapt faces in the viewscreen.

"I'm basing my orders—my entire strategy—on that belief. They can't do it. They're going to run into every problem, every financial hassle, every planetside hassle that we did, and I don't think they'll be able to take it! I think they'll fold within a year, two years at most ... If—and it's a big if—If we don't make a mistake, and right now I think fighting them would be the biggest mistake we could make! If we destroy half their fleet, the other half will have a cause to fight for, and we'll never be rid of them. If we destroy their whole fleet—"

Tambu rubbed his forehead angrily.

"If we destroy their whole fleet, we'll be making martyrs of them all. The planets will field another fleet, and another—because then we'll have given them proof of what they've been saying all along: that we're gangsters, extortionists who will squash or try to squash anyone who butts in on our territory. That's why I say lean back and wait 'em out. Logically, it's the best plan."

The faces in the screen were mostly thoughtful, though there were several head shakings and scowls.

"That's logically. Emotionally, I feel a bit different." The tone in his voice brought the heads up as if attached to strings.

"I'm Tambu. I hired and licensed every captain in that room for a peacekeeping force, and as long as my name's on it, that's what it's going to be! That's not subject to debate or a vote—that's the way it is. Period!"

He glared at them. Even though they couldn't see him, they could feel the intensity in his voice.

"Now, each of you signed on voluntarily. I can't force you to stay or to follow my orders. If you and your crews want to go caterwauling across the starlanes chasing the Defense Alliance, fine! Go ahead. You want to demand half of each planet's wealth and your pick of bed partners? Okay! It's no skin off my nose. You want to gun down every Groundhog who spits in the street when you walk by? Go get 'em! But—"

His voice took on an icy hardness.

"But you aren't going to do it in my name or under the fleet's protection! Whether I command two hundred ships or a hundred .. . or ten, or even one, the weapons at my command belong to a peacekeeping force; and if you cross my path with your games, we'll burn you down like we would any other pirate. For the record and for your information, *that* is my emotional solution, and you're right! It's not going to change!"

He paused and looked at the still, silent figures in the viewscreen.

"Now that that matter's settled," he finished conversationally, "I'll adjourn the meeting for today. Think it over, talk it over. Talk to your crews. Anyone who's leaving can contact me through normal channels to settle their severance pay. For those who are staying, we'll reconvene at 0800 hours tomorrow and see how much of a fleet we have left. Tambu out."

Interview X

"I take it most of them stayed with the fleet," Erickson observed.

"All of them did. It caused me a bit of concern at the time."

"How so? I should think you would have been pleased that they came around to your way of thinking."

"Perhaps. If I had really believed that I had changed their minds. As it was, I knew that several of the captains were dead set against my plans. If a few ships had left the fleet at that time, I might have been able to kid myself into believing that those remaining were in agreement with me. As it was, I was left knowing that I had serious dissenters in the ranks, and that trouble could flare up at any time."

"And did it?" Erickson urged.

"It did and it does," Tambu answered. "For specific examples, you need only look at your backfile newstapes. Every ship-to-ship battle that's taken place in the last three years has been the result of someone disobeying orders—in one fleet or the other. I repeat my earlier statement: neither the Alliance High Command—or I want our ships to fight. We're making a good living from the status quo, and any combat, win or lose, costs too much."

"But the Alliance was formed to destroy your fleet," the reporter protested.

"They were formed to protect the planets, just as we were," Tambu corrected. "At first they thought they could best do that by destroying us. As I predicted, they found they couldn't do it, and instead settled into a pattern of preventive patrol."

"That last part you didn't actually predict," Erickson pointed out bluntly. "As I recall, your prediction was that they would disband."

"Frankly, I didn't think they would be intelligent enough to adapt," Tambu admitted. "Of course, it's always a mistake to underestimate your opponent. In this case, however, consider it a minor error as it doesn't really matter. The settled universe is big enough for both fleets—particularly now that the Alliance has come to its senses and abandoned its aggressor role."

"You seem very sure of yourself."

"Do I? Yes, I suppose I do. It's a habit I've gotten into over the years. I often wish I was as confident as I sound."

"I suppose that's necessary in a command position."

"Quite so. Nothing is as certain to guarantee disaster as if a crew panics—and nothing will panic a crew faster than fear or uncertainty in the leaders over them. The higher you get in the chain of command, the more certain you have to appear. As the head of the fleet, part of my job is to appear infallible."

"Yet you've already admitted your own fallibility."

"There is a great difference between being infallible and seeming infallible, Mr. Erickson. While there is a great pressure on me to be infallible, fortunately, seeming to be infallible is all that is actually required."

Erickson added wryly, "Along with everything else, I must admit that before I had this opportunity to speak with you, I never stopped to think of how grueling your position actually must be. Everything you've told me so far is testimony to the constant demands on your energies and time. What I can't understand is how you stand it. How do you put up with the unending pressure?"

"The answer to that is quite simple, Mr. Erickson," Tambu replied easily. "I don't. To survive unchanged and unscarred would require a superman—and, as I have been trying to assure you, I'm quite human. Often painfully so."

Chapter Ten

Ramona awoke alone in Tambu's bed. She groped for his warmth for a few moments, then sleepily burrowed back into her pillow, assuming that he was in the bathroom. Poised on the brink of unconsciousness, her mind registered a small noise on the far side of the cabin. She snuck a lazy peek through her lashes, then blinked her eyes fully open.

The cabin was bathed in a ghostly light, illuminated by the starfield on the console's viewscreen. Silhouetted by the light, Tambu sat naked at the console, staring at the screen.

Ramona frowned as her mind struggled to analyze what she was seeing. This was highly unusual. Occasionally their sleep would be interrupted by a late-night call from a distraught captain, but then Tambu would deal with them in abrupt, terse tones, and return immediately to bed. He slept and loved seldom enough that when he did, he clung to it with an almost savage intensity. He was constantly either engaged in activity or sleeping. Sitting up quietly at night was something new for him.

"What is it, love?" Ramona called, stretching sleepily.

The figure at the console made no move to respond or to acknowledge her question.

"Tambu? Hey!"

Concerned now, she crawled to the foot of the bed and rose, moving to his side.

"Tambu?" she asked again, touching his shoulder lightly.

He turned his head and focused on her as if seeing her for the first time. "Oh! Sorry, love. Did I wake you?"

"What is it?" she pressed, ignoring his question. "Is something wrong?"

"Not really," he shrugged. "I just made a decision, is all. A hard decision."

"A decision? What is it? You haven't said anything about a major decision in the works."

"Believe it or not, I don't tell you everything," he smiled weakly. "No. This is a personal decision, one I've been thinking about for some time now."

"If you're going to tell me, tell me. Otherwise, let's go back to bed."

"Didn't mean to be melodramatic," he apologized. "It's just that it's been a rough decision to make. I didn't want to—I'm doing it again."

He ran a hand through his hair, then raised his gaze to look her squarely in the eye.

"You see, I've decided to retire. I'm going to step down as head of the fleet."

Ramona stared at him, started to speak, then sank down in a chair shaking her head.

"I—I'm sorry, love," she managed at last. "You caught me off guard. This is kind of sudden."

"Not for me," Tambu proclaimed grimly. "It's been on my mind for a long time now."

"Then you're serious?" Ramona asked incredulously, still trying to deal with his statement in her own mind. "You're really going to retire?"

He nodded slowly.

"I've got to. I've been seesawing back and forth for years, but now I don't even think I've got a choice anymore."

There was something in the tone of his voice—something new. Her shock at his decision was swept aside by a wave of concern for his well-being.

"Do you want to talk about it?" she offered gently.

For several moments he didn't respond; then he turned back to her with a sigh.

"I suppose I should. A lot of people are going to be asking a lot of questions when I make my decision public. I might as well get some practice explaining in advance."

He lapsed into silence again, frowning and pursing his lips. Ramona waited patiently.

"You know, it's funny," he said at last with a nervous smile. "I've been thinking about this so long, I could go through the problem in my sleep, but now that I've got to verbalize it, I don't know where to start."

"I'm not going anywhere," Ramona soothed, drawing her legs up under her. "Take your time and start anywhere."

"Well," he sighed. "For openers, look at this."

He extended a hand at chest height, fingers spread loosely.

Ramona peered at it, but saw nothing unusual. She shot a cautious glance at him and found him frowning at his hand.

"That's funny," he mused to himself. "A while ago, it was shaking like a leaf. I couldn't stop it."

"I know," Ramona nodded. "I've seen it before," she explained. "When you were sleeping. Sometimes you'd lie there shaking all over. I always thought it was fatigue from pushing yourself so hard. You know how sometimes I nag you about getting more sleep? Well, that's why. I get really worried about you."

"I get worried about me, too," Tambu acknowledged. "But it goes a lot deeper than fatigue. It's the main reason I'm quitting."

He paused again. Ramona waited.

"I'm tired, love," he said softly. "Not just physically, get-some-sleep tired, I mean tired all the way through. I'm tired of making decisions, tired of giving orders, tired of speaking out, tired of not speaking out . . . tired of being Tambu."

"I'd say you've got a problem," Ramona observed with mock judiciousness. "I mean, when Tambu gets tired of being Tambu, where does that leave the fleet?"

"I'll let you in on a deep, dark secret, Ramona," Tambu announced wearily. "Perhaps the most closely guarded secret in the fleet."

He looked over both shoulders with melodramatic suspicion, then leaned forward to whisper in her ear. "You see, I'm not Tambu."

"Really?" Ramona gasped, mimicking his manner. "Well, while I am shocked and horrified, I must compliment you sir, on your excellent impersonation. You look, talk, walk, drink and make love just like him. I never would have guessed if you hadn't revealed yourself."

"I'm serious," he replied with no trace of levity. "I'm not Tambu."

Ramona studied him thoughtfully for a moment.

"Okay, I'll play your game. If you aren't Tambu, who are you?"

"I'm a space bum," he announced. "A space bum who had an idea to get himself and his friends out of a bad situation. Part of the idea— a very small part—was to take on an assumed name: Tambu. By itself, the new name created no problems. But them something happened. The space bum and his friends—and a few new friends—decided to build a mythical figure around the name Tambu. You remember, love. You were there at the time."

Ramona nodded dumbly.

"It was ridiculously easy to do," he continued. "We've been conditioned by literature, Tri-D adventures, and other entertainment forms to recognize a heroic figure. All we had to do was provide a few high points and hide any contradictory information, and people would complete the picture themselves. They would see Tambu as a powerful, omnipresent, charismatic leader they could trust and follow. He must be! Otherwise, why is everybody else following him?"

Ramona dropped her eyes and gnawed on her lip. She looked up again as Tambu laid a gentle hand on her arm.

"Don't feel bad, love," he chided. "You didn't force me into anything I didn't want to do. It was a con game, and one I went along with willingly. Why not? It was fun. It was kind of like having the lead in a play, and I played my role to the hilt."

He leaned back again, his expression becoming more serious.

"The trouble is, the play never ended," he said in a low voice. "We never had the curtain call, when the players came out onstage and said 'Hey, look! We're just actors. What you've seen is just make-believe made momentarily plausible by master illusionists.' Because we've never clarified our position, the audience has accepted the illusion as reality, and by that acceptance made it reality."

"Slow up a little, love," Ramona said, shaking her head. "You lost me on that last curve."

"Let me try it from a slightly different angle. Any actor or con artist—or even a salesman—will tell you that to be successful, you have to believe what you're doing. Well, to be Tambu, I had to project myself into that character. I kept asking myself, 'What would a powerful person do in this situation?' 'What would a charismatic leader say to that problem?' I did that for years, until Tambu became more familiar to me than my own character. I got so I could do Tambu without thinking, purely by reflex. Do you see what I'm saying? I became Tambu, but Tambu isn't me!"

"I see your point," Ramona acknowledged. "But couldn't you also say Tambu is just another phase of your own development? I mean, I don't think you've done anything as Tambu that you would have been morally against in your earlier life. In a lot of ways, he's simply a projection of yourself."

"I don't know anymore," Tambu sighed. "And that's why I feel I've got to get out. Lately I find myself saying and doing things as Tambu that go completely against my grain. If I keep going, I'm afraid I'll lose myself to him completely."

"What things went against the grain? Just to satisfy my curiosity."

"Little things, mostly. But things that bother me. Remember the last captains' meeting? When Egor told us about Whitey getting killed. Part of me—the original me—wanted to get sick when I heard that. I wanted to walk away from the screen and hide for a couple of days—cry, get drunk, anything to ease the pain I felt. I mean, in a lot of ways, Whitey was like the sister I never had. She was patient, critical, supportive—more than a friend to me in every way. When I found out she was dead, and how she died, it hit me hard. So what did I do? I gave her a one-line eulogy and then told everyone her death didn't matter. That wasn't me talking, that was Tambu. Our opinions and reactions differed, and his won."

"But you were trying to make a point," Ramona argued. "An

important point about not fighting the Defense Alliance. Not only was the news of Whitey's death distracting, it could have undermined your arguments by raising emotions against the Alliance. You should take that into consideration."

"Should I?" Tambu smiled. "You know that original me I keep talking about? You know what he felt about the whole matter? He was with the captains! He wanted to go out there and smash the bastards in the Alliance and anyone else who dared to take up arms against us. That's what he wanted, but Tambu wouldn't allow it, just like he wouldn't let the captains go off half-cocked. That's the rest of my problem. I can't ease off on Tambu, let him develop into what I was originally. The fleet needs Tambu—a cold mind with an eye for the overview. If I let the original me—the one I'm fighting to save—take over the fleet, it would be disastrous. I've got to make the choice: either stay with the fleet as Tambu, or save myself and leave."

"Your concern for the fleet is touching," Ramona drawled sarcastically. "What happens to the fleet if you retire? You'll be leaving a lot of friends holding the bag."

"What friends?" Tambu challenged. "With the exception of you, I don't have any friends left in the fleet. Puck, Whitey, even Blackjack, whom I never really liked, all of them are gone. Everyone else knows me as an authoritative voice on a blank viewscreen."

"There's Egor," Ramona reminded him.

Tambu thought for a moment, then sighed. "I suppose you're right," he admitted. "Egor and I are still friends, even though we haven't gotten along too well lately. I still cover for him, and he still tries to be captain for me. It must be friendship. There's no other reason for it."

"But everyone else can go hang—if you'll pardon the pun. You must be a different person. That doesn't sound like Tambu at all."

Tambu slumped back in his chair, his eyes downcast, but his hands balled into tight fists.

"You're wrong, Ramona," he said quietly. "I *do* care what happens to the fleet. That's my problem. If I didn't care, I could just take a shuttle down at the next planet, and never look back. I do care, though, so I've been racking my brain trying to think of a way to have my cake and eat it, too. I want to be able to save myself for myself, and at the same time ensure the fleet's continued survival."

"That's a pretty tall order," Ramona said. "I don't see any way you could do it."

"I've figured a way," Tambu said quietly. "If I hadn't, I wouldn't be retiring. The fleet means a lot to me. I wouldn't sell it down the river just to save myself."

"That sounds more like the Tambu I know," Ramona said eagerly. "What's the plan? I'm all ears."

"Well . . . not all ears," Tambu smiled, leaning forward to caress her lightly.

"Stop that!" She slapped his hand. "You'll get me all distracted, and I want to hear this master plan of yours."

"See what I mean about my job getting in the way of my personal life?" Tambu sighed in mock dejection.

"Are you going to tell me the plan or not?"

"Well, I got the idea from an item on the agenda for the next captains' meeting," Tambu began.

"Swell! I haven't seen a copy of the agenda yet."

"I know. I haven't distributed them yet."

"Tell me the plan!"

Tambu yawned. "As I was saying before I was interrupted, there is an item on the agenda calling for the formation of a Captains' Council. The general idea is to select a dozen or so captains, each of whom will meet with small groups of ships throughout the year. Then, at the yearly meeting, they will represent the ships in the policy arguments with me. It's an attempt to avoid mob scenes like last year's meeting when there were too many captains, all trying to talk at once on every subject."

"Will the other captains be allowed to attend, too?" Ramona asked.

"I don't know. Hopefully, there would be enough trust in the Council that it wouldn't be necessary for the other captains to sit in. It wouldn't surprise me, though, if they insisted on attending for the first few years until that trust was built."

"What has this got to do with your plan?" Ramona pressed.

"Isn't it obvious?" Tambu blinked. "That Council could take over as the governing body of the fleet after I'm gone."

"Do you think the fleet will go along with that?" Ramona asked. "I mean, everybody's used to having one person at the top. I'm not sure they'll like switching over to rule by committee."

"I think the fleet would be better off with a council calling the shots. If you put all the weight on one person, there's too much chance that he'll fold—or worse, abuse the power. If they really want one person at the controls, though, I suppose they could choose one or let the Council choose one."

"Anyone specific in mind?" Ramona asked.

"If I had to name my successor or make a recommendation," Tambu frowned, "I'd have to go with A.C. She's shrewd as well as intelligent, and gutsy enough for three people."

"She also has a temper that won't quit," Ramona observed dryly.

"Nobody will be ideal. I'm hoping that the added responsibility would calm her down."

"There is one person who's ideal," Ramona suggested.

"Who's that?"

"You," Ramona said bluntly. "Face it, love, you invented the job and defined its range and parameters. No matter who gets picked, nobody's going to be better at being Tambu than Tambu."

"But I've told you how I feel about that," he protested.

"Yes, you have," Ramona retorted. "Now let me tell you how the fleet will feel. The captains will feel betrayed, abandoned, and shat upon. They're in the fleet because they believe in you and you believe in what you're doing. How do you think they'll feel when you try to take that away from them? I say 'try,' because I'm not sure they'll let you step down."

"How will they stop me—kill me?" Tambu laughed sardonically. "That's what it would take, and either way, they won't have Tambu at the controls anymore. No, hopefully they'll realize that if I'm not working willingly, I'll be no good to them at all."

"That's if they're thinking logically, which they don't always do," Ramona retorted. "At the very least, a lot of people are going to try to talk you out of it."

"I know. One of the things I don't know yet is how and when I'm going to make the announcement—if at all. It'll blow things wide open if I do it at the captains' meeting. Ideally, I'd like to wait until the Council idea has been passed and the members chosen, then tell them in a private meeting. That would give me some time to work with them, train them, and help organize the new structure before I left. I'll just have to wait and see what the temperature of the water is like at the meeting before I make up my mind on that. Maybe it would be easier to just establish the structure and then disappear—you know, missing in action. They can't argue with me if they can't find me."

"Well, I can't see any way you can make a popular move," Ramona said. "If you let the captains in on your decision, they'll turn on you like a pack of animals."

"So what's new?" Tambu smiled. "I've gotten used to it over the last couple years. You know, Ramona, lately I've taken to seeing the captains as opponents rather than allies. They're a force to be dealt with—and they scare me more than the Defense Alliance ever could. If the Alliance starts getting frisky, I've got the fleet to fight them with. If the captains get upset, though, it's just me and them. No one's going to intercede on my behalf."

Ramona was silent for a few moments.

At last she sighed, "If that's how you see things, it's probably just as well if you step down. One question, though. You've already made it clear you don't think I could step into your position and run the fleet. What do you think my chances would be of getting a spot on the Council?"

"You?" Tambu blinked. "But you . . . I'm sorry. I've been so busy talking about myself, I haven't said anything about my other plans. I was hoping you'd come with me when I left."

Ramona gnawed her lip for a moment.

"Thanks for the invitation," she said finally. "Listening to you talk, I wasn't sure I'd be welcome. Now, at least, I know I've got a choice."

"But will you come with me?"

"I—I don't know," Ramona admitted. "So much of what I love in you is tied into the fleet. I mean, I love Tambu—and what you've been telling me is you're not Tambu, that you're someone else. I don't know that other person. I'm not sure if I'd love you more or hate you."

"I had counted on your coming along," Tambu said softly.

"Would it change your decision if I said I wouldn't go with you?" Ramona asked.

Tambu looked at her for a long moment, then lowered his eyes and shook his head.

"Then I'll have to think about it," Ramona sighed. "Come back to bed now. I'll give you my answer before you leave the fleet."

Interview XI

"Did Ramona's argument surprise you? About your being the only one who could run the fleet?"

"I felt it was exaggerated. There is a natural tendency in any group to feel that the current leader is the only one who can hold things together—particularly if that leader is the one who formed the group originally. A more realistic attitude is found in business, where they maintain that no one is irreplaceable."

"There it is again," the reporter murmured.

"I beg your pardon?"

"Hmmm? Sorry, I was just thinking out loud. It's just that throughout the interview, in all your examples, you seem to downplay yourself as a charismatic figure. It's as if you feel that anyone could do what you've done, if given the opportunity."

"In many ways, you're correct, Mr. Erickson. For a long time I saw myself as nothing more than an opportunistic space bum who got lucky. I didn't consider myself a charismatic figure so much as a weak leader who was scrambling desperately trying to live up to the faith and trust that others had placed in him. I didn't control or manipulate circumstances, they controlled me. I dealt with situations as they arose in the manner I thought best at that time. It's been only recently that I've begun to realize how exceptional one must be to do the job I've done. That's what's given me my confidence, but it had to be built slowly over my entire career. I didn't start with it."

"So at the time you considered retiring, you still felt that any one of a number of people could run the fleet, once you turned your files over to them?" the reporter guessed.

"That is correct. Aside from the fact that I had designed the job, I didn't see why I should be singled out to serve. While a new leader would have doubtless handled things differently, I was confident that the position was transferable."

"You were just going to walk away from it?" Erickson marveled. "The power, the notoriety, everything? Just up and leave it?"

"That's correct. And believe me, the decision was every bit as hard as it sounds. You see, I like being Tambu. That's one thing that was not mentioned in that conversation. There is something giddy and addictive about having a roomful of powerful people hanging on your every word, waiting for your commands or pronouncements."

"And, of course, there's always the detail of having the power of life and death over a vast number of people," the reporter added.

"Unfortunately, yes. It's at once appealing and horrifying. I feel it speaks highly of me that I could have seriously planned to give it up."

"I assume you changed your mind again after the mood passed." Erickson smiled.

"It was more than a mood. And it wasn't the lure of power that made me change my plans."

"Did Ramona talk you out of it, then?"

"No, she didn't even try."

"Then the captains must have raised sufficient protest—"

"Mr. Erickson," Tambu interrupted, "I think you fail to realize the strength of my will. Once my mind was made up, no person or group of people could have changed it. When the yearly meeting was convened, I had every intention of carrying out my plan."

"Yet you are still obviously in command of the fleet. When you made your announcement, something must have happened to change your plans."

"As a matter of fact," Tambu reminisced softly, "the subject never came up."

Chapter Eleven

Tambu watched silently as the captains gathered for the yearly meeting. For nearly an hour now he had been sitting in front of his viewscreen, watching and listening.

Other years, he had waited until the signal came from the meeting ship that the captains were assembled and ready before activating his screen to call the group to order. Usually, his last hours before the meeting were filled with activity as he organized his notes, reviewed personnel files, and made last-minute additions to his plans for the upcoming year.

This year was different. This year, he had been watching the room when the first captains appeared and helped themselves to the coffee provided by the host crew. This year, he studied each of the captains as they entered the meeting room, observing their expression and body tension, noting whom they chose to talk with prior to the meeting.

His spying was born of nervousness and anxiety over the course of today's meeting. He wanted the Council motion to pass—smoothly if possible—but if need be, he was ready to bend a few people to push it through. If the motion didn't pass, it would delay his retirement until an alternate system could be devised and approved.

The captains would probably raise their eyebrows if they knew how closely they were being scrutinized, but the odds of them finding out were slim to nonexistent. Only Tambu and Egor knew he was watching, and Egor could be trusted to keep the secret. That was partially the reason he had chosen the *Scorpion* as the site for this year's meeting. The other reason was that he wanted to provide one final public display of his approval of Egor, hopefully to end once and for all the criticisms of his friend which abounded in the fleet.

He wondered for a moment if Egor would resign once he learned of Tambu's plans, but dismissed the thought. Egor's reaction, like those of the other captains, would be apparent soon enough when he made the announcement. Until then, it was a waste of mental energy to try to second guess what would happen.

His attention turned again to the figures on the screen. For the first time in years he viewed them as individuals rather than as business associates. A lot of his hopes were riding on the people in that room. He had picked them, trained them, argued with them, and bled with them. Could they hold the fleet together after he was gone? If anyone could, they could. There would be some changes, of course—possibly even some major policy revisions. Still, they were experienced captains, and he was confident they would rise to the challenge.

Egor came forward, moving toward the screen. He had been standing by the door, greeting each captain and checking them off on the master list as they arrived. The fact that he had abandoned his post signaled that all were in attendance now. The captains knew that, too, and began drifting toward their seats as Egor began working the viewscreen controls.

A blinking red light appeared on Tambu's console, the ready signal. He paused for a moment, looking at the expectant assemblage. This was the fleet! His creation! Realization came to him that this would be the last time he would deal with them, command them as a unit.

With leaden slowness, he leaned toward the mike. "Good morning. I trust everyone is well rested and ready for a full day's business?"

Assorted groans and grimaces greeted his words. This had come to be a traditional opening. He knew, as they did, that the yearly meetings had become a week-long social gathering and party for the crews. That, combined with the captains' own last-minute preparations, usually guaranteed that no one arrived at the meeting well rested.

"Before we begin," he continued, "I'd like to take a moment to thank Captain Egor and the *Scorpion*'s crew for hosting this year's meeting. As those of you who have hosted these meetings in the past will testify, there's a lot of work that goes into the preparations. Egor?"

Egor rose to a round of automatic applause, and gestured for silence.

"My crew has asked me to convey their regrets and apologies to you for their absence from the pre-meeting parties on board the other ships," he announced with pompous formality. "Contrary to popular belief, this is not because I've confined them to the ship."

Egor paused for a moment, but no laughter greeted his attempted joke.

"Actually," he continued, "they've been working on their own on a surprise they've cooked up for today's meeting. I don't know what it is, but they've been planning it ever since they found out the yearly meeting was going to be on the *Scorpion*—and if I know my crew, it should be memorable."

He sat down, and Tambu waited until the polite applause died.

"Thank you, Egor. Now, before we get into the agenda, I'd like to announce a change in policy as to how this meeting is to be conducted. As you recall, last year we encountered difficulty discussing points on the agenda, both from the size of the assemblage, and from my attempting to guide the discussion from the chair. Well, this year, we're going to try something different."

A low murmur rose at this, but most of the captains listened in rapt attention.

"This year, we will have a captain conduct the discussion from the floor of the meeting. If I have something to say, I'll have to wait my turn with the rest of you. In an effort to maintain complete impartiality, I have assigned a different captain to each item on the agenda. These captains were chosen at random, and their names subsequently withdrawn from the pool until every captain has conducted a discussion."

The murmur rose to a buzz as the captains discussed the announcement. As Tambu had predicted, most of the reactions were favorable.

"Now, then," Tambu said after the captains had quieted down, "I believe we're ready to start on the agenda. The first item is a proposal for a Council of Captains to replace or supplement the yearly meetings. Captain Ratso, will you conduct the discussion, please?"

The random selection of captains had been a white lie. Tambu had specifically chosen Ramona to conduct this first discussion and had briefed her carefully as to how it was to be done. He had two very important reasons for doing this. First, her handling of the discussion would set the pattern for the other discussion leaders to follow. More important, this item would be the key for his smooth retirement, and he wanted it handled carefully. While Ramona hadn't given him her answer yet whether or not she would accompany him when he left, she was as eager as he to be sure that his departure was handled with a minimum of hassle on all fronts.

"Thank you, Tambu," Ramona said, taking her place at the front of the room. "This item could have a major effect on all of us. I think we are in agreement that these meetings are getting too large to handle the problems that arise each year. We need an alternative to the mass yearly meetings to conduct our business. The question is, is this proposal the best solution? A.C.? Would you start the discussion please?"

Tambu smiled to himself as A.C. clambered onto her chair. Ramona was following his instructions to the letter. A.C. was one of the best shotgunners at the meeting, lying back quietly until everyone had committed themselves to an opinion, then cutting the legs out from under them. By setting her up to speak first, Ramona was ensuring that A.C. would be the one on the defensive instead of having the final shot.

"I don't think we need a Captain's Council at all," A.C. declared loudly. "In fact, before this item appeared on the agenda, I was going to move that we abolish the yearly meetings altogether."

An angry snarl greeted this suggestion. Tambu rocked back and forth in his chair gleefully. This was better than he had hoped. A.C.'s abrupt negativism was setting the assembly against her. That meant they would be that much more receptive to a positive proposal.

"Grow up, people!" A.C. was shouting at her decriers. "Can't you accept the facts? Didn't the boss spell it out for you last year? The captains have no power at all—we're paper dragons. Tambu calls the shots, and his word is final. All we do is provide background noise. He lets us get together and talk and argue so we'll think we've got a say in what's going on, but it doesn't really matter. He gives the orders and that's that."

She turned to face the front of the room, and for a moment Tambu had the uncomfortable feeling she could see him through the screen.

"Don't get me wrong, boss. I'm not complaining. I think you're doing a terrific job of running the show. You're fair, you're careful, and you have a better feel for what's going on in the fleet than any five or ten or twenty of us put together. Now, I don't pretend I agree wholeheartedly with all your decisions, particularly when they're shoved down my throat. In the long run, though, I've got to admit you've been right. If I didn't feel that way, I wouldn't still be with you— and neither would anyone else in this room. You're the boss, and I wouldn't have it any other way."

Tambu writhed before this display of loyalty. Without knowing it, A.C. had voiced a strong argument against his retirement. It stood as a grim warning of what he could expect when he made his announcement.

"I hate to interrupt, A.C," Ramona said, "but you're supposed to be giving your views on the proposal on the floor."

"You want my views?" A.C. snarled. "I'll give you my views. I think a Council of Captains would be a waste of time. I think these meetings are a waste of time, and a Council would only compound it. I think we should quit wasting our time and let Tambu get on with his business of running the fleet."

She sat down to a rising tide of protests. Clearly her speech was not popular with the other captains.

"I'd like to reply to that, if I might," Tambu interjected his voice through the din.

"I'm sorry, boss," Ramona apologized, "there are a couple of speakers ahead of you. Remember, it was your rule!"

A ripple of laughter greeted this, mixed with a few catcalls. But Tambu was not upset. Things were still going according to plan. Ramona had agreed that he should try to interrupt after the first speaker, only to be blocked by the discussion leader. It provided a bit of comic relief, while at the same time setting a precedent for later discussions. Top man or not, Tambu was not to be allowed to interrupt at will. More important, the discussion leader could stop him without fear of repercussions.

"Jelly?" Ramona was saying. "Would you care to speak next?"

Tambu frowned slightly as the old man rose to his feet. He wouldn't have chosen Jelly to speak next. The aging captain was still sharp enough mentally, not to mention highly respected, but he tended to be deathly slow when speaking. The pace of the meeting was bound to suffer with Jelly's speaking so early. Still, he was Ramona's choice, and Tambu was going to have to get used to things being handled differently during these discussions.

"I must take exception to Captain A.C.'s comments," Jelly was saying. "These meetings serve several functions, one of which is to force the captains to hear each other. When we do, we find that our views and opinions are shared by many others, and it becomes unnecessary for each of us to speak. This avoids repetition, and saves Tambu the trouble of hearing the same suggestion or complaint forty or fifty times."

He paused to clear his throat, coughing slightly.

"Excuse me. As to the Captains" Council," he continued, "this is also something which could potentially save us considerable time. If for example, a problem—"

He broke off suddenly, coughing hard and clutching at his chair for support.

Tambu bolted upright, staring at the screen as the room dissolved into chaos. He reached for his mike—but before he could speak, the viewscreen went blank.

He froze, blinking at the screen in disbelief. This was impossible! Communications equipment simply didn't break down. In the years of the fleet's existence, there had never been a failure of communications gear—on any ship.

Moving quickly, Tambu punched out a familiar combination of buttons and a view of immediate space filled with the ships of the fleet sprang to life on the screen. That gave him some assurance. At least the problem wasn't with his gear. Something must be malfunctioning with the equipment on the *Scorpion*. Strange that it should happen just as there was a disruption in the meeting . . . or was it a coincidence?

Tambu frowned, trying to reconstruct the scene in his mind. Had Jelly been the only one coughing? He had a flashing impression of people moving away from Jelly during the commotion—not towards him, as would be the normal reflex.

Shaking the thought from his mind, Tambu made a few adjustments to his controls and tried the *Scorpion* again.

"Calling the *Scorpion*! This is Tambu. Come in, *Scorpion*."

To his relief, the response was almost immediate. The display, however, was not of the captains' meeting. Instead, there was a bearded man on the screen with a tangle of dark, unkempt, shoulder-length hair. Tambu noted several features in the cabin behind the man, and realized he was in Egor's private quarters.

"*Scorpion* here, sir," the man announced. "We've been expecting your call."

Tambu did not recognize the man immediately and there was something in his tone which hinted of disrespect. But the situation was too pressing to prolong the conversation.

"If you're expecting my call," he snapped, "then you probably know what's going wrong. Assign someone to repair the viewscreen in the meeting room immediately. Tell Captain Egor to declare a recess until the screen is functioning. Then have him report to me."

"There's nothing wrong with the viewscreen in the meeting room," the man informed him tensely. "We deliberately overrode the transmission."

A flash of anger shot through Tambu.

"We?" he barked. "Who is 'we,' and by what authority do you—"

"We are the crew of the *Scorpion*," the man interrupted. "And it is my pleasure to inform you that we've just taken control of the ship."

Tambu's mind reeled. A mutiny! Devilishly well timed, too!

Almost without thinking, his hand activated the computer tie-in to the console, seeking the identity of his adversary in the fleet's personnel files. The search was thankfully brief, and the information appeared on a small supplemental data screen.

"I see," he said quietly, hiding his agitation. "Tell me, Hairy . . . it is Hairy, isn't it? With an 'i'? Just what do you and your friends hope to accomplish with this takeover? You're completely boxed in by the fleet, you know. I don't see much chance of your escaping."

"We—we just want a fair deal," Hairy stammered, visibly shaken by Tambu's recognition.

"A fair deal?" Tambu frowned. "You'll have to be a little clearer than that, Hairy. I was under the impression you already had a fair deal."

"Maybe that's what you call it," Hairy snarled, his nervousness overcome by his anger. "But we don't see it that way."

"Don't you think this is a bit extreme?" Tambu chided him. "There are formal channels for registering complaints. I fail to see why you feel you have to resort to such drastic methods to make your feelings known."

"Normal channels!" The man spat. "Normal channels haven't been open to us. That's one of our complaints. Our last petition to the captain got torn up in front of us. When we've tried to complain to you, either the captain hasn't relayed the messages, or you've ignored them completely."

Memories flooded Tambu's head. Memories of Egor's numerous calls, assaulting him with tales of his crew's discontent. Memories of Tambu telling him to handle it himself.

"We've even tried complaining to crews from other ships when we met them," Hairy continued. "We told them to pass the word to their captains, hoping it would reach you indirectly. That didn't get us anything but more grief when the other captains called Egor to criticize his handling of his crew."

"If the situation is as bad as that, why don't you just resign?" Tambu asked.

"Resign?" Hairy snorted. "Cheese tried to resign. The captain killed him outright. After that, no one's tried to resign. We don't get leave planetside anymore, so we don't even have a chance to jump ship."

"When was Cheese killed?" Tambu demanded. "I don't recall seeing a report on that."

"The captain reported it as a suicide, and of course, no one thought to question his word."

"So you devised this trick to get my attention," Tambu observed grimly. "When you plan a surprise for the captains, you don't kid around, do you?"

"We figured since you only listen to the captains, the best way for us to be heard was to come between you and them," Hairy sneered. "You want to see how your captains' meeting is going?"

The man leaned forward, reaching for his console's controls. Immediately the screen changed to display the *Scorpion*'s meeting room. The captains were sprawled all over the room, some crumpled on the floor, others slumped in their chairs. No one was moving.

"There are your precious captains," Hairy taunted, reappearing on the screen. "Amazing what a couple of canisters of knockout gas in the vent system can do, isn't it? All of them, sleeping like babies inside of thirty seconds."

"You think that by holding the captains hostage, you can force me to let you and your shipmates leave the fleet?" Tambu asked levelly.

"You've got us all wrong," Hairy protested. "We don't want to leave the fleet. If that was what we wanted, we could have jumped the captain anytime and just sailed away. No, we've talked to enough of the other crews to know the *Scorpion* has been the exception, not the rule in your fleet. We're willing to stay in the fleet—once we get a few of our differences resolved."

"Very well," Tambu sighed. "If you revive the captains and allow them to finish their meetings, I'll extend immunity to you from reprisals. Furthermore, I'll give you my promise to personally look into the situation on board the *Scorpion* at my earliest possible convenience. Agreed?"

"Not agreed!" Hairy shot back, shaking his head violently. "You aren't going to deal with us 'at your earliest convenience.' You're going to deal with us right now. What's more, the captains aren't going anywhere until after we've settled this. You don't seem to understand. We're dealing from a position of power. You don't tell us what to do, we tell you!"

His words hung in the air, forever irretrievable. Unseen by Hairy, Tambu's eyes narrowed, and his expression froze into icy grimness.

"Is that how it is?" he said softly. "And just what sort of orders do you and your pirates have in mind for me?"

Any of the captains could have told Hairy that when Tambu's voice went quiet like that, it was a clear danger signal. What's more, the men never wanted Tambu to think of them as pirates. Unfortunately, the captains weren't there to advise Hairy at the moment.

"Well," Hairy began confidently, "first we demand the right to choose our own captain. Even though we'll probably elect him from within our own crew, we want copies of your personnel files to see who else might be available and what their qualifications are. Second, we think the crews should have as much say in how the fleet is run as the captains do . . . including access to you for private conferences. Finally, we want your signature on an order to execute Egor for gross abuse of the authorities of a captain."

"Is that all?" Tambu asked mildly.

"Well, there are a lot of little things," Hairy admitted. "We each want a bonus to compensate us for what we've had to put up with serving under Egor—and there are some benefits we think every crewman in the fleet should have. We're still putting the list together. We figure we should make the most of this while we've got the chance."

"What chance?" Tambu pressed.

"The chance to call the shots for a change. If we set this up right, we can have a hand in all decisions from here on."

"And if I don't agree, you'll kill the captains," Tambu said slowly.

"You understand perfectly," Hairy leered. "You don't really have much of a choice, do you?"

"I have a few." Tambu smiled. "There is one thing I don't understand, though. I think you may be laboring under a misconception. Who do you think you're talking to right now?"

"Who?" Hairy blinked, taken aback by the question. "This is Tambu, isn't it? I mean, you said—"

"That's right, sonny!" Tambu exploded, his voice cracking like a whip. "You're talking to Tambu! Not some sweaty planetside official who wets his pants when you rattle your saber. I'm Tambu, and nobody tells me how to run my fleet. Not the planets, not the Defense Alliance, not the captains, and definitely not some jackass who's throwing a tantrum because he thinks he's being treated badly."

"But if you—" Hairy protested.

"You think you're in a position of power?" Tambu snarled, ignoring the interruption. "Sonny, you don't know what power is. I'd give orders to burn an entire planet to cinders, people and all, before I'd let you blackmail me into turning the fleet over to you, and you try to bargain with a roomful of hostages? You're a fool, Hairy! If my mother was in that room, I wouldn't lift a finger to save her."

Hairy's face was pale in the viewscreen. He no longer looked arrogant and confident. He looked scared.

"If you try anything, we'll open fire on the fleet. There are a lot of ships in range of the *Scorpion*'s guns, and their crews are all busy partying. We could do a lot of damage before we went down."

The fleet! Tambu's mind raced as he searched his memory for the deployment of the ships around the *Scorpion*. There were none lying close to the mutineers' ship, but over half a dozen within the maximum range of its weapons. They were too far out to muster a boarding party before the *Scorpion* could bring its guns to bear. What's more, now that he was in contact with the mutineers, there was no way he could alert the fleet or order the endangered ships to disperse without Hairy's knowing he was planning something.

Still, he couldn't surrender control of two hundred ships to save six ships any more than he could do it to save one ship—one ship!

Slowly, his hand released the double lock on one of the levers on his console.

"Hairy," Tambu said coldly. "You just made a big mistake. I was willing to listen to your complaints because I think you've got a valid case. But I can't be nice to you anymore, Hairy. You just became a danger to the fleet."

Hairy was panicky now. He wet his lips and tried to speak, but nothing came out.

"Look at the console in front of you, Hairy. Do you see the red lever? The one with the double safety lock? Do you know what that is, Hairy?"

"It's—it's the ship's self-destruct mechanism," Hairy managed at last.

"That's right, Hairy. But did you know I can activate that mechanism from right here at my console? Did you know that, Hairy?"

Hairy shook his head woodenly.

"Well, you know it now! Game time is over, Hairy. You have five seconds to call your crew to assemble in front of that screen where I can see them all, or I activate the mechanism."

Despite his firm declaration, Tambu was holding his breath, hoping. If the mutineers would only comply now—stand there so he could see they weren't manning the guns, leveling their sights on an unsuspecting fleet—

For a moment, Hairy wavered. Sweat beaded on his forehead and his eyes darted to someone off-screen. Another voice called out, its words indistinguishable, but it seemed to strengthen Hairy's resolve.

"You're bluffing," he challenged, his head coming up defiantly. "We've got all the captains on board. Even if you could do it, you wouldn't just—"

"Good-bye, Hairy," Tambu said, lowering his hand to the console's keyboard.

For a split second, Hairy's face filled the screen, his eyes wide with terror. Then, for the second time that day, the screen went blank.

Immediately, Tambu rekeyed the display, and the view of the fleet reappeared—the fleet minus the *Scorpion*. There was no trace left of the meeting ship.

The console's board lit up like a Christmas tree. The blinking red lights chased each other up and down the board as Tambu sat and stared. Idly he noted in his mind which ships took the longest to call in.

Finally, his mind focused and he lunged forward, gripping the mike with one hand as his other played rapidly over the console's keyboard.

"This is Tambu," he announced. "All ships, cancel your calls and stand by for a fleetwide announcement."

He waited as the call lights winked out.

"There has been an explosion of unknown origin on board the *Scorpion*," he announced. "We can only assume there are no survivors."

He paused for a moment to allow the message to sink in.

"First officers are to assume command of their vessels immediately," he ordered. "You are to take the rest of the day for whatever services you wish to perform for the lost personnel. Starting at 0800 hours tomorrow, I will contact each of you individually to assist in reorganizing your crews as well as to issue specific orders and assignments. Those ships closest to the *Scorpion* have one hour to conduct a damage inspection of their ships. After that, they are to call me with a status report. Acknowledge receipt of message by responding with an amber call."

He watched as the board lit up again. This time the lights were all amber—all but one. The *Scorpion* would never call in again.

"Tambu out."

The fleet secure, Tambu slumped back in his chair as the enormity of his deed washed over him.

Gone! All of them. Ramona, Egor, A.C, Jelly . . . all of them wiped out when he pressed a single button on his console.

In his shock-dulled mind, he realized he had lost his personal battle. When pressured, it was Tambu who controlled his actions, and Tambu had ended his last hope of retirement. He couldn't leave the fleet now. With the captains gone, there would be no one to pass control to. He would have to stay on, working with the new captains, reorganizing . . .

He had lost. He was Tambu.

The horror of that realization rose up and sucked him down . . . Tambu wept.

Interview XII

"I transferred ships shortly after that. I found my old quarters held too many memories for comfort. That pretty much brings us to the present. For the last two years, I have been training the new captains. The Council is now established and functioning, allowing me leisure time, which in turn enabled me to grant you this interview."

"And the fleet never found out the actual cause of the explosion on the *Scorpion*?" Erickson asked.

"Of course they found out. I told each of the new captains during their initial briefing. I felt it was a necessary lesson as to the possible repercussions of a poor captain-crew relationship."

"Didn't anyone question what you had done?" the reporter pressed. "I mean, surely someone objected to your handling of the situation."

"Remember our discussion of famous people, Mr. Erickson," Tambu instructed. "None of the new captains had ever dealt directly with me before. They had been suddenly thrust into a new position of responsibility, and were casting about for direction and approval. Preconditioned to view me with awe and fear, they readily accepted me as their authority figure, the only one between them and chaos. No one questioned my actions, but they eagerly learned the lesson of the disaster."

"Of course, you've done nothing to encourage that awe and fear," Erickson said.

"Quite the opposite," Tambu admitted easily. "I've done everything I could to build the image. Most of my work for the last two years has been establishing and maintaining the gap between myself and the fleet."

"But why?" the reporter asked. "It seems you're not only accepting your isolation, you're creating it."

"Well put, Mr. Erickson. As to why I'm doing this, remember the *Scorpion* episode. I lost a ship, a good crew, and all my captains because I had allowed my judgment to be clouded by personal friendship. I have found I function much more efficiently in isolation. As I started this latest phase without friends or confidants, it has been relatively easy to avoid forming any. I feel my judgments and appraisals have benefited from this detachment."

"Have you taken a new mistress?" Erickson said bluntly.

"No," Tambu replied after a moment's pause. "I make no pretensions of loyalty to Ramona's memory. I have no doubts that eventually I will need someone again, but it's still too soon."

"It occurred to me earlier in the interview, but now that I've heard your whole story, I feel I must make the observation out loud: You pay a terrible price for your position, Tambu."

"Don't pity me, Mr. Erickson." Tambu's voice was cold. "I do what I do willingly—just as you accept travel, cheap rooms, and restaurant food as a necessary part of your chosen occupation. Once, when I thought of stepping down, I felt regret and remorse. I mentioned at the end of that episode, however, that battle has been won—or lost, depending on your point of view. I am Tambu now, and I do what is necessary to be Tambu. I was born in the early days of the fleet's formation, and the fleet is my life now."

"Then you have no plans for retirement now that the Council is ready to assume command?" Erickson asked.

"Retire to what?" Tambu countered. "My family is dead. My friends are dead. There's nothing for me outside of the fleet."

"That's pretty definite," the reporter acknowledged. "What about the future? What do you see ahead for you and the fleet? A continuance of the status quo?"

"Nothing is forever, Mr. Erickson. The only certain thing in the universe is change. The specifics are anybody's guess. The Defense Alliance is growing larger every year. They may eventually feel they are strong enough to attempt a direct confrontation. I think it would be stupid of them to try it, but they've come a long way doing things I thought were stupid. Then again, they may simply crowd us out of the starlanes."

"You seem unconcerned about either possibility."

Tambu laughed. "If you want my real prediction of the future, I fully expect to slip on a bar of soap and crack my head open in the shower. I've led far too exciting a life to be able to expect anything but an anticlimactic death. But whatever happens in the future, I am the fleet. If I die, the fleet dies with me, and vice versa. I'll leave it to the Fates to work out the details."

"A fitting epitaph," Erickson smiled. "Well, while I could sit here for days talking with you, I've got to admit I have more than enough material for my article."

"Very well, Mr. Erickson. It has been a rare pleasure talking with you these last few hours. Can you remember the way back to the docking bay where your ship is, or shall I call for a guide?"

"I can remember the way. Just give me a moment to gather my things."

"If you don't mind, Mr. Erickson, may I ask you a question before you go?"

"Certainly," the reporter blinked. "What would you like to know?"

"Solely to satisfy my own curiosity, I'd like to know what you intend to say in your article."

A shiver of apprehension ran down Erickson's spine. The alienness of his surroundings came back to him with a rush, as did the distance he had to cover to reach his ship and safety. Taking a deep breath, he turned and faced the blank viewscreen directly.

"I'm going to try to tell your story as I see it," he said carefully. "It's the story of a forceful man with a dream, a dream that went awry and carried him with it."

He paused for a moment, but there was no rebuttal from the screen.

"The man had an incredible sense of loyalty and obligation," he continued haltingly, "a sense of loyalty so strong, it blinded him to everything else in the universe and in his mind. First he was loyal to his friends, then to the planets, and finally to the fleet . . . the business he had built. At each step, his sense of obligation was so strong, so single-minded, that it was beyond the comprehension of everyone who came in contact with him. There were people all along the way who might have swayed him from his course, but they couldn't understand what was happening, and instead of helping, actually speeded him on his way with their actions. It's the story of a man who gave so much of himself that now there's nothing human left—just the image he built with the aid of those who supported or opposed him. That's the story I intend to write, sir . . . assuming, of course, I'm allowed to leave the ship with my notes, mind, and body intact."

"That's an interesting story," Tambu said after a moment's silence. "I'll look forward to seeing it in its final form. I don't agree with all your observations, but, even if I took exception to the entire story, you would be allowed to leave. I granted you an interview and a newsman's immunity, Mr. Erickson. There were no conditions about whether or not I would like what you wrote. If I had wanted my own opinions printed, I would have simply written the article myself and released it to the news services."

"But you still controlled what you did and didn't tell me," Erickson pointed out. "I remember that earlier in our conversation, you stated that anyone being interviewed would slant the facts to create a certain impression. Would you tell me now, off the record, how much of what you've said was exaggerated or downplayed to further your own image?"

"You'll never know that for certain, Mr. Erickson. But if you're willing to believe me at all, accept that I have not knowingly slanted anything. You see, I feel that actions and reactions have been colorful enough without exaggeration. Then, too, there's the fact that I sincerely believe your article will not affect me or the fleet in any way—positive or negative. Our supporters and decriers will accept or reject different portions of your accounts depending on their preformed conception of our motives and activities. Perhaps if I truly believed your article would change people's minds, I might have become concerned enough to lie to you; but as it stands, the truth can be no more damaging to the fleet than any fabrication."

"But if my article really means so little to you, why did you bother giving me the interview at all?"

"I told you at the beginning of our conversation. Curiosity. As one who has been branded as the archvillain of contemporary times, I was curious to meet and have a prolonged conversation with someone who believes in heroes and villains. That same curiosity prompts me to ask you one more question. During our talk, you have shown both distaste and sympathy for me. I ask you now, in your opinion, am I a villain?"

Erickson frowned.

"I don't know," he admitted finally. "While I still believe in evil, I'm no longer sure of its definition. Is evil inherent in the deed, or in the intent? If it's in the deed, then you're a villain. Too many bodies can be laid at your doorstep to be ignored. Of course, if that's our sole unit of measure, then every honored general from mankind's history must be burning in hell right now."

"You are quite correct," Tambu acknowledged. "I personally tend to judge myself on a basis of intent. By that measure, I feel no guilt over my career. I wonder how many people could make the same claim? Yourself, Mr. Erickson. During our interview, I've observed you waging war with yourself—the man versus the professional. You've been constantly struggling to impose 'what you should say' over 'what you would like to say.' In that, your dilemma is not unlike my own Eisner-Tambu difficulties."

"You're quite observant," Erickson acknowledged, "but I'd like to think I'm not the only one with that problem. I'm sure a lot of reporters suffer the same dilemma."

"A lot of people suffer the same dilemma," Tambu corrected. "I was not attempting to criticize you. I was trying to point out that many people feel the need to sacrifice their normal inclinations to conform to their chosen professions. I would hazard a prophecy that if you continue with your career as a reporter, the day will come when your personal questions or statements will not even enter your mind during an interview. You will conduct yourself consciously and subconsciously as a journalist—and on that day you will have become a journalist just as I have become Tambu."

"You may be right." Erickson shrugged. "However, the standards and ethics of my profession were set long before I entered the field; and if I adhere to them, there is little or no chance I will gain your infamy. Remember, sir, you set your own standards and must therefore bear the full weight of their consequences."

"I can't deny that," Tambu admitted, "either the setting of standards or the responsibility for them. However, we were speaking of intent and guilt. Though branded a villain, throughout my career, I have acted with what in my mind were the purest of intentions. All too frequently the results went awry, but each decision made was, in my judgment, made in favor of the greatest good for others, not for myself—and was therefore in keeping with my personal ethics. That is the salve I have to use against any doubts or feelings of guilt. Do you have that same salve, Mr. Erickson? Can you say that in your career as a reporter you've never betrayed a confidence, cheated a friend, or broken a promise for the sake of a story? That you've never gone against your own principles to further your career? That you've never allowed your self-interest to overshadow your ethics?"

The reporter dropped his eyes and frowned thoughtfully, but did not answer.

Tambu concluded, "Then I ask you, Mr. Erickson, who is the bigger villain? You or I?"